GRAND OAK BOOKS

Saloon

Published by:
Grand Oak Books Publishing, Ltd

ISBN-10: 1937727092
ISBN-13: 978-1-937727-09-3

Library of Congress Cataloging-in-Publication Data:

Zola, Émile (1840-1902)/Saloon

L'ASSOMMOIR

PAR

Émile ZOLA

GERVAISE

EN VENTE CHEZ C. MARPON ET E. FLAMMARION, ÉDITEURS

GALERIES DE L'ODÉON, 1 A 7, ET RUE ROTROU, 4, PARIS

ET CHEZ TOUS LES LIBRAIRES

Frontispiece from the Illustrated Edition

Saloon

(L'Assommoir)

by Émile Zola

Introduction by
Stephen R. Pastore

🜊

Grand Oak Books
2012

The Monster in the Machine: Zola's Saloon

by
Stephen R. Pastore

Nothing could have been more calculated to arouse Zola's compassion for dispossessed humanity than those two years of poverty and misery in his youth. The scenes he witnessed – drunken wife-beatings, promiscuity, the desperation of the starved, the hopelessness of the breadwinner without work, the vicious squabbles, the battered children, sickness and brutality – were of the kind that would have sent a more fortunate visitor to those districts retreating in horror and righteous repugnance. But Zola had lived among these people, as one of them, and he soon saw that the source of their degradation was largely an accumulation of social and hereditary forces outside their control. The sympathy which grew out of those years, however, is not without a tinge of bitterness which on many occasions darkens his vision. In Saloon the intensity of this bitterness is projected through Marescot, the landlord of a big tenement building, and one of the most malignant and detestable characters the novelist ever created. A former poor worker, Marescot uses his savings to become a landlord, and then proceeds unmercifully to screw his own kind, living a life of luxury while his tenants live in fear and misery. In Marescot, Zola is portraying the worst side of human nature.

Saloon is, for most readers, a damning indictment of the evil caused by bad living and working conditions. What comes through with dramatic force is that life in the slums is far from picturesque; it is a drab and depressing incarceration from which the only escape is money – which the inhabitants can only dream about – alcohol and sex. And as they are more or less constantly sozzled few can do more than hope, by some miracle, to climb out of their sad environment. Although there was a strong steak of the reformer in Zola at the time, he resisted the urge to dogmatize; Saloon is an exposé, not a sermon, and gains enormous strength from its impartiality. In his preliminary notes for the novel Zola had written, "Do not flatter the working class for slumdwellers are neither saints nor sinners. He takes no political sides and there is a total absence of working-class martyrs. In fact the most voluble spokesman for the socialist viewpoint is the layabout and soapbox pundit, Lantier. To even the balance the Royalists are represented by Poisson, an old civil servant bore. Not surprisingly, critics from both sides of the political fence were enraged that their sacrosanct beliefs were made to look faintly ridiculous by mere association with these worthless characters.

That a novel about working-class people should have whipped up such a storm seems odd to us now. But in mid-nineteenth-century France writers of every rank, with one or two exceptions, were preoccupied with the boudoir, the salons, and the financial ambitions and crimes of passion among the rich and middle class. Zola was the first novelist to recognize that world-shaking changes were taking place; commercial capitalism was usurping feudal paternalism; craftsmen and small traders were being made redundant by mass-production; vast factories were springing up everywhere, as were new industrial towns. Yet most of his fellow writers, especially those with talent, persisted in burying their heads in the stale and perfumed haunts of fashionable society. The vapid productions of his contemporaries made it look as though Zola was ahead of his time. He wasn't; he was simply in it. What is remarkable, though, is that a middle-class writer should have produced the world's first major novel based on the working class, and which reflected so accurately, and with such genuine sympathy, the underprivileged lives and thwarted aspirations of the proletariat. Yet when it was published Zola was set upon by right, left and center; the conservatives said, well, didn't we tell you, the working class are dirty, illiterate, irresponsible scum, and quite unfit to vote; the Republicans were furious that such a bestial picture had been painted of the working man; the socialists, on the other hand, accused Zola of holding his hand, dodging the issue, of leaving unsaid what should have been written with gallons of revolutionary blood. Too few people, it seems, had the wit to deduce the cause from the effect – Zola must have wished, at times, that he had sermonized the obvious – and ironically the only faction to use the novel's reformist potential were not the campaigners for free education, better housing and fewer working hours, but the prohibitionists.

The moralists turned Saloon into a homily against alcohol, and the book became a Bible to the temperance movement which, to advance its cause, thumped its covers unceasingly in Britain and America for two or three decades. With its fearsome symbolism and horrific accounts of alcoholism and its side effects, it is easy to understand how the novel came to be called the world's greatest temperance tract. In recent years, however, thoughtful analysts of the novel have pinpointed morality, not drink, as the true cause of Gervaise's downfall. To some extent this is true, but it is also an over-reaction to the mislabeling of the novel as an exposé of the evils of cheap drink, for Coupeau's abuse of alcohol, and ultimately alcohol's abuse of Coupeau, are definite and important elements in Gervaise's tragedy. With raw brandy only a franc a liter, alcohol was just as available to poor working-class people as sex, and equally good as an opiate against hardship and despair. Zola was well aware of this and in fact promoted the novel in certain medical and religious quarters as a study of what happens when the more extreme forms of inherited instability are stimulated by excessive drinking. According to the Italian journalist de Amicis, the novelist told him that he'd intended writing a book about alcohol. He'd researched its effects, studied patients in the Sainte-Anne hospital and so forth, and defined his characters. But the plot had given him trouble; he had Lantier abandon Gervaise, who took up with Coupeau, who took up with drink, their sad ends had been plotted but somehow there was something missing in the middle. It was this void that led Zola to have Lantier return to make up the fateful ménage á trois. In the end, Zola said, the novel was "simply a lesson in morality."

This is, of course, the essence of Saloon. It is not alcohol which ruins Gervaise, nor is it promiscuity; like the grog, sex in all its forms is freely available in the slums. The poor were no less randy than the rich, but if sex for the bourgeoisie was an expression of their greed, and for the aristocracy an extravagant distraction, sex for the working classes in Zola's novels was an escape from the cruel reality of their lives. No, what brings down Gervaise is an inherited weakness of character, the cracks in which only appeared under extreme stress to be prised open by factors beyond her control. The laundress was no easy mark; her easy-going nature did not extend to sleeping around. While Lantier's mistress she remained loyal; while married to Coupeau she was virtuous; and who could blame her when, insulted, humiliated and driven from her bedroom by her husband, she hesitantly submitted to the seductive maneuvers of her former lover: Interestingly, despite Zola's neurotic belief that a former male lover has some physiological hold over his formerly beloved, Lantier's seduction of Gervaise follows a strictly logical progression from familiarity to circumstance and opportunity. Earlier, when Lantier shows up after several years' absence, the laundress is certainly disturbed: "She always felt, at the name of Lantier, a burning sensation at the pit of the stomach, as if the man had left there, under the skin, something of himself." This is the classic Zola Lover's Return Syndrome, but thereafter the author makes no further reference to it. When Gervaise finally sees Lantier, she feels "a chill strike through her, mounting from her legs to her heart"; but this, surely, is not such an unusual emotion in the event of two ex-lovers meeting unexpectedly. Thankfully Zola did not intrude his neurotic obsession into the passage describing poor Gervaise's seduction by her former lover, for it stands as one of the most superbly conceived climaxes in the novel.

From beginning to end Saloon is imbued with irony, symbolism and even humor, although for the most part the humor is grim – when, for example, the Lorilleux hang a blanket over their door when they cook rabbit stew to stop the smell reaching their starving neighbors – or bitter-sweet, as with Gervaise's wedding day. After the hurried, offhand Nuptial Mass – a subtle thrust at the church on the way – the party visits the Louvre, their only escape in the entire novel to a world beyond their own, geographically only half a mile distant but horizons away in every other sense. The Louvre visit is deliberately designed as an ironic set-piece, but mostly the ironies are set like tiny jewels in Zola's prose, becoming more concentrated as Gervaise begins her fall. Vertical incongruities play and important role here. Coupeau could have hurt himself in many ways, but it is significant that he falls. With Gervaise there is a preoccupation with verticality: we have her climbing and descending stairs, looking up, looking down, raising her eyes, tilting her chin, feeling that buildings are about to topple on her. As she descends down the ladders of poverty and morality, she climbs physically. As Zola had discovered in his own days of poverty, the top floors of walkup tenements were, for the really destitute, a franc a month ahead of damp basements and box-rooms under stairs. The rooms up there were cramped, miserably cold in winter and oppressive in summer. On one occasion Gervaise is in a stifling, fifth-floor room, and looks down to see an apparition of herself in the street below, as a young woman, looking up to examine the house for the first time, and the jump back in time makes her heart jump and awakens her momentarily to her sorry condition. There is also a cruel irony when she visits Coupeau in Sainte-Anne's hospital, the same hospital he helped to build, singing in the sun and shouting down to bystanders like a playful sparrow. But now he is locked in a padded cell in the basement, a madman. The most persistent irony, however, is Gervaise's intermittent relationship with Old Bazouge, the undertaker; with each fall she draws closer and closer to him, moving into the same slum building and finally into the room next to his, so that only the thinnest of partitions separate them. As with many of the characters and objects in Saloon, the appearances of Bazouge are symbolic. It is not fortuitous that Gervaise's beat as a first-time prostitute begins by a slaughter-house, to the wailing whistles of nearby trains; nor the feeling in the reader that the buildings she lives in are more like prisons than homes: "He led the way down a long corridor, turning twice, first to the left, then to the right. The corridor went on further still, going both ways, cramped, dilapidated and unplastered, lit at intervals by tiny gas-jets; and the doors, all of one pattern, like the doors of a prison...." And again: "...one felt the breath of starvation, the walls which resounded like empty stomachs, the doors through which ever came the sound of blows and the whining of starving children..." Even the weather is subtly used to reinforce or suggest a mood. In the courtyard of one of the tenements in which she lives is a gutter carrying the run-off from a dyer's shop; its reflections change color according to the degree of apprehension Zola wishes to invoke.

But the pre-eminent symbol in Saloon is the still in Colombe's Bar, which Zola invests with the properties of some terrible monster, with copper claws, giant jaws and intestinal coils through which pass the poison in which its victims eventually drown:

Then, suddenly, she had an uncomfortable sensation of something behind her back. She turned, and saw the still, the drinking-machine, working away under the glass of the narrow court, with the quivering motion of its wizard's kitchen. At night the coppers looked duller, they had merely a sort of big red star where they were round; and the whole apparatus flung monstrous shadows on the wall at the back, figures with tails, great beasts opening their jaws as if to swallow up everything.

The sleeping beast at first merely disturbs Gervaise, for it is introduced so casually as the "distilling apparatus", the "sozzling machine", that even we can hardly believe the terrifying powers ascribed to it. But the sleeping monster is soon aroused and the tone of Zola's descriptions of it become more violent and touched with hate and anger; it is, after all, the abomination which distils the venom responsible for misery on a vast scale, and the still eventually becomes the author's personal symbol for an evil that, unchecked, will grow until it destroys all mankind.

Zola's absorption with the environmental effects upon his characters led him to introduce a new dimension into the craft of descriptive prose. Read any of his novels and you soon become aware that for their author the place is never separate from the plot; locations are never limp backdrops, quickly painted and then ignored. Again and again they intrude, and sometimes even monopolize the narrative. It is as if, in a stage play, the scenery and props were to come to life and join in with the actors. Zola's environment is always an integral and vital part of the narrative which accounts for much of the memorable, brighter-than-bright quality of his descriptive passages. In Saloon the novelist took this welding of place and story an important stage further by infusing his prose with the argot of the environment. One of the great achievements of this novel is that it records for all time Zola's solution to the problem of blending the linguistic demands of narrative prose with the crude vocabulary, spoken and thought, of his characters. In this he departed from the tradition that the narrative style sets the tone for the characters' dialogue. In fact he turned it completely about; Saloon is the first major novel in which the idiom and the inarticulation of the characters govern the style of the narrative. We take this for granted now, but in 1876 it was positively revolutionary. Not only are the characters convincingly idiomatic in their speech, but the descriptive passages also use a vocabulary Gervaise and her friends would be quite at home with. Of course the narrative abounds with slang - "pins" for legs, "saw-bones" for doctor, "ticker" for watch and so on – and with idiomatic similes, but the significant effect of it all is that we tend not to be visitors to the pages of the novel, loftily watching all the goings-on from some remote vantage point, but intimate observers in the streets, the houses and the rooms in which Gervaise lives. With the exception of the visit to the Louvre we see all the action throughout the book as though through the eyes and mind of a working woman, and innovation which adds immeasurably to its superb parabolic unity.

While the intention was inspired, the fact that the overall effect is near-faultless is an accident of time. For all his research into contemporary slang, Zola was apparently wide of the mark in his appreciation of its subtleties. Henry James remembered one Sunday afternoon in the early 1870s at Zola's Paris home, where a group of disciples were passionately discussing their writing plans. Zola told him, "As for me, I'm engaged on a book, the study of common morals, for which I'm making a collection of the swear-words in the language, those used commonly by the people in their everyday language." The remark, according to James, was made in passing, just as though an interesting idea had occurred to the novelist, and the American was particularly impressed by the seriousness with which Zola treated the project. It was only some years after that James discovered that he had witnessed the genesis of a masterpiece. Zola had an extraordinary ear for speech patterns and idiosyncrasies that reflected a great range of emotions and human foibles, but he was never master of the working-class patois of the time. Now, a hundred years on, with the niceties blurred by time, the argument about the accuracy of the slang in Saloon is academic, and need not concern us, especially as this point is further blurred by the limitations and skill of numerous translators.

If Zola's deadpan portrait of the common working man provoked a storm among the politically conscious readers of the novel, so did the author's blunt use – or alleged misuse – of the language. Henry James's view was, as usual, two-sided, complaining of the "ferociously bad smell which blows through Saloon like an emanation from an open drain and makes the perusal of the history of Gervaise and Coupeau very much such an ordeal as a crossing of the Channel in a November gale"; but adding that "Saloon, in spite of its fetid atmosphere, is full of magnificent passages and episodes, and the sustained power of the whole thing, the art of carrying a weight, is extraordinary."

Another critic, after damning the novel as pornography, warned that its author was "about to follow in the footsteps of the Marquis de Sade". But the critics were mostly ignored by the public who loved Gervaise; she became the heroine of a popular song, and her story was pantomimed at a Parisian circus. Nor was Zola without his defenders. An exasperated Huysmans wrote, "Is it possible there are people who deny this man's priceless talent, his powerful personality, his breadth of understanding, his strength of purpose, unique in this age of weakness and languor?" Huysmans was then, of course, white hot in the cause of naturalism, from which he later defected. But the poet Mallarmé, whose admiration remained constant, wrote to Zola: "You have endowed literature with something entirely new."

Saloon had sold well over 100,000 copies in France when it was introduced to English readers with Vizetelly's 1884 translation. It was thought prudent to add a preface by the Italian writer and journalist Edmondo de Amicis. "After reading Zola's romances," he wrote, "it is like finding truth for the first time," although, he warned, "sometimes you spring back as if from a sudden whiff of bad air." The disclaimer went on to suggest that delicate persons should withdraw, because "Zola does not conceal or embellish anything… he is at once a judicious romancer, a surgeon, a casuist, a physiologist, and an expert chancellor of the exchequer, who thus raises every veil, putting his hands into everything, and calling a spade a spade. Morally he unveils in his characters those deepest feelings which are generally profound secrets, tremblingly whispered through the grating of a confessional. In language he scarcely refrains from those few unspeakable words which naughty boys stealthily seek for in the dictionary. No one has ever gone further in this extreme, and you really do not know whether you ought to admire his talent or his courage." No wonder this translation sold 162,000 copies over the ensuing twenty-five years; no modern-day cover blurb could more calculatingly rivet a reader to its contents.

From the reaction to the serialization of the novel, Zola was ready with his defence by the time the book was published some months later. Commenting on the brouhaha in a preface to the first edition, he wrote, "Saloon is without doubt the most chaste of all my books. I have often had to point out sores far more frightful. It is the style which has shocked. It is the words that have angered. My crime has been to write a novel using the language of the people." Also included in the preface is Zola's somewhat chaste view of himself: "If only it were realized that the blood-thirsty and ferocious novelist is merely a worthy citizen, a man of studious and artistic tastes, living quietly and soberly in his little corner, and whose only ambition is to leave to posterity as great and vital a work of which he is capable!" Zola need hardly have bothered, for epithets like "pornographer" and "filthy Frenchman" continued to be thrown at him for the rest of his life, and even afterwards. As for the "great and vital work", the novelist's ambitions were more extravagantly realized than he can have imagined. Saloon is one of the greatest masterpieces of literature, a work which heralded a new era in the craft of fiction, a work in which all the elements of the novelist's art are unified into one magnificent whole. Perhaps more than in any of his other novels it reveals the depth of him compassion for humanity and the breadth of his vision. In it Zola's social conscience was forged into a weapon he was to throw repeatedly into the heart of indifference and injustice. In Gervaise he created one of literature's most unforgettable heroines, richly human, weak and generous. There is a logical inevitability about her life which creates the powerful illusion of reality, an illusion which persists long after the reader has finished the book. Gervaise also pervades four of her creator's other novels, in the sense that her four children are the protagonists of Nana(Nana), Germinal (Etienne), The Masterpiece (Claude) and The Beast in Man (Jacques).

Yet only a third of the way through his daunting, self-imposed task of writing the Rougon-Macquart Chronicle, Zola created an unsurpassed story of courage and despair, tenderness and brutality, humor and sadness which is never likely to go out of print. In it his characters find, at the end of the story, no happiness, no enlightenment, no fulfillment, no reason, no purpose. They are corks in the stream of life. But through this great novel flows a magnificent passion, the quivering vibration of tremendous, purposeless energy, the shockwaves of the primal force by which man expresses his presence on earth.

A Note on the Illustrations

The enormous popularity of Saloon resulted in many editions, songs, plays and even small paperback printings suitable for the back pocket of readers. Zola counted most of the leading artists of the day has his friends so that in 1878, C. Marpon and E. Flammarion, Publishers in Paris, produced an over-sized edition illustrated profusely. Many of the artists are relatively unknown today particularly to American readers, but Pierre Auguste Renoir is one of the most well-known artists in the history of art. He produced four etchings for Saloon and, as was his practice, they are not signed. We have included copies of his illustrations in this new edition of Saloon; they appear here for the first time since the original edition in 1878.

Saloon

(L'Assommoir)

CHAPTER I

Gervaise had waited up for Lantier until two in the morning. Then, shivering from having remained in a thin loose jacket, exposed to the fresh air at the window, she had thrown herself across the bed, drowsy, feverish, and her cheeks bathed in tears.

For a week past, on leaving the "Two-Headed Calf," where they took their meals, he had sent her home with the children and never reappeared himself till late at night, alleging that he had been in search of work. That evening, while watching for his return, she thought she had seen him enter the dancing-hall of the "Grand-Balcony," the ten blazing windows of which lighted up with the glare of a conflagration the dark expanse of the exterior Boulevards; and five or six paces behind him, she had caught sight of little Adele, a burnisher, who dined at the same restaurant, swinging her hands, as if she had just quitted his arm so as not to pass together under the dazzling light of the globes at the door.

When, towards five o'clock, Gervaise awoke, stiff and sore, she broke forth into sobs. Lantier had not returned. For the first time he had slept away from home. She remained seated on the edge of the bed, under the strip of faded chintz, which hung from the rod fastened to the ceiling by a piece of string. And slowly, with her eyes veiled by tears, she glanced round the wretched lodging, furnished with a walnut chest of drawers, minus one drawer, three rush-bottomed chairs, and a little greasy table, on which stood a broken water-jug. There had been added, for the children, an iron bedstead, which prevented any one getting to the chest of drawers, and filled two-thirds of the room. Gervaise's and Lantier's trunk, wide open, in one corner, displayed its emptiness, and a man's old hat right at the bottom almost buried beneath some dirty shirts and socks; while, against the walls, above the articles of furniture, hung a shawl full of holes, and a pair of trousers begrimed with mud, the last rags which the dealers in second-hand clothes declined to buy. In the center of the mantel-piece, lying between two odd zinc candle-sticks, was a bundle of pink pawn-tickets. It was the best room of the hotel, the first floor room, looking on to the Boulevard.

The two children were sleeping side by side, with their heads on the same pillow. Claude, aged eight years, was breathing quietly, with his little hands thrown outside the coverlet; while Etienne, only four years old, was smiling, with one arm round his brother's neck. And bare-footed, without thinking to again put on the old shoes that had fallen on the floor, she resumed her position at the window, her eyes searching the pavements in the distance.

The hotel was situated on the Boulevard de la Chapelle, to the left of the Barriere Poissonniere. It was a building of two stories high, painted a red, of the color of wine dregs, up to the second floor, and with shutters all rotted by the rain. Over a lamp with starred panes of glass, one could manage to read, between the two windows, the words, "Hotel Boncoeur, kept by Marsoullier," painted in big yellow letters, several pieces of which the moldering of the plaster had carried away. The lamp preventing her seeing, Gervaise raised herself on tiptoe, still holding the handkerchief to her lips. She looked to the right, towards the Boulevard Rochechouart, where groups of butchers, in aprons smeared with blood, were hanging about in front of the slaughter-houses; and the fresh breeze wafted occasionally a stench of slaughtered beasts. Looking to the left, she scanned a long avenue that ended nearly in front of her, where the white mass of the Lariboisiere Hospital was then in course of construction. Slowly, from one end of the horizon to the other, she followed the stone wall, behind which she sometimes heard, during night time, the shrieks of persons being murdered; and she searchingly looked into the remote angles, the dark corners, black with humidity and filth, fearing to discern there Lantier's body, stabbed to death.

She looked at the endless gray wall that surrounded the city with its belt of desolation. When she raised her eyes higher, she became aware of a bright burst of sunlight. The dull hum of the city's awakening already filled the air. Craning her neck to look at the Poissonniere gate, she remained for a time watching the constant stream of men, horses, and carts which flooded down from the heights of Montmartre and La Chapelle, pouring between the two squat stone lodges. It was like a herd of plodding cattle, an endless throng widened by sudden stoppages into eddies that spilled off the sidewalks into the street, a steady procession of laborers on their way back to work with tools slung over their back and a loaf of bread under their arm. This human inundation kept pouring down into Paris to be constantly swallowed up. Gervaise leaned further out at the risk of falling when she thought she recognized Lantier among the throng. She pressed the handkerchief tighter against her mouth, as though to push back the pain within her.

The sound of a young and cheerful voice caused her to leave the window.

"So the old man isn't here, Madame Lantier?"

"Why, no, Monsieur Coupeau," she replied, trying to smile.

Coupeau, a zinc-worker who occupied a ten franc room on the top floor, having seen the door unlocked, had walked in as friends will do.

"You know," he continued, "I'm now working over there in the hospital. What beautiful May weather, isn't it? The air is rather sharp this morning."

And he looked at Gervaise's face, red with weeping. When he saw that the bed had not been slept in, he shook his head gently; then he went to the children's couch where they were sleeping, looking as rosy as cherubs, and, lowering his voice, he said, "Come, the old man's not been home, has he? Don't worry yourself, Madame Lantier. He's very much occupied with politics. When they were voting for Eugene Sue the other day, he was acting almost crazy. He has very likely spent the night with some friends criticizing old Bonaparte."

"No, no," she murmured with an effort. "You don't think that. I know where Lantier is. You see, we have our little troubles like the rest of the world."

Coupeau winked his eye, to indicate he was not a dupe of this falsehood; and he went off, after offering to fetch her milk, if she did not care to go out: she was a good and courageous woman, and might count upon him on any day of trouble.

As soon as he was gone, Gervaise again returned to the window. At the Barriere, the tramp of the drove still continued in the morning air: locksmiths in short blue blouses, masons in white jackets, house painters in overcoats over long smocks. From a distance the crowd looked like a chalky smear of neutral hue composed chiefly of faded blue and dingy gray. When one of the workers occasionally stopped to light his pipe the others kept plodding past him, without sparing a laugh or a word to a comrade. With cheeks gray as clay, their eyes were continually drawn toward Paris which was swallowing them one by one.

At both corners of the Rue des Poissonniers however, some of the men slackened their pace as they neared the doors of the two wine-dealers who were taking down their shutters; and, before entering, they stood on the edge of the pavement, looking sideways over Paris, with no strength in their arms and already inclined for a day of idleness. Inside various groups were already buying rounds of drinks, or just standing around, forgetting their troubles, crowding up the place, coughing, spitting, clearing their throats with sip after sip.

Gervaise was watching Old Man Colombe's wine shop to the left of the street, where she thought she had seen Lantier, when a stout woman, bareheaded and wearing an apron called to her from the middle of the roadway:

"Hey, Madame Lantier, you're up very early."

Gervaise leaned out. "Why. It's you, Madame Boche. I've got a lot of work today."

"Yes, things don't do themselves, do they?"

The conversation continued between roadway and window. Madame Boche was concierge of the building where the "Two-Headed Calf" was on the ground floor. Gervaise had waited for Lantier more than once in the concierge's lodge, so as not to be alone at table with all the men who ate at the restaurant. Madame Boche was going to a tailor who was late in mending an overcoat for her husband. She mentioned one of her tenants who had come in with a woman the night before and kept everybody awake past three in the morning. She looked at Gervaise with intense curiosity.

"Is Monsieur Lantier, then, still in bed?" she asked abruptly.

"Yes, he's asleep," replied Gervaise, who could not avoid blushing.

Madame Boche saw the tears come into her eyes; and, satisfied no doubt, she turned to go, declaring men to be a cursed, lazy set. As she went off, she called back:

"It's this morning you go to the wash-house, isn't it? I've something to wash, too. I'll keep you a place next to me, and we can chat together."

Then, as if moved with sudden pity, she added:

"My poor little thing, you had far better not remain there; you'll take harm. You look quite blue with cold."

Gervaise still obstinately remained at the window during two mortal hours, till eight o'clock. Now all the shops had opened. Only a few work men were still hurrying along.

The working girls now filled the boulevard: metal polishers, milliners, flower sellers, shivering in their thin clothing. In small groups they chattered gaily, laughing and glancing here and there. Occasionally there would be one girl by herself, thin, pale, serious-faced, picking her way along the city wall among the puddles and the filth.

After the working girls, the office clerks came past, breathing upon their chilled fingers and munching penny rolls. Some of them are gaunt young fellows in ill-fitting suits, their tired eyes still fogged from sleep. Others are older men, stooped and tottering, with faces pale and drawn from long hours of office work and glancing nervously at their watches for fear of arriving late.

In time the Boulevards settle into their usual morning quiet. Old folks come out to stroll in the sun. Tired young mothers in bedraggled skirts cuddle babies in their arms or sit on a bench to change diapers. Children run, squealing and laughing, pushing and shoving.

Then Gervaise felt herself choking, dizzy with anguish, all hopes gone; it seemed to her that everything was ended, even time itself, and that Lantier would return no more. Her eyes vacantly wandered from the old slaughter-house, foul with butchery and with stench, to the new white hospital which, through the yawning openings of its ranges of windows, disclosed the naked wards, where death was preparing to mow. In front of her on the other side of the stone wall the bright heavens dazzled her, with the rising sun which rose higher and higher over the vast awaking city.

The young woman was seated on a chair, no longer crying, and with her hands abandoned on her lap, when Lantier quietly entered the room.

"It's you. It's you." she cried, rising to throw herself upon his neck.

"Yes, it's me. What of it?" he replied. "You are not going to begin any of your nonsense, I hope."

He had pushed her aside. Then, with a gesture of ill-humor he threw his black felt hat to the chest of drawers. He was a young fellow of twenty-six years of age, short and very dark, with a handsome figure, and slight moustaches which his hand was always mechanically twirling. He wore a workman's overalls and an old soiled overcoat, which he had belted tightly at the waist, and he spoke with a strong Provencal accent.

Gervaise, who had fallen back on her chair, gently complained, in short sentences: "I've not had a wink of sleep. I feared some harm had happened to you. Where have you been? Where did you spend the night? For heaven's sake. Don't do it again, or I shall go crazy. Tell me Auguste, where have you been?"

"Where I had business, of course," he returned shrugging his shoulders. "At eight o'clock, I was at La Glaciere, with my friend who is to start a hat factory. We sat talking late, so I preferred to sleep there. Now, you know, I don't like being spied upon, so just shut up."

The young woman recommenced sobbing. The loud voices and the rough movements of Lantier, who upset the chairs, had awakened the children. They sat up in bed, half naked, disentangling their hair with their tiny hands and, hearing their mother weep, they uttered terrible screams, crying also with their scarcely open eyes.

"Ah. There's the music." shouted Lantier furiously. "I warn you, I'll take my hook. And it will be for good, this time. You won't shut up? Then, good morning. I'll return to the place I've just come from."

He had already taken his hat from off the chest of drawers. But Gervaise threw herself before him, stammering: "No, no."

And she hushed the little ones' tears with her caresses, smoothed their hair, and soothed them with soft words. The children, suddenly quieted, laughing on their pillow, amused themselves by punching each other. The father however, without even taking off his boots, had thrown himself on the bed looking worn out, his face bearing signs of having been up all night. He did not go to sleep; he lay with his eyes wide open, looking round the room.

"It's a mess here." he muttered. And after observing Gervaise a moment, he malignantly added: "Don't you even wash yourself now?"

Gervaise was twenty-two, tall and slim with fine features, but she was already beginning to show the strain of her hard life. She seemed to have aged ten years from the hours of agonized weeping. Lantier's mean remark made her mad.

"You're not fair," she said spiritedly. "You well know I do all I can. It's not my fault we find ourselves here. I would like to see you, with two children, in a room where there's not even a stove to heat some water. When we arrived in Paris, instead of squandering your money, you should have made a home for us at once, as you promised."

"Listen." Lantier exploded. "You cracked the nut with me; it doesn't become you to sneer at it now."

Apparently not listening, Gervaise went on with her own thought. "If we work hard we can get out of the hole we're in. Madame Fauconnier, the laundress on Rue Neuve, will start me on Monday. If you work with your friend from La Glaciere, in six months we will be doing well. We'll have enough for decent clothes and a place we can call our own. But we'll have to stick with it and work hard."

Lantier turned over towards the wall, looking greatly bored. Then Gervaise lost her temper.

"Yes, that's it; I know the love of work doesn't trouble you much. You're bursting with ambition; you want to be dressed like a gentleman. You don't think me nice enough, do you, now that you've made me pawn all my dresses? Listen, Auguste, I didn't intend to speak of it, I would have waited a bit longer, but I know where you spent the night; I saw you enter the 'Grand-Balcony' with that trollop Adele. Ah. You choose them well. She's a nice one, she is. She does well to put on the airs of a princess. She's been the ridicule of every man who frequents the restaurant."

At a bound Lantier sprang from the bed. His eyes had become as black as ink in his pale face. With this little man, rage blew like a tempest.

"Yes, yes, of every man who frequents the restaurant." repeated the young woman. "Madame Boche intends to give them notice; she and her long stick of a sister, because they've always a string of men after them on the staircase."

Lantier raised his fists; then, resisting the desire of striking her, he seized hold of her by the arms, shook her violently and sent her sprawling upon the bed of the children, who recommenced crying. And he lay down again, mumbling, like a man resolving on something that he previously hesitated to do:

"You don't know what you've done, Gervaise. You've made a big mistake; you'll see."

For an instant the children continued sobbing. Their mother, who remained bending over the bed, held them both in her embrace, and kept repeating the same words in a monotonous tone of voice.

"If it weren't for you. My poor little ones. If it weren't for you. If it weren't for you."

Stretched out quietly, his eyes raised to the faded strip of chintz, Lantier no longer listened, but seemed to be buried in a fixed idea. He remained thus for nearly an hour, without giving way to sleep, in spite of the fatigue which weighed his eyelids down.

He finally turned toward Gervaise, his face set hard in determination. She had gotten the children up and dressed and had almost finished cleaning the room. The room looked, as always, dark and depressing with its sooty black ceiling and paper peeling from the damp walls. The dilapidated furniture was always streaked and dirty despite frequent dustings. Gervaise, devouring her grief, trying to assume a look of indifference, hurried over her work.

Lantier watched as she tidied her hair in front of the small mirror hanging near the window. While she washed herself he looked at her bare arms and shoulders. He seemed to be making comparisons in his mind as his lips formed a grimace. Gervaise limped with her right leg, though it was scarcely noticeable except when she was tired. Today, exhausted from remaining awake all night, she was supporting herself against the wall and dragging her leg.

Neither one spoke, they had nothing more to say. Lantier seemed to be waiting, while Gervaise kept busy and tried to keep her countenance expressionless. Finally, while she was making a bundle of the dirty clothes thrown in a corner, behind the trunk, he at length opened his lips and asked:

"What are you doing there? Where are you going?"

She did not answer at first. Then, when he furiously repeated his question, she made up her mind, and said:

"I suppose you can see for yourself. I'm going to wash all this. The children can't live in filth."

He let her pick up two or three handkerchiefs. And, after a fresh pause, he resumed: "Have you got any money?"

At these words she stood up and looked him full in the face, without leaving go of the children's dirty clothes, which she held in her hand.

"Money. And where do you think I can have stolen any? You know well enough that I got three francs the day before yesterday on my black skirt. We've lunched twice off it, and money goes quick at the pork-butcher's. No, you may be quite sure I've no money. I've four sous for the wash-house. I don't have an extra income like some women."

He let this allusion pass. He had moved off the bed, and was passing in review the few rags hanging about the room. He ended by taking up the pair of trousers and the shawl, and searching the drawers, he added two chemises and a woman's loose jacket to the parcel; then, he threw the whole bundle into Gervaise's arms, saying:

"Here, go and pop this."

"Don't you want me to pop the children as well?" asked she. "Eh. If they lent on children, it would be a fine riddance."

She went to the pawn broker, however. When she returned at the end of half an hour, she laid a hundred sou piece on the mantel-shelf, and added the ticket to the others, between the two candlesticks.

"That's what they gave me," said she. "I wanted six francs, but I couldn't manage it . . . . They'll never ruin themselves. And there's always such a crowd there."

Lantier did not pick up the five franc piece directly. He would rather that she got change, so as to leave her some of it. But he decided to slip it into his waistcoat pocket, when he noticed a small piece of ham wrapped up in paper, and the remains of a loaf on the chest of drawers.

"I didn't dare go to the milk woman's, because we owe her a week," explained Gervaise. "But I shall be back early; you can get some bread and some chops while I'm away, and then we'll have lunch. Bring also a bottle of wine."

He did not say no. Their quarrel seemed to be forgotten. The young woman was completing her bundle of dirty clothes. But when she went to take Lantier's shirts and socks from the bottom of the trunk, he called to her to leave them alone.

"*Leave my things, d'ye hear? I don't want 'em touched.*"

"What's it you don't want touched?" she asked, rising up. "I suppose you don't mean to put these filthy things on again, do you? They must be washed."

She studied his boyishly handsome face, now so rigid that it seemed nothing could ever soften it. He angrily grabbed his things from her and threw them back into the trunk, saying:

"Just obey me, for once. I tell you I won't have 'em touched."

"But why?" she asked, turning pale, a terrible suspicion crossing her mind. "You don't need your shirts now, you're not going away. What can it matter to you if I take them?"

He hesitated for an instant, embarrassed by the piercing glance she fixed upon him. "Why—why," stammered he, "because you go and tell everyone that you keep me, that you wash and mend. Well. It worries me, there. Attend to your own business and I'll attend to mine, washerwomen don't work for dogs."

She supplicated, she protested she had never complained; but he roughly closed the trunk and sat down upon it, saying, "No." to her face. He could surely do as he liked with what belonged to him. Then, to escape from the inquiring looks she leveled at him, he went and laid down on the bed again, saying that he was sleepy, and requesting her not to make his head ache with any more of her row. This time indeed, he seemed to fall asleep. Gervaise, for a while, remained undecided. She was tempted to kick the bundle of dirty clothes on one side, and to sit down and sew. But Lantier's regular breathing ended by reassuring her. She took the ball of blue and the piece of soap remaining from her last washing, and going up to the little ones who were quietly playing with some old corks in front of the window, she kissed them, and said in a low voice:

"Be very good, don't make any noise; papa's asleep."

When she left the room, Claude's and Etienne's gentle laughter alone disturbed the great silence beneath the blackened ceiling. It was ten o'clock. A ray of sunshine entered by the half open window.

On the Boulevard, Gervaise turned to the left, and followed the Rue Neuve de la Goutte-d'Or. As she passed Madame Fauconnier's shop, she slightly bowed her head. The wash-house she was bound for was situated towards the middle of the street, at the part where the roadway commenced to ascend.

The rounded, gray contours of the three large zinc wash tanks, studded with rivets, rose above the flat-roofed building. Behind them was the drying room, a high second story, closed in on all sides by narrow-slatted lattices so that the air could circulate freely, and through which laundry could be seen hanging on brass wires. The steam engine's smokestack exhaled puffs of white smoke to the right of the water tanks.

Gervaise was used to puddles and did not bother to tuck her skirts up before making her way through the doorway, which was cluttered with jars of bleaching water. She was already acquainted with the mistress of the wash-house, a delicate little woman with red, inflamed eyes, who sat in a small glazed closet with account books in front of her, bars of soap on shelves, balls of blue in glass bowls, and pounds of soda done up in packets; and, as she passed, she asked for her beetle and her scouring-brush, which she had left to be taken care of the last time she had done her washing there. Then, after obtaining her number, she entered the wash-house.

It was an immense shed, with large clear windows, and a flat ceiling, showing the beams supported on cast-iron pillars. Pale rays of light passed through the hot steam, which remained suspended like a milky fog. Smoke arose from certain corners, spreading about and covering the recesses with a bluish veil. A heavy moisture hung around, impregnated with a soapy odor, a damp insipid smell, continuous though at moments overpowered by the more potent fumes of the chemicals. Along the washing-places, on either side of the central alley, were rows of women, with bare arms and necks, and skirts tucked up, showing colored stockings and heavy lace-up shoes. They were beating furiously, laughing, leaning back to call out a word in the midst of the din, or stooping over their tubs, all of them brutal, ungainly, foul of speech, and soaked as though by a shower, with their flesh red and reeking.

All around the women continuously flowed a river from hot-water buckets emptied with a sudden splash, cold-water faucets left dripping, soap suds spattering, and the dripping from rinsed laundry which was hung up. It splashed their feet and drained away across the sloping flagstones. The din of the shouting and the rhythmic beating was joined by the patter of steady dripping. It was slightly muffled by the moisture-soaked ceiling. Meanwhile, the steam engine could be heard as it puffed and snorted ceaselessly while cloaked in its white mist. The dancing vibration of its flywheel seemed to regulate the volume of the noisy turbulence.

Gervaise passed slowly along the alley, looking to the right and left, carrying her laundry bundle under one arm, with one hip thrust high and limping more than usual. She was jostled by several women in the hubbub.

"This way, my dear." cried Madame Boche, in her loud voice. Then, when the young woman had joined her at the very end on the left, the concierge, who was furiously rubbing a dirty sock, began to talk incessantly, without leaving off her work. "Put your things there, I've kept your place. . . . I won't be long over what I've got. Boche scarcely dirties his things at all. And you, you won't be long either, will you? Your bundle's quite a little one. Before twelve o'clock we shall have finished, and we can go off to lunch. I used to send my things to a laundress in the Rue Poulet, but she destroyed everything with her chlorine and her brushes; so now I do the washing myself. It's so much saved; it only costs the soap. I say, you should have put those shirts to soak. Those little rascal children, on my word. One would think their bodies were covered with soot."

Gervaise, having undone her bundle, was spreading out the little ones' shirts, and as Madame Boche advised her to take a pail full of lye, she answered, "warm water will do. I'm used to it." She had sorted her laundry with several colored pieces to one side. Then, after filling her tub with four pails of cold water from the tap behind her, she plunged her pile of whites into it.

"You're used to it?" repeated Madame Boche. "You were a washerwoman in your native place, weren't you, my dear?"

Gervaise, with her sleeves pushed back, displayed the graceful arms of a young blonde, as yet scarcely reddened at the elbows, and started scrubbing her laundry. She spread a shirt out on the narrow rubbing board which was water-bleached and eroded by years of use. She rubbed soap into the shirt, turned it over, and soaped the other side. Before replying to Madame Boche she grasped her beetle and began to pound away so that her shouted phrases were punctuated with loud and rhythmic thumps.

"Yes, yes, a washerwoman—When I was ten—That's twelve years ago—We used to go to the river—It smelt nicer there than it does here—You should have seen, there was a nook under the trees, with clear running water—You know, at Plassans—Don't you know Plassans? It's near Marseilles."

"How you go at it." exclaimed Madame Boche, amazed at the strength of her blows. "You could flatten out a piece of iron with your little lady-like arms."

The conversation continued in a very high volume. At times, the concierge, not catching what was said, was obliged to lean forward. All the linen was beaten, and with a will. Gervaise plunged it into the tub again, and then took it out once more, each article separately, to rub it over with soap a second time and brush it. With one hand she held the article firmly on the plank; with the other, which grasped the short couch-grass brush, she extracted from the linen a dirty lather, which fell in long drips. Then, in the slight noise caused by the brush, the two women drew together, and conversed in a more intimate way.

"No, we're not married," resumed Gervaise. "I don't hide it. Lantier isn't so nice for anyone to care to be his wife. If it weren't for the children. I was fourteen and he was eighteen when we had our first one. It happened in the usual way, you know how it is. I wasn't happy at home. Old man Macquart would kick me in the tail whenever he felt like it, for no reason at all. I had to have some fun outside. We might have been married, but—I forget why—our parents wouldn't consent."

She shook her hands, which were growing red in the white suds. "The water's awfully hard in Paris."

Madame Boche was now washing only very slowly. She kept leaving off, making her work last as long as she could, so as to remain there, to listen to that story, which her curiosity had been hankering to know for a fortnight past. Her mouth was half open in the midst of her big, fat face; her eyes, which were almost at the top of her head, were gleaming. She was thinking, with the satisfaction of having guessed right.

"That's it, the little one gossips too much. There's been a row."

Then, she observed out loud, "He isn't nice, then?"

"Don't mention it." replied Gervaise. "He used to behave very well in the country; but, since we've been in Paris, he's been unbearable. I must tell you that his mother died last year and left him some money— about seventeen hundred francs. He would come to Paris, so, as old Macquart was forever knocking me about without warning, I consented to come away with him. We made the journey with two children. He was to set me up as a laundress, and work himself at his trade of a hatter. We should have been very happy; but, you see, Lantier's ambitious and a spendthrift, a fellow who only thinks of amusing himself. In short, he's not worth much. On arriving, we went to the Hotel Montmartre, in the Rue Montmartre. And then there were dinners, and cabs, and the theatre; a watch for himself and a silk dress for me, for he's not unkind when he's got the money. You understand, he went in for everything, and so well that at the end of two months we were cleaned out. It was then that we came to live at the Hotel Boncoeur, and that this horrible life began."

She interrupted herself. A lump had suddenly risen in her throat, and she could scarcely restrain her tears. She had finished brushing the things.

"I must go and fetch my hot water," she murmured.

But Madame Boche, greatly disappointed at this break off in the disclosures, called to the wash-house boy, who was passing, "My little Charles, kindly get madame a pail of hot water; she's in a hurry."

The youth took the bucket and brought it back filled. Gervaise paid him; it was a sou the pailful. She poured the hot water into the tub, and soaped the things a last time with her hands, leaning over them in a mass of steam, which deposited small beads of gray vapor in her light hair.

"Here put some soda in, I've got some by me," said the concierge, obligingly.

And she emptied into Gervaise's tub what remained of a bag of soda which she had brought with her. She also offered her some of the chemical water, but the young woman declined it; it was only good for grease and wine stains.

"I think he's rather a loose fellow," resumed Madame Boche, returning to Lantier, but without naming him.

Gervaise, bent almost double, her hands all shriveled, and thrust in amongst the clothes, merely tossed her head.

"Yes, yes," continued the other, "I have noticed several little things." But she suddenly interrupted herself, as Gervaise jumped up, with a pale face, and staring wildly at her. Then she exclaimed, ". . . no. I don't know anything. He likes to laugh a bit, I think, that's all. For instance, you know the two girls who lodge at my place, Adele and Virginie. Well;

he larks about with 'em, but he just flirts for sport."

The young woman standing before her, her face covered with perspiration, the water dripping from her arms, continued to stare at her with a fixed and penetrating look. Then the concierge got excited, giving herself a blow on the chest, and pledging her word of honor, she cried:

"I know nothing, I mean it when I say so."

Then calming herself, she added in a gentle voice, as if speaking to a person on whom loud protestations would have no effect, "I think he has a frank look about the eyes. He'll marry you, my dear, I'm sure of it."

Gervaise wiped her forehead with her wet hand. Shaking her head again, she pulled another garment out of the water. Both of them kept silence for a moment. The wash-house was quieting down, for eleven o'clock had struck. Half of the washerwomen were perched on the edge of their tubs, eating sausages between slices of bread and drinking from open bottles of wine. Only housewives who had come to launder small bundles of family linen were hurrying to finish.

Occasional beetle blows could still be heard amid the subdued laughter and gossip half-choked by the greedy chewing of jawbones. The steam engine never stopped. Its vibrant, snorting voice seemed to fill the entire hall, though not one of the women even heard it. It was like the breathing of the wash-house, its hot breath collecting under the ceiling rafters in an eternal floating mist.

The heat was becoming intolerable. Through the tall windows on the left sunlight was streaming in, touching the steamy vapors with opalescent tints of soft pinks and grayish blues. Charles went from window to window, letting down the heavy canvas awnings. Then he crossed to the shady side to open the ventilators. He was applauded by cries and hand clapping and a rough sort of gaiety spread around. Soon even the last of the beetle-pounding stopped.

With full mouths, the washerwomen could only make gestures. It became so quiet that the grating sound of the fireman shoveling coal into the engine's firebox could be heard at regular intervals from far at the other end.

Gervaise was washing her colored things in the hot water thick with lather, which she had kept for the purpose. When she had finished, she drew a trestle towards her and hung across it all the different articles; the drippings from which made bluish puddles on the floor; and she commenced rinsing. Behind her, the cold water tap was set running into a vast tub fixed to the ground, and across which were two wooden bars whereon to lay the clothes. High up in the air were two other bars for the things to finish dripping on.

"We're almost finished, and not a bad job," said Madame Boche. "I'll wait and help you wring all that."

". . . . It's not worth while; I'm much obliged though," replied the young woman, who was kneading with her hands and sousing the colored things in some clean water. "If I'd any sheets, it would be another thing."

But she had, however, to accept the concierge's assistance. They were wringing between them, one at each end, a woolen skirt of a washed-out chestnut color, from which dribbled a yellowish water, when Madame Boche exclaimed:

"Why, there's tall Virginie. What has she come here to wash, when all her wardrobe that isn't on her would go into a pocket handkerchief?"

Gervaise jerked her head up. Virginie was a girl of her own age, taller than she was, dark and pretty in spite of her face being rather long and narrow. She had on an old black dress with flounces, and a red ribbon round her neck; and her hair was done up carefully, the chignon being enclosed in a blue silk net. She stood an instant in the middle of the central alley, screwing up her eyes as though seeking someone; then, when she caught sight of Gervaise, she passed close to her, erect, insolent, and with a swinging gait, and took a place in the same row, five tubs away from her.

"There's a freak for you." continued Madame Boche in a lower tone of voice. "She never does any laundry, not even a pair of cuffs. A seamstress who doesn't even sew on a loose button. She's just like her sister, the brass burnisher, that bitch Adele, who stays away from her job two days out of three. Nobody knows who their folks are or how they make a living. Though, if I wanted to talk . . . What on earth is she scrubbing there? A filthy petticoat. I'll wager it's seen some lovely sights, that petticoat."

Madame Boche was evidently trying to make herself agreeable to Gervaise. The truth was she often took a cup of coffee with Adele and

Virginia, when the girls had any money. Gervaise did not answer, but hurried over her work with feverish hands. She had just prepared her blue in a little tub that stood on three legs. She dipped in the linen things, and shook them an instant at the bottom of the colored water, the reflection of which had a pinky tinge; and after wringing them lightly, she spread them out on the wooden bars up above. During the time she was occupied with this work, she made a point of turning her back on Virginie. But she heard her chuckles; she could feel her side-long glances. Virginie appeared only to have come there to provoke her. At one moment, Gervaise having turned around, they both stared into each other's faces.

"Leave her alone," whispered Madame Boche. "You're not going to pull each other's hair out, I hope. When I tell you there's nothing to it. It isn't her, anyhow."

At this moment, as the young woman was hanging up the last article of clothing, there was a sound of laughter at the door of the wash-house.

"Here are two brats who want their mamma." cried Charles.

All the women leant forward. Gervaise recognized Claude and Etienne. As soon as they caught sight of her, they ran to her through the puddles, the heels of their unlaced shoes resounding on the flagstones. Claude, the eldest, held his little brother by the hand. The women, as they passed them, uttered little exclamations of affection as they noticed their frightened though smiling faces. And they stood there, in front of their mother, without leaving go of each other's hands, and holding their fair heads erect.

"Has papa sent you?" asked Gervaise.

But as she stooped to tie the laces of Etienne's shoes, she saw the key of their room on one of Claude's fingers, with the brass number hanging from it.

"Why, you've brought the key." she said, greatly surprised. "What's that for?"

The child, seeing the key which he had forgotten on his finger, appeared to recollect, and exclaimed in his clear voice:

"Papa's gone away."

"He's gone to buy the lunch, and told you to come here to fetch me?"

Claude looked at his brother, hesitated, no longer recollecting. Then he resumed all in a breath: "Papa's gone away. He jumped off the bed, he put all the things in the trunk, he carried the trunk down to a cab. He's gone away."

Gervaise, who was squatting down, slowly rose to her feet, her face ghastly pale. She put her hands to her cheeks and temples, as though she felt her head was breaking; and she could find only these words, which she repeated twenty times in the same tone of voice:

"*Ah. Good heavens.—ah. Good heavens.—ah. Good heavens.*"

Madame Boche, however, also questioned the child, quite delighted at the chance of hearing the whole story.

"Come, little one, you must tell us just what happened. It was he who locked the door and who told you to bring the key, wasn't it?" And, lowering her voice, she whispered in Claude's ear: "Was there a lady in the cab?"

The child again got confused. Then he recommenced his story in a triumphant manner: "He jumped off the bed, he put all the things in the trunk. He's gone away."

Then, when Madame Boche let him go, he drew his brother in front of the tap, and they amused themselves by turning on the water. Gervaise was unable to cry. She was choking, leaning back against her tub, her face still buried in her hands. Brief shudders rocked her body and she wailed out long sighs while pressing her hands tighter against her eyes, as though abandoning herself to the blackness of desolation, a dark, deep pit into which she seemed to be falling.

"Come, my dear, pull yourself together." murmured Madame Boche.

"If you only knew. If you only knew." said she at length very faintly. "He sent me this morning to pawn my shawl and my chemises to pay for that cab."

And she burst out crying. The memory of the events of that morning and of her trip to the pawn-place tore from her the sobs that had been choking her throat. That abominable trip to the pawn-place was the thing that hurt most in all her sorrow and despair. Tears were streaming down her face but she didn't think of using her handkerchief.

"Be reasonable, do be quiet, everyone's looking at you," Madame Boche, who hovered round her, kept repeating. "How can you worry yourself so much on account of a man? You loved him, then, all the same, did you, my poor darling? A little while ago you were saying all sorts of things against him; and now you're crying for him, and almost breaking your heart. Dear me, how silly we all are."

Then she became quite maternal.

"A pretty little woman like you. Can it be possible? One may tell you everything now, I suppose. Well. You recollect when I passed under your window, I already had my suspicions. Just fancy, last night, when Adele came home, I heard a man's footsteps with hers. So I thought I would see who it was. I looked up the staircase. The fellow was already on the second landing; but I certainly recognized Monsieur Lantier's overcoat. Boche, who was on the watch this morning, saw him tranquilly nod adieu. He was with Adele, you know. Virginie has a situation now, where she goes twice a week. Only it's highly imprudent all the same, for they've only one room and an alcove, and I can't very well say where Virginie managed to sleep."

She interrupted herself an instant, turned round, and then resumed, subduing her loud voice:

"She's laughing at seeing you cry, that heartless thing over there. I'd stake my life that her washing's all a pretense. She's packed off the other two, and she's come here so as to tell them how you take it."

Gervaise removed her hands from her face and looked. When she beheld Virginie in front of her, amidst three or four women, speaking low and staring at her, she was seized with a mad rage. Her arms in front of her, searching the ground, she stumbled forward a few paces. Trembling all over, she found a bucket full of water, grabbed it with both hands, and emptied it at Virginie.

"The bastard," yelled tall Virginie.

She had stepped back, and her boots alone got wet. The other women, who for some minutes past had all been greatly upset by Gervaise's tears, jostled each other in their anxiety to see the fight. Some, who were finishing their lunch, got on the tops of their tubs. Others hastened forward, their hands smothered with soap. A ring was formed.

"Ah. The bastard," repeated tall Virginie. "What's the matter with her? She's mad."

Gervaise, standing on the defensive, her chin thrust out, her features convulsed, said nothing, not having yet acquired the Paris gift of street gab. The other continued:

"Get out. This girl's tired of wallowing about in the country; she wasn't twelve years old when the soldiers were at her. She even lost her leg serving her country. That leg's rotting off."

The on-lookers burst out laughing. Virginie, seeing her success, advanced a couple of steps, drawing herself up to her full height, and yelling louder than ever:

"Here. Come a bit nearer, just to see how I'll settle you. Don't you come annoying us here. Do I even know her, the bitch? If she'd wetted me, I'd have pretty soon shown her battle, as you'd have seen. Let her just say what I've ever done to her. Speak, you vixen; what's been done to you?"

"Don't talk so much," stammered Gervaise. "You know well enough. Someone saw my husband last night. And shut up, because if you don't I'll most certainly strangle you."

"Her husband. That's a good one. As if cripples like her had husbands. If he's left you it's not my fault. Surely you don't think I've stolen him, do you? He was much too good for you and you made him sick. Did you keep him on a leash? Has anyone here seen her husband? There's a reward."

The laughter burst forth again. Gervaise contented herself with continually murmuring in a low tone of voice, "You know well enough, you know well enough. It's your sister. I'll strangle her—your sister."

"Yes, go and try it on with my sister," resumed Virginie sneeringly. "Ah. It's my sister. That's very likely. My sister looks a trifle different to you; but what's that to me? Can't one come and wash one's clothes in peace now? Just dry up, d'ye hear, because I've had enough of it."

But it was she who returned to the attack, after giving five or six strokes with her beetle, intoxicated by the insults she had been giving utterance to, and worked up into a passion. She left off and recommenced again, speaking in this way three times:

"Well, yes. It's my sister. There now, does that satisfy you? They adore each other. You should just see them bill and coo. And he's left you with your children. Those pretty kids with scabs all over their faces. You got one of them from a gendarme, didn't you? And you let three others die because you didn't want to pay excess baggage on your journey. It's your Lantier who told us that. Ah. He's been telling some fine things; he'd had enough of you."

"You dirty slut. You dirty slut. You dirty slut," yelled Gervaise, beside herself, and again seized with a furious trembling. She turned round, looking once more about the ground; and only observing the little tub, she seized hold of it by the legs, and flung the whole of the bluing at Virginie's face.

"The beast. She's spoilt my dress." cried the latter, whose shoulder was sopping wet and whose left hand was dripping blue. "Just wait, you wretch."

In her turn she seized a bucket, and emptied it over Gervaise. Then a formidable battle began. They both ran along the rows of tubs, seized hold of the pails that were full, and returned to dash the contents at each other's heads. And each deluge was accompanied by a volley of words. Gervaise herself answered now:

"There, you scum. You got it that time. It'll help to cool you."

"Ah. The carrion. That's for your filth. Wash yourself for once in your life."

"*Yes, yes, I'll wash the salt out of you, you cod.*"

"Another one. Brush your teeth, fix yourself up for your post tonight at the corner of the Rue Belhomme."

They ended by having to refill the buckets at the water taps, continuing to insult each other the while. The initial bucketfuls were so poorly aimed as to scarcely reach their targets, but they soon began to splash each other in earnest. Virginie was the first to receive a bucketful in the face. The water ran down, soaking her back and front. She was still staggering when another caught her from the side, hitting her left ear and drenching her chignon which then came unwound into a limp, bedraggled string of hair.

Gervaise was hit first in the legs. One pail filled her shoes full of water and splashed up to her thighs. Two more wet her even higher. Soon both of them were soaked from top to bottom and it was impossible to count the hits. Their clothes were plastered to their bodies and they looked shrunken. Water was dripping everywhere as from umbrellas in a rainstorm.

"They look jolly funny." said the hoarse voice of one of the women.

Everyone in the wash-house was highly amused. A good space was left to the combatants, as nobody cared to get splashed. Applause and jokes circulated in the midst of the sluice-like noise of the buckets emptied in rapid succession. On the floor the puddles were running one into another, and the two women were wading in them up to their ankles. Virginie, however, who had been meditating a treacherous move, suddenly seized hold of a pail of lye, which one of her neighbors had left there and threw it. The same cry arose from all. Everyone thought Gervaise was scalded; but only her left foot had been slightly touched. And, exasperated by the pain, she seized a bucket, without troubling herself to fill it this time, and threw it with all her might at the legs of Virginie, who fell to the ground. All the women spoke together.

"She's broken one of her limbs."

"Well, the other tried to cook her."

"She's right, after all, the blonde one, if her man's been taken from her." Madame Boche held up her arms to heaven, uttering all sorts of exclamations. She had prudently retreated out of the way between two tubs; and the children, Claude and Etienne, crying, choking, terrified, clung to her dress with the continuous cry of "Mamma. Mamma" broken by their sobs. When she saw Virginie fall she hastened forward, and tried to pull Gervaise away by her skirt, repeating the while, "Come now, go home. Be reasonable. On my word, it's quite upset me. Never was such a butchery seen before."

But she had to draw back and seek refuge again between the two tubs, with the children. Virginie had just flown at Gervaise's throat. She squeezed her round the neck, trying to strangle her. The latter freed herself with a violent jerk, and in her turn hung on to the other's hair, as though she was trying to pull her head off. The battle was silently resumed, without a cry, without an insult. They did not seize each other round the body, they attacked each other's faces with open hands and clawing fingers, pinching, scratching whatever they caught hold of. The tall, dark girl's red ribbon and blue silk hair net were torn off. The body of her dress, giving way at the neck, displayed a large portion of her shoulder; while the blonde, half stripped, a sleeve gone from her loose white jacket without her knowing how, had a rent in her underwear, which exposed to view the naked line of her waist. Shreds of stuff flew in all directions. It was from Gervaise that the first blood was drawn, three long scratches from the mouth to the chin; and she sought to protect her eyes, shutting them at every grab the other made, for fear of

having them torn out. No blood showed on Virginie as yet. Gervaise
aimed at her ears, maddened at not being able to reach them. At length
she succeeded in seizing hold of one of the earrings—an imitation pear
in yellow glass—which she pulled out and slit the ear, and the blood
flowed.

"They're killing each other. Separate them, the whores," exclaimed
several voices.

The other women had drawn nearer. They formed themselves into
two camps. Some were cheering the combatants on as the others were
trembling and turning their heads away saying that it was making them
sick. A large fight nearly broke out between the two camps as the
women called each other names and brandished their fists threateningly. Three loud slaps rang out.

Madame Boche, meanwhile, was trying to discover the wash-house
boy.

"Charles. Charles. Wherever has he got to?"

And she found him in the front rank, looking on with his arms
folded. He was a big fellow, with an enormous neck. He was laughing
and enjoying the sight of the skin which the two women displayed. The
little blonde was as fat as a quail. It would be fun if her chemise burst
open.

"Why," murmured he, blinking his eye, "she's got a strawberry
birthmark under her arm."

"What. You're there." cried Madame Boche, as she caught sight of
him. "Just come and help us separate them. You can easily separate
them, you can."

"No. thank you, not if I know it," said he coolly. "To get my eye
scratched like I did the other day, I suppose. I'm not here for that sort
of thing; I have enough to do without that. Don't be afraid, a little
bleeding does 'em good; it'll soften 'em."

The concierge then talked of fetching the police; but the mistress
of the wash-house, the delicate young woman with the red, inflamed
eyes, would not allow her to do this. She kept saying:

"No, no, I won't; it'll compromise my establishment."

The struggle on the ground continued. All on a sudden, Virginie
raised herself up on her knees. She had just gotten hold of a beetle and
held it on high. She had a rattle in her throat and in an altered voice, she

exclaimed, "Here's something that'll settle you. Get your dirty linen ready."

Gervaise quickly thrust out her hand, and also seized a beetle, and held it up like a club; and she too spoke in a choking voice, "Ah. You want to wash. Let me get hold of your skin that I may beat it into dishcloths."

For a moment they remained there, on their knees, menacing each other. Their hair all over their faces, their breasts heaving, muddy, swelling with rage, they watched one another, as they waited and took breath. Gervaise gave the first blow. Her beetle glided off Virginie's shoulder, and she at once threw herself on one side to avoid the latter's beetle, which grazed her hip. Then, warming to their work they struck at each other like washerwomen beating clothes, roughly, and in time. Whenever there was a hit, the sound was deadened, so that one might have thought it a blow in a tub full of water. The other women around them no longer laughed. Several had gone off saying that it quite upset them; those who remained stretched out their necks, their eyes lighted up with a gleam of cruelty, admiring the pluck displayed. Madame Boche had led Claude and Etienne away, and one could hear at the other end of the building the sound of their sobs, mingled with the sonorous shocks of the two beetles. But Gervaise suddenly yelled. Virginie had caught her a whack with all her might on her bare arm, just above the elbow. A large red mark appeared, the flesh at once began to swell. Then she threw herself upon Virginie, and everyone thought she was going to beat her to death.

"Enough. Enough." was cried on all sides.

Her face bore such a terrible expression, that no one dared approach her. Her strength seemed to have increased tenfold. She seized Virginie round the waist, bent her down and pressed her face against the flagstones. Raising her beetle she commenced beating as she used to beat at Plassans, on the banks of the Viorne, when her mistress washed the clothes of the garrison. The wood seemed to yield to the flesh with a damp sound. At each whack a red weal marked the white skin.

"Shit!" exclaimed the boy Charles, opening his eyes to their full extent and gloating over the sight.

Laughter again burst forth from the lookers-on, but soon the cry, "Enough. Enough." recommenced. Gervaise heard not, neither did she tire. She examined her work, bent over it, anxious not to leave a dry place. She wanted to see the whole of that skin beaten, covered with contusions. And she talked, seized with a ferocious gaiety, recalling a washerwoman's song,

> "Bang. Bang. Margot at her tub.
> Bang. Bang. Beating rub-a-dub.
> Bang. Bang. Tries to wash her heart.
> Bang. Bang. Black with grief to part."

> And then she resumed,
> "That's for you, that's for your sister.
> That's for Lantier.
> When you next see them,
> You can give them that.
> Attention. I'm going to begin again.
> That's for Lantier, that's for your sister.
> That's for you.
> Bang. Bang. Margot at her tub.
> Bang. Bang. Beating rub-a-dub"

The others were obliged to drag Virginie away from her. The tall, dark girl, her face bathed in tears and purple with shame, picked up her things and hastened away. She was vanquished. Gervaise slipped on the sleeve of her jacket again, and fastened up her petticoats. Her arm pained her a good deal, and she asked Madame Boche to place her bundle of clothes on her shoulder. The concierge referred to the battle, spoke of her emotions, and talked of examining the young woman's person, just to see.

"You may, perhaps, have something broken. I heard a tremendous blow."

But Gervaise wanted to go home. She made no reply to the pitying remarks and noisy ovation of the other women who surrounded her, erect in their aprons. When she was laden she gained the door, where the children awaited her.

"Two hours, that makes two sous," said the mistress of the wash-house, already back at her post in the glazed closet.

Why two sous? She no longer understood that she was asked to pay for her place there. Then she gave the two sous; and limping very much beneath the weight of the wet clothes on her shoulder, the water dripping from off her, her elbow black and blue, her cheek covered with blood, she went off, dragging Claude and Etienne with her bare arms, while they trotted along on either side of her, still trembling, and their faces besmeared with their tears.

Once she was gone, the wash-house resumed its roaring tumult. The washerwomen had eaten their bread and drunk their wine. Their faces were lit up and their spirits enlivened by the fight between Gervaise and Virginie.

The long lines of tubs were astir again with the fury of thrashing arms, of craggy profiles, of marionettes with bent backs and slumping shoulders that twisted and jerked violently as though on hinges. Conversations went on from one end to the other in loud voices. Laughter and coarse remarks crackled through the ceaseless gurgling of the water. Faucets were sputtering, buckets spilling, rivulets flowing underneath the rows of washboards. Throughout the huge shed rising wisps of steam reflected a reddish tint, pierced here and there by disks of sunlight, golden globes that had leaked through holes in the awnings. The air was stiflingly warm and odorous with soap.

Suddenly the hall was filled with a white mist. The huge copper lid of the lye-water kettle was rising mechanically along a notched shaft, and from the gaping copper hollow within its wall of bricks came whirling clouds of vapor. Meanwhile, at one side the drying machines were hard at work; within their cast-iron cylinders bundles of laundry were being wrung dry by the centrifugal force of the steam engine, which was still puffing, steaming, jolting the wash-house with the ceaseless labor of its iron limbs.

When Gervaise turned into the entry of the Hotel Boncoeur, her tears again mastered her. It was a dark, narrow passage, with a gutter for the dirty water running alongside the wall; and the stench which she again encountered there caused her to think of the fortnight she had passed in the place with Lantier—a fortnight of misery and quarrels, the recollection of which was now a bitter regret. It seemed to bring her abandonment home to her.

Upstairs the room was bare, in spite of the sunshine which entered through the open window. That blaze of light, that kind of dancing golden dust, exposed the lamentable condition of the blackened ceiling, and of the walls half denuded of paper, all the more. The only thing left hanging in the room was a woman's small neckerchief, twisted like a piece of string. The children's bedstead, drawn into the middle of the apartment, displayed the chest of drawers, the open drawers of which exposed their emptiness. Lantier had washed himself and had used up the last of the pomatum—two sous' worth of pomatum in a playing card; the greasy water from his hands filled the basin. And he had forgotten nothing. The corner which until then had been filled by the trunk seemed to Gervaise an immense empty space. Even the little mirror which hung on the window-fastening was gone. When she made this discovery, she had a presentiment. She looked on the mantel-piece. Lantier had taken away the pawn tickets; the pink bundle was no longer there, between the two odd zinc candlesticks.

She hung her laundry over the back of a chair and just stood there, gazing around at the furniture. She was so dulled and bewildered that she could no longer cry. She had only one sou left. Then, hearing Claude and Etienne laughing merrily by the window, their troubles already forgotten, she went to them and put her arms about them, losing herself for a moment in contemplation of that long gray avenue where, that very morning, she had watched the awakening of the working population, of the immense work-shop of Paris.

At this hour immense heat was rising from the pavement and from all the furnaces in the factories, setting alight a reflecting oven over the city and beyond the stone wall. Out upon this very pavement, into this furnace blast, she had been tossed, alone with her little ones. As she glanced up and down the boulevard, she was seized with a dull dread that her life would be fixed there forever, between a slaughter-house and a hospital.

CHAPTER II

Three weeks later, towards half-past eleven, one beautiful sunshiny day, Gervaise and Coupeau, the zinc-worker, were each partaking of a plum preserved in brandy, at "The Saloon" kept by Old Man Colombe. Coupeau, who had been smoking a cigarette on the pavement, had prevailed on her to go inside as she returned from taking home a customer's washing; and her big square laundress's basket was on the floor beside her, behind the little zinc covered table.

Old Man Colombe's The Saloon was at the corner of Rue des Poissonniers and Boulevard de Rochechouart. The sign, in tall blue letters stretching from one end to the other said: Distillery. Two dusty oleanders planted in half casks stood beside the doorway. A long bar with its tin measuring cups was on the left as you entered. The large room was decorated with casks painted a gay yellow, bright with varnish, and gleaming with copper taps and hoops.

On the shelves above the bar were liquor bottles, jars of fruit preserved in brandy, and flasks of all shapes. They completely covered the wall and were reflected in the mirror behind the bar as colorful spots of apple green, pale gold, and soft brown. The main feature of the establishment, however, was the distilling apparatus. It was at the rear, behind an oak railing in a glassed-in area. The customers could watch its functioning, long-necked still-pots, copper worms disappearing underground, a devil's kitchen alluring to drink-sodden work men in search of pleasant dreams.

The Saloon was nearly empty at the lunch hour. Old Man Colombe, a heavy man of forty, was serving a ten year old girl who had asked him to place four sous' worth of brandy into her cup. A shaft of sunlight came through the entrance to warm the floor which was always damp from the smokers' spitting. From everything, the casks, the bar, the entire room, a liquorish odor arose, an alcoholic aroma which seemed to thicken and befuddle the dust motes dancing in the sunlight.

Coupeau was making another cigarette. He was very neat, in a short blue linen blouse and cap, and was laughing and showing his white teeth. With a projecting under jaw and a slightly snub nose, he had handsome chestnut eyes, and the face of a jolly dog and a thorough good fellow. His coarse curly hair stood erect. His skin still preserved the softness of his twenty-six years. Opposite to him, Gervaise, in a thin black woolen dress, and bareheaded, was finishing her plum which she held by the stalk between the tips of her fingers. They were close to the street, at the first of the four tables placed alongside the barrels facing the bar.

When the zinc-worker had lit his cigarette, he placed his elbows on the table, thrust his face forward, and for an instant looked without speaking at the young woman, whose pretty fair face had that day the milky transparency of china. Then, alluding to a matter known to themselves alone, and already discussed between them, he simply asked in a low voice:

"So it's to be 'no'? You say 'no'?"

"Most decidedly 'no' Monsieur Coupeau," quietly replied Gervaise with a smile. "I hope you're not going to talk to me about that here. You know you promised me you would be reasonable. Had I known, I wouldn't have let you treat me."

Coupeau kept silence, looking at her intently with a boldness. She sat still, at ease and friendly. At the end of a brief silence she added:

"You can't really mean it. I'm an old woman; I've a big boy eight years old. Whatever could we two do together?"

"Why." murmured Coupeau, blinking his eyes, "what the others do, of course, get married."

She made a gesture of feeling annoyed. ". . . Do you think it's always pleasant? One can very well see you've never seen much of living. No, Monsieur Coupeau, I must think of serious things. Burdening oneself never leads to anything, you know. I've two mouths at home which are never tired of swallowing, I can tell you. How do you suppose I can bring up my little ones, if I only sit here talking indolently? And listen, besides that, my misfortune has been a famous lesson to me. You know I don't care a bit about men now. They won't catch me again for a long while."

She spoke with such cool objectivity that it was clear she had resolved this in her mind, turning it about thoroughly.

Coupeau was deeply moved and kept repeating: "I feel so sorry for you.

It causes me a great deal of pain."

"Yes, I know that," resumed she, "and I am sorry, Monsieur Coupeau. But you mustn't take it to heart. If I had any idea of enjoying myself, mon Dieu, I would certainly rather be with you than anyone else. You're a good boy and gentle. Only, where's the use, as I've no inclination to wed? I've been for the last fortnight, now, at Madame Fauconnier's. The children go to school. I've work, I'm contented. So the best is to remain as we are, isn't it?"

And she stooped down to take her basket.

"You're making me talk; they must be expecting me at the shop. You'll easily find someone else prettier than I, Monsieur Coupeau, and who won't have two boys to drag about with her."

He looked at the clock inserted in the frame-work of the mirror, and made her sit down again, exclaiming:

"Don't be in such a hurry. It's only eleven thirty-five. I've still twenty-five minutes. You don't have to be afraid that I shall do anything foolish; there's the table between us. So you detest me so much that you won't stay and have a little chat with me."

She put her basket down again, so as not to disoblige him; and they conversed like good friends. She had eaten her lunch before going out with the laundry. He had gulped down his soup and beef hurriedly to be able to wait for her. All the while she chatted amiably, Gervaise kept looking out the window at the activity on the street. It was now unusually crowded with the lunch time rush.

Everywhere were hurried steps, swinging arms, and pushing elbows. Some late comers, hungry and angry at being kept extra-long at the job, rushed across the street into the bakery. They emerged with a loaf of bread and went three doors farther to the Two-Headed Calf to gobble down a six-sou meat dish.

Next door to the bakery was a grocer who sold fried potatoes and mussels cooked with parsley. A procession of girls went in to get hot potatoes wrapped in paper and cups of steaming mussels. Other pretty girls brought bunches of radishes. By leaning a bit, Gervaise could see into the sausage shop from which children issued, holding a fried chop, a sausage or a piece of hot blood pudding wrapped in greasy paper.

The street was always slick with black mud, even in clear weather. A few laborers had already finished their lunch and were strolling aimlessly about, their open hands slapping their thighs, heavy from eating, slow and peaceful amid the hurrying crowd. A group formed in front of the door of The Saloon.

"Say, Bibi-the-Smoker," demanded a hoarse voice, "aren't you going to buy us a round of vitriol?"

Five laborers came in and stood by the bar.

"Ah. Here's that thief, Old Man Colombe." the voice continued. "We want the real old stuff, you know. And full sized glasses, too."

Old Man Colombe served them as three more laborers entered. More blue smocks gathered on the street corner and some pushed their way into the establishment.

"You're foolish. You only think of the present," Gervaise was saying to Coupeau. "Sure, I loved him, but after the disgusting way in which he left me."

They were talking of Lantier. Gervaise had not seen him again; she thought he was living with Virginie's sister at La Glaciere, in the house of that friend who was going to start a hat factory. She had no thought of running after him. She had been so distressed at first that she had thought of drowning herself in the river. But now that she had thought about it, everything seemed to be for the best. Lantier went through money so fast, that she probably never could have raised her children properly. . . she'd let him see his children, all right, if he bothered to come round. But as far as she was concerned, she didn't want him to touch her, not even with his fingertips.

She told all this to Coupeau just as if her plan of life was well settled. Meanwhile, Coupeau never forgot his desire to possess her. He made a jest of everything she said, turning it into ribaldry and asking some very direct questions about Lantier. But he proceeded so gaily and which such a smile that she never thought of being offended.

"So, you're the one who beat him," said he at length. ". . . You're not kind. You just go around whipping people."

She interrupted him with a hearty laugh. It was true, though, she had whipped Virginie's tall carcass. She would have delighted in strangling someone on that day. She laughed louder than ever when Coupeau told her that Virginie, ashamed at having shown so much cowardice, had left the neighborhood. Her face, however, preserved an expression of childish gentleness as she put out her plump hands, insisting she wouldn't even harm a fly.

She began to tell Coupeau about her childhood at Plassans. She had never cared overmuch for men; they had always bored her. She was fourteen when she got involved with Lantier. She had thought it was nice because he said he was her husband and she had enjoyed playing a housewife. She was too soft-hearted and too weak. She always got passionately fond of people who caused her trouble later. When she loved a man, she wasn't thinking of having fun in the present; she was dreaming about being happy and living together forever.

And as Coupeau, with a chuckle, spoke of her two children, saying they hadn't come from under a bolster, she slapped his fingers; she added that she was, no doubt made on the model of other women; women thought of their home, slaved to keep the place clean and tidy, and went to bed too tired at night not to go to sleep at once. Besides, she resembled her mother, a stout laboring woman who died at her work and who had served as beast of burden to old Macquart for more than twenty years. Her mother's shoulders had been heavy enough to smash through doors, but that didn't prevent her from being soft-hearted and madly attracted to people. And if she limped a little, she no doubt owed that to the poor woman, whom old Macquart used to belabor with blows. Her mother had told her about the times when Macquart came home drunk and brutally bruised her. She had probably been born with her lame leg as a result of one of those times.

". . . it's scarcely anything, it's hardly perceptible," said Coupeau gallantly.

She shook her head; she knew well enough that it could be seen; at forty she would look broken in two. Then she added gently, with a slight laugh: "It's a funny fancy of yours to fall in love with a cripple."

With his elbows still on the table, he thrust his face closer to hers and began complimenting her in rather dubious language as though to intoxicate her with his words. But she kept shaking her head "no," and didn't allow herself to be tempted although she was flattered by the tone of his voice. While listening, she kept looking out the window, seeming to be fascinated by the interesting crowd of people passing.

The shops were now almost empty. The grocer removed his last panfull of fried potatoes from the stove. The sausage man arranged the dishes scattered on his counter. Great bearded workmen were as playful as young boys, clumping along in their hobnailed boots. Other workmen were smoking, staring up into the sky and blinking their eyes. Factory bells began to ring in the distance, but the workers, in no hurry, relit their pipes. Later, after being tempted by one wine shop after another, they finally decided to return to their jobs, but were still dragging their feet.

Gervaise amused herself by watching three workmen, a tall fellow and two short ones who turned to look back every few yards; they ended by descending the street, and came straight to Old Man Colombe's The Saloon.

"Ah, well," murmured she, "there're three fellows who don't seem inclined for work."

"Why," said Coupeau, "I know the tall one, it's My-Boots, a comrade of mine."

Old Man Colombe's The Saloon was now full. You had to shout to be heard. Fists often pounded on the bar, causing the glasses to clink. Everyone was standing, hands crossed over belly or held behind back. The drinking groups crowded close to one another. Some groups, by the casks, had to wait a quarter of an hour before being able to order their drinks of Old Man Colombe.

"Hallo. It's that aristocrat, Young Cassis." cried My-Boots, bringing his hand down roughly on Coupeau's shoulder. "A fine gentleman, who smokes paper, and wears shirts. So we want to do the grand with our sweetheart; we stand her little treats."

"Shut up. Don't bother me." replied Coupeau, greatly annoyed.

But the other added, with a chuckle, "Right you are. We know what's what, my boy. Muffs are muffs, that's all."

He turned his back after leering terribly as he looked at Gervaise. The latter drew back, feeling rather frightened. The smoke from the pipes, the strong odor of all those men, ascended in the air, already foul with the fumes of alcohol and she felt a choking sensation in her throat, and coughed slightly.

"What a horrible thing it is to drink." said she in a low voice.

And she related that formerly at Plassans she used to drink anisette with her mother. But on one occasion it nearly killed her, and that disgusted her with it; now, she could never touch any liqueurs.

"You see," added she, pointing to her glass, "I've eaten my plum; only I must leave the juice, because it would make me ill."

For himself, Coupeau couldn't understand how anyone could drink glass after glass of cheap brandy. A brandied plum occasionally could not hurt, but as for cheap brandy, absinthe and the other strong stuff, no, not for him, no matter how much his comrades teased him about it. He stayed out on the sidewalk when his friends went into low establishments. Coupeau's father had smashed his head open one day when he fell from the eaves of No. 25 on Rue Coquenard. He was drunk. This memory kept Coupeau's entire family from the drink. Every time Coupeau passed that spot, he thought he would rather lick up water from the gutter than accept a free drink in a bar. He would always say: "In our trade, you have to have steady legs."

Gervaise had taken up her basket again. She did not rise from her seat however, but held the basket on her knees, with a vacant look in her eyes and lost in thought, as though the young workman's words had awakened within her far-off thoughts of existence. And she said again, slowly, and without any apparent change of manner:

"My God. I'm not ambitious; I don't ask for much. My desire is to work in peace, always to have bread to eat and a decent place to sleep in, you know; with a bed, a table, and two chairs, nothing more. If I can, I'd like to raise my children to be good citizens. Also, I'd like not to be beaten up, if I ever again live with a man. It's not my idea of amusement." She pondered, thinking if there was anything else she wanted, but there wasn't anything of importance. Then, after a moment she went on, "Yes, when one reaches the end, one might wish to die in one's bed. For myself, having trudged through life, I should like to die in my bed, in my own home."

And she rose from her seat. Coupeau, who cordially approved her wishes, was already standing up, anxious about the time. But they did not leave yet. Gervaise was curious enough to go to the far end of the room for a look at the big still behind the oak railing. It was chugging away in the little glassed-in courtyard. Coupeau explained its workings to her, pointing at the different parts of the machinery, showing her the trickling of the small stream of limpid alcohol. Not a single gay puff of steam was coming forth from the endless coils. The breathing could barely be heard. It sounded muffled as if from underground. It was like a somber worker, performing dark deeds in the bright daylight, strong but silent.

My-Boots, accompanied by his two comrades, came to lean on the railing until they could get a place at the bar. He laughed, looking at the machine. Tonnerre de Dieu, that's clever. There's enough stuff in its big belly to last for weeks. He wouldn't mind if they just fixed the end of the tube in his mouth, so he could feel the fiery spirits flowing down to his heels like a river. It would be better than the tiny sips doled out by Old Man Colombe. His two comrades laughed with him, saying that My-Boots was quite a guy after all.

The huge still continued to trickle forth its alcoholic sweat. Eventually it would invade the bar, flow out along the outer Boulevards, and inundate the immense expanse of Paris.

Gervaise stepped back, shivering. She tried to smile as she said, "It's foolish, but that still and the liquor gives me the creeps."

Then, returning to the idea she nursed of a perfect happiness, she resumed: "Now, ain't I right? It's much the nicest isn't it—to have plenty of work, bread to eat, a home of one's own, and to be able to bring up one's children and to die in one's bed?"

"And never to be beaten," added Coupeau gaily. "But I would never beat you, if you would only try me, Madame Gervaise. You've no cause for fear. I don't drink and then I love you too much. Come, shall it be marriage? I'll get you divorced and make you my wife."

He was speaking low, whispering at the back of her neck while she made her way through the crowd of men with her basket held before her. She kept shaking her head "no." Yet she turned around to smile at him, apparently happy to know that he never drank. Yes, certainly, she would say "yes" to him, except she had already sworn to herself never to start up with another man. Eventually they reached the door and went out.

When they left, The Saloon was packed to the door, spilling its hubbub of rough voices and its heavy smell of vitriol into the street. My-Boots could be heard railing at Old Man Colombe, calling him a scoundrel and accusing him of only half filling his glass. He didn't have to come in here. He'd never come back. He suggested to his comrades a place near the Barriere Saint-Denis where you drank good stuff straight.

"Ah," sighed Gervaise when they reached the sidewalk. "You can breathe out here. Good-bye, Monsieur Coupeau, and thank you. I must hurry now."

He seized her hand as she started along the boulevard, insisting, "Take a walk with me along Rue de la Goutte-d'Or. It's not much farther for you. I've got to see my sister before going back to work. We'll keep each other company."

In the end, Gervaise agreed and they walked beside each other along the Rue des Poissonniers, although she did not take his arm. He told her about his family. His mother, an old vest-maker, now had to do housekeeping because her eyesight was poor. Her birthday was the third of last month and she was sixty-two. He was the youngest. One of his sisters, a widow of thirty-six, worked in a flower shop and lived in the Batignolles section, on Rue des Moines. The other sister was thirty years old now. She had married a deadpan chain-maker named Lorilleux. That's where he was going now. They lived in a big tenement on the left side. He ate with them in the evenings; it saved a bit for all of them. But he had been invited out this evening and he was going to tell her not to expect him.

Gervaise, who was listening to him, suddenly interrupted him to ask, with a smile: "So you're called 'Young Cassis,' Monsieur Coupeau?"

"Yep," replied he, "it's a nickname my mates have given me because I generally drink 'cassis' when they force me to accompany them to the wine shop. It's no worse to be called Young Cassis than My-Boots, is it?"

"Of course not. Young Cassis isn't an ugly name," observed the young woman.

And she questioned him about his work. He was still working there, behind the stone wall at the new hospital. . . . There was no want of work, he would not be finished there for a year at least. There were yards and yards of gutters.

"You know," said he, "I can see the Hotel Boncoeur when I'm up there. Yesterday you were at the window, and I waved my arms, but you didn't notice me."

They had already gone about a hundred paces along the Rue de la Goutte-d'Or, when he stood still and raising his eyes, said:

"That's the house. I was born farther on, at No. 22. But this house is, all the same, a fine block of masonry. It's as big as a barrack inside."

Gervaise looked up, examining the facade. On the street side, the tenement had five stories, each with fifteen windows, whose black shutters with their broken slats gave an air of desolation to the wide expanse of wall. Four shops occupied the ground floor. To the right of the entrance, a large, greasy hash house, and to the left, a coal dealer, a notions seller, and an umbrella merchant. The building appeared even larger than it was because it had on each side a small, low building which seemed to lean against it for support. This immense, squared-off building was outlined against the sky. Its unplastered side walls were as bare as prison walls, except for rows of roughly jutting stones which suggested jaws full of decayed teeth yawning vacantly.

Gervaise was gazing at the entrance with interest. The high, arched doorway rose to the second floor and opened onto a deep porch, at the end of which could be seen the pale daylight of a courtyard. This entranceway was paved like the street, and down the center flowed a streamlet of pink-stained water.

"Come in," said Coupeau, "no one will eat you."

Gervaise wanted to wait for him in the street. However, she could not resist going through the porch as far as the concierge's room on the right. And there, on the threshold, she raised her eyes. Inside, the building was six stories high, with four identical plain walls enclosing the broad central court. The drab walls were corroded by yellowish spots and streaked by drippings from the roof gutters. The walls went straight up to the eaves with no molding or ornament except the angles on the drain pipes at each floor. Here the sink drains added their stains. The glass window panes resembled murky water. Mattresses of checkered blue ticking were hanging out of several windows to air. Clothes lines stretched from other windows with family washing hanging to dry. On a third floor line was a baby's diaper, still implanted with filth. This crowded tenement was bursting at the seams, spilling out poverty and misery through every crevice.

Each of the four walls had, at ground level, a narrow entrance, plastered without a trace of woodwork. This opened into a vestibule containing a dirt-encrusted staircase which spiraled upward. They were each labeled with one of the first four letters of the alphabet painted on the wall.

Several large work-shops with weather-blackened skylights were scattered about the court. Near the concierge's room was the dyeing establishment responsible for the pink streamlet. Puddles of water infested the courtyard, along with wood shavings and coal cinders. Grass and weeds grew between the paving stones. The unforgiving sunlight seemed to cut the court into two parts. On the shady side was a dripping water tap with three small hens scratching for worms with their filth-smeared claws.

Gervaise slowly gazed about, lowering her glance from the sixth floor to the paving stones, then raising it again, surprised at the vastness, feeling as it were in the midst of a living organ, in the very heart of a city, and interested in the house, as though it were a giant before her.

"Is madame seeking for any one?" called out the inquisitive concierge, emerging from her room.

The young woman explained that she was waiting for a friend. She returned to the street; then as Coupeau did not come, she went back to the courtyard seized with the desire to take another look. She did not think the house ugly. Amongst the rags hanging from the windows she discovered various cheerful touches—a wall-flower blooming in a pot, a cage of chirruping canaries, shaving-glasses shining like stars in the depth of the shadow. A carpenter was singing in his work-shop, accompanied by the whining of his plane. The blacksmith's hammers were ringing rhythmically.

In contrast to the apparent wretched poverty, at nearly every open window appeared the begrimed faces of laughing children. Women with peaceful faces could be seen bent over their sewing. The rooms were empty of men who had gone back to work after lunch. The whole tenement was tranquil except for the sounds from the work-shops below which served as a sort of lullaby that went on, unceasingly, always the same.

The only thing she did not like was the courtyard's dampness. She would want rooms at the rear, on the sunny side. Gervaise took a few more steps into the courtyard, inhaling the characteristic odor of the slums, comprised of dust and rotten garbage. But the sharp odor of the waste water from the dye shop was strong and Gervaise thought it smelled better here than at the Hotel Boncoeur. She chose a window for herself, the one at the far left with a small window box planted with scarlet runners.

"I'm afraid I've kept you waiting rather a long time," said Coupeau, whom she suddenly heard close beside her. "They always make an awful fuss whenever I don't dine with them, and it was worse than ever today as my sister had bought some veal."

And as Gervaise had slightly started with surprise, he continued glancing around in his turn:

"You were looking at the house. It's always all let from the top to the bottom. There are three hundred lodgers, I think. If I had any furniture, I would have secured a small room. One would be comfortable here, don't you think so?"

"Yes, one would be comfortable," murmured Gervaise. "In our street at Plassans there weren't near so many people. Look, that's pretty—that window up on the fifth floor, with the scarlet runners."

The zinc-worker's obstinate desire made him ask her once more whether she would or she wouldn't. They could rent a place here as soon as they found a bed. She hurried out the arched entranceway, asking him not to start that subject again. There was as much chance of this building collapsing as there was of her sleeping under the same blanket with him. Still, when Coupeau left her in front of Madame Fauconnier's shop, he was allowed to hold her hand for a moment.

For a month the young woman and the zinc-worker were the best of friends. He admired her courage, when he beheld her half killing herself with work, keeping her children tidy and clean, and yet finding time at night to do a little sewing. Often other women were hopelessly messy, forever nibbling or gadding about, but she wasn't like them at all. She was much too serious. Then she would laugh, and modestly defend herself. It was her misfortune that she had not always been good, having been with a man when only fourteen. Then too, she had often helped her mother empty a bottle of anisette. But she had learned a few things from experience. He was wrong to think of her as strong-willed; her will power was very weak. She had always let herself be pushed into things because she didn't want to hurt someone's feelings. Her one hope now was to live among decent people, for living among bad people was like being hit over the head. It cracks your skull. Whenever she thought of the future, she shivered. Everything she had seen in life so far, especially when a child, had given her lessons to remember.

Coupeau, however, chaffed her about her gloomy thoughts, and brought back all her courage by trying to pinch her hips. She pushed him away from her, and slapped his hands, while he called out laughingly that, for a weak woman, she was not a very easy capture. He, who always joked about everything did not trouble himself regarding the future. One day followed another, that was all. There would always be somewhere to sleep and a bite to eat. The neighborhood seemed decent enough to him, except for a gang of drunkards that ought to be cleaned out of the gutters.

Coupeau was not a bad sort of fellow. He sometimes had really sensible things to say. He was something of a dandy with his Parisian working man's gift for banter, a regular gift of gab, and besides, he was attractive.

They had ended by rendering each other all sorts of services at the Hotel Boncoeur. Coupeau fetched her milk, ran her errands, carried her bundles of clothes; often of an evening, as he got home first from work, he took the children for a walk on the exterior Boulevard. Gervaise, in return for his polite attentions, would go up into the narrow room at the top of the house where he slept, and see to his clothes, sewing buttons on his blue linen trousers, and mending his linen jackets. A great familiarity existed between them. She was never bored when he was around. The gay songs he sang amused her, and so did his continuous banter of jokes and jibes characteristic of the Paris streets, this being still new to her.

On Coupeau's side, this continual familiarity inflamed him more and more until it began to seriously bother him. He began to feel tense and uneasy. He continued with his foolish talk, never failing to ask her, "When will it be?" She understood what he meant and teased him. He would then come to visit her carrying his bedroom slippers, as if he were moving in. She joked about it and continued calmly without blushing at the allusions with which he was always surrounding her. She stood for anything from him as long as he didn't get rough. She only got angry once when he pulled a strand of her hair while trying to force a kiss from her.

Towards the end of June, Coupeau lost his liveliness. He became most peculiar. Gervaise, feeling uneasy at some of his glances, barricaded herself in at night. Then, after having sulked ever since the Sunday, he suddenly came on the Tuesday night about eleven o'clock and knocked at her room. She would not open to him; but his voice was so gentle and so trembling that she ended by removing the chest of drawers she had pushed against the door. When he entered, she thought he was ill; he looked so pale, his eyes were so red, and the veins on his face were all swollen. And he stood there, stuttering and shaking his head. No, no, he was not ill. He had been crying for two hours upstairs in his room; he wept like a child, biting his pillow so as not to be heard by the neighbors. For three nights past he had been unable to sleep. It could not go on like that.

"Listen, Madame Gervaise," said he, with a swelling in his throat and on the point of bursting out crying again; "we must end this, mustn't we? We'll go and get married. It's what I want. I've quite made up my mind."

Gervaise showed great surprise. She was very grave.

"Monsieur Coupeau," murmured she, "whatever are you thinking of? You know I've never asked you for that. I didn't care about it—that was all. . . no, no. it's serious now; think of what you're saying, I beg of you."

But he continued to shake his head with an air of unalterable resolution. He had already thought it all over. He had come down because he wanted to have a good night. She wasn't going to send him back to weep again he supposed. As soon as she said "yes," he would no longer bother her, and she could go quietly to bed. He only wanted to hear her say "yes." They could talk it over on the morrow.

"But I certainly can't say 'yes' just like that," resumed Gervaise. "I don't want you to be able to accuse me later on of having incited you to do a foolish thing. You shouldn't be so insistent, Monsieur Coupeau. You can't really be sure that you're in love with me. If you didn't see me for a week, it might fade away. Sometimes men get married and then there's day after day, stretching out into an entire lifetime, and they get pretty well bored by it all. Sit down there; I'm willing to talk it over at once."

Then until one in the morning, in the dark room and by the faint light of a smoky tallow candle which they forgot to snuff, they talked of their marriage, lowering their voices so as not to wake the two children, Claude and Etienne, who were sleeping, both heads on the same pillow. Gervaise kept pointing out the children to Coupeau, what a funny kind of dowry they were. She really shouldn't burden him with them. Besides, what would the neighbors say? She'd feel ashamed for him because everyone knew about the story of her life and her lover. They wouldn't think it decent if they saw them getting married barely two months later.

Coupeau replied by shrugging his shoulders. He didn't care about the neighbors. He never bothered about their affairs. So, there was Lantier before him, well, so what? What's so bad about that? She hadn't been constantly bringing men upstairs, as some women did, even rich ladies. The children would grow up, they'd raise them right. Never had he known before such a woman, such sound character, so good-hearted. Anyway, she could have been anything, a streetwalker, ugly, lazy and good-for-nothing, with a whole gang of dirty kids, and so what? He wanted her.

"Yes, I want you," he repeated, bringing his hand down on his knee with a continuous hammering. "You understand, I want you. There's nothing to be said to that, is there?"

Little by little, Gervaise gave way. Her emotions began to take control when faced with his encompassing desire. Still, with her hands in her lap and her face suffused with a soft sweetness, she hesitantly offered objections. From outside, through the half-open window, a lovely June night breathed in puffs of sultry air, disturbing the candle with its long wick gleaming red like a glowing coal. In the deep silence of the sleeping neighborhood the only sound was the infantile weeping of a drunkard lying in the middle of the street. Far away, in the back room of some restaurant, a violin was playing a dance tune for some late party.

Coupeau was silent. Then, knowing she had no more arguments, he smiled, took hold of her hands and pulled her toward him. She was in one of those moments of weakness she so greatly mistrusted, persuaded at last, too emotionally stirred to refuse anything or to hurt anyone's feelings. Coupeau didn't realize that she was giving way. He held her wrists so tightly as to almost crush them. Together they breathed a long sigh that to both of them meant a partial satisfaction of their desire.

"You'll say 'yes,' won't you?" asked he.

"How you worry me." she murmured. "You wish it? Well then, 'yes.' Ah. We're perhaps doing a very foolish thing."

He jumped up, and, seizing her round the waist, kissed her roughly on the face, at random. Then, as this caress caused a noise, he became anxious, and went softly and looked at Claude and Etienne.

"Hush, we must be careful," said he in a whisper, "and not wake the children. Good-bye till to-morrow."

And he went back to his room. Gervaise, all in a tremble, remained seated on the edge of her bed, without thinking of undressing herself for nearly an hour. She was touched; she felt that Coupeau was very honorable; for at one moment she had really thought it was all over, and that he would forget her. The drunkard below, under the window, was now hoarsely uttering the plaintive cry of some lost animal. The violin in the distance had left off its saucy tune and was now silent.

During the following days Coupeau sought to get Gervaise to call some evening on his sister in the Rue de la Goutte-d'Or; but the young woman, who was very timid, showed a great dread of this visit to the Lorilleux. She knew that Coupeau had a lingering fear of that household, even though he certainly wasn't dependent on his sister, who wasn't even the oldest of the family. Mamma Coupeau would certainly give her consent at once, as she never refused her only son anything. The thing was that the Lorilleuxs were supposed to be earning ten francs a day or more and that gave them a certain authority. Coupeau would never dare to get married unless his wife was acceptable to them.

"I have spoken to them of you, they know our plans," explained he to Gervaise. "Come now. What a child you are. Let's call on them this evening. I've warned you, haven't I? You'll find my sister rather stiff. Lorilleux, too, isn't always very amiable. In reality they are greatly annoyed, because if I marry, I shall no longer take my meals with them, and it'll be an economy the less. But that doesn't matter, they won't turn you out. Do this for me, it's absolutely necessary."

These words only frightened Gervaise the more. One Saturday evening, however, she gave in. Coupeau came for her at half-past eight. She had dressed herself in a black dress, a crape shawl with yellow palms, and a white cap trimmed with a little cheap lace. During the six weeks she had been working, she had saved the seven francs for the shawl, and the two and a half francs for the cap; the dress was an old one cleaned and made up afresh.

"They're expecting you," said Coupeau to her, as they went round by the Rue des Poissonniers. ". . . . They're beginning to get used to the idea of my being married. They seem nice indeed, to-night. And you know if you've never seen gold chains made, it'll amuse you to watch them. They just happen to have a pressing order for Monday."

"They've got gold in their room?" asked Gervaise.

"I should think so; there's some on the walls, on the floor, in fact everywhere."

They had passed the arched doorway and crossed the courtyard. The Lorilleuxs lived on the sixth floor, staircase B. Coupeau laughingly told her to hold the hand-rail tight and not to leave go of it. She looked up, and blinked her eyes, as she perceived the tall hollow tower of the staircase, lighted by three gas jets, one on every second landing; the last one, right up at the top looked like a star twinkling in a black sky, while the other two cast long flashes of light, of fantastic shapes, among the interminable windings of the stairs.

"By Jove," said the zinc-worker as he reached the first floor, smiling, "there's a strong smell of onion soup. Someone's having onion soup, I'm sure."

Staircase B, with its gray, dirty steps and hand-rail, its scratched walls and chipped plaster, was full of strong kitchen odors. Long corridors, echoing with noise, led away from each landing. Doors, painted yellow, gaped open, smeared black around the latch from dirty hands. A sink on each landing gave forth a fetid humidity, adding its stench to the sharp flavor of the cooking of onions. From the basement, all the way to the sixth floor, you could hear dishes clattering, saucepans being rinsed, pots being scraped and scoured.

On the first floor Gervaise saw a half-opened door with the word "Designer" written on it in large letters. Inside were two men sitting by a table, the dishes cleared away from its oilcloth cover, arguing furiously amid a cloud of pipe smoke. The second and third floors were quieter, and through cracks in the woodwork only such sounds filtered as the rhythm of a cradle rocking, the stifled crying of a child, a woman's voice sounding like the dull murmur of running water with no words distinct. Gervaise read the various signs on the doors giving the names of the occupants: "Madame Gaudron, wool-carder" and "Monsieur Madinier, cardboard boxes." There was a fight in progress on the fourth floor: a stomping of feet that shook the floor, furniture banged around, a racket of curses and blows; but this did not bother the neighbors opposite, who were playing cards with their door opened wide to admit more air.

When Gervaise reached the fifth floor, she had to stop to take a breath; she was not used to going up so high; that wall for ever turning, the glimpses she had of the lodgings following each other, made her head ache. Anyway, there was a family almost blocking the landing: the father washing the dishes over a small earthenware stove near the sink and the mother sitting with her back to the stair-rail and cleaning the baby before putting it to bed.

Coupeau kept urging Gervaise along, and they finally reached the sixth floor. He encouraged her with a smile; they had arrived. She had been hearing a voice all the way up from the bottom and she was gazing upward, wondering where it could be coming from, a voice so clear and piercing that it had dominated all the other sounds. It came from a little old woman in an attic room who sang while putting dresses on cheap dolls. When a tall girl came by with a pail of water and entered a nearby apartment, Gervaise saw a tumbled bed on which a man was sprawled, his eyes fixed on the ceiling. As the door closed behind her, Gervaise saw the hand-written card: "Mademoiselle Clemence, ironing."

Now that she had finally made it to the top, her legs weary and her breath short, Gervaise leaned over the railing to look down. Now it was the gaslight on the first floor which seemed a distant star at the bottom of a narrow well six stories deep. All the odors and all the murmurings of the immense variety of life within the tenement came up to her in one stifling breath that flushed her face as she hazarded a worried glance down into the gulf below.

"We're not there yet," said Coupeau. "It's quite a journey."

He had gone down a long corridor on the left. He turned twice, the first time also to the left, the second time to the right. The corridor still continued branching off, narrowing between walls full of crevices, with plaster peeling off, and lighted at distant intervals by a slender gas-jet; and the doors all alike, succeeded each other the same as the doors of a prison or a convent, and nearly all open, continued to display homes of misery and work, which the hot June evening filled with a reddish mist. At length they reached a small passage in complete darkness.

"We're here," resumed the zinc-worker. "Be careful, keep to the wall; there are three steps."

And Gervaise carefully took another ten steps in the obscurity. She stumbled and then counted the three steps. But at the end of the passage Coupeau had opened a door, without knocking. A brilliant light spread over the tiled floor. They entered.

It was a narrow apartment, and seemed as if it were the continuation of the corridor. A faded woolen curtain, raised up just then by a string, divided the place in two. The first part contained a bedstead pushed beneath an angle of the attic ceiling, a cast-iron stove still warm from the cooking of the dinner, two chairs, a table and a wardrobe, the cornice of which had had to be sawn off to make it fit in between the door and the bedstead. The second part was fitted up as a work-shop; at the end, a narrow forge with its bellows; to the right, a vise fixed to the wall beneath some shelves on which pieces of old iron lay scattered; to the left near the window, a small workman's bench, encumbered with greasy and very dirty pliers, shears and microscopic saws, all very dirty and grimy.

"It's us," cried Coupeau advancing as far as the woolen curtain.

But no one answered at first. Gervaise, deeply affected, moved especially by the thought that she was about to enter a place full of gold, stood behind the zinc-worker, stammering and venturing upon nods of her head by way of bowing. The brilliant light, a lamp burning on the bench, a brazier full of coals flaring in the forge, increased her confusion still more. She ended however, by distinguishing Madame Lorilleux—little, red-haired and tolerably strong, pulling with all the strength of her short arms, and with the assistance of a big pair of pincers, a thread of black metal which she passed through the holes of a draw-plate fixed to the vise. Seated in front of the bench, Lorilleux, quite as small of stature, but more slender in the shoulders, worked with the tips of his pliers, with the vivacity of a monkey, at a labor so minute, that it was impossible to follow it between his scraggy fingers. It was the husband who first raised his head—a head with scanty locks, the face of the yellow tinge of old wax, long, and with an ailing expression.

"Ah. It's you; well, well." murmured he. "We're in a hurry you know. Don't come into the work-room, you'd be in our way. Stay in the bed-room."

And he resumed his minute task, his face again in the reflection of a glass globe full of green-colored water, through which the lamp shed a circle of bright light over his work.

"Take the chairs." called out Madame Lorilleux in her turn. "It's that lady, isn't it? Very well, very well."

She had rolled the wire and she carried it to the forge, and then, reviving the fire of the brazier with a large wooden fan, she proceeded to temper the wire before passing it through the last holes of the draw-plate.

Coupeau moved the chairs forward and seated Gervaise by the curtain. The room was so narrow that he could not sit beside her, so he sat behind her, leaning over her shoulder to explain the work in progress. Gervaise was intimidated by this strange reception and felt uneasy. She had a buzzing in her ears and couldn't hear clearly. She thought the wife looked older than her thirty years and not very neat with her hair in a pigtail dangling down the back of her loosely worn wrapper. The husband, who was only a year older, appeared already an old man with mean, thin lips, as he sat there working in his shirt sleeves with his bare feet thrust into down at the heel slippers. Gervaise was dismayed by the smallness of the shop, the grimy walls, the rustiness of the tools, and the black soot spread all over what looked like the odds and ends of a scrap-iron peddler's wares.

"And the gold?" asked Gervaise in a low voice.

Her anxious glances searched the corners and sought amongst all that filth for the resplendence she had dreamed of. But Coupeau burst out laughing.

"Gold?" said he; "why there's some; there's some more, and there's some at your feet."

He pointed successively to the fine wire at which his sister was working, and to another roll of wire, similar to the ordinary iron wire, hanging against the wall close to the vise; then going down on all fours, he picked up, beneath the wooden screen which covered the tiled floor of the work-room, a piece of waste, a tiny fragment resembling the point of a rusty needle. But Gervaise protested; that couldn't be gold, that blackish piece of metal as ugly as iron. He had to bite into the piece and show her the gleaming notch made by his teeth. Then he continued his explanations: the employers provided the gold wire, already alloyed; the craftsmen first pulled it through the draw-plate to obtain the correct size, being careful to anneal it five or six times to keep it from breaking. It required a steady, strong hand, and plenty of practice. His sister would not let her husband touch the wire-drawing since he was subject to coughing spells. She had strong arms for it; he had seen her draw gold to the fineness of a hair.

Lorilleux, seized with a fit of coughing, almost doubled up on his stool. In the midst of the paroxysm, he spoke, and said in a choking voice, still without looking at Gervaise, as though he was merely mentioning the thing to himself:

"I'm making the herring-bone chain."

Coupeau urged Gervaise to get up. She might draw nearer and see. The chain-maker consented with a grunt. He wound the wire prepared by his wife round a mandrel, a very thin steel rod. Then he sawed gently, cutting the wire the whole length of the mandrel, each turn forming a link, which he soldered. The links were laid on a large piece of charcoal. He wetted them with a drop of borax, taken from the bottom of a broken glass beside him; and he made them red-hot at the lamp beneath the horizontal flame produced by the blow-pipe. Then, when he had soldered about a hundred links he returned once more to his minute work, propping his hands against the edge of the cheville, a small piece of board which the friction of his hands had polished. He bent each link almost double with the pliers, squeezed one end close, inserted it in the last link already in place and then, with the aid of a point opened out again the end he had squeezed; and he did this with a continuous regularity, the links joining each other so rapidly that the chain gradually grew beneath Gervaise's gaze, without her being able to follow, or well understand how it was done.

"That's the herring-bone chain," said Coupeau. "There's also the long link, the cable, the plain ring, and the spiral. But that's the herring-bone. Lorilleux only makes the herring-bone chain."

The latter chuckled with satisfaction. He exclaimed, as he continued squeezing the links, invisible between his black finger-nails.

"Listen to me, Young Cassis. I was making a calculation this morning. I commenced work when I was twelve years old, you know. Well. Can you guess how long a herring-bone chain I must have made up till today?"

He raised his pale face, and blinked his red eye-lids.

"Twenty-six thousand feet, do you hear? Two leagues. That's something. A herring-bone chain two leagues long. It's enough to twist round the necks of all the women of the neighborhood. And you know, it's still increasing. I hope to make it long enough to reach from Paris to Versailles."

Gervaise had returned to her seat, disenchanted and thinking everything very ugly. She smiled to be polite to the Lorilleuxs. The complete silence about her marriage bothered her. It was the sole reason for her having come. The Lorilleuxs were treating her as some stranger brought in by Coupeau. When a conversation finally did get started, it concerned the building's tenants. Madame Lorilleux asked her husband if he had heard the people on the fourth floor having a fight. They fought every day. The husband usually came home drunk and the wife had her faults too, yelling in the filthiest language. Then they spoke of the designer on the first floor, an uppity show-off with a mound of debts, always smoking, always arguing loudly with his friends. Monsieur Madinier's cardboard business was barely surviving. He had let two girl workers go yesterday. The business ate up all his money, leaving his children to run around in rags. And that Madame Gaudron was pregnant again; this was almost indecent at her age. The landlord was going to evict the Coquets on the fifth floor. They owed nine months' rent, and besides, they insisted on lighting their stove out on the landing. Last Saturday the old lady on the sixth floor, Mademoiselle Remanjou, had arrived just in time to save the Linguerlot child from being badly burned. Mademoiselle Clemence, one who took in ironing, well, she lived life as she pleased. She was so kind to animals though and had such a good heart that you couldn't say anything against her. It was a pity, a fine girl like her, the company she kept. She'd be walking the streets before long.

"Look, here's one," said Lorilleux to his wife, giving her the piece of chain he had been working on since his lunch. "You can trim it." And he added, with the persistence of a man who does not easily relinquish a joke: "Another four feet and a half. That brings me nearer to Versailles."

Madame Lorilleux, after tempering it again, trimmed it by passing it through the regulating draw-plate. Then she put it in a little copper saucepan with a long handle, full of lye-water, and placed it over the fire of the forge. Gervaise, again pushed forward by Coupeau, had to follow this last operation. When the chain was thoroughly cleansed, it appeared a dull red color. It was finished, and ready to be delivered.

"They're always delivered like that, in their rough state," the zinc-worker explained. "The polishers rub them afterwards with cloths."

Gervaise felt her courage failing her. The heat, more and more intense, was suffocating her. They kept the door shut, because Lorilleux caught cold from the least draught. Then as they still did not speak of the marriage, she wanted to go away and gently pulled Coupeau's jacket. He understood. Besides, he also was beginning to feel ill at ease and vexed at their affectation of silence.

"Well, we're off," said he. "We mustn't keep you from your work."

He moved about for a moment, waiting, hoping for a word or some allusion or other. At length he decided to broach the subject himself.

"I say, Lorilleux, we're counting on you to be my wife's witness."

The chain-maker pretended, with a chuckle, to be greatly surprised; while his wife, leaving her draw-plates, placed herself in the middle of the work-room.

"So it's serious then?" murmured he. "That confounded Young Cassis, one never knows whether he is joking or not."

"Ah. Yes, madame's the person involved," said the wife in her turn, as she stared rudely at Gervaise. "My God, We've no advice to give you, we haven't. It's a funny idea to go and get married, all the same. Anyhow, it's your own wish. When it doesn't succeed, one's only got oneself to blame, that's all. And it doesn't often succeed, not often, not often."

She uttered these last words slower and slower, and shaking her head, she looked from the young woman's face to her hands, and then to her feet as though she had wished to undress her and see the very pores of her skin. She must have found her better than she expected.

"My brother is perfectly free," she continued more stiffly. "No doubt the family might have wished—one always makes projects. But

things take such funny turns. For myself, I don't want to have any unpleasantness.

Had he brought us the lowest of the low, I should merely have said:
'Marry her and go to blazes.' He was not badly off though, here
with us. He's fat enough; one can very well see he didn't fast much; and
he always found his soup hot right on time. I say, Lorilleux, don't you
think madame's like Therese—you know who I mean, that woman who
used to live opposite, and who died of consumption?"

"Yes, there's a certain resemblance," replied the chain-maker.

"And you've got two children, madame? Now, I must admit I said
to my brother: 'I can't understand how you can want to marry a woman
who's got two children.' You mustn't be offended if I consult his in-
terests; it's only natural. You don't look strong either. Don't you think,
Lorilleux, that madame doesn't look very strong?"

"No, no, she's not strong."

They did not mention her leg; but Gervaise understood by their
side glances, and the curling of their lips, that they were alluding to it.
She stood before them, wrapped in her thin shawl with the yellow
palms, replying in monosyllables, as though in the presence of her
judges.

Coupeau, seeing she was suffering, ended by exclaiming, "All that's
nothing to do with it. What you are talking about isn't important. The
wedding will take place on Saturday, July 29. I calculated by the almanac.
Is it settled? Does it suit you?"

"It's all the same to us," said his sister. "There was no necessity to
consult us. I shan't prevent Lorilleux being witness. I only want peace
and quiet."

Gervaise, hanging her head, not knowing what to do with herself
had put the toe of her boot through one of the openings in the wooden
screen which covered the tiled floor of the work-room; then afraid of
having disturbed something when she had withdrawn it, she stooped
down and felt about with her hand. Lorilleux hastily brought the lamp,
and he examined her fingers suspiciously.

"You must be careful," said he, "the tiny bits of gold stick to the
shoes, and get carried away without one knowing it."

It was all to do with business. The employers didn't allow a single
speck for waste. He showed her the rabbit's foot he used to brush off

any flecks of gold left on the cheville and the leather he kept on his lap to catch any gold that fell. Twice weekly the shop was swept out carefully, the sweepings collected and burned and the ashes sifted. This recovered up to twenty-five or thirty francs' worth of gold a month.

Madame Lorilleux could not take her eyes from Gervaise's shoes.

"There's no reason to get angry," murmured she with an amiable smile.

"But, perhaps madame would not mind looking at the soles of her shoes."

And Gervaise, turning very red, sat down again, and holding up her feet showed that there was nothing clinging to them. Coupeau had opened the door, exclaiming: "Good-night." in an abrupt tone of voice. He called to her from the corridor. Then she in her turn went off, after stammering a few polite words: she hoped to see them again, and that they would all agree well together. Both of the Lorilleux had already gone back to their work at the far end of their dark hole of a workroom. Madame Lorilleux, her skin reflecting the red glow from the bed of coals, was drawing on another wire. Each effort swelling her neck and making the strained muscles stand out like taut cords. Her husband, hunched over beneath the greenish gleam of the globe was starting another length of chain, twisting each link with his pliers, pressing it on one side, inserting it into the next link above, opening it again with the pointed tool, continuously, mechanically, not wasting a motion, even to wipe the sweat from his face.

When Gervaise emerged from the corridor on to the landing, she could not help saying, with tears in her eyes:

"That doesn't promise much happiness."

Coupeau shook his head furiously. He would get even with Lorilleux for that evening. Had anyone ever seen such a miserly fellow? To think that they were going to walk off with two or three grains of his gold dust. All the fuss they made was from pure avarice. His sister thought perhaps that he would never marry, so as to enable her to economize four sous on her dinner every day. However, it would take place all the same on July 29. He did not care a hang for them.

Nevertheless, Gervaise still felt depressed. Tormented by a foolish fearfulness, she peered anxiously into every dark shadow along the stair-rail as she descended. It was dark and deserted at this hour, lit only by a single gas jet on the second floor. In the shadowy depths of the dark pit, it gave a spot of brightness, even with its flamed turned so low. It was now silent behind the closed doors; the weary laborers had gone to sleep after eating. However, there was a soft laugh from Mademoiselle Clemence's room and a ray of light shone through the keyhole of Mademoiselle Remanjou's door. She was still busy cutting out dresses for the dolls. Downstairs at Madame Gaudron's, a child was crying. The sinks on the landings smelled more offensive than ever in the midst of the darkness and stillness.

In the courtyard, Gervaise turned back for a last look at the tenement as Coupeau called out to the concierge. The building seemed to have grown larger under the moonless sky. The drip-drip of water from the faucet sounded loud in the quiet. Gervaise felt that the building was threatening to suffocate her and a chill went through her body. It was a childish fear and she smiled at it a moment later.

"Watch your step," warned Coupeau.

To get to the entrance, Gervaise had to jump over a wide puddle that had drained from the dye shop. The puddle was blue now, the deep blue of a summer sky. The reflections from the night light of the concierge sparkled in it like stars.

CHAPTER III

Gervaise did not want to have a wedding-party. What was the use of spending money? Besides, she still felt somewhat ashamed; it seemed to her quite unnecessary to parade the marriage before the whole neighborhood. But Coupeau cried out at that. One could not be married without having a feed. He did not care a button for the people of the neighborhood. Nothing elaborate, just a short walk and a rabbit ragout in the first eating-house they fancied. No music with dessert. Just a glass or two and then back home.

The zinc-worker, chaffing and joking, at length got the young woman to consent by promising her that there should be no larks. He would keep his eye on the glasses, to prevent sunstrokes. Then he organized a sort of picnic at five francs a head, at the "Silver Windmill," kept by Auguste, on the Boulevard de la Chapelle. It was a small cafe with moderate charges and had a dancing place in the rear, beneath the three acacias in the courtyard. They would be very comfortable on the first floor. During the next ten days, he got hold of guests in the house where his sister lived in the Rue de la Goutte-d'Or—Monsieur Madinier, Mademoiselle Remanjou, Madame Gaudron and her husband. He even ended by getting Gervaise to consent to the presence of two of his comrades—Bibi-the-Smoker and My-Boots. No doubt My-Boots was a boozer; but then he had such a fantastic appetite that he was always asked to join those sort of gatherings, just for the sight of the caterer's mug when he beheld that bottomless pit swallowing his twelve pounds of bread. The young woman on her side promised to bring her employer Madame Fauconnier and the Boches, some very agreeable people. On counting, they found there would be fifteen to sit down to table, which was quite enough. When there are too many, they always wind up by quarrelling.

Coupeau however, had no money. Without wishing to show off, he intended to behave handsomely. He borrowed fifty francs of his employer. Out of that, he first of all purchased the wedding-ring—a twelve franc gold wedding-ring, which Lorilleux procured for him at the wholesale price of nine francs. He then bought himself a frock coat, a pair of trousers and a waistcoat at a tailor's in the Rue Myrrha, to whom he gave merely twenty-five francs on account; his patent leather shoes and his hat were still good enough. When he had put by the ten francs for his and Gervaise's share of the feast—the two children not being charged for—he had exactly six francs left—the price of a low mass at the altar of the poor. He had no liking for those black crows, the priests. It would gripe him to pay his last six francs to keep their whistles wet; however, a marriage without a mass wasn't a real marriage at all.

Going to the church himself, he bargained for a whole hour with a little old priest in a dirty cassock who was as sharp at dealing as a push-cart peddler. Coupeau felt like boxing his ears. For a joke, he asked the priest if he didn't have a second-hand mass that would do for a modest young couple. The priest, mumbling that God would take small pleasure in blessing their union, finally let his have his mass for five francs. Well after all, that meant twenty sous saved.

Gervaise also wanted to look decent. As soon as the marriage was settled, she made her arrangements, worked extra time in the evenings, and managed to put thirty francs on one side. She had a great longing for a little silk mantle marked thirteen francs in the Rue du Faubourg Poissonniere. She treated herself to it, and then bought for ten francs of the husband of a washerwoman who had died in Madame Fauconnier's house a blue woolen dress, which she altered to fit herself. With the seven francs remaining she procured a pair of cotton gloves, a rose for her cap, and some shoes for Claude, her eldest boy. Fortunately the youngsters' blouses were passable. She spent four nights cleaning everything, and mending the smallest holes in her stockings and chemise.

On Friday night, the eve of the great day, Gervaise and Coupeau had still a good deal of running about to do up till eleven o'clock, after returning home from work. Then before separating for the night they spent an hour together in the young woman's room, happy at being about to be released from their awkward position. In spite of the fact that they had originally resolved not to put themselves out to impress the neighbors, they had ended by taking it seriously and working themselves till they were weary. By the time they said "Good-night," they were almost asleep on their feet. They breathed a great sigh of relief now that everything was ready.

Coupeau's witnesses were to be Monsieur Madinier and Bibi-the-Smoker. They were counting on Lorilleux and Boche for Gervaise's witnesses. They were to go quietly to the mayor's office and the church, just the six of them, without a whole procession of people trailing behind them. The bridegroom's two sisters had even declared that they would stay home, their presence not being necessary. Coupeau's mother, however, had sobbed and wailed, threatening to go ahead of them and hide herself in some corner of the church, until they had promised to take her along. The meeting of the guests was set for one o'clock at the Silver Windmill. From there, they would go to Saint-Denis, going out by railroad and returning on foot along the highway in order to work up an appetite. The party promised to be quite all right.

Saturday morning, while getting dressed, Coupeau felt a qualm of uneasiness in view of the single franc in his pocket. He began to think that it was a matter of ordinary courtesy to offer a glass of wine and a slice of ham to the witnesses while awaiting dinner. Also, there might be unforeseen expenses. So, after taking Claude and Etienne to stay with Madame Boche, who was to bring them to the dinner later that afternoon, he hurried over to the Rue de la Goutte-d'Or to borrow ten francs from Lorilleux. Having to do that griped him immensely as he could guess the attitude his brother-in-law would take. The latter did grumble a bit, but ended by lending him two five-franc pieces. However, Coupeau overheard his sister muttering under her breath, "This is a fine beginning."

The ceremony at the mayor's was to take place at half-past ten. It was beautiful weather—a magnificent sun seemed to roast the streets. So as not to be stared at the bride and bridegroom, the old mother, and the four witnesses separated into two bands. Gervaise walked in front with Lorilleux, who gave her his arm; while Monsieur Madinier followed with mother Coupeau. Then, twenty steps behind on the opposite side of the way, came Coupeau, Boche, and Bibi-the-Smoker. These three were in black frock coats, walking erect and swinging their arms. Boche's trousers were bright yellow. Bibi-the-Smoker didn't have a waistcoat so he was buttoned up to the neck with only a bit of his cravat showing. The only one in a full dress suit was Monsieur Madinier and passers-by gazed at this well-dressed gentleman escorting the huge bulk of mother Coupeau in her green shawl and black bonnet with red ribbons.

Gervaise looked very gay and sweet in her dress of vivid blue and with her new silk mantle fitted tightly to her shoulders. She listened politely to the sneering remarks of Lorilleux, who seemed buried in the depths of the immense overcoat he was wearing. From time to time, Gervaise would turn her head a little to smile brightly at Coupeau, who was rather uncomfortable under the hot sun in his new clothes.

Though they walked very slowly, they arrived at the mayor's quite half an hour too soon. And as the mayor was late, their turn was not reached till close upon eleven o'clock. They sat down on some chairs and waited in a corner of the apartment, looking by turns at the high ceiling and bare walls, talking low, and over-politely pushing back their chairs each time that one of the attendants passed. Yet among themselves they called the mayor a sluggard, saying he must be visiting his blonde to get a massage for his gout, or that maybe he'd swallowed his official sash.

However, when the mayor did put in his appearance, they rose respectfully in his honor. They were asked to sit down again and they had to wait through three other marriages. The hall was crowded with the three bourgeois wedding parties: brides all in white, little girls with carefully curled hair, bridesmaids wearing wide sashes, an endless procession of ladies and gentlemen dressed in their best and looking very stylish.

When at length they were called, they almost missed being married altogether. Bibi-the-Smoker having disappeared, Boche discovered him outside smoking his pipe. Well. They were a nice lot inside there to humbug people about like that, just because one hadn't yellow kid gloves to shove under their noses. And the various formalities—the reading of the Code, the different questions to be put, the signing of all the documents—were all got through so rapidly that they looked at each other with an idea that they had been robbed of a good half of the ceremony. Gervaise, dizzy, her heart full, pressed her handkerchief to her lips. Mother Coupeau wept bitterly. All had signed the register, writing their names in big struggling letters with the exception of the bridegroom, who not being able to write, had put his cross. They each gave four sous for the poor. When an attendant handed Coupeau the marriage certificate, the latter, prompted by Gervaise who nudged his elbow, handed him another five sous.

It was a fair walk from the mayor's office in the town hall to the church. The men stopped along the way to have a beer. Mother Coupeau and Gervaise took cassis with water. Then they had to trudge along the long street where the sun glared straight down without the relief of shade.

When they arrived at the church they were hurried along and asked if they came so late in order to make a mockery of religion. A priest came forward, his face pale and resentful from having to delay his lunch. An altar boy in a soiled surplice ran before him.

The mass went very fast, with the priest turning, bowing his head, spreading out his arms, making all the ritual gestures in haste while casting sidelong glances at the group. Gervaise and Coupeau, before the altar, were embarrassed, not knowing when they should kneel or rise or seat themselves, expecting some indication from the attendant. The witnesses, not knowing what was proper, remained standing during the ceremony. Mother Coupeau was weeping again and shedding her tears into the missal she had borrowed from a neighbor.

Meanwhile, the noon chimes had sounded and the church began to fill with noise from the shuffling feet of sacristans and the clatter of chairs being put back in place. The high altar was apparently being prepared for some special ceremony.

Thus, in the depths of this obscure chapel, amid the floating dust, the surly priest placed his withered hands on the bared heads of Gervaise and Coupeau, blessing their union amid a hubbub like that of moving day. The wedding party signed another registry, this time in the sacristy, and then found themselves out in the bright sunlight before the church doors where they stood for a moment, breathless and confused from having been carried along at such a break-neck speed.

"Voila." said Coupeau with an embarrassed laugh. "Well, it sure didn't take long. They shove it at you so; it's like being at the painless dentist's who doesn't give you time to cry out. Here you get a painless wedding."

"Yes, it's a quick job," Lorilleux smirked. "In five minutes you're tied together for the rest of your life. You poor Young Cassis, you've had it."

The four witnesses whacked Coupeau on the shoulders as he arched his back against the friendly blows. Meanwhile Gervaise was hugging and kissing mother Coupeau, her eyes moist, a smile lighting her face. She replied reassuringly to the old woman's sobbing: "Don't worry, I'll do my best. I want so much to have a happy life. If it doesn't work out it won't be my fault. Anyhow, it's done now. It's up to us to get along together and do the best we can for each other."

After that they went straight to the Silver Windmill. Coupeau had taken his wife's arm. They walked quickly, laughing as though carried away, quite two hundred steps ahead of the others, without noticing the houses or the passers-by, or the vehicles. The deafening noises of the Faubourg sounded like bells in their ears. When they reached the wine shop, Coupeau at once ordered two bottles of wine, some bread and some slices of ham, to be served in the little glazed closet on the ground floor, without plates or table cloth, simply to have a snack. Then, noticing that Boche and Bibi-the-Smoker seemed to be very hungry, he had a third bottle brought, as well as a slab of brie cheese. Mother Coupeau was not hungry, being too choked up to be able to eat. Gervaise found herself very thirsty, and drank several large glasses of water with a small amount of wine added.

"I'll settle for this," said Coupeau, going at once to the bar, where he paid four francs and five sous.

It was now one o'clock and the other guests began to arrive. Madame Fauconnier, a fat woman, still good looking, first put in an appearance; she wore a chintz dress with a flowery pattern, a pink tie and a cap over-trimmed with flowers. Next came Mademoiselle Remanjou, looking very thin in the eternal black dress which she seemed to keep on even when she went to bed; and the two Gaudrons—the husband, like some heavy animal and almost bursting his brown jacket at the slightest movement, the wife, an enormous woman, whose figure indicated evident signs of an approaching maternity and whose stiff violet colored skirt still more increased her rotundity. Coupeau explained that they were not to wait for My-Boots; his comrade would join the party on the Route de Saint-Denis.

"Well." exclaimed Madame Lerat as she entered, "it'll pour in torrents soon. That'll be pleasant."

And she called everyone to the door of the wine shop to see the clouds as black as ink which were rising rapidly to the south of Paris. Madame Lerat, eldest of the Coupeaus, was a tall, gaunt woman who talked through her nose. She was unattractively dressed in a puce-colored robe that hung loosely on her and had such long dangling fringes that they made her look like a skinny poodle coming out of the water. She brandished her umbrella like a club. After greeting Gervaise, she said, "You've no idea. The heat in the street is like a slap on the face. You'd think someone was throwing fire at you."

Everyone agreed that they knew the storm was coming. It was in the air. Monsieur Madinier said that he had seen it as they were coming out of the church. Lorilleux mentioned that his corns were aching and he hadn't been able to sleep since three in the morning. A storm was due. It had been much too hot for three days in a row.

"Well, maybe it will just be a little mist," Coupeau said several times, standing at the door and anxiously studying the sky. "Now we have to wait only for my sister. We'll start as soon as she arrives."

Madame Lorilleux was late. Madame Lerat had stopped by so they could come together, but found her only beginning to get dressed. The two sisters had argued. The widow whispered in her brother's ear, "I left her flat. She's in a dreadful mood. You'll see."

And the wedding party had to wait another quarter of an hour, walking about the wine shop, elbowed and jostled in the midst of the men who entered to drink a glass of wine at the bar. Now and again Boche, or Madame Fauconnier, or Bibi-the-Smoker left the others and went to the edge of the pavement, looking up at the sky. The storm was not passing over at all; a darkness was coming on and puffs of wind, sweeping along the ground, raised little clouds of white dust. At the first clap of thunder, Mademoiselle Remanjou made the sign of the cross. All the glances were anxiously directed to the clock over the looking-glass; it was twenty minutes to two.

"Here it goes," cried Coupeau. "It's the angels who're weeping."

A gush of rain swept the pavement, along which some women flew, holding down their skirts with both hands. And it was in the midst of this first shower that Madame Lorilleux at length arrived, furious and out of breath, and struggling on the threshold with her umbrella that would not close.

"Did anyone ever see such a thing?" she exclaimed. "It caught me just at the door. I felt inclined to go upstairs again and take my things off. I should have been wise had I done so. Ah. It's a pretty wedding. I said how it would be. I wanted to put it off till next Saturday; and it rains because they wouldn't listen to me. So much the better, so much the better. I wish the sky would burst."

Coupeau tried to pacify her without success. He wouldn't have to pay for her dress if it was spoilt. She had on a black silk dress in which she was nearly choking, the bodice, too tight fitting, was almost bursting the button-holes, and was cutting her across the shoulders; while the skirt only allowed her to take very short steps in walking. However, the ladies present were all staring at her, quite overcome by her costume.

She appeared not to notice Gervaise, who was sitting beside mother Coupeau. She asked her husband for his handkerchief. Then she went into a corner and very carefully wiped off the raindrops that had fallen on her silk dress.

The shower had abruptly ceased. The darkness increased, it was almost like night—a livid night rent at times by large flashes of lightning. Bibi-the-Smoker said laughingly that it would certainly rain priests. Then the storm burst forth with extreme violence. For half an hour the rain came down in bucketsful, and the thunder rumbled unceasingly. The men standing up before the door contemplated the gray veil of the downpour, the swollen gutters, the splashes of water caused by the rain beating into the puddles. The women, feeling frightened, had sat down again, holding their hands before their eyes. They no longer conversed, they were too upset. A jest Boche made about the thunder, saying that St. Peter was sneezing up there, failed to raise a smile. But, when the thunder-claps became less frequent and gradually died away in the distance, the wedding guests began to get impatient, enraged against the storm, cursing and shaking their fists at the clouds. A fine and interminable rain now poured down from the sky which had become an ashy gray.

"It's past two o'clock," cried Madame Lorilleux. "We can't stop here forever."

Mademoiselle Remanjou, having suggested going into the country all the same, even though they went no farther than the moat of the fortifications, the others scouted the idea: the roads would be in a nice state, one would not even be able to sit down on the grass; besides, it did not seem to be all over yet, there might perhaps be another downpour. Coupeau, who had been watching a workman, completely soaked, yet quietly walking along in the rain, murmured, "If that animal My-Boots is waiting for us on the Route de Saint-Denis, he won't catch a sunstroke."

That made some of them laugh; but the general ill-humor increased. It was becoming ludicrous. They must decide on something unless they planned to sit there, staring at each other, until time for dinner. So for the next quarter of an hour, while the persistent rain continued, they tried to think of what to do. Bibi-the-Smoker suggested that they play cards. Boche slyly suggested a most amusing game, the game of true confessions. Madame Gaudron thought of going to eat onion tarts on the Chaussee Clignancourt. Madame Lerat wanted to hear some stories. Gaudron said he wasn't a bit put out and thought they were quite well off where they were, out of the downpour. He suggested sitting down to dinner immediately.

There was a discussion after each proposal. Some said that this would put everybody to sleep or that that would make people think they were stupid. Lorilleux had to get his word in. He finally suggested a walk along the outer Boulevards to Old Man Lachaise cemetery. They could visit the tomb of Heloise and Abelard. Madame Lorilleux exploded, no longer able to control herself. She was leaving, she was. Were they trying to make fun of her? She got all dressed up and came out in the rain. And for what? To be wasting time in a wine shop. No, she had had enough of this wedding party. She'd rather be in her own home. Coupeau and Lorilleux had to get between her and the door to keep her from leaving. She kept telling them, "Get out of my way. I am leaving, I tell you."

Lorilleux finally succeeded in calming her down. Coupeau went over to Gervaise, who had been sitting quietly in a corner with mother Coupeau and Madame Fauconnier.

"You haven't suggested anything," he said to her.

"Whatever they want," she replied, laughing. "I don't mind. We can go out or stay here."

She seemed aglow with contentment. She had spoken to each guest as they arrived. She spoke sensibly, in her soft voice, not getting into any disagreements. During the downpour, she had sat with her eyes wide open, watching the lightning as though she could see the future in the sudden flashes.

Monsieur Madinier had up to this time not proposed anything. He was leaning against the bar, with the tails of his dress coat thrust apart, while he fully maintained the important air of an employer. He kept on expectorating, and rolled his big eyes about.

"My God," said he, "We might go to the Museum."

And he stroked his chin, as he blinkingly consulted the other members of the party.

"There are antiquities, pictures, paintings, a whole heap of things. It is very instructive. Perhaps you have never been there. . . . It is quite worth seeing at least once in a while."

They looked at each other interrogatively. No, Gervaise had never been;

Madame Fauconnier neither, nor Boche, nor the others. Coupeau thought he had been one Sunday, but he was not sure. They hesitated, however, when Madame Lorilleux, greatly impressed by Monsieur Madinier's importance, thought the suggestion a very worthy and respectable one. As they were wasting the day, and were all dressed up, they might as well go somewhere for their own instruction. Everyone approved. Then, as it still rained a little, they borrowed some umbrellas from the proprietor of the wine shop, old blue, green, and brown umbrellas, forgotten by different customers, and started off to the Museum.

The wedding party turned to the right, and descended into Paris along the Faubourg Saint-Denis. Coupeau and Gervaise again took the lead, almost running and keeping a good distance in front of the others. Monsieur Madinier now gave his arm to Madame Lorilleux, mother Coupeau having remained behind in the wine shop on account of her old legs. Then came Lorilleux and Madame Lerat, Boche and Madame Fauconnier, Bibi-the-Smoker and Mademoiselle Remanjou, and finally the two Gaudrons. They were twelve and made a pretty long procession on the pavement.

"I swear to you, we had nothing to do with it," Madame Lorilleux explained to Monsieur Madinier. "We don't even know how they met, or, we know only too well, but that's not for us to discuss. My husband even had to buy the wedding ring. We were scarcely out of bed this morning when he had to lend them ten francs. And, not a member of her family at her wedding, what kind of bride is that? She says she has a sister in Paris who works for a pork butcher. Why didn't she invite her?" She stopped to point at Gervaise, who was limping awkwardly because of the slope of the pavement. "Just look at her. Clump-clump."

"Clump-clump" ran through the wedding procession. Lorilleux laughed under his breath, and said they ought to call her that, but Madame Fauconnier stood up for Gervaise. They shouldn't make fun of her; she was neat as a pin and did a good job when there was washing to be done.

When the wedding procession came out of the Faubourg Saint-Denis, they had to cross the boulevard. The street had been transformed into a morass of sticky mud by the storm. It had started to pour again and they had opened the assorted umbrellas. The women picked their way carefully through the mud, holding their skirts high as the men held the sorry-looking umbrellas over their heads. The procession stretched out the width of the street.

"It's a masquerade." yelled two street urchins.

People turned to stare. These couples parading across the boulevard added a splash of vivid color against the damp background. It was a parade of a strange medley of styles showing fancy used clothing which are the luxury of the poor. The gentlemen's hats caused the most merriment, old hats preserved for years in dark and dusty cupboards, in a variety of comical forms: tall ones, flattened ones, sharply peaked ones, hats with extraordinary brims, curled back or flat, too narrow or too wide. Then at the very end, Madame Gaudron came along with her bright dress over her bulging belly and caused the smiles of the audience to grow even wider. The procession made no effort to hasten its progress. They were, in fact, rather pleased to attract so much attention and admiration.

"Look. Here comes the bride." one of the urchins shouted, pointing to Madame Gaudron. "Isn't it too bad. She must have swallowed something."

The entire wedding procession burst into laughter. Bibi-the-Smoker turned around and laughed. Madame Gaudron laughed the most of all. She wasn't ashamed as she thought more than one of the women watching had looked at her with envy.

They turned into the Rue de Clery. Then they took the Rue du Mail. On reaching the Place des Victoires, there was a halt. The bride's left shoe lace had come undone, and as she tied it up again at the foot of the statue of Louis XIV., the couples pressed behind her waiting, and joking about the bit of calf of her leg that she displayed. At length, after passing down the Rue Croix-des-Petits-Champs, they reached the Louvre.

Monsieur Madinier politely asked to be their cicerone. It was a big place, and they might lose themselves; besides, he knew the best parts, because he had often come there with an artist, a very intelligent fellow from whom a large dealer bought designs to put on his cardboard boxes. Down below, when the wedding party entered the Assyrian Museum, a slight shiver passed through it. The deuce. It was not at all warm there; the hall would have made a capital cellar. And the couples slowly advanced, their chins raised, their eyes blinking, between the gigantic stone figures, the black marble gods, dumb in their hieratic rigidity, and the monstrous beasts, half cats and half women, with death-like faces, attenuated noses, and swollen lips. They thought all these things very ugly. The stone carvings of the present day were a great deal better. An inscription in Phoenician characters amazed them. No one could possibly have ever read that scrawl. But Monsieur Madinier, already up on the first landing with Madame Lorilleux, called to them, shouting beneath the vaulted ceiling:

"Come along. They're nothing, all those things. The things to see are on the first floor."

The severe barrenness of the staircase made them very grave. An attendant, superbly attired in a red waistcoat and a coat trimmed with gold lace, who seemed to be awaiting them on the landing, increased their emotion. It was with great respect, and treading as softly as possible, that they entered the French Gallery.

Then, without stopping, their eyes occupied with the gilding of the frames, they followed the string of little rooms, glancing at the passing pictures too numerous to be seen properly. It would have required an hour before each, if they had wanted to understand it. What a number of pictures. There was no end to them. They must be worth a mint of money. Right at the end, Monsieur Madinier suddenly ordered a halt opposite the "Raft of the Medusa" and he explained the subject to them. All deeply impressed and motionless, they uttered not a word. When they started off again, Boche expressed the general feeling, saying it was marvelous.

In the Apollo Gallery, the inlaid flooring especially astonished the party—a shining floor, as clear as a mirror, and which reflected the legs of the seats. Mademoiselle Remanjou kept her eyes closed, because she could not help thinking that she was walking on water. They called to Madame Gaudron to be careful how she trod on account of her condition. Monsieur Madinier wanted to show them the gilding and paintings of the ceiling; but it nearly broke their necks to look up above, and they could distinguish nothing. Then, before entering the Square Salon, he pointed to a window, saying:

"That's the balcony from which Charles IX fired on the people."

He looked back to make sure the party was following. In the middle of the Salon Carre, he held up his hand. "There are only masterpieces here," he said, in a subdued voice, as though in church. They went all around the room. Gervaise wanted to know about "The Wedding at Cana." Coupeau paused to stare at the "Mona Lisa," saying that she reminded him of one of his aunts. Boche and Bibi-the-Smoker snickered at the nudes, pointing them out to each other and winking. The Gaudrons looked at the "Virgin" of Murillo, he with his mouth open, she with her hands folded on her belly.

When they had been all around the Salon, Monsieur Madinier wished them to go round it again, it was so worthwhile. He was very attentive to Madame Lorilleux, because of her silk dress; and each time that she questioned him he answered her gravely, with great assurance. She was curious about "Titian's Mistress" because the yellow hair resembled her own. He told her it was "La Belle Ferronniere," a mistress of Henry IV. about whom there had been a play at the Ambigu.

Then the wedding party invaded the long gallery occupied by the Italian and Flemish schools. More paintings, always paintings, saints, men and women, with faces which some of them could understand, landscapes that were all black, animals turned yellow, a medley of people and things, the great mixture of the colors of which was beginning to give them all violent headaches. Monsieur Madinier no longer talked as he slowly headed the procession, which followed him in good order, with stretched necks and upcast eyes. Centuries of art passed before their bewildered ignorance, the fine sharpness of the early masters, the splendors of the Venetians, the vigorous life, beautiful with light, of the Dutch painters. But what interested them most were the artists who were copying, with their easels planted amongst the people, painting away unrestrainedly, an old lady, mounted on a pair of high steps, working a big brush over the delicate sky of an immense painting, struck them as something most peculiar.

Slowly the word must have gone around that a wedding party was visiting the Louvre. Several painters came over with big smiles. Some visitors were so curious that they went to sit on benches ahead of the group in order to be comfortable while they watched them pass in review. Museum guards bit back comments. The wedding party was now quite weary and beginning to drag their feet.

Monsieur Madinier was reserving himself to give more effect to a surprise that he had in store. He went straight to the "Kermesse" of Rubens; but still he said nothing. He contented himself with directing the others' attention to the picture by a sprightly glance. The ladies uttered faint cries the moment they brought their noses close to the painting. Then, blushing deeply they turned away their heads. The men though kept them there, cracking jokes, and seeking for the coarser details.

"Just look." exclaimed Boche, "it's worth the money. There's one spewing, and another, he's watering the dandelions; and that one—that one. Ah, well. They're a nice clean lot, they are."

"Let us be off," said Monsieur Madinier, delighted with his success. "There is nothing more to see here."

They retraced their steps, passing again through the Salon Carre and the Apollo Gallery. Madame Lerat and Mademoiselle Remanjou complained, declaring that their legs could scarcely bear them. But the cardboard box manufacturer wanted to show Lorilleux the old jewelry. It was close by in a little room which he could find with his eyes shut. However, he made a mistake and led the wedding party astray through seven or eight cold, deserted rooms, only ornamented with severe looking-glass cases, containing numberless broken pots and hideous little figures.

While looking for an exit they stumbled into the collection of drawings. It was immense. Through room after room they saw nothing interesting, just scribblings on paper that filled all the cases and covered the walls. They thought there was no end to these drawings.

Monsieur Madinier, losing his head, not willing to admit that he did not know his way, ascended a flight of stairs, making the wedding party mount to the next floor. This time they traversed the Naval Museum, among models of instruments and cannons, plans in relief, and vessels as tiny as playthings. After going a long way, and walking for a quarter of an hour, the party came upon another staircase; and, having descended this, found itself once more surrounded by the drawings. Then despair took possession of them as they wandered at random through long halls, following Monsieur Madinier, who was furious and mopping the sweat from his forehead. He accused the government of having moved the doors around. Museum guards and visitors looked on with astonishment as the procession, still in a column of couples, passed by. They passed again through the Salon Carre, the French Gallery and then along the cases where minor Eastern divinities slumbered peacefully. It seemed they would never find their way out. They were getting tired and made a lot of noise.

"Closing time. Closing time." called out the attendants, in a loud tone of voice.

And the wedding party was nearly locked in. An attendant was obliged to place himself at the head of it, and conduct it to a door. Then in the courtyard of the Louvre, when it had recovered its umbrellas from the cloakroom, it breathed again. Monsieur Madinier regained his assurance. He had made a mistake in not turning to the left, now he recollected that the jewelry was to the left. The whole party pretended to be very pleased at having seen all they had.

Four o'clock was striking. There were still two hours to be employed before the dinner time, so it was decided they should take a stroll, just to occupy the interval. The ladies, who were very tired, would have preferred to sit down; but, as no one offered any refreshments, they started off, following the line of quays. There they encountered another shower and so sharp a one that in spite of the umbrellas, the ladies' dresses began to get wet. Madame Lorilleux, her heart sinking within her each time a drop fell upon her black silk, proposed that they should shelter themselves under the Pont-Royal; besides if the others did not accompany her, she threatened to go all by herself. And the procession marched under one of the arches of the bridge. They were very comfortable there. It was, most decidedly a capital idea. The ladies, spreading their handkerchiefs over the paving-stones, sat down with their knees wide apart, and pulled out the blades of grass that grew between the stones with both hands, while they watched the dark flowing water as though they were in the country. The men amused themselves with calling out very loud, so as to awaken the echoes of the arch. Boche and Bibi-the-Smoker shouted insults into the air at the top of their voices, one after the other. They laughed uproariously when the echo threw the insults back at them. When their throats were hoarse from shouting, they made a game of skipping flat stones on the surface of the Seine.

The shower had ceased but the whole party felt so comfortable that no one thought of moving away. The Seine was flowing by, an oily sheet carrying bottle corks, vegetable peelings, and other refuse that sometimes collected in temporary whirlpools moving along with the turbulent water. Endless traffic rumbled on the bridge overhead, the noisy bustle of Paris, of which they could glimpse only the rooftops to the left and right, as though they were in the bottom of a deep pit.

Mademoiselle Remanjou sighed; if the leaves had been out this would have reminded her of a bend of the Marne where she used to go with a young man. It still made her cry to think of him.

At last, Monsieur Madinier gave the signal for departure. They passed through the Tuileries gardens, in the midst of a little community of children, whose hoops and balls upset the good order of the couples. Then as the wedding party on arriving at the Place Vendome looked up at the column, Monsieur Madinier gallantly offered to treat the ladies to a view from the top. His suggestion was considered extremely amusing. Yes, yes, they would go up; it would give them something to laugh about for a long time. Besides, it would be full of interest for those persons who had never been higher than a cow pasture.

"Do you think Clump-clump will venture inside there with her leg all out of place?" murmured Madame Lorilleux.

"I'll go up with pleasure," said Madame Lerat, "but I won't have any men walking behind me."

And the whole party ascended. In the narrow space afforded by the spiral staircase, the twelve persons crawled up one after the other, stumbling against the worn steps, and clinging to the walls. Then, when the obscurity became complete, they almost split their sides with laughing.

The ladies screamed when the gentlemen pinched their legs. But they weren't stupid enough to say anything. The proper plan is to think that it is the mice nibbling at them. It wasn't very serious; the men knew when to stop.

Boche thought of a joke and everyone took it up. They called down to Madame Gaudron to ask her if she could squeeze her belly through. Just think. If she should get stuck there, she would completely block the passage, and how would they ever get out? They laughed so at the jokes about her belly that the column itself vibrated. Boche was now quite carried away and declared that they were growing old climbing up this chimney pipe. Was it ever coming to an end, or did it go right up to heaven? He tried to frighten the ladies by telling them the structure was shaking.

Coupeau, meanwhile, said nothing. He was behind Gervaise, with his arm around her waist, and felt that she was everything perfect to him. When they suddenly emerged again into the daylight, he was just in the act of kissing her on the cheek.

"Well. You're a nice couple; you don't stand on ceremony," said Madame Lorilleux with a scandalized air.

Bibi-the-Smoker pretended to be furious. He muttered between his teeth.

"You made such a noise together. I wasn't even able to count the steps."

But Monsieur Madinier was already up on the platform, pointing out the different monuments. Neither Madame Fauconnier nor Mademoiselle Remanjou would on any consideration leave the staircase. The thought of the pavement below made their blood curdle, and they contented themselves with glancing out of the little door. Madame Lerat, who was bolder, went round the narrow terrace, keeping close to the bronze dome; but, it gave one a rude emotion to think that one only had to slip off. The men were a little paler than usual as they stared down at the square below. You would think you were up in mid-air, detached from everything. No, it wasn't fun; it froze your very insides.

Monsieur Madinier told them to raise their eyes and look straight into the distance to avoid feeling dizzy. He went on pointing out the Invalides, the Pantheon, Notre Dame and the Montmartre hill. Madame

Lorilleux asked if they could see the place where they were to have dinner, the Silver Windmill on the Boulevard de la Chapelle. For ten minutes they tried to see it, even arguing about it. Everyone had their own idea where it was.

"It wasn't worthwhile coming up here to bite each other's noses off," said Boche, angrily as he turned to descend the staircase.

The wedding party went down, unspeaking and sulky, awakening no other sound beyond that of shoes clanking on the stone steps. When it reached the bottom, Monsieur Madinier wished to pay; but Coupeau would not permit him, and hastened to place twenty-four sous into the keeper's hand, two sous for each person. So they returned by the Boulevards and the Faubourg du Poissonniers. Coupeau, however, considered that their outing could not end like that. He bundled them all into a wine shop where they took some vermouth.

The repast was ordered for six o'clock. At the Silver Windmill, they had been waiting for the wedding party for a good twenty minutes. Madame Boche, who had got a lady living in the same house to attend to her duties for the evening, was conversing with mother Coupeau in the first floor room, in front of the table, which was all laid out; and the two youngsters, Claude and Etienne, whom she had brought with her, were playing about beneath the table and amongst the chairs. When Gervaise, on entering caught sight of the little ones, whom she had not seen all the day, she took them on her knees, and caressed and kissed them.

"Have they been good?" asked she of Madame Boche. "I hope they haven't worried you too much."

And as the latter related the things the little rascals had done during the afternoon, and which would make one die with laughing, the mother again took them up and pressed them to her breast, seized with an overpowering outburst of maternal affection.

"It's not very pleasant for Coupeau, all the same," Madame Lorilleux was saying to the other ladies, at the end of the room.

Gervaise had kept her smiling peacefulness from the morning, but after the long walk she appeared almost sad at times as she watched her husband and the Lorilleuxs in a thoughtful way. She had the feeling that Coupeau was a little afraid of his sister. The evening before, he had been talking big, swearing he would put them in their places if they did-

n't behave. However, she could see that in their presence he was hanging on their words, worrying when he thought they might be displeased. This gave the young bride some cause for worry about the future.

They were now only waiting for My-Boots, who had not yet put in an appearance.

"Fuck him," cried Coupeau, "Let's begin. You'll see, he'll soon turn up, he's got a hollow nose, he can scent the grub from afar. I say he must be amusing himself, if he's still standing like a post on the Route de Saint-Denis."

Then the wedding party, feeling very lively, sat down making a great noise with the chairs. Gervaise was between Lorilleux and Monsieur Madinier, and Coupeau between Madame Fauconnier and Madame Lorilleux. The other guests seated themselves where they liked, because it always ended with jealousies and quarrels, when one settled their places for them. Boche glided to a seat beside Madame Lerat. Bibi-the-Smoker had for neighbors Mademoiselle Remanjou and Madame Gaudron. As for Madame Boche and mother Coupeau, they were right at the end of the table, looking after the children, cutting up their meat and giving them something to drink, but not much wine.

"Does nobody say grace?" asked Boche, while the ladies arranged their skirts under the table-cloth, so as not to get them stained.

But Madame Lorilleux paid no attention to such pleasantries. The vermicelli soup, which was nearly cold, was gulped down very quickly, their lips making a hissing noise against the spoons. Two waiters served at table, dressed in little greasy jackets and not over-clean white aprons. By the four open windows overlooking the acacias of the courtyard there entered the clear light of the close of a stormy day, with the atmosphere purified thereby though without sufficiently cooling it. The light reflected from the humid corner of trees tinged the haze-filled room with green and made leaf shadows dance along the table-cloth, from which came a vague aroma of dampness and mildew.

Two large mirrors, one at each end of the room, seemed to stretch out the table. The heavy crockery with which it was set was beginning to turn yellow and the cutlery was scratched and grimed with grease. Each time a waiter came through the swinging doors from the kitchen a whiff of odorous burnt lard came with him.

"Don't all talk at once," said Boche, as everyone remained silent with his nose in his plate.

They were drinking the first glass of wine as their eyes followed two meat pies which the waiters were handing round when My-Boots entered the room.

"Well, you're a scurvy lot, you people." said he. "I've been wearing my pins out for three hours waiting on that road, and a gendarme even came and asked me for my papers. It isn't right to play such dirty tricks on a friend. You might at least have sent me word by a commissionaire. Ah. No, you know, joking apart, it's too bad. And with all that, it rained so hard that I got my pickets full of water. Honor bright, you might still catch enough fish in 'em for a meal."

The others wriggled with laughter. That animal My-Boots was just a bit on; he had certainly already stowed away his two quarts of wine, merely to prevent his being bothered by all that frog's liquor with which the storm had deluged his limbs.

"Hail, Count Leg-of-Mutton." said Coupeau, "Just go and sit yourself there, beside Madame Gaudron. You see you were expected."

. . . he did not mind, he would soon catch the others up; and he asked for three helpings of soup, platefuls of vermicelli, in which he soaked enormous slices of bread. Then, when they had attacked the meat pies, he became the profound admiration of everyone at the table. How he stowed it away. The bewildered waiters helped each other to pass him bread, thin slices which he swallowed at a mouthful. He ended by losing his temper; he insisted on having a loaf placed on the table beside him. The landlord, very anxious, came for a moment and looked in at the door. The party, which was expecting him, again wriggled with laughter. It seemed to upset the caterer. What a rum card he was that My-Boots. One day he had eaten a dozen hard-boiled eggs and drank a dozen glasses of wine while the clock was striking twelve. There are not many who can do that. And Mademoiselle Remanjou, deeply moved, watched My-Boots chew while Monsieur Madinier, seeking for a word to express his almost respectful astonishment, declared that such a capacity was extraordinary.

There was a brief silence. A waiter had just placed on the table a ragout of rabbits in a vast dish as deep as a salad-bowl. Coupeau, who liked fun, started another joke.

"I say, waiter, that rabbit's from the housetops. It still mews."

And in fact, a faint mew perfectly imitated seemed to issue from the dish. It was Coupeau who did that with his throat, without opening his lips; a talent which at all parties, met with decided success, so much so that he never ordered a dinner abroad without having a rabbit ragout. After that he purred. The ladies pressed their napkins to their mouths to try and stop their laughter. Madame Fauconnier asked for a head, she only liked that part. Mademoiselle Remanjou had a weakness for the slices of bacon. And as Boche said he preferred the little onions when they were nicely broiled, Madame Lerat screwed up her lips, and murmured:

"I can understand that."

She was a dried up stick, living the cloistered life of a hard-working woman imprisoned within her daily routine, who had never had a man stick his nose into her room since the death of her husband; yet she had an obsession with double meanings and indecent allusions that were sometimes so far off the mark that only she understood them.

As Boche leaned toward her and, in a whisper, asked for an explanation, she resumed, "Little onions; why of course. That's quite enough, I think."

The general conversation was becoming grave. Each one was talking of his trade. Monsieur Madinier raved about the cardboard business. There were some real artists. For an example, he mentioned Christmas gift boxes, of which he'd seen samples that were marvels of splendor.

Lorilleux sneered at this; he was extremely vain because of working with gold, feeling that it gave a sort of sheen to his fingers and his whole personality. "In olden times jewelers wore swords like gentlemen." He often cited the case of Bernard Palissy, even though he really knew nothing about him.

Coupeau told of a masterpiece of a weather vane made by one of his fellow workers which included a Greek column, a sheaf of wheat, a basket of fruit, and a flag, all beautifully worked out of nothing but strips of zinc shaped and soldered together.

Madame Lerat showed Bibi-the-Smoker how to make a rose by rolling the handle of her knife between her bony fingers.

All the while, their voices had been rising louder and louder, competing for attention. Shrill comments by Madame Fauconnier were heard. She complained about the girls who worked for her, especially a little apprentice who was nothing but a tart and had badly scorched some sheets the evening before.

"You may talk," Lorilleux cried, banging his fist down on the table, "but gold is gold."

And, in the midst of the silence caused by the statement of this fact, the only sound heard was Mademoiselle Remanjou's shrill voice continuing, "Then I turn up the skirt and stitch it inside. I stick a pin in the head to keep the cap on, and that's all; and they are sold for thirteen sous a piece."

She was explaining how she dressed her dolls to My-Boots, whose jaws were working slowly like grindstones. He did not listen, though he kept nodding his head, but looked after the waiters to prevent them removing any of the dishes he had not cleaned out. They had now finished a veal stew with green beans. The roast was brought in, two scrawny chickens resting on a bed of water cress which was limp from the warming oven.

Outside, only the higher branches of the acacias were touched by the setting sun. Inside, the greenish reflected light was thickened by wisps of steam rising from the table, now messy with spilled wine and gravy and the debris of the dinner. Along the wall were dirty dishes and empty bottles which the waiters had piled there like a heap of refuse. It was so hot that the men took off their jackets and continued eating in their shirt sleeves.

"Madame Boche, please don't spread their butter so thick," said Gervaise, who spoke but little, and who was watching Claude and Etienne from a distance.

She got up from her seat, and went and talked for a minute while standing behind the little ones' chairs. Children did not reason; they would eat all day long without refusing a single thing; and then she herself helped them to some chicken, a little of the breast. But mother Coupeau said they might, just for once in a while, risk an attack of indigestion. Madame Boche, in a low voice accused Boche of caressing Madame Lerat's knees. He was a sly one, but he was getting a little too gay. She had certainly seen his hand disappear. If he did it again, drat him. She wouldn't hesitate throwing a pitcher of water over his head.

In the partial silence, Monsieur Madinier was talking politics. "Their law of May 31, is an abominable one. Now you must reside in a place for two years. Three millions of citizens are struck off the voting lists. I've been told that Bonaparte is, in reality, very much annoyed for he loves the people; he has given them proofs."

He was a republican; but he admired the prince on account of his uncle, a man the like of whom would never be seen again. Bibi-the-Smoker flew into a passion. He had worked at the Elysee; he had seen Bonaparte just as he saw My-Boots in front of him over there. Well that jerk of a president was just like a jackass, that was all. It was said that he was going to travel about in the direction of Lyons; it would be a precious good riddance of bad rubbish if he fell into some hole and broke his neck. But, as the discussion was becoming too heated, Coupeau had to interfere.

"Ah, well. How simple you all are to quarrel about politics. Politics are all humbug. Do such things exist for us? Let there be any one as king, it won't prevent me earning my five francs a day, and eating and sleeping; isn't that so? No, it's too stupid to argue about."

Lorilleux shook his head. He was born on the same day as the Count of Chambord, the 29th of September, 1820. He was greatly struck with this coincidence, indulging himself in a vague dream, in which he established a connection between the king's return to France and his own private fortunes. He never said exactly what he was expecting, but he led people to suppose that when that time arrived something extraordinarily agreeable would happen to him. So whenever he had a wish too great to be gratified, he would put it off to another time, when the king came back.

"Besides," observed he. "I saw the Count de Chambord one evening."

Every face was turned towards him.

"It's quite true. A stout man in an overcoat with a good-natured air. I was at Pequignot's, one of my friends who deals in furniture in the Grand Rue de la Chapelle. The Count of Chambord had forgotten his umbrella there the day before; so he came in, and just simply said, like this, 'Will you please return me my umbrella?' Well, yes, it was him; Pequignot gave me his word of honor it was."

Not one of the guests suggested the smallest doubt. They had now arrived at dessert and the waiters were clearing the table with much clattering of dishes. Madame Lorilleux, who up to then had been very genteel, very much the lady, suddenly let fly with a curse. One of the wait-ers had spilled something wet down her neck while removing a dish. This time her silk dress would be stained for sure. Monsieur Madinier had to examine her back, but he swore there was nothing to be seen.

Two platters of cheese, two dishes of fruit, and a floating island pudding of frosted eggs in a deep salad-bowl had now been placed along the middle of the table. The pudding caused a moment of re-spectful attention even though the overdone egg whites had flattened on the yellow custard. It was unexpected and seemed very fancy.

My-Boots was still eating. He had asked for another loaf. He fin-ished what there was of the cheese; and, as there was some cream left, he had the salad-bowl passed to him, into which he sliced some large pieces of bread as though for a soup.

"The gentleman is really remarkable," said Monsieur Madinier, again giving way to his admiration.

Then the men rose to get their pipes. They stood for a moment be-hind My-Boots, patting him on the back, and asking him if he was feel-ing better. Bibi-the-Smoker lifted him up in his chair; but Mother of God, the animal had doubled in weight. Coupeau joked that My-Boots was only getting started, that now he was going to settle down and re-ally eat for the rest of the night. The waiters were startled and quickly vanished from sight.

Boche, who had gone downstairs for a moment, came up to report the proprietor's reaction. He was standing behind his bar, pale as death. His wife, dreadfully upset, was wondering if any bakeries were still open. Even the cat seemed deep in despair. This was as funny as could be, really worth the price of the dinner. It was impossible to have a proper dinner party without My-Boots, the bottomless pit. The other men eyed him with a brooding jealousy as they puffed on their pipes. Indeed, to be able to eat so much, you had to be very solidly built.

"I wouldn't care to be obliged to support you," said Madame Gaudron.

"Ah, no; you may take my word for that."

"I say, little mother, no jokes," replied My-Boots, casting a side glance at his neighbor's rotund figure. "You've swallowed more than I have."

The others applauded, shouting "Bravo."—it was well answered. It was now pitch dark outside, three gas-jets were flaring in the room, diffusing dim rays in the midst of the tobacco-smoke. The waiters, after serving the coffee and the brandy, had removed the last piles of dirty plates. Down below, beneath the three acacias, dancing had commenced, a cornet-a-piston and two fiddles playing very loud, and mingling in the warm night air with the rather hoarse laughter of women.

"We must have a punch," cried My-Boots; "two quarts of brandy, lots of lemon, and a little sugar."

But Coupeau, seeing the anxious look on Gervaise's face in front of him, got up from the table, declaring that there should be no more drink. They had emptied twenty-five quarts, a quart and a half to each person, counting the children as grown-up people; that was already too much. They had had a feed together in good fellowship, and without ceremony, because they esteemed each other, and wished to celebrate the event of the day amongst themselves. Everything had been very nice; they had had lots of fun. It wouldn't do to get cockeyed drunk now, out of respect to the ladies. That was all he had to say, they had come together to toast a marriage and they had done so.

Coupeau delivered the little speech with convincing sincerity and punctuated each phrase by placing his hand on his heart. He won whole-hearted approval from Lorilleux and Monsieur Madinier; but the other four men, especially My-Boots, were already well lit and sneered. They declared in hoarse drunken voices that they were thirsty and wanted drinks.

"Those who're thirsty are thirsty, and those who aren't thirsty aren't thirsty," remarked My-Boots. "Therefore, we'll order the punch. No one need take offence. The aristocrats can drink sugar-and-water."

And as the zinc-worker commenced another sermon, the other, who had risen on his legs, gave himself a slap, exclaiming, "Come, let's have no more of that, my boy. Waiter, two quarts of your aged stuff."

So Coupeau said very well, only they would settle for the dinner at once. It would prevent any disputes. The well-behaved people did not want to pay for the drunkards; and it just happened that My-Boots, after searching in his pockets for a long time, could only produce three francs and seven sous. Well, why had they made him wait all that time on the Route de Saint-Denis? He could not let himself be drowned and so he had broken into his five-franc piece. It was the fault of the others, that was all. He ended by giving the three francs, keeping the seven sous for the morrow's tobacco. Coupeau, who was furious, would have knocked him over had not Gervaise, greatly frightened, pulled him by his coat, and begged him to keep cool. He decided to borrow the two francs of Lorilleux, who after refusing them, lent them on the sly, for his wife would never have consented to his doing so.

Monsieur Madinier went round with a plate. The spinster and the ladies who were alone—Madame Lerat, Madame Fauconnier, Mademoiselle Remanjou—discreetly placed their five-franc pieces in it first. Then the gentlemen went to the other end of the room, and made up the accounts. They were fifteen; it amounted therefore to seventy-five francs. When the seventy-five francs were in the plate, each man added five sous for the waiters. It took a quarter of an hour of laborious calculations before everything was settled to the general satisfaction.

But when Monsieur Madinier, who wished to deal direct with the landlord, had got him to step up, the whole party became lost in astonishment on hearing him say with a smile that there was still something due to him. There were some extras; and, as the word "extras" was greeted with angry exclamations, he entered into details:—Twenty-five quarts of wine, instead of twenty, the number agreed upon beforehand; the frosted eggs, which he had added, as the dessert was rather scanty; finally, a quarter of a bottle of rum, served with the coffee, in case any one preferred rum. Then a formidable quarrel ensued. Coupeau, who was appealed to, protested against everything; he had never mentioned twenty quarts; as for the frosted eggs, they were included in the dessert, so much the worse for the landlord if he chose to add them without being asked to do so. There remained the rum, a mere nothing, just a mode of increasing the bill by putting on the table spirits that no one thought anything about.

"It was on the tray with the coffee," he cried; "therefore it goes with the coffee. Go to the deuce. Take your money, and never again will we set foot in your den."

"It's six francs more," repeated the landlord. "Pay me my six francs; and with all that I haven't counted the four loaves that gentleman ate."

The whole party, pressing forward, surrounded him with furious gestures and a yelping of voices choking with rage. The women especially threw aside all reserve, and refused to add another centime. This was some wedding dinner. Mademoiselle Remanjou vowed she would never again attend such a party. Madame Fauconnier declared she had had a very disappointing meal; at home she could have had a finger-licking dish for only two francs. Madame Gaudron bitterly complained that she had been shoved down to the worst end of the table next to My-Boots who had ignored her. These parties never turned out well, one should be more careful whom one invites. Gervaise had taken refuge with mother Coupeau near one of the windows, feeling shamed as she realized that all these recriminations would fall back upon her.

Monsieur Madinier ended by going down with the landlord. One could hear them arguing below. Then, when half an hour had gone by the cardboard box manufacturer returned; he had settled the matter by giving three francs. But the party continued annoyed and exasperated, constantly returning to the question of the extras. And the uproar increased from an act of vigor on Madame Boche's part. She had kept an eye on Boche, and at length detected him squeezing Madame Lerat round the waist in a corner. Then, with all her strength, she flung a water pitcher, which smashed against the wall.

"One can easily see that your husband's a tailor, madame," said the tall widow, with a curl of the lip, full of a double meaning. "He's a petticoat specialist, even though I gave him some pretty hard kicks under the table."

The harmony of the evening was altogether upset. Everyone became more and more ill-tempered. Monsieur Madinier suggested some singing, but Bibi-the-Smoker, who had a fine voice, had disappeared some time before; and Mademoiselle Remanjou, who was leaning out of the window, caught sight of him under the acacias, swinging round a big girl who was bare-headed. The cornet-a-piston and two fiddles were playing "Le Marchand de Moutarde." The party now began to break up. My-Boots and the Gaudrons went down to the dance with Boche sneaking along after them. The twirling couples could be seen from the windows. The night was still as though exhausted from the heat of the day. A serious conversation started between Lorilleux and Monsieur Madinier. The ladies examined their dresses carefully to see if they had been stained.

Madame Lerat's fringe looked as though it had been dipped in the coffee. Madame Fauconnier's chintz dress was spotted with gravy.

Mother Coupeau's green shawl, fallen from off a chair, was discovered in a corner, rolled up and trodden upon. But it was Madame Lorilleux especially who became more ill-tempered. She had a stain on the back of her dress; it was useless for the others to declare that she had not— she felt it. And, by twisting herself about in front of a looking-glass, she ended by catching a glimpse of it.

"What did I say?" cried she. "It's gravy from the fowl. The waiter shall pay for the dress. I will bring an action against him. Ah. This is a fit ending to such a day. I should have done better to have stayed in bed. To begin with, I'm off. I've had enough of their wretched wedding."

And she left the room in a rage, causing the staircase to shake beneath her heavy footsteps. Lorilleux ran after her. But all she would consent to was that she would wait five minutes on the pavement outside, if he wanted them to go off together. She ought to have left directly after the storm, as she wished to do. She would make Coupeau sorry for that day. Coupeau was dismayed when he heard how angry she was. Gervaise agreed to leave at once to avoid embarrassing him anymore.

There was a flurry of quick good-night kisses. Monsieur Madinier was to escort mother Coupeau home. Madame Boche would take Claude and Etienne with her for the bridal night. The children were sound asleep on chairs, stuffed full from the dinner. Just as the bridal couple and Lorilleux were about to go out the door, a quarrel broke out near the dance floor between their group and another group. Boche and My-Boots were kissing a lady and wouldn't give her up to her escorts, two soldiers.

It was scarcely eleven o'clock. On the Boulevard de la Chapelle, and in the entire neighborhood of the Goutte-d'Or, the fortnight's pay, which fell due on that Saturday, produced an enormous drunken uproar. Madame Lorilleux was waiting beneath a gas-lamp about twenty paces from the Silver Windmill. She took her husband's arm, and walked on in front without looking round, at such a rate, that Gervaise and Coupeau got quite out of breath in trying to keep up with them. Now and again they stepped off the pavement to leave room for some drunkard who had fallen there. Lorilleux looked back, endeavoring to make things pleasant.

"We will see you as far as your door," said he.

But Madame Lorilleux, raising her voice, thought it a funny thing to spend one's wedding night in such a filthy hole as the Hotel Boncoeur. Ought they not to have put their marriage off, and have saved a few sous to buy some furniture, so as to have had a home of their own on the first night? Ah. They would be comfortable, right up under the roof, packed into a little closet, at ten francs a month, where there was not even the slightest air.

"I've given notice, we're not going to use the room up at the top of the house," timidly interposed Coupeau. "We are keeping Gervaise's room, which is larger."

Madame Lorilleux forgot herself. She turned abruptly round.

"That's worse than all." cried she. "You're going to sleep in Clump-clump's room."

Gervaise became quite pale. This nickname, which she received full in the face for the first time, fell on her like a blow. And she fully understood it, too, her sister-in-law's exclamation: the Clump-clump's room was the room in which she had lived for a month with Lantier, where the shreds of her past life still hung about. Coupeau did not understand this, but merely felt hurt at the harsh nickname.

"You do wrong to christen others," he replied angrily. "You don't know perhaps, that in the neighborhood they call you Cow's-Tail, because of your hair. There, that doesn't please you, does it? Why should we not keep the room on the first floor? Tonight the children won't sleep there and we shall be very comfortable."

Madame Lorilleux added nothing further, but retired into her dignity, horribly annoyed at being called Cow's-Tail. To cheer up Gervaise, Coupeau squeezed her arm softly. He even succeeded in making her smile by whispering into her ear that they were setting up housekeeping with the grand sum of seven sous, three big two-sou pieces and one little sou, which he jingled in his pocket.

When they reached the Hotel Boncoeur, the two couples wished each other good-night, with an angry air; and as Coupeau pushed the two women into each other's arms, calling them a couple of ninnies, a drunken fellow, who seemed to want to go to the right, suddenly slipped to the left and came tumbling between them.

"Why, it's old Bazouge." said Lorilleux. "He's had his fill today."

Gervaise, frightened, squeezed up against the door of the hotel. Old Bazouge, an undertaker's helper of some fifty years of age, had his black trousers all stained with mud, his black cape hooked on to his shoulder, and his black feather hat knocked in by some tumble he had taken.

"Don't be afraid, he's harmless," continued Lorilleux. "He's a neighbor of ours—the third room in the passage before us. He would find himself in a nice mess if his people were to see him like this."

Old Bazouge, however, felt offended at the young woman's evident terror.

"Well, what." hiccoughed he, "we ain't going to eat any one. I'm as good as another any day, my little woman. No doubt I've had a drop. When work's plentiful one must grease the wheels. It's not you, nor your friends, who would have carried down the stiff 'un of forty-seven stone whom I and a pal brought from the fourth floor to the pavement, and without smashing him too. I like jolly people."

But Gervaise retreated further into the doorway, seized with a longing to cry, which spoilt her day of sober-minded joy. She no longer thought of kissing her sister-in-law, she implored Coupeau to get rid of the drunkard. Then Bazouge, as he stumbled about, made a gesture of philosophical disdain.

"That won't prevent you passing through our hands, my little woman. You'll perhaps be glad to do so, one of these days. Yes, I know some women who'd be much obliged if we did carry them off."

And, as Lorilleux led him away, he turned around, and stuttered out a last sentence, between two burps.

"When you're dead—listen to this—when you're dead, it's for a long, long time."

CHAPTER IV

Then followed four years of hard work. In the neighborhood, Gervaise and Coupeau had the reputation of being a happy couple, living in retirement without quarrels, and taking a short walk regularly every Sunday in the direction of St. Ouen. The wife worked twelve hours a day at Madame Fauconnier's, and still found means to keep their lodging as clean and bright as a new coined sou and to prepare the meals for all her little family, morning and evening. The husband never got drunk, brought his wages home every fortnight, and smoked a pipe at his window in the evening, to get a breath of fresh air before going to bed. They were frequently alluded to on account of their nice, pleasant ways; and as between them they earned close upon nine francs a day, it was reckoned that they were able to put by a good deal of money.

However, during their first months together they had to struggle hard to get by. Their wedding had left them owing two hundred francs. Also, they detested the Hotel Boncoeur as they didn't like the other occupants. Their dream was to have a home of their own with their own furniture. They were always figuring how much they would need and decided three hundred and fifty francs at least, in order to be able to buy little items that came up later.

They were in despair at ever being able to collect such a large sum when a lucky chance came their way. An old gentleman at Plassans offered to take the older boy, Claude, and send him to an academy down there. The old man, who loved art, had previously been much impressed by Claude's sketches. Claude had already begun to cost them quite a bit. Now, with only Etienne to support, they were able to accumulate the money in a little over seven months. One day they were finally able to buy their own furniture from a second-hand dealer on Rue Belhomme. Their hearts filled with happiness, they celebrated by walking home along the exterior Boulevards.

They had purchased a bed, a night table, a chest of drawers with a marble top, a wardrobe, a round table covered with oilcloth, and six chairs. All were of dark mahogany. They also bought blankets, linen, and kitchen utensils that were scarcely used. It meant settling down and giving themselves a status in life as property owners, as persons to be respected.

For two months past they had been busy seeking some new apartments. At first they wanted above everything to hire these in the big house of the Rue de la Goutte-d'Or. But there was not a single room to let there; so that they had to relinquish their old dream. To tell the truth, Gervaise was rather glad in her heart; the neighborhood of the Lorilleux almost door to door, frightened her immensely. Then, they looked about elsewhere. Coupeau, very properly did not wish to be far from Madame Fauconnier's so that Gervaise could easily run home at any hour of the day. And at length they met with exactly what suited them, a large room with a small closet and a kitchen, in the Rue Neuve de la Goutte-d'Or, almost opposite the laundress's. This was in a small two-story building with a very steep staircase. There were two apartments on the second floor, one to the left, the other to the right. The ground floor was occupied by a man who rented out carriages, which filled the sheds in the large stable yard by the street.

Gervaise was delighted with this as it made her feel she was back in a country town. With no close neighbors there would be no gossip to worry about in this little corner. It reminded her of a small lane outside the ramparts of Plassans. She could even see her own window while ironing at the laundry by just tilting her head to the side.

They took possession of their new abode at the April quarter. Gervaise was then eight months advanced. But she showed great courage, saying with a laugh that the baby helped her as she worked; she felt its influence growing within her and giving her strength. Ah, well. She just laughed at Coupeau whenever he wanted her to lie down and rest herself. She would take to her bed when the labor pains came. That would be quite soon enough as with another mouth to feed, they would have to work harder than ever.

She made their new place bright and shiny before helping her husband install the furniture. She loved the furniture, polishing it and becoming almost heart-broken at the slightest scratch. Any time she knocked into the furniture while cleaning she would stop with a sudden shock as though she had hurt herself.

The chest of drawers was especially dear to her. She thought it handsome, sturdy and most respectable-looking. The dream that she hadn't dared to mention was to get a clock and put it right in the middle of the marble top. It would make a splendid effect. She probably would have bought one right away except for the expected baby.

The couple was thoroughly enchanted with their new home. Etienne's bed occupied the small closet, where there was still room to put another child's crib. The kitchen was a very tiny affair and as dark as night, but by leaving the door wide open, one could just manage to see; besides, Gervaise had not to cook meals for thirty people, all she wanted was room to make her soup. As for the large room, it was their pride. The first thing in the morning, they drew the curtains of the alcove, white calico curtains; and the room was thus transformed into a dining-room, with the table in the center, and the wardrobe and chest of drawers facing each other.

They stopped up the chimney since it burned as much as fifteen sous of coal a day. A small cast-iron stove on the marble hearth gave them enough warmth on cold days for only seven sous. Coupeau had also done his best to decorate the walls. There was a large engraving showing a marshal of France on horseback with a baton in his hand. Family photographs were arranged in two rows on top of the chest of drawers on each side of an old holy-water basin in which they kept matches. Busts of Pascal and Beranger were on top of the wardrobe. It was really a handsome room.

"Guess how much we pay here?" Gervaise would ask of every visitor she had.

And whenever they guessed too high a sum, she triumphed and delighted at being so well suited for such a little money, cried:

"One hundred and fifty francs; not a sou more. Isn't it almost like having it for nothing."

The street, Rue Neuve de la Goutte d'Or, played an important part in their contentment. Gervaise's whole life was there, as she traveled back and forth endlessly between her home and Madame Fauconnier's laundry. Coupeau now went down every evening and stood on the doorstep to smoke his pipe. The poorly-paved street rose steeply and had no sidewalks. Toward Rue de la Goutte d'Or there were some gloomy shops with dirty windows. There were shoemakers, coopers, a run-down grocery, and a bankrupt cafe whose closed shutters were covered with posters. In the opposite direction, toward Paris, four-story buildings blocked the sky. Their ground floor shops were all occupied by laundries with one exception—a green-painted store front typical of a small-town hair-dresser. Its shop windows were full of variously colored flasks. It lighted up this drab corner with the gay brightness of its copper bowls which were always shining.

The most pleasant part of the street was in between, where the buildings were fewer and lower, letting in more sunlight. The carriage sheds, the plant which manufactured soda water, and the wash-house opposite made a wide expanse of quietness. The muffled voices of the washerwomen and the rhythmic puffing of the steam engine seemed to deepen the almost religious silence. Open fields and narrow lanes vanishing between dark walls gave it the air of a country village. Coupeau, always amused by the infrequent pedestrians having to jump over the continuous streams of soapy water, said it reminded him of a country town where his uncle had taken him when he was five years old. Gervaise's greatest joy was a tree growing in the courtyard to the left of their window, an acacia that stretched out a single branch and yet, with its meager foliage, lent charm to the entire street.

It was on the last day of April that Gervaise was confined. The pains came on in the afternoon, towards four o'clock, as she was ironing a pair of curtains at Madame Fauconnier's. She would not go home at once, but remained there wriggling about on a chair, and continuing her ironing every time the pain allowed her to do so; the curtains were wanted quickly and she obstinately made a point of finishing them. Besides, perhaps after all it was only colic; it would never do to be frightened by a bit of a stomach-ache. But as she was talking of starting on some shirts, she became quite pale. She was obliged to leave the workshop, and cross the street doubled in two, holding on to the walls. One of the workwomen offered to accompany her; she declined, but begged her to go instead for the midwife, close by, in the Rue de la Charbonniere. This was only a false alarm; there was no need to make a fuss. She would be like that no doubt all through the night. It was not going to prevent her getting Coupeau's dinner ready as soon as she was indoors; then she might perhaps lie down on the bed a little, but without undressing. On the staircase she was seized with such a violent pain, that she was obliged to sit down on one of the stairs; and she pressed her two fists against her mouth to prevent herself from crying out, for she would have been ashamed to have been found there by any man, had one come up. The pain passed away; she was able to open her door, feeling relieved, and thinking that she had decidedly been mistaken. That evening she was going to make a stew with some neck chops. All went well while she peeled the potatoes. The chops were cooking in a saucepan when the pains returned. She mixed the gravy as she stamped about in front of the stove, almost blinded with her tears. If she was going to give birth, that was no reason why Coupeau should be kept without his dinner. At length the stew began to simmer on a fire covered with cinders. She went into the other room, and thought she would have time to lay the cloth at one end of the table. But she was obliged to put down the bottle of wine very quickly; she no longer had strength to reach the bed; she fell prostrate, and she had more pains on a mat on the floor. When the midwife arrived, a quarter of an hour later, she found mother and baby lying there on the floor.

The zinc-worker was still employed at the hospital. Gervaise would not have him disturbed. When he came home at seven o'clock, he found her in bed, well covered up, looking very pale on the pillow, and the child crying, swathed in a shawl at its mother's feet.

"Ah, my poor wife." said Coupeau, kissing Gervaise. "And I was joking only an hour ago, while you were crying with pain. I say, you don't make much fuss about it—the time to sneeze and it's all over."

She smiled faintly; then she murmured: "It's a girl."

"Right." the zinc-worker replied, joking so as to enliven her, "I ordered a girl. Well, now I've got what I wanted. You do everything I wish." And, taking the child up in his arms, he continued: "Let's have a look at you, miss. You've got a very black little mug. It'll get whiter, never fear. You must be good, never run about the streets, and grow up sensible like your papa and mamma."

Gervaise looked at her daughter very seriously, with wide open eyes, slowly overshadowed with sadness, for she would rather have had a boy. Boys can talk care of themselves and don't have to run such risks on the streets of Paris as girls do. The midwife took the infant from Coupeau. She forbade Gervaise to do any talking; it was bad enough there was so much noise around her.

Then the zinc-worker said that he must tell the news to mother Coupeau and the Lorilleuxs, but he was dying with hunger, he must first of all have his dinner. It was a great worry to the invalid to see him have to wait on himself, run to the kitchen for the stew, eat it out of a soup plate, and not be able to find the bread. In spite of being told not to do so, she bewailed her condition, and fidgeted about in her bed. It was stupid of her not to have managed to set the cloth, the pains had laid her on her back like a blow from a bludgeon. Her poor old man would not think it kind of her to be nursing herself up there while he was dining so badly. At least were the potatoes cooked enough? She no longer remembered whether she had put salt in them.

"Keep quiet." cried the midwife.

"Ah. If only you could stop her from wearing herself out." said Coupeau with his mouth full. "If you were not here, I'd bet she'd get up to cut my bread. Keep on your back, you big goose. You mustn't move about, otherwise it'll be a fortnight before you'll be able to stand on your legs. Your stew's very good. Madame will eat some with me, won't you, Madame?"

The midwife declined; but she was willing to accept a glass of wine, because it had upset her, said she to find the poor woman with the baby on the mat. Coupeau at length went off to tell the news to his relations. Half an hour later he returned with all of them, mother Coupeau, the Lorilleuxs, and Madame Lerat, whom he had met at the latter's.

"I've brought you the whole gang." cried Coupeau. "It can't be helped. They wanted to see you. Don't open your mouth, it's forbidden. They'll stop here and look at you without ceremony, you know. As for me, I'm going to make them some coffee, and of the right sort."

He disappeared into the kitchen. Mother Coupeau after kissing Gervaise, became amazed at the child's size. The two other women also kissed the invalid on her cheeks. And all three, standing before the bed, commented with exclamations on the details of the confinement—a most remarkable confinement, just like having a tooth pulled, nothing more.

Madame Lerat examined the baby all over, declared she was well formed, even added that she could grow up into an attractive woman. Noticing that the head had been squeezed into a point on top, she kneaded it gently despite the infant's cries, trying to round it a bit. Madame Lorilleux grabbed the baby from her; that could be enough to give the poor little thing all sorts of vicious tendencies, meddling with it like that while her skull was still soft. She then tried to figure out who the baby resembled. This almost led to a quarrel. Lorilleux, peering over the women's shoulders, insisted that the little girl didn't look the least bit like Coupeau. Well, maybe a little around the nose, nothing more. She was her mother all over again, with big eyes like hers. Certainly there were no eyes like that in the Coupeau family.

Coupeau, however, had failed to reappear. One could hear him in the kitchen struggling with the grate and the coffee-pot. Gervaise was worrying herself frightfully; it was not the proper thing for a man to make coffee; and she called and told him what to do, without listening to the midwife's energetic "hush."

"Here we are." said Coupeau, entering with the coffee-pot in his hand. "Didn't I just have a bother with it. It all went wrong on purpose. Now we'll drink out of glasses, won't we? Because you know, the cups are still at the shop."

They seated themselves around the table, and the zinc-worker insisted on pouring out the coffee himself. It smelt very strong; it was none of that weak stuff. When the midwife had sipped hers up, she went off; everything was going on nicely, she was not required. If the young woman did not pass a good night they were to send for her on the morrow. She was scarcely down the staircase, when Madame Lorilleux called her a glutton and a good-for-nothing. She put four lumps of sugar in her coffee, and charged fifteen francs for leaving you with your baby all by yourself. But Coupeau took her part; he would willingly fork out the fifteen francs. After all those sort of women spent their youth in studying, they were right to charge a good price.

It was then Lorilleux who got into a quarrel with Madame Lerat by maintaining that, in order to have a son, the head of the bed should be turned to the north. She shrugged her shoulders at such nonsense, offering another formula which consisted in hiding under the mattress, without letting your wife know, a handful of fresh nettles picked in bright sunlight.

The table had been pushed over close to the bed. Until ten o'clock Gervaise lay there, smiling although she was only half awake. She was becoming more and more weary, her head turned sideways on the pillow. She no longer had the energy to venture a remark or a gesture. It seemed to her that she was dead, a very sweet death, from the depths of which she was happy to observe the others still in the land of the living. The thin cries of her baby daughter rose above the hum of heavy voices that were discussing a recent murder on Rue du Bon Puits, at the other end of La Chapelle.

Then, as the visitors were thinking of leaving, they spoke of the christening. The Lorilleux had promised to be godfather and godmother; they looked very glum over the matter. However, if they had not been asked to stand they would have felt rather peculiar. Coupeau did not see any need for christening the little one; it certainly would not procure her an income of ten thousand francs, and besides she might catch a cold from it. The less one had to do with priests the better. But mother Coupeau called him a heathen. The Lorilleux, without going and eating consecrated bread in church, plumed themselves on their religious sentiments.

"It shall be next Sunday, if you like," said the chain-maker.

And Gervaise having consented by a nod, everyone kissed her and told her to take good care of herself. They also wished the baby goodbye. Each one went and leant over the little trembling body with smiles and loving words as though she were able to understand. They called her Nana, the pet name for Anna, which was her godmother's name.

"Good night, Nana. Come be a good girl, Nana."

When they had at length gone off, Coupeau drew his chair close up to the bed and finished his pipe, holding Gervaise's hand in his. He smoked slowly, deeply affected and uttering sentences between the puffs.

"Well, old woman, they've made your head ache, haven't they? You see I couldn't prevent them coming. After all, it shows their friendship. But we're better alone, aren't we? I wanted to be alone like this with you. It has seemed such a long evening to me. Poor little thing, she's had a lot to go through. Those shrimps, when they come out into the world, have no idea of the pain they cause. It must really almost be like being split in two. Where is does it hurt the most, that I may kiss it and make it well?"

He had carefully slid one of his big hands under her back, and now he drew her toward him, bending over to kiss her stomach through the covers, touched by a rough man's compassion for the suffering of a woman in childbirth. He inquired if he was hurting her. Gervaise felt very happy, and answered him that it didn't hurt any more at all. She was only worried about getting up as soon as possible, because there was no time to lie about now. He assured her that he'd be responsible for earning the money for the new little one. He would be a real bum if he abandoned her and the little rascal. The way he figured it, what really counted was bringing her up properly. Wasn't that so?

Coupeau did not sleep much that night. He covered up the fire in the stove. Every hour he had to get up to give the baby spoonfuls of lukewarm sugar and water. That did not prevent his going off to his work in the morning as usual. He even took advantage of his lunchhour to make a declaration of the birth at the mayor's. During this time Madame Boche, who had been informed of the event, had hastened to go and pass the day with Gervaise. But the latter, after ten hours of sleep, bewailed her position, saying that she already felt pains all over her through having been so long in bed. She would become quite ill if they did not let her get up. In the evening, when Coupeau returned home, she told him all her worries; no doubt she had confidence in Madame Boche, only it put her beside herself to see a stranger installed in her room, opening the drawers, and touching her things.

On the morrow the concierge, on returning from some errand, found her up, dressed, sweeping and getting her husband's dinner ready; and it was impossible to persuade her to go to bed again. They were trying to make a fool of her perhaps. It was all very well for ladies to pretend to be unable to move. When one was not rich one had no time for that sort of thing. Three days after her confinement she was ironing petticoats at Madame Fauconnier's, banging her irons and all in a perspiration from the great heat of the stove.

On the Saturday evening, Madame Lorilleux brought her presents for her godchild—a cup that cost thirty-five sous, and a christening dress, plaited and trimmed with some cheap lace, which she had got for six francs, because it was slightly soiled. On the morrow, Lorilleux, as godfather, gave the mother six pounds of sugar. They certainly did things properly. At the baptism supper which took place at the Coupeaus that evening, they did not come empty-handed. Lorilleux carried a bottle of fine wine under each arm and his wife brought a large custard pie from a famous pastry shop on Chaussee Clignancourt. But the Lorilleuxs made sure that the entire neighborhood knew they had spent twenty francs. As soon as Gervaise learned of their gossiping, furious, she stopped giving them credit for generosity.

It was at the christening feast that the Coupeaus ended by becoming intimately acquainted with their neighbors on the opposite side of the landing. The other lodging in the little house was occupied by two persons, mother and son, the Goujets as they were called. Until then the two families had merely nodded to each other on the stairs and in the street, nothing more; the Coupeaus thought their neighbors seemed rather bearish. Then the mother, having carried up a pail of water for Gervaise on the morrow of her confinement, the latter had thought it the proper thing to invite them to the feast, more especially as she considered them very respectable people. And naturally, they there became well acquainted with each other.

The Goujets came from the Departement du Nord. The mother mended lace; the son, a blacksmith, worked at an iron bolt factory. They had lived in their lodging for five years. Behind the quiet peacefulness of their life, a long standing sorrow was hidden. Goujet the father, one day when furiously drunk at Lille, had beaten a comrade to death with an iron bar and had afterwards strangled himself in prison with his handkerchief. The widow and child, who had come to Paris after their misfortune, always felt the tragedy hanging over their heads, and atoned for it by a strict honesty and an unvarying gentleness and courage. They had a certain amount of pride in their attitude and regarded themselves as better than other people.

Madame Goujet, dressed in black as usual, her forehead framed in a nun's hood, had a pale, calm, matronly face, as if the whiteness of the lace and the delicate work of her fingers had cast a glow of serenity over her. Goujet was twenty-three years old, huge, magnificently built, with deep blue eyes and rosy cheeks, and the strength of Hercules. His comrades at the shop called him "Golden Mouth" because of his handsome blonde beard.

Gervaise at once felt a great friendship for these people. When she entered their home for the first time, she was amazed at the cleanliness of the lodging. There was no denying it, one might blow about the place without raising a grain of dust; and the tiled floor shone like a mirror. Madame Goujet made her enter her son's room, just to see it. It was pretty and white like the room of a young girl; an iron bedstead with muslin curtains, a table, a washstand, and a narrow bookcase hanging against the wall. Then there were pictures all over the place, figures cut out, colored engravings nailed up with four tacks, and portraits of all kinds of persons taken from the illustrated papers.

Madame Goujet said with a smile that her son was a big baby. He found that reading in the evening put him to sleep, so he amused himself looking at pictures. Gervaise spent an hour with her neighbor without noticing the passing of time. Madame Goujet had gone to sit by the window and work on her lace. Gervaise was fascinated by the hundreds of pins that held the lace, and she felt happy to be there, breathing in the good clean atmosphere of this home where such a delicate task enforced a sort of meditative silence.

The Goujets were worth visiting. They worked long hours, and placed more than a quarter of their fortnight's earnings in the savings-bank. In the neighborhood everyone nodded to them, everyone talked of their savings. Goujet never had a hole in his clothes, always went out in a clean short blue blouse, without a stain. He was very polite, and even a trifle timid, in spite of his broad shoulders. The washer-women at the end of the street laughed to see him hold down his head when he passed them. He did not like their oaths, and thought it disgusting that women should be constantly uttering foul words. One day, however, he came home tipsy. Then Madame Goujet, for sole reproach, held his father's portrait before him, a daub of a painting hidden away at the bottom of a drawer; and, ever since that lesson, Goujet never drank more than was good for him, without however, any hatred of wine, for wine is necessary to the workman. On Sundays he walked out with his mother, who took hold of his arm. He would generally conduct her to Vincennes; at other times they would go to the theatre. His mother remained his passion. He still spoke to her as though he were a little child. Square-headed, his skin toughened by the wielding of the heavy hammer, he somewhat resembled the larger animals: dull of intellect, though good-natured all the same.

In the early days of their acquaintance, Gervaise embarrassed him immensely. Then in a few weeks he became accustomed to her. He watched for her that he might carry up her parcels, treated her as a sister, with an abrupt familiarity, and cut out pictures for her. One morning, however, having opened her door without knocking, he beheld her half undressed, washing her neck; and, for a week, he did not dare to look her in the face, so much so that he ended by making her blush herself.

Young Cassis, with the casual wit of a born Parisian, called Golden Mouth a dolt. It was all right not to get drunk all the time or chase women, but still, a man must be a man, or else he might as well wear skirts. Coupeau teased him in front of Gervaise, accusing him of making up to all the women in the neighborhood. Goujet vigorously defended himself against the charge.

But this didn't prevent the two workingmen from becoming best of friends. They went off to work together in the mornings and sometimes had a glass of beer together on the way home.

It eventually came about that Golden Mouth could render a service to Young Cassis, one of those favors that is remembered forever.

It was the second of December. The zinc-worker decided, just for the fun of it, to go into the city and watch the rioting. He didn't really care about the Republic, or Napoleon or anything like that, but he liked the smell of gunpowder and the sound of the rifles firing. He would have been arrested as a rioter if the blacksmith hadn't turned up at the barricade at just that moment and helped him escape. Goujet was very serious as they walked back up the Rue du Faubourg Poissonniere. He was interested in politics and believed in the Republic. But he had never fired a gun because the common people were getting tired of fighting battles for the middle classes who always seemed to get the benefit of them.

As they reached the top of the slope of the Rue du Faubourg Poissonniere, Goujet turned to look back at Paris and the mobs. After all, someday people would be sorry that they just stood by and did nothing. Coupeau laughed at this, saying you would be pretty stupid to risk your neck just to preserve the twenty-five francs a day for the lazybones in the Legislative Assembly. That evening the Coupeaus invited the Goujets to dinner. After desert Young Cassis and Golden Mouth kissed each other on the cheek. Their lives were joined till death.

For three years the existence of the two families went on, on either side of the landing, without an event. Gervaise was able to take care of her daughter and still work most of the week. She was now a skilled worker on fine laundry and earned up to three francs a day. She decided to put Etienne, now nearly eight, into a small boarding-school on Rue de Chartres for five francs a week. Despite the expenses for the two children, they were able to save twenty or thirty francs each month. Once they had six hundred francs saved, Gervaise often lay awake thinking of her ambitious dream: she wanted to rent a small shop, hire workers, and go into the laundry business herself. If this effort worked, they would have a steady income from savings in twenty years. They could retire and live in the country.

Yet she hesitated, saying she was looking for the right shop. She was giving herself time to think it over. Their savings were safe in the bank, and growing larger. So, in three years' time she had only fulfilled one of her dreams—she had bought a clock. But even this clock, made of rosewood with twined columns and a pendulum of gilded brass, was being paid for in installments of twenty-two sous each Monday for a year. She got upset if Coupeau tried to wind it; she liked to be the only one to lift off the glass dome. It was under the glass dome, behind the clock, that she hid her bank book. Sometimes, when she was dreaming of her shop, she would stare fixedly at the clock, lost in thought.

The Coupeaus went out nearly every Sunday with the Goujets. They were pleasant little excursions, sometimes to have some fried fish at Saint-Ouen, at others a rabbit at Vincennes, in the garden of some eating-house keeper without any grand display. The men drank sufficient to quench their thirst, and returned home as right as nine-pins, giving their arms to the ladies. In the evening before going to bed, the two families made up accounts and each paid half the expenses; and there was never the least quarrel about a sou more or less.

The Lorilleuxs became jealous of the Goujets. It seemed strange to them to see Young Cassis and Clump-clump going places all the time with strangers instead of their own relations. But, that's the way it was; some folks didn't care a bit about their family. Now that they had saved a few sous, they thought they were really somebody. Madame Lorilleux was much annoyed to see her brother getting away from her influence and begin to continually run down Gervaise to everyone. On the other hand, Madame Lerat took the young wife's side. Mother Coupeau tried to get along with everybody. She only wanted to be welcomed by all three of her children. Now that her eyesight was getting dimmer and dimmer she only had one regular house cleaning job but she was able to pick up some small jobs now and again.

On the day on which Nana was three years old, Coupeau, on returning home in the evening, found Gervaise quite upset. She refused
to talk about it; there was nothing at all the matter with her, she said.
But, as she had the table all wrong, standing still with the plates in her
hands, absorbed in deep reflection, her husband insisted upon knowing what was the matter.

"Well, it is this," she ended by saying, "the little draper's shop in the
Rue de la Goutte-d'Or, is to let. I saw it only an hour ago, when going
to buy some cotton. It gave me quite a turn."

It was a very decent shop, and in that big house where they dreamed
of living in former days. There was the shop, a back room, and two
other rooms to the right and left; in short, just what they required. The
rooms were rather small, but well placed. Only, she considered they
wanted too much; the landlord talked of five hundred francs.

"So you've been over the place, and asked the price?" said Coupeau.

". . . . You know, only out of curiosity." replied she, affecting an air
of indifference. "One looks about, and goes in wherever there's a bill
up—that doesn't bind one to anything. But that shop is altogether too
dear. Besides, it would perhaps be foolish of me to set up in business."

However, after dinner, she again referred to the draper's shop. She
drew a plan of the place on the margin of a newspaper. And, little by
little, she talked it over, measuring the corners, and arranging the rooms,
as though she were going to move all her furniture in there on the morrow. Then Coupeau advised her to take it, seeing how she wanted to do
so; she would certainly never find anything decent under five hundred
francs; besides they might perhaps get a reduction. He knew only one
objection to it and that was living in the same house as the Lorilleux,
whom she could not bear.

Gervaise declared that she wasn't mad at anybody. So much did she
want her own shop that she even spoke up for the Lorilleuxs, saying that
they weren't mean at heart and that she would be able to get along just
fine with them. When they went to bed, Coupeau fell asleep immediately, but she stayed awake, planning how she could arrange the new
place even though she hadn't yet made up her mind completely.

On the morrow, when she was alone, she could not resist removing the glass cover from the clock, and taking a peep at the savings-bank book. To think that her shop was there, in those dirty pages, covered with ugly writing. Before going off to her work, she consulted Madame Goujet, who highly approved her project of setting up in business for herself; with a husband like hers, a good fellow who did not drink, she was certain of getting on, and of not having her earnings squandered. At the luncheon hour Gervaise even called on the Lorilleuxs to ask their advice; she did not wish to appear to be doing anything unknown to the family. Madame Lorilleux was struck all of a heap. What. Clump-clump was going in for a shop now. And her heart bursting with envy, she stammered, and tried to pretend to be pleased: no doubt the shop was a convenient one—Gervaise was right in taking it. However, when she had somewhat recovered, she and her husband talked of the dampness of the courtyard, of the poor light of the rooms on the ground floor. . . . It was a good place for rheumatism. Yet, if she had made up her mind to take it, their observations, of course, would not make her alter her decision.

That evening Gervaise frankly owned with a laugh that she would have fallen ill if she had been prevented from having the shop. Nevertheless, before saying "it's done." she wished to take Coupeau to see the place, and try and obtain a reduction in the rent.

"Very well, then, to-morrow, if you like," said her husband. "You can come and fetch me towards six o'clock at the house where I'm working, in the Rue de la Nation, and we'll call in at the Rue de la Goutte-d'Or on our way home."

Coupeau was then finishing the roofing of a new three-storied house. It so happened that on that day he was to fix the last sheets of zinc. As the roof was almost flat, he had set up his bench on it, a wide shutter supported on two trestles. A beautiful May sun was setting, giving a golden hue to the chimney-pots. And, right up at the top, against the clear sky, the workman was quietly cutting up his zinc with a big pair of shears, leaning over the bench, and looking like a tailor in his shop cutting out a pair of trousers. Close to the wall of the next house, his boy, a youngster of seventeen, thin and fair, was keeping the fire of the chafing dish blazing by the aid of an enormous pair of bellows, each puff of which raised a cloud of sparks.

"Hi. Zidore, put in the irons." cried Coupeau.

The boy stuck the soldering irons into the midst of the charcoal, which looked a pale rose color in the daylight. Then he resumed blowing. Coupeau held the last sheet of zinc. It had to be placed at the edge of the roof, close to the gutter-pipe; there was an abrupt slant there, and the gaping void of the street opened beneath. The zinc-worker, just as though in his own home, wearing his list-shoes, advanced, dragging his feet, and whistling the air, ". . . the little lambs." Arrived in front of the opening, he let himself down, and then, supporting himself with one knee against the masonry of a chimney-stack, remained half-way out over the pavement below. One of his legs dangled. When he leant back to call that young viper, Zidore, he held on to a corner of the masonry, on account of the street beneath him.

"You confounded dawdler. Give me the irons. It's no use looking up in the air, you skinny beggar. The larks won't tumble into your mouth already cooked."

But Zidore did not hurry himself. He was interested in the neighboring roofs, and in a cloud of smoke which rose from the other side of Paris, close to Grenelle; it was very likely a fire. However, he came and laid down on his stomach, his head over the opening, and he passed the irons to Coupeau. Then the latter commenced to solder the sheet. He squatted, he stretched, always managing to balance himself, sometimes seated on one side, at other times standing on the tip of one foot, often only holding on by a finger. He had a confounded assurance, the devil's own cheek, familiar with danger, and braving it. It knew him. It was the street that was afraid, not he. As he kept his pipe in his mouth, he turned round every now and then to spit onto the pavement.

"Look, there's Madame Boche," he suddenly exclaimed and called down to her. "Hi. Madame Boche."

He had just caught sight of the concierge crossing the road. She raised her head and recognized him, and a conversation ensured between them. She hid her hands under her apron, her nose elevated in the air. He, standing up now, his left arm passed round a chimney-pot, leaned over.

"Have you seen my wife?" asked he.

"No, I haven't," replied the concierge. "Is she around here?"

"She's coming to fetch me. And are they all well at home?"

"Why, yes, thanks; I'm the most ill, as you see. I'm going to the

Chaussee Clignancourt to buy a small leg of mutton. The butcher near the Moulin-Rouge only charges sixteen sous."

They raised their voices, because a vehicle was passing. In the wide, deserted Rue de la Nation, their words, shouted out with all their might, had only caused a little old woman to come to her window; and this little old woman remained there leaning out, giving herself the treat of a grand emotion by watching that man on the roof over the way, as though she expected to see him fall, from one minute to another.

"Well. Good evening," cried Madame Boche. "I won't disturb you."

Coupeau turned round, and took back the iron that Zidore was holding for him. But just as the concierge was moving off, she caught sight of Gervaise on the other side of the way, holding Nana by the hand. She was already raising her head to tell the zinc-worker, when the young woman closed her mouth by an energetic gesture, and, in a low voice, so as not to be heard up there, she told her of her fear: she was afraid, by showing herself suddenly, of giving her husband a shock which might make him lose his balance. During the four years, she had only been once to fetch him at his work. That day was the second time. She could not witness it, her blood turned cold when she beheld her old man between heaven and earth, in places where even the sparrows would not venture.

"No doubt, it's not pleasant," murmured Madame Boche. "My husband's a tailor, so I have none of these terrors."

"If you only knew, in the early days," said Gervaise again, "I had frights from morning till night. I was always seeing him on a stretcher, with his head smashed. Now, I don't think of it so much. One gets used to everything. Bread must be earned. All the same, it's a precious dear loaf, for one risks one's bones more than is fair."

And she left off speaking, hiding Nana in her skirt, fearing a cry from the little one. Very pale, she looked up in spite of herself. At that moment Coupeau was soldering the extreme edge of the sheet close to the gutter; he slid down as far as possible, but without being able to reach the edge. Then, he risked himself with those slow movements peculiar to workmen. For an instant he was immediately over the pavement, no long holding on, all absorbed in his work; and, from below, one could see the little white flame of the solder frizzling up beneath the carefully wielded iron. Gervaise, speechless, her throat contracted with anguish, had clasped her hands together, and held them up in mechanical gesture of prayer. But she breathed freely as Coupeau got up and returned back along the roof, without hurrying himself, and taking the time to spit once more into the street.

"So you've been playing the spy on me." cried he, gaily, on beholding her. "She's been making a stupid of herself, eh, Madame Boche? She wouldn't call to me. Wait a bit, I shall have finished in ten minutes."

All that remained to do was to fix the top of the chimney—a mere nothing. The laundress and the concierge waited on the pavement, discussing the neighborhood, and giving an eye to Nana, to prevent her from dabbling in the gutter, where she wanted to look for little fishes; and the two women kept glancing up at the roof, smiling and nodding their heads, as though to imply that they were not losing patience. The old woman opposite had not left her window, had continued watching the man, and waiting.

"Whatever can she have to look at, that old she-goat?" said Madame Boche. "What a mug she has."

One could hear the loud voice of the zinc-worker up above singing, "Ah. It's nice to gather strawberries." Bending over his bench, he was now artistically cutting out his zinc. With his compasses he traced a line, and he detached a large fan-shaped piece with the aid of a pair of curved shears; then he lightly bent this fan with his hammer into the form of a pointed mushroom. Zidore was again blowing the charcoal in the chafing-dish. The sun was setting behind the house in a brilliant rosy light, which was gradually becoming paler, and turning to a delicate lilac. And, at this quiet hour of the day, right up against the sky, the silhouettes of the two workmen, looking inordinately large, with the dark line of the bench, and the strange profile of the bellows, stood out from the limpid back-ground of the atmosphere.

When the chimney-top was got into shape, Coupeau called out: "Zidore. The irons."

But Zidore had disappeared. The zinc-worker swore, and looked about for him, even calling him through the open skylight of the loft. At length he discovered him on a neighboring roof, two houses off. The young rogue was taking a walk, exploring the environs, his fair scanty locks blowing in the breeze, his eyes blinking as they beheld the immensity of Paris.

"I say, lazy bones. Do you think you're having a day in the country?" asked Coupeau, in a rage. "You're like Monsieur Beranger, composing verses, perhaps. Will you give me those irons. Did anyone ever see such a thing. Strolling about on the house-tops. Why not bring your sweetheart at once, and tell her of your love? Will you give me those irons? You confounded little shirker."

He finished his soldering, and called to Gervaise: "There, it's done. I'm coming down."

The chimney-pot to which he had to fix the flue was in the middle of the roof. Gervaise, who was no longer uneasy, continued to smile as she followed his movements. Nana, amused all on a sudden by the view of her father, clapped her little hands. She had seated herself on the pavement to see the better up there.

"Papa. Papa." called she with all her might. "Papa. Just look."

The zinc-worker wished to lean forward, but his foot slipped. Then suddenly, stupidly, like a cat with its legs entangled, he rolled and descended the slight slope of the roof without being able to grab hold of anything.

"My God," he cried in a choked voice.

And he fell. His body described a gentle curve, turned twice over on itself, and came smashing into the middle of the street with the dull thud of a bundle of clothes thrown from on high.

Gervaise, stupefied, her throat rent by one great cry, stood holding up her arms. Some passers-by hastened to the spot; a crowd soon formed. Madame Boche, utterly upset, her knees bending under her, took Nana in her arms, to hide her head and prevent her seeing. Meanwhile, the little old woman opposite quietly closed her window, as though satisfied.

Four men ended by carrying Coupeau into a chemist's, at the corner of the Rue des Poissonniers; and he remained there on a blanket, in the middle of the shop, whist they sent to the Lariboisiere Hospital for a stretcher. He was still breathing.

Gervaise, sobbing, was kneeling on the floor beside him, her face smudged with tears, stunned and unseeing. Her hands would reach to feel her husband's limbs with the utmost gentleness. Then she would draw back as she had been warned not to touch him. But a few seconds later she would touch him to assure herself that he was still warm, feeling somehow that she was helping him.

When the stretcher at length arrived, and they talked of starting for the hospital, she got up, saying violently:

"No, no, not to the hospital. We live in the Rue Neuve de la Goutte-d'Or."

It was useless for them to explain to her that the illness would cost her a great deal of money, if she took her husband home. She obstinately repeated:

"Rue Neuve de la Goutte-d'Or; I will show you the house. What can it matter to you? I've got money. He's my husband, isn't he? He's mine, and I want him at home."

And they had to take Coupeau to his own home. When the stretcher was carried through the crowd which was crushing up against the chemist's shop, the women of the neighborhood were excitedly talking of Gervaise. She limped, the dolt, but all the same she had some pluck. She would be sure to save her old man; while at the hospital the doctors let the patients die who were very bad, so as not to have the bother of trying to cure them. Madame Boche, after taking Nana home with her, returned, and gave her account of the accident, with interminable details, and still feeling agitated with the emotion she had passed through.

"I was going to buy a leg of mutton; I was there, I saw him fall," repeated she. "It was all through the little one; he turned to look at her, and bang. Ah. Good heavens. I never want to see such a sight again. However, I must be off to get my leg of mutton."

For a week Coupeau was very bad. The family, the neighbors, everyone, expected to see him turn for the worse at any moment. The doctor—a very expensive doctor, who charged five francs for each visit—apprehended internal injuries, and these words filled everyone with fear. It was said in the neighborhood that the zinc-worker's heart had been injured by the shock. Gervaise alone, looking pale through her nights of watching, serious and resolute, shrugged her shoulders. Her old man's right leg was broken, everyone knew that; it would be set for him, and that was all. As for the rest, the injured heart, that was nothing. She knew how to restore a heart with ceaseless care. She was certain of getting him well and displayed magnificent faith. She stayed close by him and caressed him gently during the long bouts of fever without a moment of doubt. She was on her feet continuously for a whole week, completely absorbed by her determination to save him. She forgot the street outside, the entire city, and even her own children. On the ninth day, the doctor finally said that Coupeau would live. Gervaise collapsed into a chair, her body limp from fatigue. That night she consented to sleep for two hours with her head against the foot of the bed.

Coupeau's accident had created quite a commotion in the family. Mother Coupeau passed the nights with Gervaise; but as early as nine o'clock she fell asleep on a chair. Every evening, on returning from work, Madame Lerat went a long round out of her way to inquire how her brother was getting on. At first the Lorilleuxs had called two or three times a day, offering to sit up and watch, and even bringing an easy-chair for Gervaise. Then it was not long before there were disputes as to the proper way to nurse invalids. Madame Lorilleux said that she had saved enough people's lives to know how to go about it. She accused the young wife of pushing her aside, of driving her away from her own brother's bed. Certainly that Clump-clump ought to be concerned about Coupeau's getting well, for if she hadn't gone to Rue de la Nation to disturb him at his job, he would never had fallen. Only, the way she was taking care of him, she would certainly finish him.

When Gervaise saw that Coupeau was out of danger, she ceased guarding his bedside with so much jealous fierceness. Now, they could no longer kill him, and she let people approach without mistrust. The family invaded the room. The convalescence would be a very long one; the doctor had talked of four months. Then, during the long hours the zinc-worker slept, the Lorilleux talked of Gervaise as of a fool. She hadn't done any good by having her husband at home. At the hospital they would have cured him twice as quickly. Lorilleux would have liked to have been ill, to have caught no matter what, just to show her that he did not hesitate for a moment to go to Lariboisiere. Madame Lorilleux knew a lady who had just come from there. Well. She had had chicken to eat morning and night.

Again and again the two of them went over their estimate of how much four months of convalescence would cost; workdays lost, the doctor and the medicines, and afterward good wine and fresh meat. If the Coupeaus only used up their small savings, they would be very lucky indeed. They would probably have to do into debt. Well, that was to be expected and it was their business. They had no right to expect any help from the family, which couldn't afford the luxury of keeping an invalid at home. It was just Clump-clump's bad luck, wasn't it? Why couldn't she have done as others did and let her man be taken to hospital? This just showed how stuck up she was.

One evening Madame Lorilleux had the spitefulness to ask Gervaise suddenly:

"Well. And your shop, when are you going to take it?"

"Yes," chuckled Lorilleux, "the landlord's still waiting for you."

Gervaise was astonished. She had completely forgotten the shop; but she saw the wicked joy of those people, at the thought that she would no longer be able to take it, and she was bursting with anger. From that evening, in fact, they watched for every opportunity to twit her about her hopeless dream. When any one spoke of some impossible wish, they would say that it might be realized on the day that Gervaise started in business, in a beautiful shop opening onto the street. And behind her back they would laugh fit to split their sides. She did not like to think such an unkind thing, but, really, the Lorilleuxs now seemed to be very pleased at Coupeau's accident, as it prevented her setting up as a laundress in the Rue de la Goutte-d'Or.

Then she also wished to laugh, and show them how willingly she parted with the money for the sake of curing her husband. Each time she took the savings-bank book from beneath the glass clock-tower in their presence, she would say gaily:

"I'm going out; I'm going to rent my shop."

She had not been willing to withdraw the money all at once. She took it out a hundred francs at a time, so as not to keep such a pile of gold and silver in her drawer; then, too, she vaguely hoped for some miracle, some sudden recovery, which would enable them not to part with the entire sum. At each journey to the savings-bank, on her return home, she added up on a piece of paper the money they had still left there. It was merely for the sake of order. Their bank account might be getting smaller all the time, yet she went on with her quiet smile and common-sense attitude, keeping the account straight. It was a consolation to be able to use this money for such a good purpose, to have had it when faced with their misfortune.

While Coupeau was bed-ridden the Goujets were very kind to Gervaise. Madame Goujet was always ready to assist. She never went to shop without stopping to ask Gervaise if there was anything she needed, sugar or butter or salt. She always brought over hot bouillon on the evenings she cooked pot au feu. Sometimes, when Gervaise seemed to have too much to do, Madame Goujet helped her do the dishes, or cleaned the kitchen herself. Goujet took her water pails every morning and filled them at the tap on Rue des Poissonniers, saving her two sous a day. After dinner, if no family came to visit, the Goujets would come over to visit with the Coupeaus.

Until ten o'clock, the blacksmith would smoke his pipe and watch Gervaise busy with her invalid. He would not speak ten words the entire evening. He was moved to pity by the sight of her pouring Coupeau's tea and medicine into a cup, or stirring the sugar in it very carefully so as to make no sound with the spoon. It stirred him deeply when she would lean over Coupeau and speak in her soft voice. Never before had he known such a fine woman. Her limp increased the credit due her for wearing herself out doing things for her husband all day long. She never sat down for ten minutes, not even to eat. She was always running to the chemist's. And then she would still keep the house clean, not even a speck of dust. She never complained, no matter how exhausted she became. Goujet developed a very deep affection for Gervaise in this atmosphere of unselfish devotion.

One day he said to the invalid, "Well, old man, now you're patched up again. I wasn't worried about you. Your wife works miracles."

Goujet was supposed to be getting married. His mother had found a suitable girl, a lace-mender like herself, whom she was urging him to marry. He had agreed so as not to hurt her feelings and the wedding had been set for early September. Money had long since been saved to set them up in housekeeping. However, when Gervaise referred to his coming marriage, he shook his head, saying, "Not every woman is like you, Madame Coupeau. If all women were like you, I'd marry ten of them."

At the end of two months, Coupeau was able to get up. He did not go far, only from the bed to the window, and even then Gervaise had to support him. There he would sit down in the easy-chair the Lorilleuxs had brought, with his right leg stretched out on a stool. This joker, who used to laugh at the people who slipped down on frosty days, felt greatly put out by his accident. He had no philosophy. He had spent those two months in bed, in cursing, and in worrying the people about him. It was not an existence, really, to pass one's life on one's back, with a pin all tied up and as stiff as a sausage. Ah, he certainly knew the ceiling by heart; there was a crack, at the corner of the alcove, that he could have drawn with his eyes shut. Then, when he was made comfortable in the easy-chair, it was another grievance. Would he be fixed there for long, just like a mummy?

Nobody ever passed along the street, so it was no fun to watch. Besides, it stank of bleach water all day. No, he was just growing old; he'd have given ten years of his life just to go see how the fortifications were getting along. He kept going on about his fate. It wasn't right, what had happened to him. A good worker like him, not a loafer or a drunkard, he could have understood in that case.

"Papa Coupeau," said he, "broke his neck one day that he'd been boozing. I can't say that it was deserved, but anyhow it was explainable. I had had nothing since my lunch, was perfectly quiet, and without a drop of liquor in my body; and yet I came to grief just because I wanted to turn round to smile at Nana. Don't you think that's too much? If there is a Providence, it certainly arranges things in a very peculiar manner. I, for one, shall never believe in it."

And when at last he was able to use his legs, he retained a secret grudge against work. It was a handicraft full of misfortunes to pass one's days, like the cats, on the roofs of the houses. The employers were no fools. They sent you to your death—being far too cowardly to venture themselves on a ladder—and stopped at home in safety at their fire-sides without caring a hang for the poorer classes; and he got to the point of saying that everyone ought to fix the zinc himself on his own house. My God. It was the only fair way to do it. If you don't want the rain to come in, do the work yourself. He regretted he hadn't learned another trade, something more pleasant, something less dangerous, maybe cabinetmaking. It was really his father's fault. Lots of fathers have the foolish habit of shoving their sons into their own line of work.

For another two months Coupeau hobbled about on crutches. He had first of all managed to get as far as the street, and smoke his pipe in front of the door. Then he had managed to reach the exterior Boulevard, dragging himself along in the sunshine, and remaining for hours on one of the seats. Gaiety returned to him; his infernal tongue got sharper in these long hours of idleness. And with the pleasure of living, he gained there a delight in doing nothing, an indolent feeling took possession of his limbs, and his muscles gradually glided into a very sweet slumber. It was the slow victory of laziness, which took advantage of his convalescence to obtain possession of his body and unnerve him with its tickling. He regained his health, as thorough a banterer as before, thinking life beautiful, and not seeing why it should not last forever.

As soon as he could get about without the crutches, he made longer walks, often visiting construction jobs to see old comrades. He would stand with his arms folded, sneering and shaking his head, ridiculing the workers slaving at the job, stretching out his leg to show them what you got for wearing yourself out. Being able to stand about and mock others while they were working satisfied his spite against hard work. No doubt he'd have to go back to it, but he'd put it off as long as possible. He had a reason now to be lazy. Besides, it seemed good to him to loaf around like a bum.

On the afternoons when Coupeau felt dull, he would call on the Lorilleuxs. The latter would pity him immensely, and attract him with all sorts of amiable attentions. During the first years following his marriage, he had avoided them, thanks to Gervaise's influence. Now they regained their sway over him by twitting him about being afraid of his wife. He was no man, that was evident. The Lorilleuxs, however, showed great discretion, and were loud in their praise of the laundress's good qualities. Coupeau, without as yet coming to wrangling, swore to the latter that his sister adored her, and requested that she would behave more amiably to her. The first quarrel which the couple had occurred one evening on account of Etienne. The zinc-worker had passed the afternoon with the Lorilleuxs. On arriving home, as the dinner was not quite ready, and the children were whining for their soup, he suddenly turned upon Etienne, and boxed his ears soundly. And during an hour he did not cease to grumble; the brat was not his; he did not know why he allowed him to be in the place; he would end by turning him out into the street. Up till then he had tolerated the youngster without all that fuss. On the morrow he talked of his dignity. Three days after, he kept kicking the little fellow, morning and evening, so much so that the child, whenever he heard him coming, bolted into the Goujets' where the old lace-mender kept a corner of the table clear for him to do his lessons.

Gervaise had for some time past, returned to work. She no longer had the trouble of looking under the glass cover of the clock; all the savings were gone; and she had to work hard, work for four, for there were four to feed now. She alone maintained them. Whenever she heard people pitying her, she at once found excuses for Coupeau. Recollect. He had suffered so much; it was not surprising if his disposition had soured. But it would pass off when his health returned. And if any one hinted that Coupeau seemed all right again, that he could very well re-turn to work, she protested: No, no; not yet. She did not want to see him take to his bed again. They would allow her to know best what the doctor said, perhaps. It was she who prevented him returning to work, telling him every morning to take his time and not to force himself. She even slipped twenty sou pieces into his waistcoat pocket. Coupeau ac-cepted this as something perfectly natural. He was always complaining of aches and pains so that she would coddle him. At the end of six months he was still convalescing.

Now, whenever he went to watch others working, he was always ready to join his comrades in downing a shot. It wasn't so bad, after all. They had their fun, and they never stayed more than five minutes. That couldn't hurt anybody. Only a hypocrite would say he went in because he wanted a drink. No wonder they had laughed at him in the past. A glass of wine never hurt anybody. He only drank wine though, never brandy. Wine never made you sick, didn't get you drunk, and helped you to live longer. Soon though, several times, after a day of idleness in going from one building job to another, he came home half drunk. On those occasions Gervaise pretended to have a terrible headache and kept their door closed so that the Goujets wouldn't hear Coupeau's drunken babblings.

Little by little, the young woman lost her cheerfulness. Morning and evening she went to the Rue de la Goutte-d'Or to look at the shop, which was still to be let; and she would hide herself as though she were committing some childish prank unworthy of a grown-up person. This shop was beginning to turn her brain. At night-time, when the light was out she experienced the charm of some forbidden pleasure by thinking of it with her eyes open. She again made her calculations; two hundred and fifty francs for the rent, one hundred and fifty francs for utensils and moving, one hundred francs in hand to keep them going for a fortnight—in all five hundred francs at the very lowest figure. If she was not continually thinking of it aloud, it was for fear she should be suspected of regretting the savings swallowed up by Coupeau's illness. She often became quite pale, having almost allowed her desire to escape her and catching back her words, quite confused as though she had been thinking of something wicked. Now they would have to work for four or five years before they would succeed in saving such a sum. Her regret was at not being able to start in business at once; she would have earned all the home required, without counting on Coupeau, letting him take months to get into the way of work again; she would no longer have been uneasy, but certain of the future and free from the secret fears which sometimes seized her when he returned home very gay and singing, and relating some joke of that animal My-Boots, whom he had treated to a drink.

One evening, Gervaise being at home alone, Goujet entered, and did not hurry off again, according to his habit. He seated himself, and smoked as he watched her. He probably had something very serious to say; he thought it over, let it ripen without being able to put it into suitable words. At length, after a long silence, he appeared to make up his mind, and took his pipe out of his mouth to say all in a breath:

"Madame Gervaise, will you allow me to lend you some money?"

She was leaning over an open drawer, looking for some dish-cloths. She got up, her face very red. He must have seen her then, in the morning, standing in ecstasy before the shop for close upon ten minutes. He was smiling in an embarrassed way, as though he had made some insulting proposal. But she hastily refused. Never would she accept money from any one without knowing when she would be able to return it. Then also it was a question of too large an amount. And as he insisted, in a frightened manner, she ended by exclaiming:

"But your marriage? I certainly can't take the money you've been saving for your marriage."

"Don't let that bother you," he replied, turning red in his turn. "I'm not going to be married now. That was just an idea, you know.

Really, I would much sooner lend you the money."

Then they both held down their heads. There was something very pleasant between them to which they did not give expression. And Gervaise accepted. Goujet had told his mother. They crossed the landing, and went to see her at once. The lace-mender was very grave, and looked rather sad as she bent her face over her tambour-frame. She would not thwart her son, but she no longer approved Gervaise's project; and she plainly told her why. Coupeau was going to the bad; Coupeau would swallow up her shop. She especially could not forgive the zinc-worker for having refused to learn to read during his convalescence. The blacksmith had offered to teach him, but the other had sent him to the right about, saying that learning made people get thin. This had almost caused a quarrel between the two workmen; each went his own way. Madame Goujet, however, seeing her big boy's beseeching glances, behaved very kindly to Gervaise. It was settled that they would lend their neighbors five hundred francs; the latter were to repay the amount by installments of twenty francs a month; it would last as long as it lasted.

"I say, the blacksmith's sweet on you," exclaimed Coupeau, laughing, when he heard what had taken place. "I'm quite easy; he's too big a muff. We'll pay him back his money. But, really, if he had to deal with some people, he'd find himself pretty well duped."

On the morrow the Coupeaus took the shop. All day long, Gervaise was running from Rue Neuve de la Goutte-d'Or. When the neighbors beheld her pass thus, nimble and delighted to the extent that she no longer limped, they said she must have undergone some operation.

CHAPTER V

It so happened that the Boches had left the Rue des Poissonniers at the April quarter, and were now taking charge of the great house in the Rue de la Goutte-d'Or. It was a curious coincidence, all the same. One thing that worried Gervaise who had lived so quietly in her lodgings in the Rue Neuve, was the thought of again being under the subjection of some unpleasant person, with whom she would be continually quarrelling, either on account of water spilt in the passage or of a door shut too noisily at night-time. Concierges are such a disagreeable class. But it would be a pleasure to be with the Boches. They knew one another— they would always get on well together. It would be just like members of the same family.

On the day the Coupeaus went to sign their lease, Gervaise felt her heart swollen with pride as she passed through the high doorway. She was then at length going to live in that house as vast as a little town, with its interminable staircases, and passages as long and winding as streets. She was excited by everything: the gray walls with varicolored rugs hanging from windows to dry in the sun, the dingy courtyard with as many holes in its pavement as a public square, the hum of activity coming through the walls. She felt joy that she was at last about to realize her ambition. She also felt fear that she would fail and be crushed in the endless struggle against the poverty and starvation she could feel breathing down her neck. It seemed to her that she was doing something very bold, throwing herself into the midst of some machinery in motion, as she listened to the blacksmith's hammers and the cabinet-makers' planes, hammering and hissing in the depths of the work-shops on the ground floor. On that day the water flowing from the dyer's under the entrance porch was a very pale apple green. She smilingly stepped over it; to her the color was a pleasant omen.

The meeting with the landlord was to take place in the Boches' room. Monsieur Marescot, a wealthy cutler of the Rue de la Paix, had at one time turned a grindstone through the streets. He was now stated to be worth several millions. He was a man of fifty-five, large and big-boned. Even though he now wore a decoration in his button-hole, his huge hands were still those of a former workingman. It was his joy to carry off the scissors and knives of his tenants, to sharpen them himself, for the fun of it. He often stayed for hours with his concierges, closed up in the darkness of their lodges, going over the accounts. That's where he did all his business. He was now seated by Madame Boche's kitchen table, listening to her story of how the dressmaker on the third floor, staircase A, had used a filthy word in refusing to pay her rent. He had had to work precious hard once upon a time. But work was the high road to everything. And, after counting the two hundred and fifty francs for the first two quarters in advance, and dropping them into his capacious pocket, he related the story of his life, and showed his decoration.

Gervaise, however, felt rather ill at ease on account of the Boches' behavior. They pretended not to know her. They were most assiduous in their attentions to the landlord, bowing down before him, watching for his least words, and nodding their approval of them. Madame Boche suddenly ran out and dispersed a group of children who were paddling about in front of the cistern, the tap of which they had turned full on, causing the water to flow over the pavement; and when she returned, upright and severe in her skirts, crossing the courtyard and glancing slowly up at all the windows, as though to assure herself of the good behavior of the household, she pursed her lips in a way to show with what authority she was invested, now that she reigned over three hundred tenants. Boche again spoke of the dressmaker on the second floor; he advised that she should be turned out; he reckoned up the number of quarters she owed with the importance of a steward whose management might be compromised. Monsieur Marescot approved the suggestion of turning her out, but he wished to wait till the half quarter. It was hard to turn people out into the street, more especially as it did not put a sou into the landlord's pocket. And Gervaise asked herself with a shudder if she too would be turned out into the street the day that some misfortune rendered her unable to pay.

The concierge's lodge was as dismal as a cellar, black from smoke and crowded with dark furniture. All the sunlight fell upon the tailor's workbench by the window. An old frock coat that was being reworked lay on it. The Boches' only child, a four-year-old redhead named

Pauline, was sitting on the floor, staring quietly at the veal simmering on the stove, delighted with the sharp odor of cooking that came from the frying pan.

Monsieur Marescot again held out his hand to the zinc-worker, when the latter spoke of the repairs, recalling to his mind a promise he had made to talk the matter over later on. But the landlord grew angry, he had never promised anything; besides, it was not usual to do any repairs to a shop. However, he consented to go over the place, followed by the Coupeaus and Boche. The little linen-draper had carried off all his shelves and counters; the empty shop displayed its blackened ceiling and its cracked wall, on which hung strips of an old yellow paper. In the sonorous emptiness of the place, there ensued a heated discussion. Monsieur Marescot exclaimed that it was the business of shopkeepers to embellish their shops, for a shopkeeper might wish to have gold put about everywhere, and he, the landlord, could not put out gold. Then he related that he had spent more than twenty thousand francs in fitting up his premises in the Rue de la Paix. Gervaise, with her woman's obstinacy, kept repeating an argument which she considered unanswerable. He would re-paper a lodging, would he not? Then, why did he not treat the shop the same as a lodging? She did not ask him for anything else—only to whitewash the ceiling, and put some fresh paper on the walls.

Boche, all this while, remained dignified and impenetrable; he turned about and looked up in the air, without expressing an opinion. Coupeau winked at him in vain; he affected not to wish to take advantage of his great influence over the landlord. He ended, however, by making a slight grimace—a little smile accompanied by a nod of the head. Just then Monsieur Marescot, exasperated, and seemingly very unhappy, and clutching his fingers like a miser being despoiled of his gold, was giving way to Gervaise, promising to do the ceiling and repaper the shop on condition that she paid for half of the paper. And he hurried away declining to discuss anything further.

Now that Boche was alone with the Coupeaus, the concierge became quite talkative and slapped them on the shoulders. Well, well, see what they had gotten. Without his help, they would never have gotten the concessions. Didn't they notice how the landlord had looked to him out of the corner of his eye for advice and how he'd made up his mind suddenly when he saw Boche smile? He confessed to them confidentially that he was the real boss of the building. It was he who decided who got eviction notices and who could become tenants. He collected all the rents and kept them for a couple of weeks in his bureau drawer.

That evening the Coupeaus, to express their gratitude to the Boches, sent them two bottles of wine as a present.

The following Monday the workmen started doing up the shop. The purchasing of the paper turned out especially to be a very big affair. Gervaise wanted a gray paper with blue flowers, so as to enliven and brighten the walls. Boche offered to take her to the dealers, so that she might make her own selection. But the landlord had given him formal instructions not to go beyond the price of fifteen sous the piece. They were there an hour. The laundress kept looking in despair at a very pretty chintz pattern costing eighteen sous the piece, and thought all the other papers hideous. At length the concierge gave in; he would arrange the matter, and, if necessary, would make out there was a piece more used than was really the case. So, on her way home, Gervaise purchased some tarts for Pauline. She did not like being behindhand—one always gained by behaving nicely to her.

The shop was to be ready in four days. The workmen were there three weeks. At first it was arranged that they should merely wash the paint. But this paint, originally maroon, was so dirty and so sad-looking, that Gervaise allowed herself to be tempted to have the whole of the frontage painted a light blue with yellow moldings. Then the repairs seemed as though they would last forever. Coupeau, as he was still not working, arrived early each morning to see how things were going. Boche left the overcoat or trousers on which he was working to come and supervise. Both of them would stand and watch with their hands behind their backs, puffing on their pipes.

The painters were very merry fellows who would often desert their work to stand in the middle of the shop and join the discussion, shaking their heads for hours, admiring the work already done. The ceiling had been whitewashed quickly, but the paint on the walls never seemed to dry in a hurry.

Around nine o'clock the painters would arrive with their paint pots which they stuck in a corner. They would look around and then disappear. Perhaps they went to eat breakfast. Sometimes Coupeau would take everyone for a drink—Boche, the two painters and any of Coupeau's friends who were nearby. This meant another afternoon wasted.

Gervaise's patience was thoroughly exhausted, when, suddenly, everything was finished in two days, the paint varnished, the paper hung, and the dirt all cleared away. The workmen had finished it off as though they were playing, whistling away on their ladders, and singing loud enough to deafen the whole neighborhood.

The moving in took place at once. During the first few days Gervaise felt as delighted as a child. Whenever she crossed the road on returning from some errand, she lingered to smile at her home. From a distance her shop appeared light and gay with its pale blue signboard, on which the word "Laundress" was painted in big yellow letters, amidst the dark row of the other frontages. In the window, closed in behind by little muslin curtains, and hung on either side with blue paper to show off the whiteness of the linen, some shirts were displayed, with some women's caps hanging above them on wires. She thought her shop looked pretty, being the same color as the heavens.

Inside there was more blue; the paper, in imitation of a Pompadour chintz, represented a trellis overgrown with morning-glories. A huge table, taking up two-thirds of the room, was her ironing-table. It was covered with thick blanketing and draped with a strip of cretonne patterned with blue flower sprays that hid the trestles beneath.

Gervaise was enchanted with her pretty establishment and would often seat herself on a stool and sigh with contentment, delighted with all the new equipment. Her first glance always went to the cast-iron stove where the irons were heated ten at a time, arranged over the heat on slanting rests. She would kneel down to look into the stove to make sure the apprentice had not put in too much coke.

The lodging at the back of the shop was quite decent. The Coupeaus slept in the first room, where they also did the cooking and took their meals; a door at the back opened on to the courtyard of the house. Nana's bed was in the right hand room, which was lighted by a little round window close to the ceiling. As for Etienne, he shared the left hand room with the dirty clothes, enormous bundles of which lay about on the floor. However, there was one disadvantage—the Coupeaus would not admit it at first—but the damp ran down the walls, and it was impossible to see clearly in the place after three o'clock in the afternoon.

In the neighborhood the new shop produced a great sensation. The Coupeaus were accused of going too fast, and making too much fuss. They had, in fact, spent the five hundred francs lent by the Goujets in fitting up the shop and in moving, without keeping sufficient to live upon for a fortnight, as they had intended doing. The morning that Gervaise took down her shutters for the first time, she had just six francs in her purse. But that did not worry her, customers began to arrive, and things seemed promising. A week later on the Saturday, before going to bed, she remained two hours making calculations on a piece of paper, and she awoke Coupeau to tell him, with a bright look on her face, that there were hundreds and thousands of francs to be made, if they were only careful.

"Ah, well." said Madame Lorilleux all over the Rue de la Goutte-d'Or, "my fool of a brother is seeing some funny things. All that was wanting was that Clump-clump should go about so haughty. It becomes her well, doesn't it?"

The Lorilleuxs had declared a feud to the death against Gervaise. To begin with, they had almost died of rage during the time while the repairs were being done to the shop. If they caught sight of the painters from a distance, they would walk on the other side of the way, and go up to their rooms with their teeth set. A blue shop for that "nobody," it was enough to discourage all honest, hard-working people. Besides, the second day after the shop opened the apprentice happened to throw out a bowl of starch just at the moment when Madame Lorilleux was passing. The zinc-worker's sister caused a great commotion in the street, accusing her sister-in-law of insulting her through her employees. This broke off all relations. Now they only exchanged terrible glares when they encountered each other.

"Yes, she leads a pretty life." Madame Lorilleux kept saying. "We all know where the money came from that she paid for her wretched shop. She borrowed it from the blacksmith; and he springs from a nice family too. Didn't the father cut his own throat to save the guillotine the trouble of doing so? Anyhow, there was something disreputable of that sort."

She bluntly accused Gervaise of flirting with Goujet. She lied—she pretended she had surprised them together one night on a seat on the exterior Boulevards. The thought of this liaison, of pleasures that her sister-in-law was no doubt enjoying, exasperated her still more, because of her own ugly woman's strict sense of propriety. Every day the same cry came from her heart to her lips.

"What does she have, that wretched cripple, for people to fall in love with her? Why doesn't anyone want me?"

She busied herself in endless gossiping among the neighbors. She told them the whole story. The day the Coupeaus got married she turned up her nose at her . . . she had a keen nose, she could smell in advance how it would turn out. Then, Clump-clump pretended to be so sweet, what a hypocrite. She and her husband had only agreed to be Nana's godparents for the sake of her brother. What a bundle it had cost, that fancy christening. If Clump-clump were on her deathbed she wouldn't give her a glass of water, no matter how much she begged.

She didn't want anything to do with such a shameless baggage. Little Nana would always be welcome when she came up to see her godparents. The child couldn't be blamed for her mother's sins. But there was no use trying to tell Coupeau anything. Any real man in his situation would have beaten his wife and put a stop to it all. All they wanted was for him to insist on respect for his family. My God. If she, Madame Lorilleux, had acted like that, Coupeau wouldn't be so complacent. He would have stabbed her for sure with his shears.

The Boches, however, who sternly disapproved of quarrels in their building, said that the Lorilleuxs were in the wrong. The Lorilleuxs were no doubt respectable persons, quiet, working the whole day long, and paying their rent regularly. But, really, jealousy had driven them mad. And they were mean enough to skin an egg, real misers. They were so stingy that they'd hide their bottle when any one came in, so as not to have to offer a glass of wine—not regular people at all.

Gervaise had brought over cassis and soda water one day to drink with the Boches. When Madame Lorilleux went by, she acted out spitting before the concierge's door. Well, after that when Madame Boches swept the corridors on Saturdays, she always left a pile of trash before the Lorilleuxs' door.

"It isn't to be wondered at." Madame Lorilleux would exclaim, "Clump-clump's always stuffing them, the gluttons. Ah. They're all alike; but they had better not annoy me. I'll complain to the landlord. Only yesterday I saw that sly old Boche chasing after Madame Gaudron's skirts. Just fancy. A woman of that age, and who has half a dozen children, too; it's positively disgusting. If I catch them at anything of the sort again, I'll tell Madame Boche, and she'll give them both a hiding. It'll be something to laugh at."

Mother Coupeau continued to visit the two houses, agreeing with everybody and even managing to get asked oftener to dinner, by complaisantly listening one night to her daughter and the next night to her daughter-in-law.

However, Madame Lerat did not go to visit the Coupeaus because she had argued with Gervaise about a Zouave who had cut the nose of his mistress with a razor. She was on the side of the Zouave, saying it was evidence of a great passion, but without explaining further her thought. Then, she had made Madame Lorilleux even more angry by telling her that Clump-clump had called her "Cow Tail" in front of fifteen or twenty people. Yes, that's what the Boches and all the neighbors called her now, "Cow Tail."

Gervaise remained calm and cheerful among all these goings-on. She often stood by the door of her shop greeting friends who passed by with a nod and a smile. It was her pleasure to take a moment between batches of ironing to enjoy the street and take pride in her own stretch of sidewalk.

She felt that the Rue de la Goutte d'Or was hers, and the neighboring streets, and the whole neighborhood. As she stood there, with her blonde hair slightly damp from the heat of the shop, she would look left and right, taking in the people, the buildings, and the sky. To the left Rue de la Goutte d'Or was peaceful and almost empty, like a country town with women idling in their doorways. While, to the right, only a short distance away, Rue des Poissonniers had a noisy throng of people and vehicles.

The stretch of gutter before her own shop became very important in her mind. It was like a wide river which she longed to see neat and clean. It was a lively river, colored by the dye shop with the most fanciful of hues which contrasted with the black mud beside it.

Then there were the shops: a large grocery with a display of dried fruits protected by mesh nets; a shop selling work clothes which had white tunics and blue smocks hanging before it with arms that waved at the slightest breeze. Cats were purring on the counters of the fruit store and the tripe shop. Madame Vigouroux, the coal dealer next door, returned her greetings. She was a plump, short woman with bright eyes in a dark face who was always joking with the men while standing at her doorway. Her shop was decorated in imitation of a rustic chalet. The neighbors on the other side were a mother and daughter, the Cudorges. The umbrella sellers kept their door closed and never came out to visit.

Gervaise always looked across the road, too, through the wide carriage entrance of the windowless wall opposite her, at the blacksmith's forge. The courtyard was cluttered with vans and carts. Inscribed on the wall was the word "Blacksmith."

At the lower end of the wall between the small shops selling scrap iron and fried potatoes was a watchmaker. He wore a frock coat and was always very neat. His cuckoo clocks could be heard in chorus against the background noise of the street and the blacksmith's rhythmic clanging.

The neighborhood in general thought Gervaise very nice. There was, it is true, a good deal of scandal related regarding her; but everyone admired her large eyes, small mouth and beautiful white teeth. In short she was a pretty blonde, and had it not been for her crippled leg she might have ranked amongst the comeliest. She was now in her twenty-eighth year, and had grown considerably plumper. Her fine features were becoming puffy, and her gestures were assuming a pleasant indolence.

At times she occasionally seemed to forget herself on the edge of a chair, while she waited for her iron to heat, smiling vaguely and with an expression of greedy joy upon her face. She was becoming fond of good living, everybody said so; but that was not a very grave fault, but rather the contrary. When one earns sufficient to be able to buy good food, one would be foolish to eat potato parings. All the more so as she continued to work very hard, slaving to please her customers, sitting up late at night after the place was closed, whenever there was anything urgent.

She was lucky as all her neighbors said; everything worked out for her. She did the washing for everyone in the house—M. Madinier, Mademoiselle Remanjou, the Boches. She even secured some of the customers of her old employer, Madame Fauconnier, Parisian ladies living in the Rue du Faubourg-Poissonniere. As early as the third week she was obliged to engage two workwomen, Madame Putois and tall Clemence, the girl who used to live on the sixth floor; counting her apprentice, that little squint-eyed Augustine, who was as ugly as a beggar's behind, that made three persons in her employ. Others would certainly have lost their heads at such a piece of good fortune. It was excusable for her to slack a little on Monday after drudging all through the week. Besides, it was necessary to her. She would have had no courage left, and would have expected to see the shirts iron themselves, if she had not been able to dress up in some pretty thing.

Gervaise was always so amiable, meek as a lamb, sweet as sugar. There wasn't any one she disliked except Madame Lorilleux. While she was enjoying a good meal and coffee, she could be indulgent and forgive everybody saying: "We have to forgive each other—don't we?—unless we want to live like savages." Hadn't all her dreams come true? She remembered her old dream: to have a job, enough bread to eat and a corner in which to sleep, to bring up her children, not to be beaten, and to die in her own bed. She had everything she wanted now and more than she had ever expected. She laughed, thinking of delaying dying in her own bed as long as possible.

It was to Coupeau especially that Gervaise behaved nicely. Never an angry word, never a complaint behind her husband's back. The zincworker had at length resumed work; and as the job he was engaged on was at the other side of Paris, she gave him every morning forty sous for his luncheon, his glass of wine and his tobacco. Only, two days out of every six, Coupeau would stop on the way, spend the forty sous in drink with a friend, and return home to lunch, with some cock-and-bull story. Once even he did not take the trouble to go far; he treated himself, My-Boots and three others to a regular feast—snails, roast meat, and some sealed bottles of wine—at the "Capuchin," on the Barriere de la Chapelle. Then, as his forty sous were not sufficient, he had sent the waiter to his wife with the bill and the information that he was in pawn. She laughed and shrugged her shoulders. Where was the harm if her old man amused himself a bit? You must give men a long rein if you want to live peaceably at home. From one word to another, one soon arrived at blows. My God. It was easy to understand. Coupeau still suffered from his leg; besides, he was led astray. He was obliged to do as the others did, or else he would be thought a cheap skate. And it was really a matter of no consequence. If he came home a bit elevated, he went to bed, and two hours afterwards he was all right again.

It was now the warm time of the year. One June afternoon, a Saturday when there was a lot of work to get through, Gervaise herself had piled the coke into the stove, around which ten irons were heating, while a rumbling sound issued from the chimney. At that hour the sun was shining full on the shop front, and the pavement reflected the heat waves, causing all sorts of quaint shadows to dance over the ceiling, and that blaze of light which assumed a bluish tinge from the color of the paper on the shelves and against the window, was almost blinding in the intensity with which it shone over the ironing-table, like a golden dust shaken among the fine linen. The atmosphere was stifling. The shop door was thrown wide open, but not a breath of air entered; the clothes which were hung up on brass wires to dry, steamed and became as stiff as shavings in less than three quarters of an hour. For some little while past an oppressive silence had reigned in that furnace-like heat, interrupted only by the smothered sound of the banging down of the irons on the thick blanket covered with calico.

"Ah, well." said Gervaise, "it's enough to melt one. We might have to take off our chemises."

She was sitting on the floor, in front of a basin, starching some things. Her sleeves were rolled up and her camisole was slipping down her shoulders. Little curls of golden hair stuck were stuck to her skin by perspiration. She carefully dipped caps, shirt-fronts, entire petticoats, and the trimmings of women's drawers into the milky water. Then she rolled the things up and placed them at the bottom of a square basket, after dipping her hand in a pail and shaking it over the portions of the shirts and drawers which she had not starched.

"This basketful's for you, Madame Putois," she said. "Look sharp, now.

It dries at once, and will want doing all over again in an hour."

Madame Putois, a thin little woman of forty-five, was ironing. Though she was buttoned up in an old chestnut-colored dress, there was not a drop of perspiration to be seen. She had not even taken her cap off, a black cap trimmed with green ribbons turned partly yellow. And she stood perfectly upright in front of the ironing-table, which was too high for her, sticking out her elbows, and moving her iron with the jerky evolutions of a puppet. On a sudden she exclaimed:

"Ah, no. Mademoiselle Clemence, you mustn't take your camisole off. You know I don't like such indecencies. While you're about it, you'd better show everything. There's already three men over the way stopping to look."

Tall Clemence called her an old beast between her teeth. She was suffocating; she might certainly make herself comfortable; everyone was not gifted with a skin as dry as touchwood. Besides no one could see anything; and she held up her arms, while her opulent bosom almost ripped her chemise, and her shoulders were bursting through the straps. At the rate she was going, Clemence was not likely to have any marrow left in her bones long before she was thirty years old. Mornings after big parties she was unable to feel the ground she trod upon, and fell asleep over her work, while her head and her stomach seemed as though stuffed full of rags. But she was kept on all the same, for no other work-woman could iron a shirt with her style. Shirts were her specialty.

"This is mine, isn't it?" she declared, tapping her bosom. "And it doesn't bite; it hurts nobody."

"Clemence, put your wrapper on again," said Gervaise. "Madame Putois is right, it isn't decent. People will begin to take my house for what it isn't."

So tall Clemence dressed herself again, grumbling the while. "My God There's prudery for you."

And she vented her rage on the apprentice, that squint-eyed Augustine who was ironing some stockings and handkerchiefs beside her. She jostled her and pushed her with her elbow; but Augustine who was of a surly disposition, and slyly spiteful in the way of an animal and a drudge, spat on the back of the other's dress just out of revenge, without being seen. Gervaise, during this incident, had commenced a cap belonging to Madame Boche, which she intended to take great pains with. She had prepared some boiled starch to make it look new again. She was gently passing a little iron rounded at both ends over the inside of the crown of the cap, when a bony-looking woman entered the shop, her face covered with red blotches and her skirts sopping wet. It was a washerwoman who employed three assistants at the wash-house in the Rue de la Goutte-d'Or.

"You've come too soon, Madame Bijard." cried Gervaise. "I told you to call this evening. I'm too busy to attend to you now."

But as the washerwoman began lamenting and fearing that she would not be able to put all the things to soak that day, she consented to give her the dirty clothes at once. They went to fetch the bundles in the left hand room where Etienne slept, and returned with enormous armfuls which they piled up on the floor at the back of the shop. The sorting lasted a good half hour. Gervaise made heaps all round her, throwing the shirts in one, the chemises in another, the handkerchiefs, the socks, the dish-cloths in others. Whenever she came across anything belonging to a new customer, she marked it with a cross in red cotton thread so as to know it again. And from all this dirty linen which they were throwing about there issued an offensive odor in the warm atmosphere.

". . . . La, la. What a stench." said Clemence, holding her nose. "Of course there is. If it were clean they wouldn't send it to us," quietly explained Gervaise. "It smells as one would expect it to, that's all. We said fourteen chemises, didn't we, Madame Bijard? Fifteen, sixteen, seventeen—"

And she continued counting aloud. Used to this kind of thing she evinced no disgust. She thrust her bare pink arms deep into the piles of laundry: shirts yellow with grime, towels stiff from dirty dish water, socks threadbare and eaten away by sweat. The strong odor which slapped her in the face as she sorted the piles of clothes made her feel drowsy. She seemed to be intoxicating herself with this stench of humanity as she sat on the edge of a stool, bending far over, smiling vaguely, her eyes slightly misty. It was as if her laziness was started by a kind of smothering caused by the dirty clothes which poisoned the air in the shop. Just as she was shaking out a child's dirty diaper, Coupeau came in.

"By Jove." he stuttered, "what a sun. It shines full on your head."

The zinc-worker caught hold of the ironing-table to save himself from falling. It was the first time he had been so drunk. Until then he had sometimes come home slightly tipsy, but nothing more. This time, however, he had a black eye, just a friendly slap he had run up against in a playful moment. His curly hair, already streaked with gray, must have dusted a corner in some low wine shop, for a cobweb was hanging to one of his locks over the back of his neck. He was still as attractive as ever, though his features were rather drawn and aged, and his under jaw projected more; but he was always lively, as he would sometimes say, with a complexion to be envied by a duchess.

"I'll just explain it to you," he resumed, addressing Gervaise.

"It was Celery-Root, you know him, the bloke with a wooden leg. Well, as he was going back to his native place, he wanted to treat us. . . We were all right, if it hadn't been for that devil of a sun. In the street everybody looks shaky. Really, all the world's drunk."

And as tall Clemence laughed at his thinking that the people in the street were drunk, he was himself seized with an intense fit of gaiety which almost strangled him.

"Look at them. The blessed tipplers. Aren't they funny?" he cried. "But it's not their fault. It's the sun that's causing it."

All the shop laughed, even Madame Putois, who did not like drunkards. That squint-eyed Augustine was cackling like a hen, suffocating with her mouth wide open. Gervaise, however, suspected Coupeau of not having come straight home, but of having passed an hour with the Lorilleuxs who were always filling his head with unpleasant ideas. When he swore he had not been near them she laughed also, full of indulgence and not even reproaching him with having wasted another day.

"My God What nonsense he does talk," she murmured. "How does he manage to say such stupid things?" Then in a maternal tone of voice she added, "Now go to bed, won't you? You see we're busy; you're in our way. That makes thirty-two handkerchiefs, Madame Bijard; and two more, thirty-four."

But Coupeau was not sleepy. He stood there wagging his body from side to side like the pendulum of a clock and chuckling in an obstinate and teasing manner. Gervaise, wanting to finish with Madame Bijard, called to Clemence to count the laundry while she made the list. Tall Clemence made a dirty remark about every item that she touched. She commented on the customers' misfortunes and their bedroom adventures. She had a wash-house joke for every rip or stain that passed through her hands. Augustine pretended that she didn't understand, but her ears were wide open. Madame Putois compressed her lips, thinking it a disgrace to say such things in front of Coupeau. It's not a man's business to have anything to do with dirty linen. It's just not done among decent people.

Gervaise, serious and her mind fully occupied with what she was about, did not seem to notice. As she wrote she gave a glance to each article as it passed before her, so as to recognize it; and she never made a mistake; she guessed the owner's name just by the look or the color. Those napkins belonged to the Goujets, that was evident; they had not been used to wipe out frying-pans. That pillow-case certainly came from the Boches on account of the pomatum with which Madame Boche always smeared her things. There was no need to put your nose close to the flannel vests of Monsieur Madinier; his skin was so oily that it clogged up his woolens.

She knew many peculiarities, the cleanliness of some, the ragged underclothes of neighborhood ladies who appeared on the streets in silk dresses; how many items each family soiled weekly; the way some people's garments were always torn at the same spot. . . she had many tales to tell. For instance, the chemises of Mademoiselle Remanjou provided material for endless comments: they wore out at the top first because the old maid had bony, sharp shoulders; and they were never really dirty, proving that you dry up by her age, like a stick of wood out of which it's hard to squeeze a drop of anything. It was thus that at every sorting of the dirty linen in the shop they undressed the whole neighborhood of the Goutte-d'Or.

". . . here's something luscious." cried Clemence, opening another bundle.

Gervaise, suddenly seized with a great repugnance, drew back.

"Madame Gaudron's bundle?" said she. "I'll no longer wash for her, I'll find some excuse. No, I'm not more particular than another. I've handled some most disgusting linen in my time; but really, that lot I can't stomach. What can the woman do to get her things into such a state?"

And she requested Clemence to look sharp. But the girl continued her remarks, thrusting the clothes sullenly about her, with complaints on the soiled caps she waved like triumphal banners of filth. Meanwhile the heaps around Gervaise had grown higher. Still seated on the edge of the stool, she was now disappearing between the petticoats and chemises. In front of her were the sheets, the table cloths, a veritable mass of dirtiness.

She seemed even rosier and more languid than usual within this spreading sea of soiled laundry. She had regained her composure, forgetting Madame Gaudron's laundry, stirring the various piles of clothing to make sure there had been no mistake in sorting. Squint-eyed Augustine had just stuffed the stove so full of coke that its cast-iron sides were bright red. The sun was shining obliquely on the window; the shop was in a blaze. Then, Coupeau, whom the great heat intoxicated all the more, was seized with a sudden fit of tenderness. He advanced towards Gervaise with open arms and deeply moved.

"You're a good wife," he stammered. "I must kiss you."

But he caught his foot in the garments which barred the way and nearly fell.

"What a nuisance you are." said Gervaise without getting angry. "Keep still, we're nearly done now."

No, he wanted to kiss her. He must do so because he loved her so much. While he stuttered he tried to get round the heap of petticoats and stumbled against the pile of chemises; then as he obstinately persisted his feet caught together and he fell flat, his nose in the midst of the dish-cloths. Gervaise, beginning to lose her temper pushed him, saying that he was mixing all the things up. But Clemence and even Madame Putois maintained that she was wrong. It was very nice of him after all. He wanted to kiss her. She might very well let herself be kissed.

"You're lucky, you are, Madame Coupeau," said Madame Bijard, whose drunkard of a husband, a locksmith, was nearly beating her to death each evening when he came in. "If my old man was like that when he's had a drop, it would be a real pleasure."

Gervaise had calmed down and was already regretting her hastiness. She helped Coupeau up on his legs again. Then she offered her cheek with a smile. But the zinc-worker, without caring a button for the other people being present, seized her bosom.

"It's not for the sake of saying so," he murmured; "but your dirty linen stinks tremendously. Still, I love you all the same, you know."

"Leave off, you're tickling me," cried she, laughing the louder. "What a great silly you are. How can you be so absurd?"

He had caught hold of her and would not let her go. She gradually abandoned herself to him, dizzy from the slight faintness caused by the heap of clothes and not minding Coupeau's foul-smelling breath. The long kiss they exchanged on each other's mouths in the midst of the filth of the laundress's trade was perhaps the first tumble in the slow downfall of their life together.

Madame Bijard had meanwhile been tying the laundry up into bundles and talking about her daughter, Eulalie, who at two was as smart as a grown woman. She could be left by herself; she never cried or played with matches. Finally Madame Bijard took the laundry away a bundle at a time, her face splotched with purple and her tall form bent under the weight.

"This heat is becoming unbearable, we're roasting," said Gervaise, wiping her face before returning to Madame Boche's cap.

They talked of boxing Augustine's ears when they saw that the stove was red-hot. The irons, also, were getting in the same condition. She must have the very devil in her body. One could not turn one's back a moment without her being up to some of her tricks. Now they would have to wait a quarter of an hour before they would be able to use their irons. Gervaise covered the fire with two shovelfuls of cinders. Then she thought to hang some sheets on the brass wires near the ceiling to serve as curtains to keep out the sunlight.

Things were now better in the shop. The temperature was still high, but you could imagine it was cooler. Footsteps could still be heard outside but you were free to make yourself comfortable. Clemence removed her camisole again. Coupeau still refused to go to bed, so they allowed him to stay, but he had to promise to be quiet in a corner, for they were very busy.

"Whatever has that vermin done with my little iron?" murmured Gervaise, speaking of Augustine.

They were forever seeking the little iron, which they found in the most out-of-the-way places, where the apprentice, so they said, hid it out of spite. Gervaise could now finish Madame Boche's cap. First she roughly smoothed the lace, spreading it out with her hand, and then she straightened it up by light strokes of the iron. It had a very fancy border consisting of narrow puffs alternating with insertions of embroidery. She was working on it silently and conscientiously, ironing the puffs and insertions.

Silence prevailed for a time. Nothing was to be heard except the soft thud of irons on the ironing pad. On both sides of the huge rectangular table Gervaise, her two employees, and the apprentice were bending over, slaving at their tasks with rounded shoulders, their arms moving incessantly. Each had a flat brick blackened by hot irons near her. A soup plate filled with clean water was on the middle of the table with a moistening rag and a small brush soaking in it.

A bouquet of large white lilies bloomed in what had once been a brandied cherry jar. Its cluster of snowy flowers suggested a corner of a royal garden. Madame Putois had begun the basket that Gervaise had brought to her filled with towels, wrappers, cuffs and underwear. Augustine was dawdling with the stockings and washcloths, gazing into the air, seemingly fascinated by a large fly that was buzzing around. Clemence had done thirty-four men's shirts so far that day.

"Always wine, never spirits." suddenly said the zinc-worker, who felt the necessity of making this declaration. "Spirits make me drunk, I'll have none of them."

Clemence took an iron from the stove with her leather holder in which a piece of sheet iron was inserted, and held it up to her cheek to see how hot it was. She rubbed it on her brick, wiped it on a piece of rag hanging from her waist-band and started on her thirty-fifth shirt, first of all ironing the shoulders and the sleeves.

"Bah. Monsieur Coupeau," said she after a minute or two, "a little glass of brandy isn't bad. It sets me going. Besides, the sooner you're merry, the jollier it is . . . . I don't make any mistake; I know that I shan't make old bones."

"What a nuisance you are with your funeral ideas." interrupted Madame Putois who did not like hearing people talk of anything sad.

Coupeau had arisen and was becoming angry thinking that he had been accused of drinking brandy. He swore on his own head and on the heads of his wife and child that there was not a drop of brandy in his veins. And he went up to Clemence and blew in her face so that she might smell his breath. Then he began to giggle because her bare shoulders were right under his nose. He thought maybe he could see more. Clemence, having folded over the back of the shirt and ironed it on both sides, was now working on the cuffs and collar. However, as he was shoving against her, he caused her to make a wrinkle, obliging her to reach for the brush soaking in the soup plate to smooth it out.

"Madame," said she, "do make him leave off bothering me."

"Leave her alone; it's stupid of you to go on like that," quietly observed Gervaise. "We're in a hurry, do you hear?"

They were in a hurry, well. What? It was not his fault. He was doing no harm. He was not touching, he was only looking. Was it no longer allowed to look at the beautiful things that God had made? All the same, she had precious fine arms, that artful Clemence. She might exhibit herself for two sous and nobody would have to regret his money. The girl allowed him to go on, laughing at these coarse compliments of a drunken man. And she soon commenced joking with him. He fiddled her about the shirts. So she was always doing shirts? Why yes, she practically lived in them. My God, she knew them pretty well. Hundreds and hundreds of them had passed through her hands. Just about every man in the neighborhood was wearing her handiwork on his body. Her shoulders were shaking with laughter through all this, but she managed to continue ironing.

"That's the banter." said she, laughing harder than ever.

That squint-eyed Augustine almost burst, the joke seemed to her so funny. The others bullied her. There was a brat for you who laughed at words she ought not to understand. Clemence handed her her iron; the apprentice finished up the irons on the stockings and the dish-cloths when they were not hot enough for the starched things. But she took hold of this one so clumsily that she made herself a cuff in the form of a long burn on the wrist. And she sobbed and accused Clemence of having burnt her on purpose. The latter who had gone to fetch a very hot iron for the shirt-front consoled her at once by threatening to iron her two ears if she did not leave off. Then she placed a piece of flannel under the front and slowly passed the iron over it giving the starch time to show up and dry. The shirt-front became as stiff and as shiny as cardboard.

"By golly." swore Coupeau, who was treading behind her with the obstinacy of a drunkard.

He raised himself up with a shrill laugh that resembled a pulley in want of grease. Clemence, leaning heavily over the ironing-table, her wrists bent in, her elbows sticking out and wide apart was bending her neck in a last effort; and all her muscles swelled, her shoulders rose with the slow play of the muscles beating beneath the soft skin, her breasts heaved, wet with perspiration in the rosy shadow of the half open chemise. Then Coupeau thrust out his hands, trying to touch her bare flesh.

"Madame. Madame." cried Clemence, "do make him leave off. I shall go away if it continues. I won't be intimated."

Gervaise glanced over just as her husband's hands began to explore inside the chemise.

"Really, Coupeau, you're too foolish," said she, with a vexed air, as though she were scolding a child who persisted in eating his jam without bread. "You must go to bed."

"Yes, go to bed, Monsieur Coupeau; it will be far better," exclaimed Madame Putois.

"Ah. Well," stuttered he, without ceasing to chuckle, "you're all precious particular. So one mustn't amuse oneself now? Women, I know how to handle them; I'll only kiss them, no more. One admires a lady, you know, and wants to show it. And, besides, when one displays one's goods, it's that one may make one's choice, isn't it? Why does the tall blonde show everything she's got? It's not decent."

And turning towards Clemence, he added: "You know, my lovely, you're wrong to be to very insolent. If it's because there are others here."

But he was unable to continue. Gervaise very calmly seized hold of him with one hand, and placed the other on his mouth. He struggled, just by way of a joke, while she pushed him to the back of the shop, towards the bedroom. He got his mouth free and said that he was willing to go to bed, but that the tall blonde must come and warm his feet.

Then Gervaise could be heard taking off his shoes. She removed his clothes too, bullying him in a motherly way. He burst out laughing after she had removed his trousers and kicked about, pretending that she was tickling him. At last she tucked him in carefully like a child. Was he comfortable now? But he did not answer; he called to Clemence:

"I say, my lovely, I'm here, and waiting for you."

When Gervaise went back into the shop, the squint-eyed Augustine was being properly chastised by Clemence because of a dirty iron that Madame Putois had used and which had caused her to soil a camisole. Clemence, in defending herself for not having cleaned her iron, blamed Augustine, swearing that it wasn't hers, in spite of the spot of burned starch still clinging to the bottom. The apprentice, outraged at the injustice, openly spat on the front of Clemence's dress, earning a slap for her boldness. Now, as Augustine went about cleaning the iron, she saved up her spit and each time she passed Clemence spat on her back and laughed to herself.

Gervaise continued with the lace of Madame Boche's cap. In the sudden calm which ensued, one could hear Coupeau's husky voice issuing from the depths of the bedroom. He was still jolly, and was laughing to himself as he uttered bits of phrases.

"How stupid she is, my wife. How stupid of her to put me to bed. Really, it's too absurd, in the middle of the day, when one isn't sleepy."

But, all on a sudden, he snored. Then Gervaise gave a sigh of relief, happy in knowing that he was at length quiet and sleeping off his intoxication on two good mattresses. And she spoke out in the silence, in a slow and continuous voice, without taking her eyes off her work.

"You see, he hasn't his reason, one can't be angry. Were I to be harsh with him, it would be of no use. I prefer to agree with him and get him to bed; then, at least, it's over at once and I'm quiet. Besides, he isn't ill-natured, he loves me very much. You could see that just a moment ago when he was desperate to give me a kiss. That's quite nice of him. There are plenty of men, you know, who after drinking a bit don't come straight home but stay out chasing women. . . he may fool around with the women in the shop, but it doesn't lead to anything. Clemence, you mustn't feel insulted. You know how it is when a man's had too much to drink. He could do anything and not even remember it."

She spoke composedly, not at all angry, being quite used to Coupeau's sprees and not holding them against him. A silence settled down for a while when she stopped talking. There was a lot of work to get done. They figured they would have to keep at it until eleven, working as fast as they could. Now that they were undisturbed, all of them were pounding away. Bare arms were moving back and forth, showing glimpses of pink among the whiteness of the laundry.

More coke had been put into the stove and the sunlight slanted in between the sheets onto the stove. You could see the heat rising up through the rays of the sun. It became so stifling that Augustine ran out of spit and was forced to lick her lips. The room smelled of the heat and of the working women. The white lilies in the jar were beginning to fade, yet they still exuded a pure and strong perfume. Coupeau's heavy snores were heard like the regular ticking of a huge clock, setting the tempo for the heavy labor in the shop.

On the morrow of his carouses, the zinc-worker always had a headache, a splitting headache which kept him all day with his hair uncombed, his breath offensive, and his mouth all swollen and askew. He got up late on those days, not shaking the fleas off till about eight o'clock; and he would hang about the shop, unable to make up his mind to start off to his work. It was another day lost. In the morning he would complain that his legs bent like pieces of thread, and would call himself a great fool to guzzle to such an extent, as it broke one's constitution. Then, too, there were a lot of lazy bums who wouldn't let you go and you'd get to drinking more in spite of yourself. No, no, no more for him.

After lunch he would always begin to perk up and deny that he had been really drunk the night before. Maybe just a bit lit up. He was rock solid and able to drink anything he wanted without even blinking an eye.

When he had thoroughly badgered the workwomen, Gervaise would give him twenty sous to clear out. And off he would go to buy his tobacco at the "Little Civet," in the Rue des Poissonniers, where he generally took a plum in brandy whenever he met a friend. Then, he spent the rest of the twenty sous at old Francois's, at the corner of the Rue de la Goutte-d'Or, where there was a famous wine, quite young, which tickled your gullet. This was an old-fashioned place with a low ceiling. There was a smoky room to one side where soup was served. He would stay there until evening drinking because there was an understanding that he didn't have to pay right away and they would never send the bill to his wife. Besides he was a jolly fellow, who would never do the least harm—a chap who loved a spree sure enough, and who colored his nose in his turn but in a nice manner, full of contempt for those pigs of men who have succumbed to alcohol, and whom one never sees sober. He always went home as gay and as gallant as a lark.

"Has your lover been?" he would sometimes ask Gervaise by way of teasing her. "One never sees him now; I must go and rout him out."

The lover was Goujet. He avoided, in fact, calling too often for fear of being in the way, and also of causing people to talk. Yet he frequently found a pretext, such as bringing the washing; and he would pass no end of time on the pavement in front of the shop. There was a corner right at the back in which he liked to sit, without moving for hours, and smoke his short pipe. Once every ten days, in the evening after his dinner, he would venture there and take up his favorite position. And he was no talker, his mouth almost seemed sewn up, as he sat with his eyes fixed on Gervaise, and only removed his pipe to laugh at everything she said. When they were working late on a Saturday he would stay on, and appeared to amuse himself more than if he had gone to a theatre.

Sometimes the women stayed in the shop ironing until three in the morning. A lamp hung from the ceiling and spread a brilliant light making the linen look like fresh snow. The apprentice would put up the shop shutters, but since these July nights were scorching hot, the door would be left open. The later the hour the more casual the women became with their clothes while trying to be comfortable. The lamplight flecked their rosy skin with gold specks, especially Gervaise who was so pleasantly rounded.

On these nights Goujet would be overcome by the heat from the stove and the odor of linen steaming under the hot irons. He would drift into a sort of giddiness, his thinking slowed and his eyes obsessed by these hurrying women as their naked arms moved back and forth, working far into the night to have the neighborhood's best clothes ready for Sunday.

Everything around the laundry was slumbering, settled into sleep for the night. Midnight rang, then one o'clock, then two o'clock. There were no vehicles or pedestrians. In the dark and deserted street, only their shop door let out any light. Once in a while, footsteps would be heard and a man would pass the shop. As he crossed the path of light he would stretch his neck to look in, startled by the sound of the thudding irons, and carry with him the quick glimpse of bare-shouldered laundresses immersed in a rosy mist.

Goujet, seeing that Gervaise did not know what to do with Etienne, and wishing to deliver him from Coupeau's kicks, had engaged him to go and blow the bellows at the factory where he worked. The profession of bolt-maker, if not one to be proud of on account of the dirt of the forge and of the monotony of constantly hammering on pieces of iron of a similar kind, was nevertheless a well-paid one, at which ten and even twelve francs a day could be earned. The youngster, who was then twelve years old, would soon be able to go in for it, if the calling was to his liking. And Etienne had thus become another link between the laundress and the blacksmith. The latter would bring the child home and speak of his good conduct. Everyone laughingly said that Goujet was smitten with Gervaise. She knew it, and blushed like a young girl, the flush of modesty coloring her cheeks with the bright tints of an apple. The poor fellow, he was never any trouble. He never made a bold gesture or an indelicate remark. You didn't find many men like him. Gervaise didn't want to admit it, but she derived a great deal of pleasure from being adored like this. Whenever a problem arose she thought immediately of the blacksmith and was consoled. There was never any awkward tension when they were alone together. They just looked at each other and smiled happily with no need to talk. It was a very sensible kind of affection.

Towards the end of the summer, Nana quite upset the household. She was six years old and promised to be a thorough good-for-nothing. So as not to have her always under her feet her mother took her every morning to a little school in the Rue Polonceau kept by Mademoiselle Josse. She fastened her playfellows' dresses together behind, she filled the school-mistress's snuff-box with ashes, and invented other tricks much less decent which could not be mentioned. Twice Mademoiselle Josse expelled her and then took her back again so as not to lose the six francs a month. Directly lessons were over Nana avenged herself for having been kept in by making an infernal noise under the porch and in the courtyard where the ironers, whose ears could not stand the racket, sent her to play. There she would meet Pauline, the Boches' daughter, and Victor, the son of Gervaise's old employer—a big booby of ten who delighted in playing with very little girls. Madame Fauconnier who had not quarreled with the Coupeaus would herself send her son. In the house, too, there was an extraordinary swarm of brats, flights of children who rolled down the four staircases at all hours of the day and alighted on the pavement of the courtyard like troops of noisy pillaging sparrows. Madame Gaudron was responsible for nine of them, all with uncombed hair, runny noses, hand-me-down clothes, saggy stockings and ripped jackets. Another woman on the sixth floor had seven of them. This hoard that only got their faces washed when it rained were in all shapes and sizes, fat, thin, big and barely out of the cradle.

Nana reigned supreme over this host of urchins; she ordered about girls twice her own size, and only deigned to relinquish a little of her power in favor of Pauline and Victor, intimate confidants who enforced her commands. This precious chit was forever wanting to play at being mamma, undressing the smallest ones to dress them again, insisting on examining the others all over, messing them about and exercising the capricious despotism of a grown-up person with a vicious disposition. Under her leadership they got up tricks for which they should have been well spanked. The troop paddled in the colored water from the dyer's and emerged from it with legs stained blue or red as high as the knees; then off it flew to the locksmith's where it purloined nails and filings and started off again to alight in the midst of the carpenter's shavings, enormous heaps of shavings, which delighted it immensely and in which it rolled head over heels exposing their behinds.

The courtyard was her kingdom. It echoed with the clatter of little shoes as they stampeded back and forth with piercing cries. On some days the courtyard was too small for them and the troop would dash down into the cellar, race up a staircase, run along a corridor, then dash up another staircase and follow another corridor for hours. They never got tired of their yelling and clambering.

"Aren't they abominable, those little toads?" cried Madame Boche. "Really, people can have but very little to do to have time get so many brats. And yet they complain of having no bread."

Boche said that children pushed up out of poverty like mushrooms out of manure. All day long his wife was screaming at them and chasing them with her broom. Finally she had to lock the door of the cellar when she learned from Pauline that Nana was playing doctor down there in the dark, viciously finding pleasure in applying remedies to the others by beating them with sticks.

Well, one afternoon there was a frightful scene. It was bound to have come sooner or later. Nana had thought of a very funny little game. She had stolen one of Madame Boche's wooden shoes from outside the concierge's room. She tied a string to it and began dragging it about like a cart. Victor on his side had had the idea to fill it with potato parings. Then a procession was formed. Nana came first dragging the wooden shoe. Pauline and Victor walked on her right and left. Then the entire crowd of urchins followed in order, the big ones first, the little ones next, jostling one another; a baby in long skirts about as tall as a boot with an old tattered bonnet cocked on one side of its head, brought up the rear. And the procession chanted something sad with plenty of ohs and ahs. Nana had said that they were going to play at a funeral; the potato parings represented the body. When they had gone the round of the courtyard, they recommenced. They thought it immensely amusing.

"What can they be up to?" murmured Madame Boche, who emerged from her room to see, ever mistrustful and on the alert.

And when she understood: "But it's my shoe." cried she furiously. "Ah, the rogues."

She distributed some smacks, clouted Nana on both cheeks and administered a kick to Pauline, that great goose who allowed the others to steal her mother's shoe. It so happened that Gervaise was filling a bucket at the top. When she beheld Nana, her nose bleeding and choking with sobs, she almost sprang at the concierge's chignon. It was not right to hit a child as though it were an ox. One could have no heart; one must be the lowest of the low if one did so. Madame Boche naturally replied in a similar strain. When one had a beast of a girl like that one should keep her locked up. At length Boche himself appeared in the doorway to call his wife to come in and not to enter into so many explanations with a filthy thing like her. There was a regular quarrel.

As a matter of fact things had not gone on very pleasantly between the Boches and the Coupeaus for a month past. Gervaise, who was of a very generous nature, was continually bestowing wine, broth, oranges and slices of cake on the Boches. One night she had taken the remains of an endive and beetroot salad to the concierge's room, knowing that the latter would have done anything for such a treat. But on the morrow she became quite pale with rage on hearing Mademoiselle Remanjou relate how Madame Boche had thrown the salad away in the presence of several persons with an air of disgust and under the pretext that she, thank goodness, was not yet reduced to feeding on things which others had messed about. From that time Gervaise took no more presents to the Boches—nothing. Now the Boches seemed to think that Gervaise was stealing something which was rightfully theirs. Gervaise saw that she had made a mistake. If she hadn't catered to them so much in the beginning, they wouldn't have gotten into the habit of expecting it and might have remained on good terms with her.

Now the concierge began to spread slander about Gervaise. There was a great fuss with the landlord, Monsieur Marescot, at the October rental period, because Gervaise was a day late with the rent. Madame Boche accused her of eating up all her money in fancy dishes. Monsieur Marescot charged into the laundry demanding to be paid at once. He didn't even bother to remove his hat. The money was ready and was paid to him immediately. The Boches had now made up with the Lorilleuxs who now came and did their guzzling in the concierge's lodge. They assured each other that they never would have fallen out if it hadn't been for Clump-clump. She was enough to set mountains to fighting. Ah. The Boches knew her well now, they could understand how much the Lorilleuxs must suffer. And whenever she passed beneath the doorway they all affected to sneer at her.

One day, Gervaise went up to see the Lorilleuxs in spite of this. It was with respect to mother Coupeau who was then sixty-seven years old. Mother Coupeau's eyesight was almost completely gone. Her legs too were no longer what they used to be. She had been obliged to give up her last cleaning job and now threatened to die of hunger if assistance were not forthcoming. Gervaise thought it shameful that a woman of her age, having three children should be thus abandoned by heaven and earth. And as Coupeau refused to speak to the Lorilleuxs on the subject saying that she, Gervaise, could very well go and do so, the latter went up in a fit of indignation with which her heart was almost bursting.

When she reached their door she entered without knocking. Nothing had been changed since the night when the Lorilleuxs, at their first meeting had received her so ungraciously. The same strip of faded woolen stuff separated the room from the workshop, a lodging like a gun barrel, and which looked as though it had been built for an eel. Right at the back Lorilleux, leaning over his bench, was squeezing together one by one the links of a piece of chain, while Madame Lorilleux, standing in front of the vise was passing a gold wire through the draw-plate. In the broad daylight the little forge had a rosy reflection.

"Yes, it's I." said Gervaise. "I daresay you're surprised to see me as we're at daggers drawn. But I've come neither for you nor myself, you may be quite sure. It's for mother Coupeau that I've come. Yes, I have come to see if we're going to let her beg her bread from the charity of others."

"Ah, well, that's a fine way to burst in upon one." murmured Madame Lorilleux. "One must have a rare cheek."

And she turned her back and resumed drawing her gold wire, affecting to ignore her sister-in-law's presence. But Lorilleux raised his pale face and cried:

"What's that you say?"

Then, as he had heard perfectly well, he continued:

"More back-bitings, eh? She's nice, mother Coupeau, to go and cry starvation everywhere. Yet only the day before yesterday she dined here. We do what we can. We haven't got all the gold of Peru. Only if she goes about gossiping with others she had better stay with them, for we don't like spies."

He took up the piece of chain and turned his back also, adding as though with regret:

"When everyone gives five francs a month, we'll give five francs."

Gervaise had calmed down and felt quite chilled by the wooden looking faces of the Lorilleux. She had never once set foot in their rooms without experiencing a certain uneasiness. With her eyes fixed on the floor, staring at the holes of the wooden grating through which the waste gold fell, she now explained herself in a reasonable manner. Mother Coupeau had three children; if each one gave five francs it would only make fifteen francs, and really that was not enough, one could not live on it; they must at least triple the sum. But Lorilleux cried out. Where did she think he could steal fifteen francs a month? It was quite amusing; people thought he was rich simply because he had gold in his place. He began then to criticize mother Coupeau: she had to have her morning coffee, she took a sip of brandy now and then, she was as demanding as if she were rich. My God. Sure, everyone liked the good things of life. But if you've never saved a sou, you had to do what other folks did and do without. Besides, mother Coupeau wasn't too old to work. She could see well enough when she was trying to pick a choice morsel from the platter. She was just an old spendthrift trying to get others to provide her with comforts. Even had he had the means, he would have considered it wrong to support any one in idleness.

Gervaise remained conciliatory, and peaceably argued against all this bad reasoning. She tried to soften the Lorilleuxs. But the husband ended by no longer answering her. The wife was now at the forge scouring a piece of chain in the little, long-handled brass saucepan full of lye-water. She still affectedly turned her back, as though a hundred leagues away. And Gervaise continued speaking, watching them pretending to be absorbed in their labor in the midst of the black dust of the workshop, their bodies distorted, their clothes patched and greasy, both become stupidly hardened like old tools in the pursuit of their narrow mechanical task. Then suddenly anger again got the better of her and she exclaimed:

"Very well, I'd rather it was so; keep your money. I'll give mother Coupeau a home, do you hear? I picked up a cat the other evening, so I can at least do the same for your mother. And she shall be in want of nothing; she shall have her coffee and her drop of brandy. Good heavens. What a vile family."

At these words Madame Lorilleux turned round. She brandished the saucepan as though she was about to throw the lye-water in her sister-in-law's face. She stammered with rage:

"Be off, or I shall do you an injury. And don't count on the five francs because I won't give a radish. No, not a radish. Ah well, yes, five francs. Mother would be your servant and you would enjoy yourself with my five francs. If she goes to live with you, tell her this, she may croak, I won't even send her a glass of water. Now off you go. Clear out."

"What a monster of a woman." said Gervaise violently slamming the door.

On the morrow she brought mother Coupeau to live with her, putting her bed in the inner room where Nana slept. The moving did not take long, for all the furniture mother Coupeau had was her bed, an ancient walnut wardrobe which was put in the dirty-clothes room, a table, and two chairs. They sold the table and had the chairs recaned. From the very first the old lady took over the sweeping. She washed the dishes and made herself useful, happy to have settled her problem.

The Lorilleux were furious enough to explode, especially since Madame Lerat was now back on good terms with the Coupeaus. One day the two sisters, the flower-maker and the chain-maker came to blows about Gervaise because Madame Lerat dared to express approval of the way she was taking care of their mother. When she noticed how this upset the other, she went on to remark that Gervaise had magnificent eyes, eyes warm enough to set paper on fire. The two of them commenced slapping each other and swore they never would see each other again. Nowadays Madame Lerat often spent her evenings in the shop, laughing to herself at Clemence's spicy remarks.

Three years passed by. There were frequent quarrels and reconciliations. Gervaise did not care a straw for the Lorilleux, the Boches and all the others who were not of her way of thinking. If they did not like it, they could forget it. She earned what she wished, that was her principal concern. The people of the neighborhood had ended by greatly esteeming her, for one did not find many customers so kind as she was, paying punctually, never caviling or haggling. She bought her bread of Madame Coudeloup, in the Rue des Poissonniers; her meat of stout Charles, a butcher in the Rue Polonceau; her groceries at Lehongre's, in the Rue de la Goutte-d'Or, almost opposite her own shop. Francois, the wine merchant at the corner of the street, supplied her with wine in baskets of fifty bottles. Her neighbor Vigouroux, whose wife's hips must have been black and blue, the men pinched her so much, sold coke to her at the same price as the gas company. And, in all truth, her tradespeople served her faithfully, knowing that there was everything to gain by treating her well.

Besides, whenever she went out around the neighborhood, she was greeted everywhere. She felt quite at home. Sometimes she put off doing a laundry job just to enjoy being outdoors among her good friends. On days when she was too rushed to do her own cooking and had to go out to buy something already cooked, she would stop to gossip with her arms full of bowls. The neighbor she respected the most was still the watchmaker. Often she would cross the street to greet him in his tiny cupboard of a shop, taking pleasure in the gaiety of the little cuckoo clocks with their pendulums ticking away the hours in chorus.

CHAPTER VI

One afternoon in the autumn Gervaise, who had been taking some washing home to a customer in the Rue des Portes-Blanches, found herself at the bottom of the Rue des Poissonniers just as the day was declining. It had rained in the morning, the weather was very mild and an odor rose from the greasy pavement; and the laundress, burdened with her big basket, was rather out of breath, slow of step, and inclined to take her ease as she ascended the street with the vague preoccupation of a longing increased by her weariness. She would have liked to have had something to eat. Then, on raising her eyes she beheld the name of the Rue Marcadet, and she suddenly had the idea of going to see Goujet at his forge. He had no end of times told her to look in any day she was curious to see how iron was wrought. Besides in the presence of other workmen she would ask for Etienne, and make believe that she had merely called for the youngster.

The factory was somewhere on this end of the Rue Marcadet, but she didn't know exactly where and street numbers were often lacking on those ramshackle buildings separated by vacant lots. She wouldn't have lived on this street for all the gold in the world. It was a wide street, but dirty, black with soot from factories, with holes in the pavement and deep ruts filled with stagnant water. On both sides were rows of sheds, workshops with beams and brickwork exposed so that they seemed unfinished, a messy collection of masonry. Beside them were dubious lodging houses and even more dubious taverns. All she could recall was that the bolt factory was next to a yard full of scrap iron and rags, a sort of open sewer spread over the ground, storing merchandise worth hundreds of thousands of francs, according to Goujet.

The street was filled with a noisy racket. Exhaust pipes on roofs puffed out violent jets of steam; an automatic sawmill added a rhythmic screeching; a button factory shook the ground with the rumbling of its machines. She was looking up toward the Montmartre height, hesitant, uncertain whether to continue, when a gust of wind blew down a mass of sooty smoke that covered the entire street. She closed her eyes and held her breath. At that moment she heard the sound of hammers in cadence. Without realizing it, she had arrived directly in front of the bolt factory which she now recognized by the vacant lot beside it full of piles of scrap iron and old rags.

She still hesitated, not knowing where to enter. A broken fence opened a passage which seemed to lead through the heaps of rubbish from some buildings recently pulled down. Two planks had been thrown across a large puddle of muddy water that barred the way. She ended by venturing along them, turned to the left and found herself lost in the depths of a strange forest of old carts, standing on end with their shafts in the air, and of hovels in ruins, the wood-work of which was still standing. Toward the back, stabbing through the half-light of sundown, a flame gleamed red. The clamor of the hammers had ceased. She was advancing carefully when a workman, his face blackened with coal-dust and wearing a goatee passed near her, casting a side-glance with his pale eyes.

"Sir," asked she, "it's here is it not that a boy named Etienne works? He's my son."

"Etienne, Etienne," repeated the workman in a hoarse voice as he twisted himself about. "Etienne; no I don't know him."

An alcoholic reek like that from old brandy casks issued from his mouth. Meeting a woman in this dark corner seemed to be giving the fellow ideas, and so Gervaise drew back saying:

"But yet it's here that Monsieur Goujet works, isn't it?"

"Ah. Goujet, yes." said the workman; "I know Goujet. If you come for Goujet, go right to the end."

And turning round he called out at the top of his voice, which had a sound of cracked brass:

"I say Golden-Mug, here's a lady wants you."

But a clanging of iron drowned the cry. Gervaise went to the end. She reached a door and stretching out her neck looked in. At first she could distinguish nothing. The forge had died down, but there was still a little glow which held back the advancing shadows from its corner. Great shadows seemed to float in the air. At times black shapes passed before the fire, shutting off this last bit of brightness, silhouettes of men so strangely magnified that their arms and legs were indistinct. Gervaise, not daring to venture in, called from the doorway in a faint voice:

"Monsieur Goujet. Monsieur Goujet."

Suddenly all became lighted up. Beneath the puff of the bellows a jet of white flame had ascended and the whole interior of the shed could be seen, walled in by wooden planks, with openings roughly plastered over, and brick walls reinforcing the corners. Coal-ash had painted the whole expanse a sooty gray. Spider webs hung from the beams like rags hung up to dry, heavy with the accumulated dust of years. On shelves along the walls, or hanging from nails, or tossed into corners, she saw rusty iron, battered implements and huge tools. The white flame flared higher, like an explosion of dazzling sunlight revealing the trampled dirt underfoot, where the polished steel of four anvils fixed on blocks took on a reflection of silver sprinkled with gold.

Then Gervaise recognized Goujet in front of the forge by his beautiful yellow beard. Etienne was blowing the bellows. Two other workmen were there, but she only beheld Goujet and walked forward and stood before him.

"Why it's Madame Gervaise." he exclaimed with a bright look on his face.

"What a pleasant surprise."

But as his comrades appeared to be rather amused, he pushed Etienne towards his mother and resumed:

"You've come to see the youngster. He behaves himself well, he's beginning to get some strength in his wrists."

"Well." she said, "it isn't easy to find your way here. I thought I was going to the end of the world."

After telling about her journey, she asked why no one in the shop knew Etienne's name. Goujet laughed and explained to her that everybody called him "Little Zouzou" because he had his hair cut short like that of a Zouave. While they were talking together Etienne stopped working the bellows and the flame of the forge dwindled to a rosy glow amid the gathering darkness. Touched by the presence of this smiling young woman, the blacksmith stood gazing at her.

Then, as neither continued speaking, he seemed to recollect and broke the silence:

"Excuse me, Madame Gervaise, I've something that has to be finished.

You'll stay, won't you? You're not in anybody's way."

She remained. Etienne returned to the bellows. The forge was soon ablaze again with a cloud of sparks; the more so as the youngster, wanting to show his mother what he could do, was making the bellows blow a regular hurricane. Goujet, standing up watching a bar of iron heating, was waiting with the tongs in his hand. The bright glare illuminated him without a shadow—sleeves rolled back, shirt neck open, bare arms and chest. When the bar was at white heat he seized it with the tongs and cut it with a hammer on the anvil, in pieces of equal length, as though he had been gently breaking pieces of glass. Then he put the pieces back into the fire, from which he took them one by one to work them into shape. He was forging hexagonal rivets. He placed each piece in a tool-hole of the anvil, bent down the iron that was to form the head, flattened the six sides and threw the finished rivet still red-hot on to the black earth, where its bright light gradually died out; and this with a continuous hammering, wielding in his right hand a hammer weighing five pounds, completing a detail at every blow, turning and working the iron with such dexterity that he was able to talk to and look at those about him. The anvil had a silvery ring. Without a drop of perspiration, quite at his ease, he struck in a good-natured sort of a way, not appearing to exert himself more than on the evenings when he cut out pictures at home.

". . . . These are little rivets of twenty millimeters," said he in reply to Gervaise's questions. "A fellow can do his three hundred a day. But it requires practice, for one's arm soon grows weary."

And when she asked him if his wrist did not feel stiff at the end of the day he laughed aloud. Did she think him a young lady? His wrist had had plenty of drudgery for fifteen years past; it was now as strong as the iron implements it had been so long in contact with. She was right though; a gentleman who had never forged a rivet or a bolt, and who would try to show off with his five pound hammer, would find himself precious stiff in the course of a couple of hours. It did not seem much, but a few years of it often did for some very strong fellows. During this conversation the other workmen were also hammering away all together. Their tall shadows danced about in the light, the red flashes of the iron that the fire traversed, the gloomy recesses, clouds of sparks darted out from beneath the hammers and shone like suns on a level with the anvils. And Gervaise, feeling happy and interested in the movement round the forge, did not think of leaving. She was going a long way round to get nearer to Etienne without having her hands burnt, when she saw the dirty and bearded workman, whom she had spoken to outside, enter.

"So you've found him, madame?" asked he in his drunken bantering way.

"You know, Golden-Mug, it's I who told madame where to find you."

He was called Salted-Mouth, otherwise Drink-without-Thirst, the brick of bricks, a dab hand at bolt forging, who wetted his iron every day with a pint and a half of brandy. He had gone out to have a drop, because he felt he wanted greasing to make him last till six o'clock. When he learnt that Little Zouzou's real name was Etienne, he thought it very funny; and he showed his black teeth as he laughed. Then he recognized Gervaise. Only the day before he had had a glass of wine with Coupeau. You could speak to Coupeau about Salted-Mouth, otherwise Drink-without-Thirst; he would at once say: "He's a jolly dog." Ah. That joker Coupeau. He was one of the right sort; he stood treat oftener than his turn.

"I'm awfully glad to know you're his missus," added he.

"He deserves to have a pretty wife. Eh, Golden-Mug, madame is a fine woman, isn't she?"

He was becoming quite gallant, sidling up towards the laundress, who took hold of her basket and held it in front of her so as to keep him at a distance. Goujet, annoyed and seeing that his comrade was joking because of his friendship for Gervaise, called out to him:

"I say, lazybones, what about the forty millimeter bolts? Do you think you're equal to them now that you've got your gullet full, you confounded guzzler?"

The blacksmith was alluding to an order for big bolts which necessitated two beaters at the anvil.

"I'm ready to start at this moment, big baby." replied Salted-Mouth, otherwise Drink-without-Thirst. "It sucks it's thumb and thinks itself a man. In spite of your size I'm equal to you."

"Yes, that's it, at once. Look sharp and off we go."

"Right you are, my boy."

They taunted each other, stimulated by Gervaise's presence. Goujet placed the pieces of iron that had been cut beforehand in the fire, then he fixed a tool-hole of large bore on an anvil. His comrade had taken from against the wall two sledge-hammers weighing twenty pounds each, the two big sisters of the factory whom the workers called Fifine and Dedele. And he continued to brag, talking of a half-gross of rivets which he had forged for the Dunkirk lighthouse, regular jewels, things to be put in a museum, they were so daintily finished off. Hang it all, no. he did not fear competition; before meeting with another chap like him, you might search every factory in the capital. They were going to have a laugh; they would see what they would see.

"Madame will be judge," said he, turning towards the young woman.

"Enough chattering," cried Goujet. "Now then, Zouzou, show your muscle.

It's not hot enough, my lad."

But Salted-Mouth, otherwise Drink-without-Thirst, asked: "So we strike together?"

"Not a bit of it. Each his own bolt, my friend."

This statement operated as a damper, and Goujet's comrade, on hearing it, remained speechless, in spite of his boasting. Bolts of forty millimeters fashioned by one man had never before been seen; the more so as the bolts were to be round-headed, a work of great difficulty, a real masterpiece to achieve.

The three other workmen came over, leaving their jobs, to watch. A tall, lean one wagered a bottle of wine that Goujet would be beaten. Meanwhile the two blacksmiths had chosen their sledge hammers with eyes closed, because Fifine weighed a half pound more than Dedele. Salted-Mouth, otherwise Drink-without-Thirst, had the good luck to put his hand on Dedele; Fifine fell to Golden-Mug.

While waiting for the iron to get hot enough, Salted-Mouth, otherwise Drink-without-Thirst, again showing off, struck a pose before the anvil while casting side glances toward Gervaise. He planted himself solidly, tapping his feet impatiently like a man ready for a fight, throwing all his strength into practice swings with Dedele. My God. He was good at this; he could have flattened the Vendome column like a pancake.

"Now then, off you go." said Goujet, placing one of the pieces of iron, as thick as a girl's wrist, in the tool-hole.

Salted-Mouth, otherwise Drink-without-Thirst, leant back, and swung Dedele round with both hands. Short and lean, with his goatee bristling, and with his wolf-like eyes glaring beneath his unkempt hair, he seemed to snap at each swing of the hammer, springing up from the ground as though carried away by the force he put into the blow. He was a fierce one, who fought with the iron, annoyed at finding it so hard, and he even gave a grunt whenever he thought he had planted a fierce stroke. Perhaps brandy did weaken other people's arms, but he needed brandy in his veins, instead of blood. The drop he had taken a little while before had made his carcass as warm as a boiler; he felt he had the power of a steam-engine within him. And the iron seemed to be afraid of him this time; he flattened it more easily than if it had been a quid of tobacco. And it was a sight to see how Dedele waltzed. She cut such capers, with her tootsies in the air, just like a little dancer at the Elysee Montmartre, who exhibits her fine underclothes; for it would never do to dawdle, iron is so deceitful, it cools at once, just to spite the hammer. With thirty blows, Salted-Mouth, otherwise Drink-without-Thirst, had fashioned the head of his bolt. But he panted, his eyes were half out of his head, and got into a great rage as he felt his arms growing tired. Then, carried away by wrath, jumping about and yelling, he gave two more blows, just out of revenge for his trouble. When he took the bolt from the hole, it was deformed, its head being askew like a hunchback's.

"Come now. Isn't that quickly beaten into shape?" said he all the same, with his self-confidence, as he presented his work to Gervaise.

"I'm no judge, sir," replied the laundress, reservedly.

But she saw plainly enough the marks of Dedele's last two kicks on the bolt, and she was very pleased. She bit her lips so as not to laugh, for now Goujet had every chance of winning.

It was now Golden-Mug's turn. Before commencing, he gave the laundress a look full of confident tenderness. Then he did not hurry himself. He measured his distance, and swung the hammer from on high with all his might and at regular intervals. He had the classic style, accurate, evenly balanced, and supple. Fifine, in his hands, did not cut capers, like at a dance-hall, but made steady, certain progress; she rose and fell in cadence, like a lady of quality solemnly leading some ancient minuet.

There was no brandy in Golden-Mug's veins, only blood, throbbing powerfully even into Fifine and controlling the job. That stalwart fellow. What a magnificent man he was at work. The high flame of the forge shone full on his face. His whole face seemed golden indeed with his short hair curling over his forehead and his splendid yellow beard. His neck was as straight as a column and his immense chest was wide enough for a woman to sleep across it. His shoulders and sculptured arms seemed to have been copied from a giant's statue in some museum. You could see his muscles swelling, mountains of flesh rippling and hardening under the skin; his shoulders, his chest, his neck expanded; he seemed to shed light about him, becoming beautiful and all-powerful like a kindly god.

He had now swung Fifine twenty times, his eyes always fixed on the iron, drawing a deep breath with each blow, yet showing only two great drops of sweat trickling down from his temples. He counted: "Twenty-one, twenty-two, twenty-three…" calmly Fifine continued, like a noble lady dancing.

"What a show-off," jeeringly murmured Salted-Mouth, otherwise Drink-without-Thirst.

Gervaise, standing opposite Goujet, looked at him with an affectionate smile. My God. What fools men are. Here these two men were, pounding on their bolts to pay court to her. She understood it. They were battling with hammer blows, like two big red roosters vying for the favors of a little white hen. Sometimes the human heart has fantastic ways of expressing itself. This thundering of Dedele and Fifine upon the anvil was for her, this forge roaring and overflowing was for her. They were forging their love before her, battling over her.

To be honest, she rather enjoyed it. All women are happy to receive compliments. The mighty blows of Golden-Mug found echoes in her heart; they rang within her, a crystal-clear music in time with the throbbing of her pulse. She had the feeling that this hammering was driving something deep inside of her, something solid, something hard as the iron of the bolt.

She had no doubt Goujet would win. Salted-Mouth, otherwise Drink-without-Thirst, was much too ugly in his dirty tunic, jumping around like a monkey that had escaped from a zoo. She waited, blushing red, happy that the heat could explain the blush.

Goujet was still counting.

"And twenty-eight." cried he at length, laying the hammer on the ground.

"It's finished; you can look."

The head of the bolt was clean, polished, and without a flaw, regular goldsmith's work, with the roundness of a marble cast in a mold. The other men looked at it and nodded their heads; there was no denying it was lovely enough to be worshipped. Salted-Mouth, otherwise Drink-without-Thirst, tried indeed to chuff; but it was no use, and ended by returning to his anvil, with his nose put out of joint. Gervaise had squeezed up against Goujet, as though to get a better view. Etienne having let go the bellows, the forge was once more becoming enveloped in shadow, like a brilliant red sunset suddenly giving way to black night. And the blacksmith and the laundress experienced a sweet pleasure in feeling this gloom surround them in that shed black with soot and filings, and where an odor of old iron prevailed. They could not have thought themselves more alone in the Bois de Vincennes had they met there in the depths of some copse. He took her hand as though he had conquered her.

Outside, they scarcely exchanged a word. All he could find to say was that she might have taken Etienne away with her, had it not been that there was still another half-hour's work to get through. When she started away he called her back, wanting a few more minutes with her.

"Come along. You haven't seen all the place. It's quite interesting."

He led her to another shed where the owner was installing a new machine. She hesitated in the doorway, oppressed by an instinctive dread. The great hall was vibrating from the machines and black shadows filled the air. He reassured her with a smile, swearing that there was nothing to fear, only she should be careful not to let her skirts get caught in any of the gears. He went first and she followed into the deafening hubbub of whistling, amid clouds of steam peopled by human shadows moving busily.

The passages were very narrow and there were obstacles to step over, holes to avoid, passing carts to move back from. She couldn't distinguish anything clearly or hear what Goujet was saying.

Gervaise looked up and stopped to stare at the leather belts hanging from the roof in a gigantic spider web, each strip ceaselessly revolving. The steam engine that drove them was hidden behind a low brick wall so that the belts seemed to be moving by themselves. She stumbled and almost fell while looking up.

Goujet raised his voice with explanations. There were the tapping machines operated by women, which put threads on bolts and nuts. Their steel gears were shining with oil. She could follow the entire process. She nodded her head and smiled.

She was still a little tense, however, feeling uneasy at being so small among these rough metalworkers. She jumped back more than once, her blood suddenly chilled by the dull thud of a machine.

Goujet had stopped before one of the rivet machines. He stood there brooding, his head lowered, his gaze fixed. This machine forged forty millimeter rivets with the calm ease of a giant. Nothing could be simpler. The stoker took the iron shank from the furnace; the striker put it into the socket, where a continuous stream of water cooled it to prevent softening of the steel. The press descended and the bolt flew out onto the ground, its head as round as though cast in a mold. Every twelve hours this machine made hundreds of kilograms of bolts.

Goujet was not a mean person, but there were moments when he wanted to take Fifine and smash this machine to bits because he was angry to see that its arms were stronger than his own. He reasoned with himself, telling himself that human flesh cannot compete with steel. But he was still deeply hurt. The day would come when machinery would destroy the skilled worker. Their day's pay had already fallen from twelve francs to nine francs. There was talk of cutting it again. He stared at it, frowning, for three minutes without saying a word. His yellow beard seemed to bristle defiantly. Then, gradually an expression of resignation came over his face and he turned toward Gervaise who was clinging tightly to him and said with a sad smile:

"Well. That machine would certainly win a contest. But perhaps it will be for the good of mankind in the long run."

Gervaise didn't care a bit about the welfare of mankind. Smiling, she said to Goujet:

"I like yours better, because they show the hand of an artist."

Hearing this gave him great happiness because he had been afraid that she might be scornful of him after seeing the machines. My God. He might be stronger than Salted-Mouth, otherwise Drink-without-Thirst, but the machines were stronger yet. When Gervaise finally took her leave, Goujet was so happy that he almost crushed her with a hug.

The laundress went every Saturday to the Goujets to deliver their washing. They still lived in the little house in the Rue Neuve de la Goutte-d'Or. During the first year she had regularly repaid them twenty francs a month; so as not to jumble up the accounts, the washing-book was only made up at the end of each month, and then she added to the amount whatever sum was necessary to make the twenty francs, for the Goujets' washing rarely came to more than seven or eight francs during that time. She had therefore paid off nearly half the sum owing, when one quarter day, not knowing what to do, some of her customers not having kept their promises, she had been obliged to go to the Goujets and borrow from them sufficient for her rent. On two other occasions she had also applied to them for the money to pay her workwomen, so that the debt had increased again to four hundred and twenty-five francs. Now, she no longer gave a halfpenny; she worked off the amount solely by the washing. It was not that she worked less, or that her business was not so prosperous. But something was going wrong in her home; the money seemed to melt away, and she was glad when she was able to make both ends meet. My God. What's the use of complaining as long as one gets by. She was putting on weight and this caused her to become a bit lazy. She no longer had the energy that she had in the past. . . . Well, there was always something coming in.

Madame Goujet felt a motherly concern for Gervaise and sometimes reprimanded her. This wasn't due to the money owed but because she liked her and didn't want to see her get into difficulties. She never mentioned the debt. In short, she behaved with the utmost delicacy.

The morrow of Gervaise's visit to the forge happened to be the last Saturday of the month. When she reached the Goujets, where she made a point of going herself, her basket had so weighed on her arms that she was quite two minutes before she could get her breath. One would hardly believe how heavy clothes are, especially when there are sheets among them.

"Are you sure you've brought everything?" asked Madame Goujet. She was very strict on that point. She insisted on having her washing brought home without a single article being kept back for the sake of order, as she said. She also required the laundress always to come on the day arranged and at the same hour; in that way there was no time wasted.

". . . yes, everything is here," replied Gervaise smiling. "You know I never leave anything behind."

"That's true," admitted Madame Goujet; "you've got into many bad habits but you're still free of that one."

And while the laundress emptied her basket, laying the linen on the bed, the old woman praised her; she never burnt the things nor tore them like so many others did, neither did she pull the buttons off with the iron; only she used too much blue and made the shirt-fronts too stiff with starch.

"Just look, it's like cardboard," continued she, making one crackle between her fingers. "My son does not complain, but it cuts his neck. To-morrow his neck will be all scratched when we return from Vincennes."

"No, don't say that." exclaimed Gervaise, quite grieved. "To look nice, shirts must be rather stiff, otherwise it's as though one had a rag on one's body. You should just see what the gentlemen wear. I do all your things myself. The workwomen never touch them and I assure you I take great pains. I would, if necessary, do everything over a dozen times, because it's for you, you know."

She slightly blushed as she stammered out the last words. She was afraid of showing the great pleasure she took in ironing Goujet's shirts. She certainly had no wicked thoughts, but she was none the less a little bit ashamed.

". . . . I'm not complaining of your work; I know it's perfection," said Madame Goujet. "For instance, you've done this cap splendidly, only you could bring out the embroidery like that. And the flutings are all so even . . . . I recognize your hand at once. When you give even a dish-cloth to one of your workwomen I detect it at once. In future, use a little less starch, that's all. Goujet does not care to look like a stylish gentleman."

She had taken out her notebook and was crossing off the various items. Everything was in order. She noticed that Gervaise was charging six sous for each bonnet. She protested, but had to agree that it was in

line with present prices. Men's shirts were five sous, women's underwear four sous, pillow-cases a sou and a half, and aprons one sou. No,
the prices weren't high. Some laundresses charged a sou more for each
item.

Gervaise was now calling out the soiled clothes, as she packed them
in her basket, for Madame Goujet to list. Then she lingered on, embarrassed by a request which she wished to make.

"Madame Goujet," she said at length, "if it does not inconvenience
you, I would like to take the money for the month's washing."

It so happened that that month was a very heavy one, the account
they had made up together amounting to ten francs, seven sous.
Madame Goujet looked at her a moment in a serious manner, then she
replied:

"My child, it shall be as you wish. I will not refuse you the money
as you are in need of it. Only it's scarcely the way to pay off your debt;
I say that for your sake, you know. Really now, you should be careful."

Gervaise received the lecture with bowed head and stammering excuses. The ten francs were to make up the amount of a bill she had
given her coke merchant. But on hearing the word "bill," Madame Goujet became severer still. She gave herself as an example; she had reduced her expenditure ever since Goujet's wages had been lowered
from twelve to nine francs a day. When one was wanting in wisdom
while young, one dies of hunger in one's old age. But she held back
and didn't tell Gervaise that she gave her their laundry only in order to
help her pay off the debt. Before that she had done all her own washing, and she would have to do it herself again if the laundry continued
taking so much cash out of her pocket. Gervaise spoke her thanks and
left quickly as soon as she had received the ten francs seven sous. Outside on the landing she was so relieved she wanted to dance. She was
becoming used to the annoying, unpleasant difficulties caused by a
shortage of money and preferred to remember not the embarrassment
but the joy in escaping from them.

It was also on that Saturday that Gervaise met with a rather strange
adventure as she descended the Goujets' staircase. She was obliged to
stand up close against the stair-rail with her basket to make way for a
tall bare-headed woman who was coming up, carrying in her hand a

very fresh mackerel, with bloody gills, in a piece of paper. She recognized Virginie, the girl whose face she had slapped at the wash-house. They looked each other full in the face. Gervaise shut her eyes. She thought for a moment that she was going to be hit in the face with the fish. But no, Virginie even smiled slightly. Then, as her basket was blocking the staircase, the laundress wished to show how polite she, too, could be.

"I beg your pardon," she said.

"You are completely excused," replied the tall brunette.

And they remained conversing together on the stairs, reconciled at once without having ventured on a single allusion to the past. Virginie, then twenty-nine years old, had become a superb woman of strapping proportions, her face, however, looking rather long between her two plaits of jet black hair. She at once began to relate her history just to show off. She had a husband now; she had married in the spring an ex-journeyman cabinetmaker, who recently left the army, and who had applied to be admitted into the police, because a post of that kind is more to be depended upon and more respectable. She had been out to buy the mackerel for him.

"He adores mackerel," said she. "We must spoil them, those naughty men, mustn't we? But come up. You shall see our home. We are standing in a draught here."

After Gervaise had told of her own marriage and that she had formerly occupied the very apartment Virginie now had, Virginie urged her even more strongly to come up since it is always nice to visit a spot where one had been happy.

Virginie had lived for five years on the Left Bank at Gros-Caillou. That was where she had met her husband while he was still in the army. But she got tired of it, and wanted to come back to the Goutte-d'Or neighborhood where she knew everyone. She had only been living in the rooms opposite the Goujets for two weeks . . . . Everything was still a mess, but they were slowly getting it in order.

Then, still on the staircase, they finally told each other their names.

"Madame Coupeau."

"Madame Poisson."

And from that time forth, they called each other on every possible occasion Madame Poisson and Madame Coupeau, solely for the pleasure of being madame, they who in former days had been acquainted when occupying rather questionable positions. However, Gervaise felt rather mistrustful at heart. Perhaps the tall brunette had made it up the better to avenge herself for the beating at the wash-house by concocting some plan worthy of a spiteful hypocritical creature. Gervaise determined to be upon her guard. For the time being, as Virginie behaved so nicely, she would be nice also.

In the room upstairs, Poisson, the husband, a man of thirty-five, with a cadaverous-looking countenance and carroty moustaches and beard, was seated working at a table near the window. He was making little boxes. His only tools were a knife, a tiny saw the size of a nail file and a pot of glue. He was using wood from old cigar boxes, thin boards of unfinished mahogany upon which he executed fretwork and embellishments of extraordinary delicacy. All year long he worked at making the same size boxes, only varying them occasionally by inlay work, new designs for the cover, or putting compartments inside. He did not sell his work, he distributed it in presents to persons of his acquaintance. It was for his own amusement, a way of occupying his time while waiting for his appointment to the police force. It was all that remained with him from his former occupation of cabinetmaking.

Poisson rose from his seat and politely bowed to Gervaise, when his wife introduced her as an old friend. But he was no talker; he at once returned to his little saw. From time to time he merely glanced in the direction of the mackerel placed on the corner of the chest of drawers. Gervaise was very pleased to see her old lodging once more. She told them whereabouts her own furniture stood, and pointed out the place on the floor where Nana had been born. How strange it was to meet like this again, after so many years. They never dreamed of running into each other like this and even living in the same rooms.

Virginie added some further details. Her husband had inherited a little money from an aunt and he would probably set her up in a shop before long. Meanwhile she was still sewing. At length, at the end of a full half hour, the laundress took her leave. Poisson scarcely seemed to notice her departure. While seeing her to the door, Virginie promised to return the visit. And she would have Gervaise do her laundry. While Virginie was keeping her in further conversation on the landing, Gervaise had the feeling that she wanted to say something about Lantier and her sister Adele, and this notion upset her a bit. But not a word was uttered respecting those unpleasant things; they parted, wishing each other good-bye in a very amiable manner.

"Good-bye, Madame Coupeau."

"Good-bye, Madame Poisson."

That was the starting point of a great friendship. A week later, Virginie never passed Gervaise's shop without going in; and she remained there gossiping for hours together, to such an extent indeed that Poisson, filled with anxiety, fearing she had been run over, would come and seek her with his expressionless and death-like countenance. Now that she was seeing the dressmaker every day Gervaise became aware of a strange obsession. Every time Virginie began to talk Gervaise had the feeling Lantier was going to be mentioned. So she had Lantier on her mind throughout all of Virginie's visits. This was silly because, in fact, she didn't care a bit about Lantier or Adele at this time. She was quite certain that she had no curiosity as to what had happened to either of them. But this obsession got hold of her in spite of herself. Anyway, she didn't hold it against Virginie, it wasn't her fault, surely. She enjoyed being with her and looked forward to her visits.

Meanwhile winter had come, the Coupeaus' fourth winter in the Rue de la Goutte-d'Or. December and January were particularly cold. It froze hard as it well could. After New Year's Day the snow remained three weeks without melting. It did not interfere with work, but the contrary, for winter is the best season for the ironers. It was very pleasant inside the shop. There was never any ice on the window-panes like there was at the grocer's and the hosier's opposite. The stove was always stuffed with coke and kept things as hot as a Turkish bath. With the laundry steaming overhead you could almost imagine it was summer. You were quite comfortable with the doors closed and so much warmth everywhere that you were tempted to doze off with your eyes open. Gervaise laughed and said it reminded her of summer in the country. The street traffic made no noise in the snow and you could hardly hear the pedestrians who passed by. Only children's voices were heard in the silence, especially the noisy band of urchins who had made a long slide in the gutter near the blacksmith's shop.

Gervaise would sometimes go over to the door, wipe the moisture from one of the panes with her hand, and look out to see what was happening to her neighborhood due to this extraordinary cold spell. Not one nose was being poked out of the adjacent shops. The entire neighborhood was muffled in snow. The only person she was able to exchange nods with was the coal-dealer next door, who still walked out bare-headed despite the severe freeze.

What was especially enjoyable in this awful weather was to have some nice hot coffee in the middle of the day. The workwomen had no cause for complaint. The mistress made it very strong and without a grain of chicory. It was quite different to Madame Fauconnier's coffee, which was like ditch-water. Only whenever mother Coupeau undertook to make it, it was always an interminable time before it was ready, because she would fall asleep over the kettle. On these occasions, when the workwomen had finished their lunch, they would do a little ironing while waiting for the coffee.

It so happened that on the morrow of Twelfth-day half-past twelve struck and still the coffee was not ready. It seemed to persist in declining to pass through the strainer. Mother Coupeau tapped against the pot with a tea-spoon; and one could hear the drops falling slowly, one by one, and without hurrying themselves any the more.

"Leave it alone," said tall Clemence; "you'll make it thick. Today there'll be as much to eat as to drink."

Tall Clemence was working on a man's shirt, the plaits of which she separated with her finger-nail. She had caught a cold, her eyes were frightfully swollen and her chest was shaken with fits of coughing, which doubled her up beside the work-table. With all that she had not even a handkerchief round her neck and she was dressed in some cheap flimsy woolen stuff in which she shivered. Close by, Madame Putois, wrapped up in flannel muffled up to her ears, was ironing a petticoat which she turned round the skirt-board, the narrow end of which rested on the back of a chair; while a sheet laid on the floor prevented the petticoat from getting dirty as it trailed along the tiles. Gervaise alone occupied half the work-table with some embroidered muslin curtains, over which she passed her iron in a straight line with her arms stretched out to avoid making any creases. All on a sudden the coffee running through noisily caused her to raise her head. It was that squint-eyed Augustine who had just given it an outlet by thrusting a spoon through the strainer.

"Leave it alone." cried Gervaise. "Whatever is the matter with you? It'll be like drinking mud now."

Mother Coupeau had placed five glasses on a corner of the work-table that was free. The women now left their work. The mistress always poured out the coffee herself after putting two lumps of sugar into each glass. It was the moment that they all looked forward to. On this occasion, as each one took her glass and squatted down on a little stool in front of the stove, the shop-door opened. Virginie entered, shivering all over.

"Ah, my children," said she, "it cuts you in two. I can no longer feel my ears. The cold is something awful."

"Why, it's Madame Poisson." exclaimed Gervaise. "Ah, well. You've come at the right time. You must have some coffee with us."

"On my word, I can't say no. One feels the frost in one's bones merely by crossing the street."

There was still some coffee left, luckily. Mother Coupeau went and fetched a sixth glass, and Gervaise let Virginie help herself to sugar out of politeness. The workwomen moved to give Virginie a small space close to the stove. Her nose was very red, she shivered a bit, pressing her hands which were stiff with cold around the glass to warm them. She had just come from the grocery store where you froze to death waiting for a quarter-pound of cheese and so she raved about the warmth of the shop. It felt so good on one's skin. After warming up, she stretched out her long legs and the six of them relaxed together, supping their coffee slowly, surround by all the work still to be done. Mother Coupeau and Virginie were the only ones on chairs, the others, on low benches, seemed to be sitting on the floor. Squint-eyed Augustine had pulled over a corner of the cloth below the skirt, stretching herself out on it.

No one spoke at first; all kept their noses in their glasses, enjoying their coffee.

"It's not bad, all the same," declared Clemence.

But she was seized with a fit of coughing, and almost choked. She leant her head against the wall to cough with more force.

"That's a bad cough you've got," said Virginie. "Wherever did you catch it?"

"One never knows." replied Clemence, wiping her face with her sleeve. "It must have been the other night. There were two girls who were flaying each other outside the 'Grand-Balcony.' I wanted to see, so I stood there while the snow was falling. Ah, what a drubbing. It was enough to make one die with laughing. One had her nose almost pulled off; the blood streamed on the ground. When the other, a great long stick like me, saw the blood, she slipped away as quick as she could. And I coughed nearly all night. Besides that too, men are so stupid in bed, they don't let you have any covers over you half the time."

"Pretty conduct that," murmured Madame Putois. "You're killing yourself, my girl."

"And if it pleases me to kill myself. Life isn't so very amusing. Slaving all the blessed day long to earn fifty-five sous, cooking one's blood from morning to night in front of the stove; no, you know, I've had enough of it. All the same though, this cough won't do me the service of making me croak. It'll go off the same way it came."

A short silence ensued. The good-for-nothing Clemence, who led riots in low dancing establishments, and shrieked like a screech-owl at work, always saddened everyone with her thoughts of death. Gervaise knew her well, and so merely said:

"You're never very gay the morning after a night of high living."

The truth was that Gervaise did not like this talk about women fighting. Because of the flogging at the wash-house it annoyed her whenever anyone spoke before her and Virginie of kicks with wooden shoes and of slaps in the face. It so happened, too, that Virginie was looking at her and smiling.

"By the way," she said quietly, "yesterday I saw some hair-pulling. They almost tore each other to pieces."

"Who were they?" Madame Putois inquired.

"The midwife and her maid, you know, a little blonde. What a pest the girl is. She was yelling at her employer that she had got rid of a child for the fruit woman and that she was going to tell the police if she wasn't paid to keep quiet. So the midwife slapped her right in the face and then the little blonde jumped on her and started scratching her and pulling her hair, really—by the roots. The sausage-man had to grab her to put a stop to it."

The workwomen laughed. Then they all took a sip of coffee.

"Do you believe that she really got rid of a child?" Clemence asked.

". . . yes. The rumor was all round the neighborhood," Virginie answered. "I didn't see it myself, you understand, but it's part of the job. All midwives do it."

"Well." exclaimed Madame Putois. "You have to be pretty stupid to put yourself in their hands. No thanks, you could be maimed for life. But there's a sure way to do it. Drink a glass of holy water every evening and make the sign of the cross three times over your stomach with your thumb. Then your troubles will be over."

Everyone thought mother Coupeau was asleep, but she shook her head in protest. She knew another way and it was infallible. You had to eat a hard-cooked egg every two hours, and put spinach leaves on your loins. Squint-eyed Augustine set up a hen-cackling when she heard this. They had forgotten about her. Gervaise lifted up the petticoat that was being ironed and found her rolling on the floor with laughter. She jerked her upright. What was she laughing about? Was it right for her to be eavesdropping when older people were talking, the little goose? Anyway it was time for her to deliver the laundry to a friend of Madame Lerat at Les Batignolles. So Gervaise hung a basket on her arm and pushed her toward the door. Augustine went off, sobbing and sniveling, dragging her feet in the snow.

Meanwhile mother Coupeau, Madame Putois and Clemence were discussing the effectiveness of hard-cooked eggs and spinach leaves. Then Virginie said softly:

"My God you have a fight, and then you make it up, if you have a generous heart." She leaned toward Gervaise with a smile and added, "Really, I don't hold any grudge against you for that business at the wash-house. You remember it, don't you?"

This was what Gervaise had been dreading. She guessed that the subject of Lantier and Adele would now come up.

Virginie had moved close to Gervaise so as not to be overheard by the others. Gervaise, lulled by the excessive heat, felt so limp that she couldn't even summon the willpower to change the subject. She foresaw what the tall brunette would say and her heart was stirred with an emotion which she didn't want to admit to herself.

"I hope I'm not hurting your feelings," Virginie continued. "Often I've had it on the tip of my tongue. But since we are now on the subject, word of honor, I don't have any grudge against you."

She stirred her remaining coffee and then took a small sip. Gervaise, with her heart in her throat, wondered if Virginie had really forgiven her as completely as she said, for she seemed to observe sparks in her dark eyes.

"You see," Virginie went on, "you had an excuse. They played a really rotten, dirty trick on you. To be fair about it, if it had been me, I'd have taken a knife to her."

She drank another small sip, then added rapidly without a pause:

"Anyway, it didn't bring them happiness, mon Dieu. Not a bit of it. They went to live over at La Glaciere, in a filthy street that was always muddy. I went two days later to have lunch with them. I can tell you, it was quite a trip by bus. Well, I found them already fighting. Really, as I came in they were boxing each other's ears. Fine pair of love birds. Adele isn't worth the rope to hang her. I say that even if she is my own sister. It would take too long to relate all the nasty tricks she played on me, and anyhow, it's between the two of us. As for Lantier—well, he's no good either. He'd beat the hide off you for anything, and with his fist closed too. They fought all the time. The police even came once."

Virginie went on about other fights . . . she knew of things that would make your hair stand up. Gervaise listened in silence, her face pale. It was nearly seven years since she had heard a word about Lantier. She hadn't realized what a strong curiosity she had as to what had become of the poor man, even though he had treated her badly. And she never would have believed that just the mention of his name could put such a glowing warmth in the pit of her stomach. She certainly had no reason to be jealous of Adele any more but she rejoiced to think of her body all bruised from the beatings. She could have listened to Virginie all night, but she didn't ask any questions, not wanting to appear much interested.

Virginie stopped to sip at her coffee. Gervaise, realizing that she was expected to say something, asked, with a pretense of indifference:

"*Are they still living at La Glaciere?*"

"No." the other replied. "Didn't I tell you? They separated last week.

One morning, Adele moved out and Lantier didn't chase after her."

"So they're separated." Gervaise exclaimed.

"Who are you talking about?" Clemence asked, interrupting her conversation with mother Coupeau and Madame Putois.

"Nobody you know," said Virginie.

She was looking at Gervaise carefully and could see that she was upset. She moved still closer, maliciously finding pleasure in bringing up these old stories. Of a sudden she asked Gervaise what she would do if Lantier came round here. Men were really such strange creatures, he might decide to return to his first love. This caused Gervaise to sit up very straight and dignified. She was a married woman; she would send Lantier off immediately. There was no possibility of anything further between them, not even a handshake. She would not even want to look that man in the face.

"I know that Etienne is his son, and that's a relationship that re-mains," she said. "If Lantier wants to see his son, I'll send the boy to him because you can't stop a father from seeing his child. But as for myself, I don't want him to touch me even with the tip of his finger. That is all finished."

Desiring to break off this conversation, she seemed to awake with a start and called out to the women:

"You ladies. Do you think all these clothes are going to iron them-selves? Get to work."

The workwomen, slow from the heat and general laziness, didn't hurry themselves, but went right on talking, gossiping about other peo-ple they had known.

Gervaise shook herself and got to her feet. Couldn't earn money by sitting all day. She was the first to return to the ironing, but found that her curtains had been spotted by the coffee and she had to rub out the stains with a damp cloth. The other women were now stretching and getting ready to begin ironing.

Clemence had a terrible attack of coughing as soon as she moved. Finally she was able to return to the shirt she had been doing. Madame Putois began to work on the petticoat again.

"Well, good-bye," said Virginie. "I only came out for a quarter-pound of Swiss cheese. Poisson must think I've frozen to death on the way."

She had only just stepped outside when she turned back to say that Augustine was at the end of the street, sliding on the ice with some urchins. The squint-eyed imp rushed in all red-faced and out of breath with snow all in her hair. She didn't mind the scolding she received, merely saying that she hadn't been able to walk fast because of the ice and then some brats threw snow at her.

The afternoons were all the same these winter days. The laundry was the refuge for anyone in the neighborhood who was cold. There was an endless procession of gossiping women. Gervaise took pride in the comforting warmth of her shop and welcomed those who came in, "holding a salon," as the Lorilleuxs and the Boches remarked meanly.

Gervaise was always thoughtful and generous. Sometimes she even invited poor people in if she saw them shivering outside. A friendship sprang up with an elderly house-painter who was seventy. He lived in an attic room and was slowly dying of cold and hunger. His three sons had been killed in the war. He survived the best he could, but it had been two years since he had been able to hold a paint-brush in his hand. Whenever Gervaise saw Old Man Bru walking outside, she would call him in and arrange a place for him close to the stove. Often she gave him some bread and cheese. Old Man Bru's face was as wrinkled as a withered apple. He would sit there, with his stooping shoulders and his white beard, without saying a word, just listening to the coke sputtering in the stove. Maybe he was thinking of his fifty years of hard work on high ladders, his fifty years spent painting doors and whitewashing ceilings in every corner of Paris.

"Well, Old Man Bru," Gervaise would say, "what are you thinking of now?"

"Nothing much. All sorts of things," he would answer quietly.

The workwomen tried to joke with him to cheer him up, saying he was worrying over his love affairs, but he scarcely listened to them before he fell back into his habitual attitude of meditative melancholy.

Virginie now frequently spoke to Gervaise of Lantier. She seemed to find amusement in filling her mind with ideas of her old lover just for the pleasure of embarrassing her by making suggestions. One day she related that she had met him; then, as the laundress took no notice, she said nothing further, and it was only on the morrow that she added he had spoken about her for a long time, and with a great show of affection. Gervaise was much upset by these reports whispered in her ear in a corner of the shop. The mention of Lantier's name always caused a worried sensation in the pit of her stomach. She certainly thought herself strong; she wished to lead the life of an industrious woman, because labor is the half of happiness. So she never considered Coupeau in this matter, having nothing to reproach herself with as regarded her husband, not even in her thoughts. But with a hesitating and suffering heart, she would think of the blacksmith. It seemed to her that the memory of Lantier—that slow possession which she was resuming—rendered her unfaithful to Goujet, to their unavowed love, sweet as friendship. She passed sad days whenever she felt herself guilty towards her good friend. She would have liked to have had no affection for anyone but him outside of her family. It was a feeling far above all carnal thoughts, for the signs of which upon her burning face Virginie was ever on the watch.

As soon as spring came Gervaise often went and sought refuge with Goujet. She could no longer sit musing on a chair without immediately thinking of her first lover; she pictured him leaving Adele, packing his clothes in the bottom of their old trunk, and returning to her in a cab. The days when she went out, she was seized with the most foolish fears in the street; she was ever thinking she heard Lantier's footsteps behind her. She did not dare turn round, but tremblingly fancied she felt his hands seizing her round the waist. He was, no doubt, spying upon her; he would appear before her some afternoon; and the bare idea threw her into a cold perspiration, because he would to a certainty kiss her on the ear, as he used to do in former days solely to tease her. It was this kiss which frightened her; it rendered her deaf beforehand; it filled her with a buzzing amidst which she could only distinguish the sound of her heart beating violently. So, as soon as these fears seized upon her, the forge was her only shelter; there, under Goujet's protection, she once more became easy and smiling, as his sonorous hammer drove away her disagreeable reflections.

What a happy time. The laundress took particular pains with the washing of her customer in the Rue des Portes-Blanches; she always took it home herself because that errand, every Friday, was a ready excuse for passing through the Rue Marcadet and looking in at the forge. The moment she turned the corner of the street she felt light and gay, as though in the midst of those plots of waste land surrounded by gray factories, she were out in the country; the roadway black with coal-dust, the plumage of steam over the roofs, amused her as much as a moss-covered path leading through masses of green foliage in a wood in the environs; and she loved the dull horizon, streaked by the tall factory-chimneys, the Montmartre heights, which hid the heavens from view, the chalky white houses pierced with the uniform openings of their windows. She would slacken her steps as she drew near, jumping over the pools of water, and finding a pleasure in traversing the deserted ins and outs of the yard full of old building materials. Right at the further end the forge shone with a brilliant light, even at mid-day. Her heart leapt with the dance of the hammers. When she entered, her face turned quite red, the little fair hairs at the nape of her neck flew about like those of a woman arriving at some lovers' meeting. Goujet was expecting her, his arms and chest bare, while he hammered harder on the anvil on those days so as to make himself heard at a distance. He divined her presence, and greeted her with a good silent laugh in his yellow beard. But she would not let him leave off his work; she begged him to take up his hammer again, because she loved him the more when he wielded it with his big arms swollen with muscles. She would go and give Etienne a gentle tap on the cheek, as he hung on to the bellows, and then remain for an hour watching the rivets.

The two did not exchange a dozen words. They could not have more completely satisfied their love if alone in a room with the door double-locked. The snickering of Salted-Mouth, otherwise Drink-without-Thirst, did not bother them in the least, for they no longer even heard him. At the end of a quarter of an hour she would begin to feel slightly oppressed; the heat, the powerful smell, the ascending smoke, made her dizzy, while the dull thuds of the hammers shook her from the crown of her head to the soles of her feet. Then she desired nothing more; it was her pleasure. Had Goujet pressed her in his arms it would not have procured her so sweet an emotion. She drew close to him that she might feel the wind raised by his hammer beat upon her cheek, and become, as it were, a part of the blow he struck. When the sparks made her soft hands smart, she did not withdraw them; on the contrary, she enjoyed the rain of fire which stung her skin. He for certain, divined the happiness which she tasted there; he always kept the most difficult work for the Fridays, so as to pay his court to her with all his strength and all his skill; he no longer spared himself at the risk of splitting the anvils in two, as he panted and his loins vibrated with the joy he was procuring her. All one spring-time their love thus filled Goujet with the rumbling of a storm. It was an idyll amongst giant-like labor in the midst of the glare of the coal fire, and of the shaking of the shed, the cracking carcass of which was black with soot. All that beaten iron, kneaded like red wax, preserved the rough marks of their love. When on the Fridays the laundress parted from Golden-Mug, she slowly re-ascended the Rue des Poissonniers, contented and tired, her mind and her body alike tranquil.

Little by little, her fear of Lantier diminished; her good sense got the better of her. At that time she would still have led a happy life, had it not been for Coupeau, who was decidedly going to the bad. One day she just happened to be returning from the forge, when she fancied she recognized Coupeau inside Old Man Colombe's The Saloon, in the act of treating himself to a round of vitriol in the company of My-Boots, Bibi-the-Smoker, and Salted-Mouth, otherwise Drink-without-Thirst. She passed quickly by, so as not to seem to be spying on them. But she glanced back; it was indeed Coupeau who was tossing his little glass of bad brandy down his throat with a gesture already familiar. He lied then; so he went in for brandy now. She returned home in despair; all her old dread of brandy took possession of her. She forgave the wine, because wine nourishes the workman; all kinds of spirit, on the contrary, were filth, poisons which destroyed in the workman the taste for bread. Ah. The government ought to prevent the manufacture of such horrid stuff.

On arriving at the Rue de la Goutte-d'Or, she found the whole house upset. Her workwomen had left the shop, and were in the court-yard looking up above. She questioned Clemence.

"It's old Bijard who's giving his wife a hiding," replied the ironer. "He was in the doorway, as drunk as a trooper, watching for her return from the wash-house. He whacked her up the stairs, and now he's finishing her off up there in their room. Listen, can't you hear her shrieks?"

Gervaise hastened to the spot. She felt some friendship for her washer-woman, Madame Bijard, who was a very courageous woman. She had hoped to put a stop to what was going on. Upstairs, on the sixth floor the door of the room was wide open, some lodgers were shouting on the landing, while Madame Boche, standing in front of the door, was calling out:

"Will you leave off? I shall send for the police; do you hear?"

No one dared to venture inside the room, because it was known that Bijard was like a brute beast when he was drunk. As a matter of fact, he was scarcely ever sober. The rare days on which he worked, he placed a bottle of brandy beside his blacksmith's vise, gulping some of it down every half hour. He could not keep himself going any other way. He would have blazed away like a torch if anyone had placed a lighted match close to his mouth.

"But we mustn't let her be murdered." said Gervaise, all in a tremble.

And she entered. The room, an attic, and very clean, was bare and cold, almost emptied by the drunken habits of the man, who took the very sheets from the bed to turn them into liquor. During the struggle the table had rolled away to the window, the two chairs, knocked over, had fallen with their legs in the air. In the middle of the room, on the tile floor, lay Madame Bijard, all bloody, her skirts, still soaked with the water of the wash-house, clinging to her thighs, her hair straggling in disorder. She was breathing heavily, with a rattle in her throat, as she muttered prolonged . . . s. each time she received a blow from the heel of Bijard's boot. He had knocked her down with his fists, and now he stamped upon her.

"Ah, strumpet. Ah, strumpet. Ah strumpet." grunted he in a choking voice, accompanying each blow with the word, taking a delight in repeating it, and striking all the harder the more he found his voice failing him.

Then when he could no longer speak, he madly continued to kick with a dull sound, rigid in his ragged blue blouse and overalls, his face turned purple beneath his dirty beard, and his bald forehead streaked with big red blotches. The neighbors on the landing related that he was beating her because she had refused him twenty sous that morning. Boche's voice was heard at the foot of the staircase. He was calling Madame Boche, saying:

"Come down; let them kill each other, it'll be so much scum the less."

Meanwhile, Old Man Bru had followed Gervaise into the room. Between them they were trying to get him towards the door. But he turned round, speechless and foaming at the lips, and in his pale eyes the alcohol was blazing with a murderous glare. The laundress had her wrist injured; the old workman was knocked against the table. On the floor, Madame Bijard was breathing with greater difficulty, her mouth wide open, her eyes closed. Now Bijard kept missing her. He had madly returned to the attack, but blinded by rage, his blows fell on either side, and at times he almost fell when his kicks went into space. And during all this onslaught, Gervaise beheld in a corner of the room little Lalie, then four years old, watching her father murdering her mother. The child held in her arms, as though to protect her, her sister Henriette, only recently weaned. She was standing up, her head covered with a cotton cap, her face very pale and grave. Her large black eyes gazed with a fixedness full of thought and were without a tear.

When at length Bijard, running against a chair, stumbled onto the tiled floor, where they left him snoring, Old Man Bru helped Gervaise to raise Madame Bijard. The latter was now sobbing bitterly; and Lalie, drawing near, watched her crying, being used to such sights and already resigned to them. As the laundress descended the stairs, in the silence of the now quieted house, she kept seeing before her that look of this child of four, as grave and courageous as that of a woman.

"Monsieur Coupeau is on the other side of the street," called out Clemence as soon as she caught sight of her. "He looks awfully drunk."

Coupeau was just then crossing the street. He almost smashed a pane of glass with his shoulder as he missed the door. He was in a state of complete drunkenness, with his teeth clinched and his nose inflamed. And Gervaise at once recognized the vitriol of The Saloon in the poisoned blood which paled his skin. She tried to joke and get him to bed, the same as on the days when the wine had made him merry; but he pushed her aside without opening his lips, and raised his fist in passing as he went to bed of his own accord. He made Gervaise think of the other—the drunkard who was snoring upstairs, tired out by the blows he had struck. A cold shiver passed over her. She thought of the men she knew—of her husband, of Goujet, of Lantier—her heart breaking, despairing of ever being happy.

CHAPTER VII

Gervaise's saint's day fell on the 19th of June. On such occasions, the Coupeaus always made a grand display; they feasted till they were as round as balls, and their stomachs were filled for the rest of the week. There was a complete clear out of all the money they had. The moment there were a few sous in the house they went in gorging. They invented saints for those days which the almanac had not provided with any, just for the sake of giving themselves a pretext for gormandizing. Virginie highly commended Gervaise for stuffing herself with all sorts of savory dishes. When one has a husband who turns all he can lay hands on into drink, it's good to line one's stomach well, and not to let everything go off in liquids. Since the money would disappear anyway, surely it was better to pay it to the butcher. Gervaise used that excuse to justify overeating, saying it was Coupeau's fault if they could no longer save a sou. She had grown considerably fatter, and she limped more than before because her leg, now swollen with fat, seemed to be getting gradually shorter.

That year they talked about her saint's day a good month beforehand. They thought of dishes and smacked their lips in advance. All the shop had a confounded longing to junket. They wanted a merrymaking of the right sort—something out of the ordinary and highly successful. One does not have so many opportunities for enjoyment. What most troubled the laundress was to decide whom to invite; she wished to have twelve persons at table, no more, no less. She, her husband, mother Coupeau, and Madame Lerat, already made four members of the family. She would also have the Goujets and the Poissons. Originally, she had decided not to invite her workwomen, Madame Putois and Clemence, so as not to make them too familiar; but as the projected feast was being constantly spoken of in their presence, and their mouths watered, she ended by telling them to come. Four and four, eight, and two are ten. Then, wishing particularly to have twelve, she became reconciled with the Lorilleuxs, who for some time past had been hovering around her; at least it was agreed that the Lorilleuxs should come to dinner, and that peace should be made with glasses in hand. You really shouldn't keep family quarrels going forever. When the Boches heard that a reconciliation was planned, they also sought to make up with Gervaise, and so they had to be invited to the dinner too. That would make fourteen, not counting the children. Never before had she given such a large dinner and the thought frightened and excited her at the same time.

The saint's day happened to fall on a Monday. It was a piece of luck. Gervaise counted on the Sunday afternoon to begin the cooking. On the Saturday, while the workwomen hurried with their work, there was a long discussion in the shop with the view of finally deciding upon what the feast should consist of. For three weeks past one thing alone had been chosen—a fat roast goose. There was a gluttonous look on every face whenever it was mentioned. The goose was even already bought. Mother Coupeau went and fetched it to let Clemence and Madame Putois feel its weight. And they uttered all kinds of exclamations; it looked such an enormous bird, with its rough skin all swelled out with yellow fat.

"Before that there will be the pot-au-feu," said Gervaise, "the soup and just a small piece of boiled beef, it's always good. Then we must have something in the way of a stew."

Tall Clemence suggested rabbit, but they were always having that, everyone was sick of it. Gervaise wanted something more distinguished. Madame Putois having spoken of stewed veal, they looked at one another with broad smiles. It was a real idea, nothing would make a better impression than a veal stew.

"And after that," resumed Gervaise, "we must have some other dish with a sauce."

Mother Coupeau proposed fish. But the others made a grimace, as they banged down their irons. None of them liked fish; it was not a bit satisfying; and besides that it was full of bones. Squint-eyed Augustine, having dared to observe that she liked skate, Clemence shut her mouth for her with a good sound clout. At length the mistress thought of stewed pig's back and potatoes, which restored the smiles to every countenance. Then Virginie entered like a puff of wind, with a strange look on her face.

"You've come just at the right time." exclaimed Gervaise. "Mother

Coupeau, do show her the bird."

And mother Coupeau went a second time and fetched the goose, which Virginie had to take in her hands. She uttered no end of exclamations. By Jove. It was heavy. But she soon laid it down on the work-table, between a petticoat and a bundle of shirts. Her thoughts were elsewhere. She dragged Gervaise into the back-room.

"I say, little one," murmured she rapidly, "I've come to warn you. You'll never guess who I just met at the corner of the street. Lantier, my dear. He's hovering about on the watch; so I hastened here at once. It frightened me on your account, you know."

The laundress turned quite pale. What could the wretched man want with her? Coming, too, like that, just in the midst of the preparations for the feast. She had never had any luck; she could not even be allowed to enjoy herself quietly. But Virginie replied that she was very foolish to put herself out about it like that. Why. If Lantier dared to follow her about, all she had to do was to call a policeman and have him locked up. In the month since her husband had been appointed a policeman, Virginie had assumed rather lordly manners and talked of arresting everybody. She began to raise her voice, saying that she wished some passer-by would pinch her bottom so that she could take the fresh fellow to the police station herself and turn him over to her husband. Gervaise signaled her to be quiet since the workwomen were listening and led the way back into the shop, reopening the discussion about the dinner.

"Now, don't we need a vegetable?"

"Why not peas with bacon?" said Virginie. "I like nothing better."

"Yes, peas with bacon." The others approved. Augustine was so enthusiastic that she jabbed the poker into the stove harder than ever.

By three o'clock on the morrow, Sunday, mother Coupeau had lighted their two stoves and also a third one of earthenware which they had borrowed from the Boches. At half-past three the pot-au-feu was boiling away in an enormous earthenware pot lent by the eating-house keeper next door, the family pot having been found too small. They had decided to cook the veal and the pig's back the night before, since both of those dishes are better when reheated. But the cream sauce for the veal would not be prepared until just before sitting down for the feast.

There was still plenty of work left for Monday: the soup, the peas with bacon, the roast goose. The inner room was lit by three fires. Butter was sizzling in the pans and emitting a sharp odor of burnt flour.

Mother Coupeau and Gervaise, with white aprons tied on, were bustling all around, cleaning parsley, dashing for salt and pepper, turning the meat. They had sent Coupeau away so as not to have him underfoot, but they still had plenty of people looking in throughout the afternoon. The luscious smells from the kitchen had spread through the entire building so that neighboring ladies came into the shop on various pretexts, very curious to see what was being cooked.

Virginie put in an appearance towards five o'clock. She had again seen Lantier; really, it was impossible to go down the street now without meeting him. Madame Boche also had just caught sight of him standing at the corner of the pavement with his head thrust forward in an uncommonly sly manner. Then Gervaise who had at that moment intended going for a sou's worth of burnt onions for the pot-au-feu, began to tremble from head to foot and did not dare leave the house; the more so, as the concierge and the dressmaker put her into a terrible fright by relating horrible stories of men waiting for women with knives and pistols hidden beneath their overcoats. Well, yes. One reads of such things every day in the newspapers. When one of those scoundrels gets his monkey up on discovering an old love leading a happy life he becomes capable of everything. Virginie obligingly offered to run and fetch the burnt onions. Women should always help one another, they could not let that little thing be murdered. When she returned she said that Lantier was no longer there; he had probably gone off on finding he was discovered. In spite of that thought, he was the subject of conversation around the saucepans until night-time. When Madame Boche advised her to inform Coupeau, Gervaise became really terrified, and implored her not to say a word about it . . . yes, wouldn't that be a nice situation. Her husband must have become suspicious already because for the last few days, at night, he would swear to himself and bang the wall with his fists. The mere thought that the two men might destroy each other because of her made her shudder. She knew that Coupeau was jealous enough to attack Lantier with his shears.

While the four of them had been deep in contemplating this drama, the saucepans on the banked coals of the stoves had been quietly simmering. When mother Coupeau lifted the lids, the veal and the pig's back were discreetly bubbling. The pot-au-feu was steadily steaming with snore-like sounds. Eventually each of them dipped a piece of bread into the soup to taste the bouillon.

At length Monday arrived. Now that Gervaise was going to have fourteen persons at table, she began to fear that she would not be able to find room for them all. She decided that they should dine in the shop; and the first thing in the morning she took measurements so as to settle which way she should place the table. After that they had to remove all the clothes and take the ironing-table to pieces; the top of this laid on to some shorter trestles was to be the dining-table. But just in the midst of all this moving a customer appeared and made a scene because she had been waiting for her washing ever since the Friday; they were humbugging her, she would have her things at once. Then Gervaise tried to excuse herself and lied boldly; it was not her fault, she was cleaning out her shop, the workmen would not be there till the morrow; and she pacified her customer and got rid of her by promising to busy herself with her things at the earliest possible moment. Then, as soon as the woman had left, she showed her temper. Really, if you listened to all your customers, you'd never have time to eat. You could work yourself to death like a dog on a leash. Well. No matter who came in today, even if they offered one hundred thousand francs, she wouldn't touch an iron on this Monday, because it was her turn to enjoy herself.

The entire morning was spent in completing the purchases. Three times Gervaise went out and returned laden like a mule. But just as she was going to order wine she noticed that she had not sufficient money left. She could easily have got it on credit; only she could not be without money in the house, on account of the thousand little expenses that one is liable to forget. And mother Coupeau and she had lamented together in the back-room as they reckoned that they required at least twenty francs. How could they obtain them, those four pieces of a hundred sous each? Mother Coupeau who had at one time done the charring for a little actress of the Theatre des Batignolles, was the first to suggest the pawn-shop. Gervaise laughed with relief. How stupid she was not to have thought of it. She quickly folded her black silk dress upon a towel which she then pinned together. Then she hid the bundle under mother Coupeau's apron, telling her to keep it very flat against her stomach, on account of the neighbors who had no need to know; and she went and watched at the door to see that the old woman was not followed. But the latter had only gone as far as the charcoal dealer's when she called her back.

"Mamma. Mamma."

She made her return to the shop, and taking her wedding-ring off her finger said:

"Here, put this with it. We shall get all the more."

When mother Coupeau brought her twenty-five francs, she danced for joy. She would order an extra six bottles of wine, sealed wine to drink with the roast. The Lorilleuxs would be crushed.

For a fortnight past it had been the Coupeaus' dream to crush the Lorilleuxs. Was it not true that those sly ones, the man and his wife, a truly pretty couple, shut themselves up whenever they had anything nice to eat as though they had stolen it? Yes, they covered up the window with a blanket to hide the light and make believe that they were already asleep in bed. This stopped anyone from coming up, and so the Lorilleuxs could stuff everything down, just the two of them. They were even careful the next day not to throw the bones into the garbage so that no one would know what they had eaten. Madame Lorilleux would walk to the end of the street to toss them into a sewer opening. One morning Gervaise surprised her emptying a basket of oyster shells there . . . those penny-pinchers were never open-handed, and all their mean contrivances came from their desire to appear to be poor. Well, we'd show them, we'd prove to them what we weren't mean.

Gervaise would have laid her table in the street, had she been able to, just for the sake of inviting each passer-by. Money was not invented that it should be allowed to grow moldy, was it? It is pretty when it shines all new in the sunshine. She resembled them so little now, that on the days when she had twenty sous she arranged things to let people think that she had forty.

Mother Coupeau and Gervaise talked of the Lorilleuxs while they laid the cloth about three o'clock. They had hung some big curtains at the windows; but as it was very warm the door was left open and the whole street passed in front of the little table. The two women did not place a decanter, or a bottle, or a salt-cellar, without trying to arrange them in such a way as to annoy the Lorilleuxs. They had arranged their seats so as to give them a full view of the superbly laid cloth, and they had reserved the best crockery for them, well knowing that the porcelain plates would create a great effect.

"No, no, mamma," cried Gervaise; "don't give them those napkins. I've two damask ones."

"Ah, good." murmured the old woman; "that'll break their hearts, that's certain."

And they smiled to each other as they stood up on either side of that big white table on which the fourteen knives and forks, placed all round, caused them to swell with pride. It had the appearance of the altar of some chapel in the middle of the shop.

"That's because they're so stingy themselves." resumed Gervaise. "You know they lied last month when the woman went about everywhere saying that she had lost a piece of gold chain as she was taking the work home. The idea. There's no fear of her ever losing anything. It was simply a way of making themselves out very poor and of not giving you your five francs."

"As yet I've only seen my five francs twice," said mother Coupeau.

"I'll bet next month they'll concoct some other story. That explains why they cover their window up when they have a rabbit to eat. Don't you see? One would have the right to say to them: 'As you can afford a rabbit you can certainly give five francs to your mother.' . . . . They're just rotten. What would have become of you if I hadn't taken you to live with us?"

Mother Coupeau slowly shook her head. That day she was all against the Lorilleuxs, because of the great feast the Coupeaus were giving. She loved cooking, the little gossipings round the saucepans, the place turned topsy-turvy by the revels of saints' days. Besides she generally got on pretty well with Gervaise. On other days when they plagued one another as happens in all families, the old woman grumbled saying she was wretchedly unfortunate in thus being at her daughter-in-law's mercy. In point of fact she probably had some affection for Madame Lorilleux who after all was her daughter.

"Ah." continued Gervaise, "you wouldn't be so fat, would you, if you were living with them? And no coffee, no snuff, no little luxuries of any sort. Tell me, would they have given you two mattresses to your bed?"

"No, that's very certain," replied mother Coupeau. "When they arrive I shall place myself so as to have a good view of the door to see the faces they'll make."

Thinking of the faces they would make gave them pleasure ahead of time. However, they couldn't remain standing there admiring the table. The Coupeaus had lunched very late on just a bite or two, because the stoves were already in use, and because they did not want to dirty any dishes needed for the evening. By four o'clock the two women were working very hard. The huge goose was being cooked on a spit. Squint-eyed Augustine was sitting on a low bench solemnly basting the goose with a long-handled spoon. Gervaise was busy with the peas with bacon. Mother Coupeau, kept spinning around, a bit confused, waiting for the right time to begin reheating the pork and the veal.

Towards five o'clock the guests began to arrive. First of all came the two workwomen, Clemence and Madame Putois, both in their Sunday best, the former in blue, the latter in black; Clemence carried a geranium, Madame Putois a heliotrope, and Gervaise, whose hands were just then smothered with flour, had to kiss each of them on both cheeks with her arms behind her back. Then following close upon their heels entered Virginie dressed like a lady in a printed muslin costume with a sash and a bonnet though she had only a few steps to come. She brought a pot of red carnations. She took the laundress in her big arms and squeezed her tight. At length Boche appeared with a pot of pansies and Madame Boche with a pot of mignonette; then came Madame Lerat with a balm-mint, the pot of which had dirtied her violet merino dress. All these people kissed each other and gathered together in the back-room in the midst of the three stoves and the roasting apparatus, which gave out a stifling heat. The noise from the saucepans drowned the voices. A dress catching in the Dutch oven caused quite an emotion. The smell of roast goose was so strong that it made their mouths water. And Gervaise was very pleasant, thanking everyone for their flowers without however letting that interfere with her preparing the thickening for the stewed veal at the bottom of a soup plate. She had placed the pots in the shop at one end of the table without removing the white paper that was round them. A sweet scent of flowers mingled with the odor of cooking.

"Do you want any assistance?" asked Virginie. "Just fancy, you've been three days preparing all this feast and it will be gobbled up in no time."

"Well, you know," replied Gervaise, "it wouldn't prepare itself. No, don't dirty your hands. You see everything's ready. There's only the soup to warm."

Then they all made themselves comfortable. The ladies laid their shawls and their caps on the bed and pinned up their skirts so as not to soil them. Boche sent his wife back to the concierge's lodge until time to eat and had cornered Clemence in a corner trying to find out if she was ticklish. She was gasping for breath, as the mere thought of being tickled sent shivers through her. So as not to bother the cooks, the other ladies had gone into the shop and were standing against the wall facing the table. They were talking through the door though, and as they could not hear very well, they were continually invading the back-room and crowding around Gervaise, who would forget what she was doing to answer them.

There were a few stories which brought sly laughter. When Virginie mentioned that she hadn't eaten for two days in order to have more room for today's feast, tall Clemence said that she had cleaned herself out that morning with an enema like the English do. Then Boche suggested a way of digesting the food quickly by squeezing oneself after each course, another English custom. After all, when you were invited to dinner, wasn't it polite to eat as much as you could? Veal and pork and goose are placed out for the cats to eat. The hostess didn't need to worry a bit, they were going to clean their plates so thoroughly that she wouldn't have to wash them.

All of them kept coming to smell the air above the saucepans and the roaster. The ladies began to act like young girls, scurrying from room to room and pushing each other.

Just as they were all jumping about and shouting by way of amusement, Goujet appeared. He was so timid he scarcely dared enter, but stood still, holding a tall white rose-tree in his arms, a magnificent plant with a stem that reached to his face and entangled the flowers in his beard. Gervaise ran to him, her cheeks burning from the heat of the stoves. But he did not know how to get rid of his pot; and when she had taken it from his hands he stammered, not daring to kiss her. It was she who was obliged to stand on tip-toe and place her cheek against his lips; he was so agitated that even then he kissed her roughly on the eye almost blinding her. They both stood trembling.

". . . . Monsieur Goujet, it's too lovely." said she, placing the rose-tree beside the other flowers which it overtopped with the whole of its tuft of foliage.

"Not at all, not at all." repeated he, unable to say anything else.

Then, after sighing deeply, he slightly recovered himself and stated that she was not to expect his mother; she was suffering from an attack of sciatica. Gervaise was greatly grieved; she talked of putting a piece of the goose on one side as she particularly wished Madame Goujet to have a taste of the bird. No one else was expected. Coupeau was no doubt strolling about in the neighborhood with Poisson whom he had called for directly after his lunch; they would be home directly, they had promised to be back punctually at six. Then as the soup was almost ready, Gervaise called to Madame Lerat, saying that she thought it was time to go and fetch the Lorilleuxs. Madame Lerat became at once very grave; it was she who had conducted all the negotiations and who had settled how everything should pass between the two families. She put her cap and shawl on again and went upstairs very stiffly in her skirts, looking very stately. Down below the laundress continued to stir her vermicelli soup without saying a word. The guests suddenly became serious and solemnly waited.

It was Madame Lerat who appeared first. She had gone round by the street so as to give more pomp to the reconciliation. She held the shop-door wide open while Madame Lorilleux, wearing a silk dress, stopped at the threshold. All the guests had risen from their seats; Gervaise went forward and kissing her sister-in-law as had been agreed, said, "Come in. It's all over, isn't it? We'll both be nice to each other."

And Madame Lorilleux replied, "I shall be only too happy if we're so always."

When she had entered Lorilleux also stopped at the threshold and he likewise waited to be embraced before penetrating into the shop. Neither the one nor the other had brought a bouquet. They had decided not to do so as they thought it would look too much like giving way to Clump-Clump if they carried flowers with them the first time they set foot in her home. Gervaise called to Augustine to bring two bottles of wine. Then, filling some glasses on a corner of the table, she called everyone to her. And each took a glass and drank to the good friendship of the family. There was a pause while the guests were drinking, the ladies raising their elbows and emptying their glasses to the last drop.

"Nothing is better before soup," declared Boche, smacking his lips.

Mother Coupeau had placed herself opposite the door to see the faces the Lorilleuxs would make. She pulled Gervaise by the skirt and dragged her into the back-room. And as they both leant over the soup they conversed rapidly in a low voice.

"Huh. What a sight." said the old woman. "You couldn't see them; but I was watching. When she caught sight of the table her face twisted around like that, the corners of her mouth almost touched her eyes; and as for him, it nearly choked him, he coughed and coughed. Now just look at them over there; they've no saliva left in their mouths, they're chewing their lips."

"It's quite painful to see people as jealous as that," murmured Gervaise.

Really the Lorilleuxs had a funny look about them. No one of course likes to be crushed; in families especially when the one succeeds, the others do not like it; that is only natural. Only one keeps it in, one does not make an exhibition of oneself. Well. The Lorilleuxs could not keep it in. It was more than a match for them. They squinted—their mouths were all on one side. In short it was so apparent that the other guests looked at them, and asked them if they were unwell. Never would they be able to stomach this table with its fourteen place-settings, its white linen table cloth, its slices of bread cut in advance, all in the style of a first-class restaurant. Mme. Lorilleux went around the table, surreptitiously fingering the table cloth, tortured by the thought that it was a new one.

"Everything's ready." cried Gervaise as she reappeared with a smile, her arms bare and her little fair curls blowing over her temples.

"If the boss would only come," resumed the laundress, "we might begin."

"Ah, well." said Madame Lorilleux, "the soup will be cold by then. Coupeau always forgets. You shouldn't have let him go off."

It was already half-past six. Everything was burning now; the goose would be overdone. Then Gervaise, feeling quite dejected, talked of sending someone to all the wine shops in the neighborhood to find Coupeau. And as Goujet offered to go, she decided to accompany him. Virginie, anxious about her husband went also. The three of them, bare-headed, quite blocked up the pavement. The blacksmith who wore his frock-coat, had Gervaise on his left arm and Virginie on his right; he was doing the two-handled basket as he said; and it seemed to them such a funny thing to say that they stopped, unable to move their legs for laughing. They looked at themselves in the pork-butcher's glass and laughed more than ever. Beside Goujet, all in black, the two women looked like two speckled hens—the dressmaker in her muslin costume, sprinkled with pink flowers, the laundress in her white cambric dress with blue spots, her wrists bare, and wearing round her neck a little gray silk scarf tied in a bow. People turned round to see them pass, looking so fresh and lively, dressed in their Sunday best on a week day and jostling the crowd which hung about the Rue des Poissonniers, on that warm June evening. But it was not a question of amusing themselves. They went straight to the door of each wine shop, looked in and sought amongst the people standing before the counter. Had that animal Coupeau gone to the Arc de Triomphe to get his dram? They had already done the upper part of the street, looking in at all the likely places; at the "Little Civet," renowned for its preserved plums; at old mother Baquet's, who sold Orleans wine at eight sous; at the "Butterfly," the coachmen's house of call, gentlemen who were not easy to please. But no Coupeau. Then as they were going down towards the Boulevard, Gervaise uttered a faint cry on passing the eating-house at the corner kept by Francois.

"What's the matter?" asked Goujet.

The laundress no longer laughed. She was very pale, and laboring under so great an emotion that she had almost fallen. Virginie understood it all as she caught a sight of Lantier seated at one of Francois's tables quietly dining. The two women dragged the blacksmith along.

"My ankle twisted," said Gervaise as soon as she was able to speak.

At length they discovered Coupeau and Poisson at the bottom of the street inside Old Man Colombe's Saloon. They were standing up in the midst of a number of men; Coupeau, in a gray blouse, was shout-

ing with furious gestures and banging his fists down on the counter.
Poisson, not on duty that day and buttoned up in an old brown coat,
was listening to him in a dull sort of way and without uttering a word,
bristling his carroty moustaches and beard the while. Goujet left the
women on the edge of the pavement, and went and laid his hand on the
zinc-worker's shoulder. But when the latter caught sight of Gervaise
and Virginie outside he grew angry. Why was he badgered with such fe-
males as those? Petticoats had taken to tracking him about now. Well.
He declined to stir, they could go and eat their beastly dinner all by
themselves. To quiet him Goujet was obliged to accept a drop of something; and even then Coupeau took a fiendish delight in dawdling a
good five minutes at the counter. When he at length came out he said
to his wife:

"I don't like this. It's my business where I go. Do you understand?"

She did not answer. She was all in a tremble. She must have said
something about Lantier to Virginie, for the latter pushed her husband
and Goujet ahead, telling them to walk in front. The two women got on
each side of Coupeau to keep him occupied and prevent him seeing
Lantier. He wasn't really drunk, being more intoxicated from shouting
than from drinking. Since they seemed to want to stay on the left side,
to tease them, he crossed over to the other side of the street. Worried,
they ran after him and tried to block his view of the door of Francois's.
But Coupeau must have known that Lantier was there. Gervaise almost
went out of her senses on hearing him grunt:

"Yes, my duck, there's a young fellow of our acquaintance inside
there. You mustn't take me for a ninny. Don't let me catch you galli-
vanting about again with your side glances."

And he made use of some very coarse expressions. It was not him
that she had come to look for with her bare elbows and her mealy
mouth; it was her old beau. Then he was suddenly seized with a mad
rage against Lantier. Ah. The brigand. Ah. The filthy hound. One or the
other of them would have to be left on the pavement, emptied of his
guts like a rabbit. Lantier, however, did not appear to notice what was
going on and continued slowly eating some veal and sorrel. A crowd
began to form. Virginie led Coupeau away and he calmed down at once
as soon as he had turned the corner of the street. All the same they returned to the shop far less lively than when they left it.

The guests were standing round the table with very long faces. The zinc-worker shook hands with them, showing himself off before the ladies. Gervaise, feeling rather depressed, spoke in a low voice as she directed them to their places. But she suddenly noticed that, as Madame Goujet had not come, a seat would remain empty—the one next to Madame Lorilleux.

"We are thirteen." said she, deeply affected, seeing in that a fresh omen of the misfortune with which she had felt herself threatened for some time past.

The ladies already seated rose up looking anxious and annoyed. Madame Putois offered to retire because according to her it was not a matter to laugh about; besides she would not touch a thing, the food would do her no good. As to Boche, he chuckled. He would sooner be thirteen than fourteen; the portions would be larger, that was all.

"Wait." resumed Gervaise. "I can manage it."

And going out on to the pavement she called Old Man Bru who was just then crossing the roadway. The old workman entered, stooping and stiff and his face without expression.

"Seat yourself there, my good fellow," said the laundress. "You won't mind eating with us, will you?"

He simply nodded his head. He was willing; he did not mind.

"As well him as another," continued she, lowering her voice. "He doesn't often eat his fill. He will at least enjoy himself once more. We shall feel no remorse in stuffing ourselves now."

This touched Goujet so deeply that his eyes filled with tears. The others were also moved by compassion and said that it would bring them all good luck. However, Madame Lorilleux seemed unhappy at having the old man next to her. She cast glances of disgust at his work-roughened hands and his faded, patched smock, and drew away from him.

Old Man Bru sat with his head bowed, waiting. He was bothered by the napkin that was on the plate before him. Finally he lifted it off and placed it gently on the edge of the table, not thinking to spread it over his knees.

Now at last Gervaise served the vermicelli soup; the guests were taking up their spoons when Virginie remarked that Coupeau had disappeared. He had perhaps returned to Old Man Colombe's. This time

the company got angry. So much the worse. One would not run after
him; he could stay in the street if he was not hungry; and as the spoons
touched the bottom of the plates, Coupeau reappeared with two pots
of flowers, one under each arm, a stock and a balsam. They all clapped
their hands. He gallantly placed the pots, one on the right, the other on
the left of Gervaise's glass; then bending over and kissing her, he said:

"I had forgotten you, my lamb. But in spite of that, we love each
other all the same, especially on such a day as this."

"Monsieur Coupeau's very nice this evening," murmured Clemence
in Boche's ear. "He's just got what he required, sufficient to make him
amiable."

The good behavior of the master of the house restored the gaiety
of the proceedings, which at one moment had been compromised. Gervaise, once more at her ease, was all smiles again. The guests finished
their soup. Then the bottles circulated and they drank their first glass
of wine, just a drop pure, to wash down the vermicelli. One could hear
the children quarrelling in the next room. There were Etienne, Pauline,
Nana and little Victor Fauconnier. It had been decided to lay a table
for the four of them, and they had been told to be very good. That
squint-eyed Augustine who had to look after the stoves was to eat off
her knees.

"Mamma. Mamma," suddenly screamed Nana, "Augustine is dipping her bread in the Dutch oven."

The laundress hastened there and caught the squint-eyed one in the
act of burning her throat in her attempts to swallow without loss of
time a slice of bread soaked in boiling goose fat. She boxed her ears
when the young monkey called out that it was not true. When, after the
boiled beef, the stewed veal appeared, served in a salad-bowl, as they did
not have a dish large enough, the party greeted it with a laugh.

"It's becoming serious," declared Poisson, who seldom spoke.

It was half-past seven. They had closed the shop door, so as not to
be spied upon by the whole neighborhood; the little clockmaker opposite especially was opening his eyes to their full size and seemed to
take the pieces from their mouths with such a gluttonous look that it almost prevented them from eating. The curtains hung before the windows admitted a great white uniform light which bathed the entire table
with its symmetrical arrangement of knives and forks and its pots of

flowers enveloped in tall collars of white paper; and this pale fading light, this slowly approaching dusk, gave to the party somewhat of an air of distinction. Virginie looked round the closed apartment hung with muslin and with a happy criticism declared it to be very cozy. Whenever a cart passed in the street the glasses jingled together on the table cloth and the ladies were obliged to shout out as loud as the men. But there was not much conversation; they all behaved very respectably and were very attentive to each other. Coupeau alone wore a blouse, because as he said one need not stand on ceremony with friends and besides which the blouse was the workman's garb of honor. The ladies, laced up in their bodices, wore their hair in plaits greasy with pomatum in which the daylight was reflected; while the gentlemen, sitting at a distance from the table, swelled out their chests and kept their elbows wide apart for fear of staining their frock coats.

Ah. Thunder. What a hole they were making in the stewed veal. If they spoke little, they were chewing in earnest. The salad-bowl was becoming emptier and emptier with a spoon stuck in the midst of the thick sauce—a good yellow sauce which quivered like a jelly. They fished pieces of veal out of it and seemed as though they would never come to the end; the salad-bowl journeyed from hand to hand and faces bent over it as forks picked out the mushrooms. The long loaves standing against the wall behind the guests appeared to melt away. Between the mouthfuls one could hear the sound of glasses being replaced on the table. The sauce was a trifle too salty. It required four bottles of wine to drown that blessed stewed veal, which went down like cream, but which afterwards lit up a regular conflagration in one's stomach. And before one had time to take a breath, the pig's back, in the middle of a deep dish surrounded by big round potatoes, arrived in the midst of a cloud of smoke. There was one general cry. By Jove. It was just the thing. Everyone liked it. They would do it justice; and they followed the dish with a side glance as they wiped their knives on their bread so as to be in readiness. Then as soon as they were helped they nudged one another and spoke with their mouths full. It was just like butter. Something sweet and solid which one could feel run through one's guts right down into one's boots. The potatoes were like sugar. It was not a bit salty; only, just on account of the potatoes, it required a wetting every few minutes. Four more bottles were placed on the table. The plates were wiped so clean that they also served for the green peas and bacon . . . . Vegetables were of no consequence. They playfully gulped them down in spoonfuls. The best part of the dish was the small pieces of bacon just nicely grilled and smelling like horse's hoof. Two bottles were sufficient for them.

"Mamma. Mamma." called out Nana suddenly, "Augustine's putting her fingers in my plate."

"Don't bother me. Give her a slap." replied Gervaise, in the act of stuffing herself with green peas.

At the children's table in the back-room, Nana was playing the role of lady of the house, sitting next to Victor and putting her brother Etienne beside Pauline so they could play house, pretending they were two married couples. Nana had served her guests very politely at first, but now she had given way to her passion for grilled bacon, trying to keep every piece for herself. While Augustine was prowling around the children's table, she would grab the bits of bacon under the pretext of dividing them amongst the children. Nana was so furious that she bit Augustine on the wrist.

"Ah. You know," murmured Augustine, "I'll tell your mother that after the veal you asked Victor to kiss you."

But all became quiet again as Gervaise and mother Coupeau came in to get the goose. The guests at the big table were leaning back in their chairs taking a breather. The men had unbuttoned their waistcoats, the ladies were wiping their faces with their napkins. The repast was, so to say, interrupted; only one or two persons, unable to keep their jaws still, continued to swallow large mouthfuls of bread, without even knowing that they were doing so. The others were waiting and allowing their food to settle while waiting for the main course. Night was slowly coming on; a dirty ashy gray light was gathering behind the curtains. When Augustine brought two lamps and placed one at each end of the table, the general disorder became apparent in the bright glare— the greasy forks and plates, the table cloth stained with wine and covered with crumbs. A strong stifling odor pervaded the room. Certain warm fumes, however, attracted all the noses in the direction of the kitchen.

"Can I help you?" cried Virginie.

She left her chair and passed into the inner room. All the women followed one by one. They surrounded the Dutch oven, and watched with profound interest as Gervaise and mother Coupeau tried to pull the bird out. Then a clamor arose, in the midst of which one could distinguish the shrill voices and the joyful leaps of the children. And there was a triumphal entry. Gervaise carried the goose, her arms stiff, and her perspiring face expanded in one broad silent laugh; the women walked behind her, laughing in the same way; while Nana, right at the end, raised herself up to see, her eyes open to their full extent. When the enormous golden goose, streaming with gravy, was on the table, they did not attack it at once. It was a wonder, a respectful wonderment, which for a moment left everyone speechless. They drew one another's attention to it with winks and nods of the head. Golly. What a bird.

"That one didn't get fat by licking the walls, I'll bet." said Boche.

Then they entered into details respecting the bird. Gervaise gave the facts. It was the best she could get at the poulterer's in the Faubourg Poissonniers; it weighed twelve and a half pounds on the scales at the charcoal-dealer's; they had burnt nearly half a bushel of charcoal in cooking it, and it had given three bowls full of drippings.

Virginie interrupted her to boast of having seen it before it was cooked. "You could have eaten it just as it was," she said, "its skin was so fine, like the skin of a blonde." All the men laughed at this, smacking their lips. Lorilleux and Madame Lorilleux sniffed disdainfully, almost choking with rage to see such a goose on Clump-Clump's table.

"Well. We can't eat it whole," the laundress observed. "Who'll cut it up? No, no, not me. It's too big; I'm afraid of it."

Coupeau offered his services. My God. It was very simple. You caught hold of the limbs, and pulled them off; the pieces were good all the same. But the others protested; they forcibly took possession of the large kitchen knife which the zinc-worker already held in his hand, saying that whenever he carved he made a regular graveyard of the platter. Finally, Madame Lerat suggested in a friendly tone:

"Listen, it should be Monsieur Poisson; yes, Monsieur Poisson."

But, as the others did not appear to understand, she added in a more flattering manner still, "Why, yes, of course, it should be Monsieur Poisson, who's accustomed to the use of arms."

And she passed the kitchen knife to the policeman. All round the table they laughed with pleasure and approval. Poisson bowed his head with military stiffness, and moved the goose before him. When he thrust the knife into the goose, which cracked, Lorilleux was seized with an outburst of patriotism.

"Ah. If it was a Cossack." he cried.

"Have you ever fought with Cossacks, Monsieur Poisson?" asked Madame Boche.

"No, but I have with Bedouins," replied the policeman, who was cutting off a wing. "There are no more Cossacks."

A great silence ensued. Necks were stretched out as every eye followed the knife. Poisson was preparing a surprise. Suddenly he gave a last cut; the hind-quarter of the bird came off and stood up on end, rump in the air, making a bishop's miter. Then admiration burst forth. None were so agreeable in company as retired soldiers.

The policeman allowed several minutes for the company to admire the bishop's miter and then finished cutting the slices and arranging them on the platter. The carving of the goose was now complete.

When the ladies complained that they were getting rather warm, Coupeau opened the door to the street and the gaiety continued against the background of cabs rattling down the street and pedestrians bustling along the pavement. The goose was attacked furiously by the rested jaws. Boche remarked that just having to wait and watch the goose being carved had been enough to make the veal and pork slide down to his ankles.

Then ensued a famous tuck-in; that is to say, not one of the party recollected ever having before run the risk of such a stomach-ache. Gervaise, looking enormous, her elbows on the table, ate great pieces of breast, without uttering a word, for fear of losing a mouthful, and merely felt slightly ashamed and annoyed at exhibiting herself thus, as gluttonous as a cat before Goujet. Goujet, however, was too busy stuffing himself to notice that she was all red with eating. Besides, in spite of her greediness, she remained so nice and good. She did not speak, but she troubled herself every minute to look after Old Man Bru, and place some dainty bit on his plate. It was even touching to see this glutton take a piece of wing almost from her mouth to give it to the old fellow, who did not appear to be very particular, and who swallowed everything with bowed head, almost besotted from having gobbled so much after he had forgotten the taste of bread. The Lorilleuxs expended their rage on the roast goose; they ate enough to last them three days; they would have stowed away the dish, the table, the very shop, if they could have ruined Clump-Clump by doing so. All the ladies had wanted a piece of the breast, traditionally the ladies' portion. Madame Lerat, Madame Boche, Madame Putois, were all picking bones; while mother Coupeau, who adored the neck, was tearing off the flesh with her two last teeth. Virginie liked the skin when it was nicely browned, and the other guests gallantly passed their skin to her; so much so, that Poisson looked at his wife severely, and bade her stop, because she had had enough as it was. Once already, she had been a fortnight in bed, with her stomach swollen out, through having eaten too much roast goose. But Coupeau got angry and helped Virginie to the upper part of a leg, saying that, by Jove's thunder. If she did not pick it, she wasn't a proper woman. Had roast goose ever done harm to anybody? On the contrary, it cured all complaints of the spleen. One could eat it without bread, like dessert. He could go on swallowing it all night without being the least bit inconvenienced; and, just to show off, he stuffed a whole drum-stick into his mouth. Meanwhile, Clemence had got to the end of the rump, and was sucking it with her lips, while she wriggled with laughter on her chair because Boche was whispering all sorts of smutty things to her. Ah, by Jove. Yes, there was a dinner. When one's at it, one's at it, you know; and if one only has the chance now and then, one would be precious stupid not to stuff oneself up to one's ears. Really, one could see their sides puff out by degrees. They were cracking in their skins, the blessed gormandizers. With their mouths open, their chins besmeared with grease, they had such bloated red faces that one would have said they were bursting with prosperity.

As for the wine, well, that was flowing as freely around the table as water flows in the Seine. It was like a brook overflowing after a rainstorm when the soil is parched. Coupeau raised the bottle high when pouring to see the red jet foam in the glass. Whenever he emptied a bottle, he would turn it upside down and shake it. One more dead solder. In a corner of the laundry the pile of dead soldiers grew larger and larger, a veritable cemetery of bottles onto which other debris from the table was tossed.

Coupeau became indignant when Madame Putois asked for water.

He took all the water pitchers from the table. Do respectable citizens ever drink water? Did she want to grow frogs in her stomach?

Many glasses were emptied at one gulp. You could hear the liquid gurgling its way down the throats like rainwater in a drainpipe after a storm. One might say it was raining wine. My God, the juice of the grape was a remarkable invention. Surely the workingman couldn't get along without his wine. Papa Noah must have planted his grapevine for the benefit of zinc-workers, tailors and blacksmiths. It brightened you up and refreshed you after a hard day's work.

Coupeau was in a high mood. He proclaimed that all the ladies present were very cute, and jingled the three sous in his pocket as if they had been five-franc pieces.

Even Goujet, who was ordinarily very sober, had taken plenty of wine. Boche's eyes were narrowing, those of Lorilleux were paling, and Poisson was developing expressions of stern severity on his soldierly face. All the men were as drunk as lords and the ladies had reached a certain point also, feeling so warm that they had to loosen their clothes. Only Clemence carried this a bit too far.

Suddenly Gervaise recollected the six sealed bottles of wine. She had forgotten to put them on the table with the goose; she fetched them, and all the glasses were filled. Then Poisson rose, and holding his glass in the air, said:

"I drink to the health of the missus."

All of them stood up, making a great noise with their chairs as they moved. Holding out their arms, they clinked glasses in the midst of an immense uproar.

"Here's to this day fifty years hence." cried Virginie.

"No, no," replied Gervaise, deeply moved and smiling; "I shall be too old. Ah. A day comes when one's glad to go."

Through the door, which was wide open, the neighborhood was looking on and taking part in the festivities. Passers-by stopped in the broad ray of light which shone over the pavement, and laughed heartily at seeing all these people stuffing away so jovially.

The aroma from the roasted goose brought joy to the whole street. The clerks on the sidewalk opposite thought they could almost taste the bird. Others came out frequently to stand in front of their shops, sniffing the air and licking their lips. The little jeweler was unable to work, dizzy from having counted so many bottles. He seemed to have lost his head among his merry little cuckoo clocks.

Yes, the neighbors were devoured with envy, as Coupeau said. But why should there be any secret made about the matter? The party, now fairly launched, was no longer ashamed of being seen at table; on the contrary, it felt flattered and excited at seeing the crowd gathered there, gaping with gluttony; it would have liked to have knocked out the shop-front and dragged the table into the road-way, and there to have enjoyed the dessert under the very nose of the public, and amidst the commotion of the thoroughfare. Nothing disgusting was to be seen in them, was there? Then there was no need to shut themselves in like selfish people. Coupeau, noticing the little clockmaker looked very thirsty, held up a bottle; and as the other nodded his head, he carried him the bottle and a glass. A fraternity was established in the street. They drank to anyone who passed. They called in any chaps who looked the right sort. The feast spread, extending from one to another, to the degree that the entire neighborhood of the Goutte-d'Or sniffed the grub, and held its stomach, amidst a rumpus worthy of the devil and all his demons. For some minutes, Madame Vigouroux, the charcoal-dealer, had been passing to and fro before the door.

"Hi. Madame Vigouroux. Madame Vigouroux." yelled the party.

She entered with a broad grin on her face, which was washed for once, and so fat that the body of her dress was bursting. The men liked pinching her, because they might pinch her all over without ever encountering a bone. Boche made room for her beside him and reached slyly under the table to grab her knee. But she, being accustomed to that sort of thing, quietly tossed off a glass of wine, and related that all the neighbors were at their windows, and that some of the people of the house were beginning to get angry.

". . . that's our business," said Madame Boche. "We're the concierges, aren't we? Well, we're answerable for good order. Let them come and complain to us, we'll receive them in a way they don't expect."

In the back-room there had just been a furious fight between Nana and Augustine, on account of the Dutch oven, which both wanted to scrape out. For a quarter of an hour, the Dutch oven had rebounded over the tile floor with the noise of an old saucepan. Nana was now nursing little Victor, who had a goose-bone in his throat. She pushed her fingers under his chin, and made him swallow big lumps of sugar by way of a remedy. That did not prevent her keeping an eye on the big table. At every minute she came and asked for wine, bread, or meat, for Etienne and Pauline, she said.

"Here. Burst," her mother would say to her. "Perhaps you'll leave us in peace now."

The children were scarcely able to swallow any longer, but they continued to eat all the same, banging their forks down on the table to the tune of a canticle, in order to excite themselves.

In the midst of the noise, however, a conversation was going on between Old Man Bru and mother Coupeau. The old fellow, who was ghastly pale in spite of the wine and the food, was talking of his sons who had died in the Crimea. Ah. If the lads had only lived, he would have had bread to eat every day. But mother Coupeau, speaking thickly, leant towards him and said:

"Ah. One has many worries with children. For instance, I appear to be happy here, don't I? Well. I cry more often than you think. No, don't wish you still had your children."

Old Man Bru shook his head.

"I can't get work anywhere," murmured he. "I'm too old. When I enter a workshop the young fellows joke, and ask me if I polished Henri IV's boots. Today it's all over; they won't have me anywhere. Last year I could still earn thirty sous a day painting a bridge. I had to lie on my back with the river flowing under me. I've had a bad cough ever since then. Now, I'm finished."

He looked at his poor stiff hands and added:

"It's easy to understand, I'm no longer good for anything. They're right; were I in their place I should do the same. You see, the misfortune is that I'm not dead. Yes, it's my fault. One should lie down and croak when one's no longer able to work."

"Really," said Lorilleux, who was listening, "I don't understand why the Government doesn't come to the aid of the invalids of labor. I was reading that in a newspaper the other day."

But Poisson thought it his duty to defend the Government.

"Workmen are not soldiers," declared he. "The Invalides is for soldiers.

You must not ask for what is impossible."

Dessert was now served. In the center of the table was a Savoy cake in the form of a temple, with a dome fluted with melon slices; and this dome was surmounted by an artificial rose, close to which was a silver paper butterfly, fluttering at the end of a wire. Two drops of gum in the center of the flower imitated dew. Then, to the left, a piece of cream cheese floated in a deep dish; while in another dish to the right, were piled up some large crushed strawberries, with the juice running from them. However, there was still some salad left, some large coss lettuce leaves soaked with oil.

"Come, Madame Boche," said Gervaise, coaxingly, "a little more salad. I know how fond you are of it."

"No, no, thank you. I've already had as much as I can manage," replied the concierge.

The laundress turning towards Virginie, the latter put her finger in her mouth, as though to touch the food she had taken.

"Really, I'm full," murmured she. "There's no room left. I couldn't swallow a mouthful."

". . . but if you tried a little," resumed Gervaise with a smile. "One can always find a tiny corner empty. Once doesn't need to be hungry to be able to eat salad. You're surely not going to let this be wasted?"

"You can eat it to-morrow," said Madame Lerat; "it's nicer when it's wilted."

The ladies sighed as they looked regretfully at the salad-bowl. Clemence related that she had one day eaten three bunches of watercress at her lunch. Madame Putois could do more than that, she would take a coss lettuce and munch it up with some salt just as it was without separating the leaves. They could all have lived on salad, would have treated themselves to tub-fulls. And, this conversation aiding, the ladies cleaned out the salad-bowl.

"I could go on all fours in a meadow," observed the concierge with her mouth full.

Then they chuckled together as they eyed the dessert. Dessert did not count. It came rather late but that did not matter; they would nurse it all the same. When you're that stuffed, you can't let yourself be stopped by strawberries and cake. There was no hurry. They had the entire night if they wished. So they piled their plates with strawberries and cream cheese. Meanwhile the men lit their pipes. They were drinking the ordinary wine while they smoked since the special wine had been finished. Now they insisted that Gervaise cut the Savoy cake. Poisson got up and took the rose from the cake and presented it in his most gallant manner to the hostess amidst applause from the other guests. She pinned it over her left breast, near the heart. The silver butterfly fluttered with her every movement.

"Well, look," exclaimed Lorilleux, who had just made a discovery, "it's your work-table that we're eating off. Ah, well. I daresay it's never seen so much work before."

This malicious joke had a great success. Witty allusions came from all sides. Clemence could not swallow a spoonful of strawberries without saying that it was another shirt ironed; Madame Lerat pretended that the cream cheese smelt of starch; while Madame Lorilleux said between her teeth that it was capital fun to gobble up the money so quickly on the very boards on which one had had so much trouble to earn it. There was quite a tempest of shouts and laughter.

But suddenly a loud voice called for silence. It was Boche who, standing up in an affected and vulgar way, was commencing to sing "The Volcano of Love, or the Seductive Trooper."

A thunder of applause greeted the first verse. Yes, yes, they would sing songs. Everyone in turn. It was more amusing than anything else. And they all put their elbows on the table or leant back in their chairs, nodding their heads at the best parts and sipping their wine when they came to the choruses. That rogue Boche had a special gift for comic songs. He would almost make the water pitchers laugh when he imitated the raw recruit with his fingers apart and his hat on the back of his head. Directly after "The Volcano of Love," he burst out into "The Baroness de Follebiche," one of his greatest successes. When he reached the third verse he turned towards Clemence and almost murmured it in a slow and voluptuous tone of voice, "The baroness had people there, her sisters four, oh rare surprise; And three were dark, and one was fair; between them, eight bewitching eyes."

Then the whole party, carried away, joined in the chorus. The men beat time with their heels, while the ladies did the same with their knives against their glasses. All of them singing at the top of their voices:

"By Jingo. Who on earth will pay

A drink to the pa—to the pa—pa—?
By Jingo. Who on earth will pay
A drink to the pa—to the pa—tro—o—l?"

The panes of glass of the shop-front resounded, the singers' great volume of breath agitated the muslin curtains. While all this was going on, Virginie had already twice disappeared and each time, on returning, had leant towards Gervaise's ear to whisper a piece of information. When she returned the third time, in the midst of the uproar, she said to her:

"My dear, he's still at Francois's; he's pretending to read the newspaper. He's certainly meditating some evil design."

She was speaking of Lantier. It was him that she had been watching. At each fresh report Gervaise became more and more grave.

"Is he drunk?" asked she of Virginie.

"No," replied the tall brunette. "He looks as though he had merely had what he required. It's that especially which makes me anxious. Why does he remain there if he's had all he wanted? My God. I hope nothing is going to happen."

The laundress, greatly upset, begged her to leave off. A profound silence suddenly succeeded the clamor. Madame Putois had just risen and was about to sing "The Boarding of the Pirate." The guests, silent and thoughtful, watched her; even Poisson had laid his pipe down on the edge of the table the better to listen to her. She stood up to the full height of her little figure, with a fierce expression about her, though her face looked quite pale beneath her black cap; she thrust out her left fist with a satisfied pride as she thundered in a voice bigger than herself:

"If the pirate audacious
Should o'er the waves chase us,
The buccaneer slaughter,
Accord him no quarter.
To the guns every man,
And with rum fill each can.
While these pests of the seas
Dangle from the cross-trees."

That was something serious. By Jove, it gave one a fine idea of the real thing. Poisson, who had been on board ship nodded his head in approval of the description. One could see too that that song was in accordance with Madame Putois's own feeling. Coupeau then told how Madame Putois, one evening on Rue Poulet, had slapped the face of four men who sought to attack her virtue.

With the assistance of mother Coupeau, Gervaise was now serving the coffee, though some of the guests had not yet finished their Savoy cake. They would not let her sit down again, but shouted that it was her turn. With a pale face, and looking very ill at ease, she tried to excuse herself; she seemed so queer that someone inquired whether the goose had disagreed with her. She finally gave them " . . . let me slumber." in a sweet and feeble voice. When she reached the chorus with its wish for a sleep filled with beautiful dreams, her eyelids partly closed and her rapt gaze lost itself in the darkness of the street.

Poisson stood next and with an abrupt bow to the ladies, sang a drinking song: "The Wines of France." But his voice wasn't very musical and only the final verse, a patriotic one mentioning the tricolor flag, was a success. Then he raised his glass high, juggled it a moment, and poured the contents into his open mouth.

Then came a string of ballads; Madame Boche's barcarolle was all about Venice and the gondoliers; Madame Lorilleux sang of Seville and the Andalusians in her bolero; while Lorilleux went so far as to allude to the perfumes of Arabia, in reference to the loves of Fatima the dancer.

Golden horizons were opening up all around the heavily laden table. The men were smoking their pipes and the women unconsciously smiling with pleasure. All were dreaming they were far away.

Clemence began to sing softly "Let's Make a Nest" with a tremolo in her voice which pleased them greatly for it made them think of the open country, of songbirds, of dancing beneath an arbor, and of flowers. In short, it made them think of the Bois de Vincennes when they went there for a picnic.

But Virginie revived the joking with "My Little Drop of Brandy." She imitated a camp follower, with one hand on her hip, the elbow arched to indicate the little barrel; and with the other hand she poured out the brandy into space by turning her fist round. She did it so well that the party then begged mother Coupeau to sing "The Mouse." The old woman refused, vowing that she did not know that naughty song. Yet she started off with the remnants of her broken voice; and her wrinkled face with its lively little eyes underlined the allusions, the terrors of Mademoiselle Lise drawing her skirts around her at the sight of a mouse. All the table laughed; the women could not keep their countenances, and continued casting bright glances at their neighbors; it was not indecent after all, there were no coarse words in it. All during the song Boche was playing mouse up and down the legs of the lady coaldealer. Things might have gotten a bit out of line if Goujet, in response to a glance from Gervaise, had not brought back the respectful silence with "The Farewell of Abdul-Kader," which he sang out loudly in his bass voice. The song rang out from his golden beard as if from a brass trumpet. All the hearts skipped a beat when he cried, "Ah, my noble comrade." referring to the warrior's black mare. They burst into applause even before the end.

"Now, Old Man Bru, it's your turn." said mother Coupeau. "Sing your song.

The old ones are the best any day."

And everybody turned towards the old man, pressing him and encouraging him. He, in a state of torpor, with his immovable mask of tanned skin, looked at them without appearing to understand. They asked him if he knew the "Five Vowels." He held down his head; he could not recollect it; all the songs of the good old days were mixed up in his head. As they made up their minds to leave him alone, he seemed to remember, and began to stutter in a cavernous voice:

"Trou la la, trou la la,
Trou la, trou la, trou la la."

His face assumed an animated expression, this chorus seemed to awake some far-off gaieties within him, enjoyed by himself alone, as he listened with a childish delight to his voice which became more and more hollow.

"Say there, my dear," Virginie came and whispered in Gervaise's ear, "I've just been there again, you know. It worried me. Well. Lantier has disappeared from Francois's."

"You didn't meet him outside?" asked the laundress.

"No, I walked quickly, not as if I was looking for him."

But Virginie raised her eyes, interrupted herself and heaved a smothered sigh.

"Ah. My God. He's there, on the pavement opposite; he's looking this way."

Gervaise, quite beside herself, ventured to glance in the direction indicated. Some persons had collected in the street to hear the party sing. And Lantier was indeed there in the front row, listening and coolly looking on. It was rare cheek, everything considered. Gervaise felt a chill ascend from her legs to her heart, and she no longer dared to move, while old Bru continued:

"Trou la la, trou la la,
Trou la, trou la, trou la la."

"Very good. Thank you, my ancient one, that's enough." said Coupeau. "Do you know the whole of it? You shall sing it for us another day when we need something sad."

This raised a few laughs. The old fellow stopped short, glanced round the table with his pale eyes and resumed his look of a meditative animal. Coupeau called for more wine as the coffee was finished. Clemence was eating strawberries again. With the pause in singing, they began to talk about a woman who had been found hanging that morning in the building next door. It was Madame Lerat's turn, but she required to prepare herself. She dipped the corner of her napkin into a glass of water and applied it to her temples because she was too hot. Then, she asked for a thimbleful of brandy, drank it, and slowly wiped her lips.

"The 'Child of God,' shall it be?" she murmured, "the 'Child of God.'"

And, tall and masculine-looking, with her bony nose and her shoulders as square as a grenadier's she began, "The lost child left by its mother alone Is sure of a home in Heaven above, God sees and protects it on earth from His throne, The child that is lost is the child of God's love."

Her voice trembled at certain words, and dwelt on them in liquid notes; she looked out of the corner of her eyes to heaven, while her right hand swung before her chest or pressed against her heart with an impressive gesture. Then Gervaise, tortured by Lantier's presence, could

not restrain her tears; it seemed to her that the song was relating her own suffering, that she was the lost child, abandoned by its mother, and whom God was going to take under his protection. Clemence was now very drunk and she burst into loud sobbing and placed her head down onto the table in an effort to smother her gasps. There was a hush vibrant with emotion.

The ladies had pulled out their handkerchiefs, and were drying their eyes, with their heads erect from pride. The men had bowed their heads and were staring straight before them, blinking back their tears. Poisson bit off the end of his pipe twice while gulping and gasping. Boche, with two large tears trickling down his face, wasn't even bothering to squeeze the coal-dealer's knee any longer. All these drunk revelers were as soft-hearted as lambs. Wasn't the wine almost coming out of their eyes? When the refrain began again, they all let themselves go, blubbering into their plates.

But Gervaise and Virginie could not, in spite of themselves, take their eyes off the pavement opposite. Madame Boche, in her turn, caught sight of Lantier and uttered a faint cry without ceasing to be-smear her face with her tears. Then all three had very anxious faces as they exchanged involuntary signs. My God.. If Coupeau were to turn round, if Coupeau caught sight of the other. What a butchery. What carnage. And they went on to such an extent that the zinc-worker asked them:

"Whatever are you looking at?"

He leant forward and recognized Lantier.

"Damnation. It's too much," muttered he. "Ah. The dirty scoundrel—ah. The dirty scoundrel. No, it's too much, it must come to an end."

And as he rose from his seat muttering most atrocious threats, Gervaise, in a low voice, implored him to keep quiet.

"Listen to me, I implore you. Leave the knife alone. Remain where you are, don't do anything dreadful."

Virginie had to take the knife which he had picked up off the table from him. But she could not prevent him leaving the shop and going up to Lantier.

Those around the table saw nothing of this, so involved were they in weeping over the song as Madame Lerat sang the last verse. It sounded like a moaning wail of the wind and Madame Putois was so moved that she spilled her wine over the table. Gervaise remained frozen with fright, one hand tight against her lips to stifle her sobs. She expected at any moment to see one of the two men fall unconscious in the street.

As Coupeau rushed toward Lantier, he was so astonished by the fresh air that he staggered, and Lantier, with his hands in his pockets, merely took a step to the side. Now the two men were almost shouting at each other, Coupeau calling the other a lousy pig and threatening to make sausage of his guts. They were shouting loudly and angrily and waving their arms violently. Gervaise felt faint and as it continued for a while, she closed her eyes. Suddenly, she didn't hear any shouting and opened her eyes. The two men were chatting amiably together.

Madame Lerat's voice rose higher and higher, warbling another verse.

Gervaise exchanged a glance with Madame Boche and Virginie. Was it going to end amicably then? Coupeau and Lantier continued to converse on the edge of the pavement. They were still abusing each other, but in a friendly way. As people were staring at them, they ended by strolling leisurely side by side past the houses, turning round again every ten yards or so. A very animated conversation was now taking place. Suddenly Coupeau appeared to become angry again, while the other was refusing something and required to be pressed. And it was the zinc-worker who pushed Lantier along and who forced him to cross the street and enter the shop.

"I tell you, you're quite welcome." shouted he. "You'll take a glass of wine. Men are men, you know. We ought to understand each other."

Madame Lerat was finishing the last chorus. The ladies were singing all together as they twisted their handkerchiefs.

"The child that is lost is the child of God's love."

The singer was greatly complimented and she resumed her seat affecting to be quite broken down. She asked for something to drink because she always put too much feeling into that song and she was constantly afraid of straining her vocal chords. Everyone at the table now had their eyes fixed on Lantier who, quietly seated beside Coupeau, was devouring the last piece of Savoy cake which he dipped in his glass of wine. With the exception of Virginie and Madame Boche none of the guests knew him. The Lorilleuxs certainly scented some underhand business, but not knowing what, they merely assumed their most conceited air. Goujet, who had noticed Gervaise's emotion, gave the newcomer a sour look. As an awkward pause ensued Coupeau simply said:

"A friend of mine." And turning to his wife, added, "Come, stir yourself. Perhaps there's still some hot coffee left."

Gervaise, feeling meek and stupid, looked at them one after the other. At first, when her husband pushed her old lover into the shop, she buried her head between her hands, the same as she instinctively did on stormy days at each clap of thunder. She could not believe it possible; the walls would fall in and crush them all. Then, when she saw the two sitting together peacefully, she suddenly accepted it as quite natural. A happy feeling of languor benumbed her, retained her all in a heap at the edge of the table, with the sole desire of not being bothered. My God what is the use of putting oneself out when others do not, and when things arrange themselves to the satisfaction of everybody? She got up to see if there was any coffee left.

In the back-room the children had fallen asleep. That squint-eyed Augustine had tyrannized over them all during the dessert, pilfering their strawberries and frightening them with the most abominable threats. Now she felt very ill, and was bent double upon a stool, not uttering a word, her face ghastly pale. Fat Pauline had let her head fall against Etienne's shoulder, and he himself was sleeping on the edge of the table. Nana was seated with Victor on the rug beside the bedstead, she had passed her arm round his neck and was drawing him towards her; and, succumbing to drowsiness and with her eyes shut, she kept repeating in a feeble voice:

" . . . Mamma, I'm not well . . . . Mamma, I'm not well."

"No wonder." murmured Augustine, whose head was rolling about on her shoulders, "they're drunk; they've been singing like grown up persons."

Gervaise received another blow on beholding Etienne. She felt as though she would choke when she thought of the youngster's father being there in the other room, eating cake, and that he had not even expressed a desire to kiss the little fellow. She was on the point of rousing Etienne and of carrying him there in her arms. Then she again felt that the quiet way in which matters had been arranged was the best. It would not have been proper to have disturbed the harmony of the end of the dinner. She returned with the coffee-pot and poured out a glass of coffee for Lantier, who, by the way, did not appear to take any notice of her.

"Now, it's my turn," stuttered Coupeau, in a thick voice. "You've been keeping the best for the last. Well. I'll sing you 'That Piggish Child.'"

"Yes, yes, 'That Piggish Child,'" cried everyone.

The uproar was beginning again. Lantier was forgotten. The ladies prepared their glasses and their knives for accompanying the chorus. They laughed beforehand, as they looked at the zinc-worker, who steadied himself on his legs as he put on his most vulgar air. Mimicking the hoarse voice of an old woman, he sang:

"When out of bed each morn I hop,
I'm always precious queer;
I send him for a little drop
To the drinking-ken that's near.
A good half hour or more he'll stay,
And that makes me so riled,
  He swigs it half upon his way:
  What a piggish child."

And the ladies, striking their glasses, repeated in chorus in the midst of a formidable gaiety:

"What a piggish child.
What a piggish child."

Even the Rue de la Goutte-d'Or itself joined in now. The whole neighborhood was singing "What a piggish child." The little clockmaker, the grocery clerks, the tripe woman and the fruit woman all knew the song and joined in the chorus. The entire street seemed to be getting drunk on the odors from the Coupeau party. In the reddish haze from the two lamps, the noise of the party was enough to shut out the rumbling of the last vehicles in the street. Two policemen rushed over, thinking there was a riot, but on recognizing Poisson, they saluted him smartly and went away between the darkened buildings.

Coupeau was now singing this verse:

"On Sundays at Petite Villette,
Whene'er the weather's fine,
We call on uncle, old Tinette,
Who's in the dustman line.
To feast upon some cherry stones
The young un's almost wild,
And rolls amongst the dust and bones,
What a piggish child.
What a piggish child."

Then the house almost collapsed, such a yell ascended in the calm warm night air that the shouters applauded themselves, for it was useless their hoping to be able to bawl any louder.

Not one of the party could ever recollect exactly how the carouse terminated. It must have been very late, it's quite certain, for not a cat was to be seen in the street. Possibly too, they had all joined hands and danced round the table. But all was submerged in a yellow mist, in which red faces were jumping about, with mouths slit from ear to ear. They had probably treated themselves to something stronger than wine towards the end, and there was a vague suspicion that someone had played them the trick of putting salt into the glasses. The children must have undressed and put themselves to bed. On the morrow, Madame Boche boasted of having treated Boche to a couple of clouts in a corner, where he was conversing a great deal too close to the charcoal-dealer; but Boche, who recollected nothing, said she must have dreamed it. Everyone agreed that it wasn't very decent the way Clemence had carried on. She had ended by showing everything she had and then been so sick that she had completely ruined one of the muslin curtains. The men had at least the decency to go into the street; Lorilleux and Poisson, feeling their stomachs upset, had stumblingly glided as far as the pork-butcher's shop. It is easy to see when a person has been well brought up. For instance, the ladies, Madame Putois, Madame Lerat, and Virginie, indisposed by the heat, had simply gone into the back-room and taken their stays off; Virginie had even desired to lie on the bed for a minute, just to obviate any unpleasant effects. Thus the party had seemed to melt away, some disappearing behind the others, all accompanying one another, and being lost sight of in the surrounding

darkness, to the accompaniment of a final uproar, a furious quarrel between the Lorilleuxs, and an obstinate and mournful "trou la la, trou la
la," of old Bru's. Gervaise had an idea that Goujet had burst out sobbing when bidding her good-bye; Coupeau was still singing; and as for
Lantier, he must have remained till the end. At one moment even, she
could still feel a breath against her hair, but she was unable to say
whether it came from Lantier or if it was the warm night air.

Since Madame Lerat didn't want to return to Les Batignolles at such
a late hour, they took one of the mattresses off the bed and spread it
for her in a corner of the shop, after pushing back the table. She slept
right there amid all the dinner crumbs. All night long, while the Coupeaus were sleeping, a neighbor's cat took advantage of an open window and was crunching the bones of the goose with its sharp teeth,
giving the bird its final resting place.

CHAPTER VIII

On the following Saturday Coupeau, who had not come home to dinner, brought Lantier with him towards ten o'clock. They had had some sheep's trotters at Chez Thomas at Montmartre.

"You mustn't scold, wife," said the zinc-worker. "We're sober, as you can see. . . . There's no fear with him; he keeps one on the straight road."

And he related how they happened to meet in the Rue Rochechouart. After dinner Lantier had declined to have a drink at the "Black Ball," saying that when one was married to a pretty and worthy little woman, one ought not to go liquoring-up at all the wine shops. Gervaise smiled slightly as she listened . . . . She was not thinking of scolding, she felt too much embarrassed for that. She had been expecting to see her former lover again someday ever since their dinner party; but at such an hour, when she was about to go to bed, the unexpected arrival of the two men had startled her. Her hands were quivering as she pinned back the hair which had slid down her neck.

"You know," resumed Coupeau, "as he was so polite as to decline a drink outside, you must treat us to one here. Ah. You certainly owe us that."

The workwomen had left long ago. Mother Coupeau and Nana had just gone to bed. Gervaise, who had been just about to put up the shutters when they appeared, left the shop open and brought some glasses which she placed on a corner of the work-table with what was left of a bottle of brandy.

Lantier remained standing and avoided speaking directly to her. However, when she served him, he exclaimed, "Only a thimbleful, madame, if you please."

Coupeau looked at them and then spoke his mind very plainly. They were not going to behave like a couple of geese he hoped. The past was past was it not? If people nursed grudges for nine and ten years together one would end by no longer seeing anybody. No, no, he carried his heart in his hand, he did. First of all, he knew who he had to deal with, a worthy woman and a worthy man—in short two friends. He felt easy; he knew he could depend upon them.

" . . . that's certain, quite certain," repeated Gervaise, looking on the ground and scarcely understanding what she said.

"She is a sister now—nothing but a sister." murmured Lantier in his turn.

"My God shake hands," cried Coupeau, "and let those who don't like it go to blazes. When one has proper feelings one is better off than millionaires. For myself I prefer friendship before everything because friendship is friendship and there's nothing to beat it."

He dealt himself heavy blows on the chest, and seemed so moved that they had to calm him. They all three silently clinked glasses, and drank their drop of brandy. Gervaise was then able to look at Lantier at her ease; for on the night of her saint's day, she had only seen him through a fog. He had grown more stout, his arms and legs seeming too heavy because of his small stature. His face was still handsome even though it was a little puffy now due to his life of idleness. He still took great pains with his narrow moustache. He looked about his actual age. He was wearing gray trousers, a heavy blue overcoat, and a round hat. He even had a watch with a silver chain on which a ring was hanging as a keepsake. He looked quite like a gentleman.

"I'm off," said he. "I live no end of a distance from here."

He was already on the pavement when the zinc-worker called him back to make him promise never to pass the door without looking in to wish them good day. Meanwhile Gervaise, who had quietly disappeared, returned pushing Etienne before her. The child, who was in his shirt-sleeves and half asleep, smiled as he rubbed his eyes. But when he beheld Lantier he stood trembling and embarrassed, and casting anxious glances in the direction of his mother and Coupeau.

"Don't you remember this gentleman?" asked the latter.

The child held down his head without replying. Then he made a slight sign which meant that he did remember the gentleman.

"Well. Then, don't stand there like a fool; go and kiss him."

Lantier gravely and quietly waited. When Etienne had made up his mind to approach him, he stooped down, presented both his cheeks, and then kissed the youngster on the forehead himself. At this the boy ventured to look at his father; but all on a sudden he burst out sobbing and scampered away like a mad creature with his clothes half falling off him, while Coupeau angrily called him a young savage.

"The emotion's too much for him," said Gervaise, pale and agitated herself.

". . . . He's generally very gentle and nice," exclaimed Coupeau. "I've brought him up properly, as you'll see. He'll get used to you. He must learn to know people. We can't stay mad. We should have made up a long time ago for his sake. I'd rather have my head cut off than keep a father from seeing his own son."

Having thus delivered himself, he talked of finishing the bottle of brandy. All three clinked glasses again. Lantier showed no surprise, but remained perfectly calm. By way of repaying the zinc-worker's politeness he persisted in helping him put up the shutters before taking his departure. Then rubbing his hands together to get rid of the dust on them, he wished the couple good-night.

"Sleep well. I shall try and catch the last bus. I promise you I'll look in again soon."

After that evening Lantier frequently called at the Rue de la Goutte-d'Or. He came when the zinc-worker was there, inquiring after his health the moment he passed the door and affecting to have solely called on his account. Then clean-shaven, his hair nicely combed and always wearing his overcoat, he would take a seat by the window and converse politely with the manners of an educated man. It was thus that the Coupeaus learnt little by little the details of his life. During the last eight years he had for a while managed a hat factory; and when they asked him why he had retired from it he merely alluded to the rascality of a partner, a fellow from his native place, a scoundrel who had squandered all the takings with women. His former position as an employer continued to affect his entire personality, like a title of nobility that he could not abandon. He was always talking of concluding a magnificent deal with some hat-makers who were going to set him up in business. While waiting for this he did nothing but stroll around all day like one of the idle rich. If anyone dared to mention a hat factory looking for workers, he smiled and said he was not interested in breaking his back working for others.

A smart fellow like Lantier, according to Coupeau, knew how to take care of himself. He always looked prosperous and it took money to look thus. He must have some deal going. One morning Coupeau had seen him having his shoes shined on the Boulevard Montmartre. Lantier was very talkative about others, but the truth was that he told lies about himself. He would not even say where he lived, only that he was staying with a friend and there was no use in coming to see him because he was never in.

It was now early November. Lantier would gallantly bring bunches of violets for Gervaise and the workwomen. He was now coming almost every day. He won the favor of Clemence and Madame Putois with his little attentions. At the end of the month they adored him. The Boches, whom he flattered by going to pay his respects in their concierge's lodge, went into ecstasies over his politeness.

As soon as the Lorilleuxs knew who he was, they howled at the impudence of Gervaise in bringing her former lover into her home. However, one day Lantier went to visit them and made such a good impression when he ordered a necklace for a lady of his acquaintance that they invited him to sit down. He stayed an hour and they were so charmed by his conversation that they wondered how a man of such distinction had ever lived with Clump-Clump. Soon Lantier's visits to the Coupeaus were accepted as perfectly natural; he was in the good graces of everyone along the Rue de la Goutte-d'Or. Goujet was the only one who remained cold. If he happened to be there when Lantier arrived, he would leave at once as he didn't want to be obliged to be friendly to him.

In the midst, however, of all this extraordinary affection for Lantier, Gervaise lived in a state of great agitation for the first few weeks. She felt that burning sensation in the pit of her stomach which affected her on the day when Virginie first alluded to her past life. Her great fear was that she might find herself without strength, if he came upon her all alone one night and took it into his head to kiss her. She thought of him too much; she was forever thinking of him. But she gradually became calmer on seeing him behave so well, never looking her in the face, never even touching her with the tips of his fingers when no one was watching. Then Virginie, who seemed to read within her, made her ashamed of all her wicked thoughts. Why did she tremble? Once could not hope to come across a nicer man. She certainly had nothing to fear now. And one day the tall brunette maneuvered in such a way as to get them both into a corner, and to turn the conversation to the subject of love. Lantier, choosing his words, declared in a grave voice that his heart was dead, that for the future he wished to consecrate his life solely for his son's happiness. Every evening he would kiss Etienne on the forehead, yet he was apt to forget him in teasing back and forth with Clemence. And he never mentioned Claude who was still in the south. Gervaise began to feel at ease. Lantier's actual presence overshadowed her memories, and seeing him all the time, she no longer dreamed about him. She even felt a certain repugnance at the thought of their former relationship. Yes, it was over. If he dared to approach her, she'd box his ears, or even better, she'd tell her husband. Once again her thoughts turned to Goujet and his affection for her.

One morning Clemence reported that the previous night, at about eleven o'clock, she had seen Monsieur Lantier with a woman. She told about it maliciously and in coarse terms to see how Gervaise would react. Yes, Monsieur Lantier was on the Rue Notre Dame de Lorette with a blonde and she followed them. They had gone into a shop where the worn-out and used-up woman had bought some shrimps. Then they went to the Rue de La Rochefoucauld. Monsieur Lantier had waited on the pavement in front of the house while his lady friend went in alone. Then she had beckoned to him from the window to join her.

No matter how Clemence went on with the story Gervaise went on peacefully ironing a white dress. Sometimes she smiled faintly. These southerners, she said, are all crazy about women; they have to have them no matter what, even if they come from a dung heap. When Lantier came in that evening, Gervaise was amused when Clemence teased him about the blonde. He seemed to feel flattered that he had been seen. My God. She was just an old friend, he explained. He saw her from time to time. She was quite stylish. He mentioned some of her former lovers, among them a count, an important merchant and the son of a lawyer. He added that a bit of playing around didn't mean a thing, his heart was dead. In the end Clemence had to pay a price for her meanness. She certainly felt Lantier pinching her hard two or three times without seeming to do so. She was also jealous because she didn't reek of musk like that boulevard work-horse.

When spring came, Lantier, who was now quite one of the family, talked of living in the neighborhood, so as to be nearer his friends. He wanted a furnished room in a decent house. Madame Boche, and even Gervaise herself went searching about to find it for him. They explored the neighboring streets. But he was always too difficult to please; he required a big courtyard, a room on the ground floor; in fact, every luxury imaginable. And then every evening, at the Coupeaus', he seemed to measure the height of the ceilings, study the arrangement of the rooms, and covet a similar lodging . . . he would never have asked for anything better, he would willingly have made himself a hole in that warm, quiet corner. Then each time he wound up his inspection with these words:

"By Jove, you are comfortably situated here."

One evening, when he had dined there, and was making the same remark during the dessert, Coupeau, who now treated him most familiarly, suddenly exclaimed:

"You must stay here, old boy, if it suits you. It's easily arranged."

And he explained that the dirty-clothes room, cleaned out, would make a nice apartment. Etienne could sleep in the shop, on a mattress on the floor; that was all.

"No, no," said Lantier, "I cannot accept. It would inconvenience you too much. I know that it's willingly offered, but we should be too warm all jumbled up together. Besides, you know, each one likes his liberty. I should have to go through your room, and that wouldn't be exactly funny."

"Ah, the rogue." resumed the zinc-worker, choking with laughter, banging his fist down on the table, "he's always thinking of something smutty. But, you joker, we're of an inventive turn of mind. There're two windows in the room, aren't there? Well, we'll knock one out and turn it into a door. Then, you understand you come in by way of the courtyard, and we can even stop up the other door, if we like. Thus you'll be in your home, and we in ours."

A pause ensued. At length the hatter murmured:

"Ah, yes, in that manner perhaps we might. And yet no, I should be too much in your way."

He avoided looking at Gervaise. But he was evidently waiting for a word from her before accepting. She was very much annoyed at her husband's idea; not that the thought of seeing Lantier living with them wounded her feelings, or made her particularly uneasy, but she was wondering where she would be able to keep the dirty clothes. Coupeau was going on about the advantages of the arrangement. Their rent, five hundred francs, had always been a bit steep. Their friend could pay twenty francs a month for a nicely furnished room and it would help them with the rent. He would be responsible for fixing up a big box under their bed that would be large enough to hold all the dirty clothes. Gervaise still hesitated. She looked toward mother Coupeau for guidance. Lantier had won over mother Coupeau months ago by bringing her gum drops for her cough.

"You would certainly not be in our way," Gervaise ended by saying. "We could so arrange things…."

"No, no, thanks," repeated the hatter. "You're too kind; it would be asking too much."

Coupeau could no longer restrain himself. Was he going to continue making objections when they told him it was freely offered? He would be obliging them. There, did he understand? Then in an excited tone of voice he yelled:

"Etienne. Etienne."

The youngster had fallen asleep on the table. He raised his head with a start.

"Listen, tell him that you wish it. Yes, that gentleman there. Tell him as loud as you can: 'I wish it'"

"I wish it." stuttered Etienne, his voice thick with sleep.

Everyone laughed. But Lantier resumed his grave and impressive air. He squeezed Coupeau's hand across the table as he said, "I accept. It's in all good fellowship on both sides, is it not? Yes, I accept for the child's sake."

The next day when the landlord, Monsieur Marescot, came to spend an hour with the Boches, Gervaise mentioned the matter to him. He refused angrily at first. Then, after a careful inspection of the premises, particularly gazing upward to verify that the upper floors would not be weakened, he finally granted permission on condition there would be no expense to him. He had the Coupeaus sign a paper saying they would restore everything to its original state on the expiration of the lease.

Coupeau brought in some friends of his that very evening—a mason, a carpenter and a painter. They would do this job in the evenings as a favor to him. Still, installing the door and cleaning up the room cost over one hundred francs, not counting the wine that kept the work going. Coupeau told his friends he'd pay them something later, out of the rent from his tenant.

Then the furniture for the room had to be sorted out. Gervaise left mother Coupeau's wardrobe where it was, and added a table and two chairs taken from her own room. She had to buy a washing-stand and a bed with mattress and bedclothes, costing one hundred and thirty francs, which she was to pay off at ten francs a month. Although Lantier's twenty francs would be used to pay off these debts for ten months, there would be a nice little profit later.

It was during the early days of June that the hatter moved in. The day before, Coupeau had offered to go with him and fetch his box, to save him the thirty sous for a cab. But the other became quite embarrassed, saying that the box was too heavy, as though he wished up to the last moment to hide the place where he lodged. He arrived in the afternoon towards three o'clock. Coupeau did not happen to be in. And Gervaise, standing at the shop door became quite pale on recognizing the box outside the cab. It was their old box, the one with which they had journeyed from Plassans, all scratched and broken now and held together by cords. She saw it return as she had often dreamed it would and it needed no great stretch of imagination to believe that the same cab, that cab in which that whore of a burnisher had played her such a foul trick, had brought the box back again. Meanwhile Boche was giving Lantier a helping hand. The laundress followed them in silence and feeling rather dazed. When they had deposited their burden in the middle of the room she said for the sake of saying something:

"Well. That's a good thing finished, isn't it?"

Then pulling herself together, seeing that Lantier, busy in undoing the cords was not even looking at her, she added, "Monsieur Boche, you must have a drink."

And she went and fetched a quart of wine and some glasses.

Just then Poisson passed along the pavement in uniform. She signaled to him, winking her eye and smiling. The policeman understood perfectly. When he was on duty and anyone winked their eye to him it meant a glass of wine. He would even walk for hours up and down before the laundry waiting for a wink. Then so as not to be seen, he would pass through the courtyard and toss off the liquor in secret.

"Ah. ah." said Lantier when he saw him enter, "it's you, Badingue."

He called him Badingue for a joke, just to show how little he cared for the Emperor. Poisson put up with it in his stiff way without one knowing whether it really annoyed him or not. Besides the two men, though separated by their political convictions, had become very good friends.

"You know that the Emperor was once a policeman in London," said Boche in his turn. "Yes, on my word. He used to take the drunken women to the station-house."

Gervaise had filled three glasses on the table. She would not drink herself, she felt too sick at heart, but she stood there longing to see what the box contained and watching Lantier remove the last cords. Before raising the lid Lantier took his glass and clinked it with the others.

"Good health."

"Same to you," replied Boche and Poisson.

The laundress filled the glasses again. The three men wiped their lips on the backs of their hands. And at last the hatter opened the box. It was full of a jumble of newspapers, books, old clothes and underwear, in bundles. He took out successively a saucepan, a pair of boots, a bust of Ledru-Rollin with the nose broken, an embroidered shirt and a pair of working trousers. Gervaise could smell the odor of tobacco and that of a man whose linen wasn't too clean, one who took care only of the outside, of what people could see.

The old hat was no longer in the left corner. There was a pincushion she did not recognize, doubtless a present from some woman. She became calmer, but felt a vague sadness as she continued to watch the objects that appeared, wondering if they were from her time or from the time of others.

"I say, Badingue, do you know this?" resumed Lantier.

He thrust under his nose a little book printed at Brussels. *The Amours of Napoleon III. Illustrated with engravings.* It related, among other anecdotes, how the Emperor had seduced a girl of thirteen, the daughter of a cook; and the picture represented Napoleon III., bare-legged, and also wearing the grand ribbon of the Legion of Honor, pursuing a little girl who was trying to escape his lust.

"Ah. That's it exactly." exclaimed Boche, whose slyly ridiculous instincts felt flattered by the sight. "It always happens like that."

Poisson was seized with consternation, and he could not find a word to say in the Emperor's defense. It was in a book, so he could not deny it. Then, Lantier, continuing to push the picture under his nose in a jeering way, he extended his arms and exclaimed:

"Well, so what?"

Lantier didn't reply, He busied himself arranging his books and newspapers on a shelf in the wardrobe. He seemed upset not to have a small bookshelf over his table, so Gervaise promised to get him one. He had *The History of Ten Years* by Louis Blanc (except for the first volume), Lamartine's *The Girondins* in installments, *The Mysteries of Paris* and *The Wandering Jew* by Eugene Sue, and a quantity of booklets on philosophic and humanitarian subjects picked up from used book dealers.

His newspapers were his prized possessions, a collection made over a number of years. Whenever he read an article in a cafe that seemed to him to agree with his own ideas, he would buy that newspaper and keep it. He had an enormous bundle of them, papers of every date and every title, piled up in no discernible order. He patted them and said to the other two:

"You see that? No one else can boast of having anything to match it. You can't imagine all that's in there. I mean, if they put into practice only half the ideas, it would clean up the social order overnight. That would be good medicine for your Emperor and all his stool pigeons."

The policeman's red mustache and beard began to bristle on his pale face and he interrupted:

"And the army, tell me, what are you going to do about that?"

Lantier flew into a passion. He banged his fists down on the newspapers as he yelled:

"I require the suppression of militarism, the fraternity of peoples. I require the abolition of privileges, of titles, and of monopolies. I require the equality of salaries, the division of benefits, the glorification of the protectorate. All liberties, do you hear? All of them. And divorce."

"Yes, yes, divorce for morality." insisted Boche.

Poisson had assumed a majestic air.

"Yet if I won't have your liberties, I'm free to refuse them," he answered.

Lantier was choking with passion.

"If you don't want them—if you don't want them—"he replied. "No, you're not free at all. If you don't want them, I'll send you off to Devil's Island. Yes, Devil's Island with your Emperor and all the rats of his crew."

They always quarreled thus every time they met. Gervaise, who did not like arguments, usually interfered. She roused herself from the torpor into which the sight of the box, full of the stale perfume of her past love, had plunged her, and she drew the three men's attention to the glasses.

"Ah, yes," said Lantier, becoming suddenly calm and taking his glass. "Good health."

"Good health." replied Boche and Poisson, clinking glasses with him.

Boche, however, was moving nervously about, troubled by an anxiety as he looked at the policeman out of the corner of his eye.

"All this between ourselves, eh, Monsieur Poisson?" murmured he at length. "We say and show you things to show off."

But Poisson did not let him finish. He placed his hand upon his heart, as though to explain that all remained buried there. He certainly did not go spying about on his friends. Coupeau arriving, they emptied a second quart. Then the policeman went off by way of the courtyard and resumed his stiff and measured tread along the pavement.

At the beginning of the new arrangement, the entire routine of the establishment was considerably upset. Lantier had his own separate room, with his own entrance and his own key. However, since they had decided not to close off the door between the rooms, he usually came and went through the shop. Besides, the dirty clothes were an inconvenience to Gervaise because her husband never made the case he had promised and she had to tuck the dirty laundry into any odd corner she could find. They usually ended up under the bed and this was not very pleasant on warm summer nights. She also found it a nuisance having to make up Etienne's bed every evening in the shop. When her employees worked late, the lad had to sleep in a chair until they finished.

Goujet had mentioned sending Etienne to Lille where a machinist he knew was looking for apprentices. As the boy was unhappy at home and eager to be out on his own, Gervaise seriously considered the proposal. Her only fear was that Lantier would refuse. Since he had come to live with them solely to be near his son, surely he wouldn't want to lose him only two weeks after he moved in. However he approved whole-heartedly when she timidly broached the matter to him. He said that young men needed to see a bit of the country. The morning that Etienne left Lantier made a speech to him, kissed him and ended by saying:

"Never forget that a workingman is not a slave, and that whoever is not a workingman is a lazy drone."

The household was now able to get into the new routine. Gervaise became accustomed to having dirty laundry lying all around. Lantier was forever talking of important business deals. Sometimes he went out, wearing fresh linen and neatly combed. He would stay out all night and on his return pretend that he was completely exhausted because he had been discussing very serious matters. Actually he was merely taking life easy. He usually slept until ten. In the afternoons he would take a walk if the weather was nice. If it was raining, he would sit in the shop reading his newspaper. This atmosphere suited him. He always felt at his ease with women and enjoyed listening to them.

Lantier first took his meals at Francois's, at the corner of the Rue des Poissonniers. But of the seven days in the week he dined with the Coupeaus on three or four; so much so that he ended by offering to board with them and to pay them fifteen francs every Saturday. From that time he scarcely ever left the house, but made himself completely at home there. Morning to night he was in the shop, even giving orders and attending to customers.

Lantier didn't like the wine from Francois's, so he persuaded Gervaise to buy her wine from Vigouroux, the coal-dealer. Then he decided that Coudeloup's bread was not baked to his satisfaction, so he sent Augustine to the Viennese bakery on the Faubourg Poissonniers for their bread. He changed from the grocer Lehongre but kept the butcher, fat Charles, because of his political opinions. After a month he wanted all the cooking done with olive oil. Clemence joked that with a Provencal like him you could never wash out the oil stains. He wanted his omelets fried on both sides, as hard as pancakes. He supervised mother Coupeau's cooking, wanting his steaks cooked like shoe leather and with garlic on everything. He got angry if she put herbs in the salad.

"They're just weeds and some of them might be poisonous," he declared. His favorite soup was made with over-boiled vermicelli. He would pour in half a bottle of olive oil. Only he and Gervaise could eat this soup, the others being too used to Parisian cooking.

Little by little Lantier also came to mixing himself up in the affairs of the family. As the Lorilleuxs always grumbled at having to part with the five francs for mother Coupeau, he explained that an action could be brought against them. They must think that they had a set of fools to deal with. It was ten francs a month which they ought to give. And he would go up himself for the ten francs so boldly and yet so amiably that the chain-maker never dared refuse them. Madame Lerat also gave two five-franc pieces now. Mother Coupeau could have kissed Lantier's hands. He was, moreover, the grand arbiter in all the quarrels between the old woman and Gervaise. Whenever the laundress, in a moment of impatience, behaved roughly to her mother-in-law and the latter went and cried on her bed, he hustled them about and made them kiss each other, asking them if they thought themselves amusing with their bad tempers.

And Nana, too; she was being brought up badly, according to his idea. In that he was right, for whenever the father spanked the child, the mother took her part, and if the mother, in her turn, boxed her ears, the father made a disturbance. Nana delighted at seeing her parents abuse each other, and knowing that she was forgiven beforehand, was up to all kinds of tricks. Her latest mania was to go and play in the blacksmith shop opposite; she would pass the entire day swinging on the shafts of the carts; she would hide with bands of urchins in the remotest corners of the gray courtyard, lighted up with the red glare of the forge; and suddenly she would reappear, running and shouting, unkempt and dirty and followed by the troop of urchins, as though a sudden clash of the hammers had frightened the ragamuffins away. Lantier alone could scold her; and yet she knew perfectly well how to get over him. This tricky little girl of ten would walk before him like a lady, swinging herself about and casting side glances at him, her eyes already full of vice. He had ended by undertaking her education: he taught her to dance and to talk patois.

A year passed thus. In the neighborhood it was thought that Lantier had a private income, for this was the only way to account for the Coupeaus' grand style of living. No doubt Gervaise continued to earn money; but now that she had to support two men in doing nothing, the shop certainly could not suffice; more especially as the shop no longer had so good a reputation, customers were leaving and the work-women were tippling from morning till night. The truth was that Lantier paid nothing, neither for rent nor board. During the first months he had paid sums on account, then he had contented himself with speaking of a large amount he was going to receive, with which later on he would pay off everything in a lump sum. Gervaise no longer dared ask him for a centime. She had the bread, the wine, the meat, all on credit. The bills increased everywhere at the rate of three and four francs a day. She had not paid a sou to the furniture dealer nor to the three comrades, the mason, the carpenter and the painter. All these people commenced to grumble, and she was no longer greeted with the same politeness at the shops.

She was as though intoxicated by a mania for getting into debt; she tried to drown her thoughts, ordered the most expensive things, and gave full freedom to her gluttony now that she no longer paid for anything; she remained withal very honest at heart, dreaming of earning from morning to night hundreds of francs, though she did not exactly know how, to enable her to distribute handfuls of five-franc pieces to her tradespeople. In short, she was sinking, and as she sank lower and lower she talked of extending her business. Instead she went deeper into debt. Clemence left around the middle of the summer because there was no longer enough work for two women and she had not been paid in several weeks.

During this impending ruin, Coupeau and Lantier were, in effect, devouring the shop and growing fat on the ruin of the establishment. At table they would challenge each other to take more helpings and slap their rounded stomachs to make more room for dessert.

The great subject of conversation in the neighborhood was as to whether Lantier had really gone back to his old footing with Gervaise. On this point opinions were divided. According to the Lorilleuxs, Clump-Clump was doing everything she could to hook Lantier again, but he would no longer have anything to do with her because she was getting old and faded and he had plenty of younger girls that were prettier. On the other hand, according to the Boches, Gervaise had gone back to her former mate the very first night, just as soon as poor Coupeau had gone to sleep. The picture was not pretty, but there were a lot of worse things in life, so folks ended by accepting the threesome as altogether natural. In fact, they thought them rather nice since there were never any fights and the outward decencies remained. Certainly if you stuck your nose into some of the other neighborhood households you could smell far worse things. So what if they slept together like a nice little family. It never kept the neighbors awake. Besides, everyone was still very much impressed by Lantier's good manners. His charm helped greatly to keep tongues from wagging. Indeed, when the fruit dealer insisted to the tripe seller that there had been no intimacies, the latter appeared to feel that this was really too bad, because it made the Coupeaus less interesting.

Gervaise was quite at her ease in this matter, and not much troubled with these thoughts. Things reached the point that she was accused of being heartless. The family did not understand why she continued to bear a grudge against the hatter. Madame Lerat now came over every evening. She considered Lantier as utterly irresistible and said that most ladies would be happy to fall into his arms. Madame Boche declared that her own virtue would not be safe if she were ten years younger. There was a sort of silent conspiracy to push Gervaise into the arms of Lantier, as if all the women around her felt driven to satisfy their own longings by giving her a lover. Gervaise didn't understand this because she no longer found Lantier seductive. Certainly he had changed for the better. He had gotten a sort of education in the cafes and political meetings but she knew him well. She could pierce to the depths of his soul and she found things there that still gave her the shivers. Well, if the others found him so attractive, why didn't they try it themselves. In the end she suggested this one day to Virginie who seemed the most eager. Then, to excite Gervaise, Madame Lerat and Virginie told her of the love of Lantier and tall Clemence. Yes, she had not noticed anything herself; but as soon as she went out on an errand, the hatter would bring the helper into his room. Now people met them out together; he probably went to see her at her own place.

"Well," said the laundress, her voice trembling slightly, "what can it matter to me?"

She looked straight into Virginie's eyes. Did this woman still have it in for her?

Virginie replied with an air of innocence, "It can't matter to you, of course. Only, you ought to advise him to break off with that girl, who is sure to cause him some unpleasantness."

The worst of it was that Lantier, feeling himself supported by public opinion, changed altogether in his behavior towards Gervaise. Now, whenever he shook hands with her, he held her fingers for a minute between his own. He tried her with his glance, fixing a bold look upon her, in which she clearly read that he wanted her. If he passed behind her, he dug his knees into her skirt, or breathed upon her neck. Yet he waited a while before being rough and openly declaring himself. But one evening, finding himself alone with her, he pushed her before him without a word, and viewed her all trembling against the wall at the back of the shop, and tried to kiss her. It so chanced that Goujet entered just at that moment. Then she struggled and escaped. And all three exchanged a few words, as though nothing had happened. Goujet, his face deadly pale, looked on the ground, fancying that he had disturbed them, and that she had merely struggled so as not to be kissed before a third party.

The next day Gervaise moved restlessly about the shop. She was miserable and unable to iron even a single handkerchief. She only wanted to see Goujet and explain to him how Lantier happened to have pinned her against the wall. But since Etienne had gone to Lille, she had hesitated to visit Goujet's forge where she felt she would be greeted by his fellow workers with secret laughter. This afternoon, however, she yielded to the impulse. She took an empty basket and went out under the pretext of going for the petticoats of her customer on Rue des Portes-Blanches. Then, when she reached Rue Marcadet, she walked very slowly in front of the bolt factory, hoping for a lucky meeting. Goujet must have been hoping to see her, too, for within five minutes he came out as if by chance.

"You have been on an errand," he said, smiling. "And now you are on your way home."

Actually Gervaise had her back toward Rue des Poissonniers. He only said that for something to say. They walked together up toward Montmartre, but without her taking his arm. They wanted to get a bit away from the factory so as not to seem to be having a rendezvous in front of it. They turned into a vacant lot between a sawmill and a button factory. It was like a small green meadow. There was even a goat tied to a stake.

"It's strange," remarked Gervaise. "You'd think you were in the country."

The went to sit under a dead tree. Gervaise placed the laundry basket by her feet.

"Yes," Gervaise said, "I had an errand to do, and so I came out."

She felt deeply ashamed and was afraid to try to explain. Yet she realized that they had come here to discuss it. It remained a troublesome burden.

Then, all in a rush, with tears in her eyes, she told him of the death that morning of Madame Bijard, her washerwoman. She had suffered horrible agonies.

"Her husband caused it by kicking her in the stomach," she said in a monotone. "He must have damaged her insides. My God. She was in agony for three days with her stomach all swelled up. Plenty of scoundrels have been sent to the galleys for less than that, but the courts won't concern themselves with a wife-beater. Especially since the woman said she had hurt herself falling. She wanted to save him from the scaffold, but she screamed all night long before she died."

Goujet clenched his hands and remained silent.

"She weaned her youngest only two weeks ago, little Jules," Gervaise went on. "That's lucky for the baby, he won't have to suffer. Still, there's the child Lalie and she has two babies to look after. She isn't eight yet, but she's already sensible. Her father will beat her now even more than before."

Goujet gazed at her silently. Then, his lips trembling:

"You hurt me yesterday, yes, you hurt me badly."

Gervaise turned pale and clasped her hands as he continued. "I thought it would happen. You should have told me, you should have trusted me enough to confess what was happening, so as not to leave me thinking that…."

Goujet could not finish the sentence. Gervaise stood up, realizing that he thought she had gone back with Lantier as the neighbors asserted.

Stretching her arms toward him, she cried, "No, no, I swear to you.

He was pushing against me, trying to kiss me, but his face never even touched mine. It's true, and that was the first time he tried. . . . I swear on my life, on the life of my children . . . believe me."

Goujet was shaking his head. Gervaise said slowly, "Monsieur Goujet, you know me well. You know that I do not lie. On my word of honor, it never happened, and it never will, do you understand? Never. I'd be the lowest of the low if it ever happened, and I wouldn't deserve the friendship of an honest man like you."

She seemed so sincere that he took her hand and made her sit down again. He could breathe freely; his heart rejoiced. This was the first time he had ever held her hand like this. He pressed it in his own and they both sat quietly for a time.

"I know your mother doesn't like me," Gervaise said in a low voice. "Don't bother to deny it. We owe you so much money."

He squeezed her hand tightly. He didn't want to talk of money. Finally he said:

"I've been thinking of something for a long time. You are not happy where you are. My mother tells me things are getting worse for you. Well, then, we can go away together."

She didn't understand at first and stared at him, startled by this sudden declaration of a love that he had never mentioned.

Finally she asked, "What do you mean?"

"We'll get away from here," he said, looking down at the ground. "We'll go live somewhere else, in Belgium, if you wish. With both of us working, we would soon be very comfortable."

Gervaise flushed. She thought she would have felt less shame if he had taken her in his arms and kissed her. Goujet was an odd fellow, proposing to elope, just the way it happens in novels. Well, she had seen plenty of workingmen making up to married women, but they never took them even as far as Saint-Denis.

"Ah, Monsieur Goujet," she murmured, not knowing what else to say.

"Don't you see?" he said. "There would only be the two of us. It annoys me having others around."

Having regained her self-possession, however, she refused his proposal.

"It's impossible, Monsieur Goujet. It would be very wrong. I'm a married woman and I have children. We'd soon regret it. I know you care for me, and I care for you also, too much to let you do anything foolish. It's much better to stay just as we are. We have respect for each other and that's a lot. It's been a comfort to me many times. When people in our situation stay on the straight, it is better in the end."

He nodded his head as he listened. He agreed with her and was unable to offer any arguments. Suddenly he pulled her into his arms and kissed her, crushing her. Then he let her go and said nothing more about their love. She wasn't angry. She felt they had earned that small moment of pleasure.

Goujet now didn't know what to do with his hands, so he went around picking dandelions and tossing them into her basket. This amused him and gradually soothed him. Gervaise was becoming relaxed and cheerful. When they finally left the vacant lot they walked side by side and talked of how much Etienne liked being at Lille. Her basket was full of yellow dandelions.

Gervaise, at heart, did not feel as courageous when with Lantier as she said. She was, indeed, perfectly resolved not to hear his flattery, even with the slightest interest; but she was afraid, if ever he should touch her, of her old cowardice, of that feebleness and gloominess into which she allowed herself to glide, just to please people. Lantier, however, did not avow his affection. He several times found himself alone with her and kept quiet. He seemed to think of marrying the tripe-seller, a woman of forty-five and very well preserved. Gervaise would talk of the tripe-seller in Goujet's presence, so as to set his mind at ease. She would say to Virginie and Madame Lerat, whenever they were ringing the hatter's praises, that he could very well do without her admiration, because all the women of the neighborhood were smitten with him.

Coupeau went braying about everywhere that Lantier was a friend and a true one. People might jabber about them; he knew what he knew and did not care a straw for their gossip, for he had respectability on his side. When they all three went out walking on Sundays, he made his wife and the hatter walk arm-in-arm before him, just by way of swaggering in the street; and he watched the people, quite prepared to administer a drubbing if anyone had ventured on the least joke. It was true that he regarded Lantier as a bit of a high flyer. He accused him of avoiding hard liquor and teased him because he could read and spoke like an educated man. Still, he accepted him as a regular comrade. They were ideally suited to each other and friendship between men is more substantial than love for a woman.

Coupeau and Lantier were forever going out junketing together. Lantier would now borrow money from Gervaise—ten francs, twenty francs at a time, whenever he smelt there was money in the house. Then on those days he would keep Coupeau away from his work, talk of some distant errand and take him with him. Then seated opposite to each other in the corner of some neighboring eating house, they would guzzle fancy dishes which one cannot get at home and wash them down with bottles of expensive wine. The zinc-worker would have preferred to booze in a less pretentious place, but he was impressed by the aristocratic tastes of Lantier, who would discover on the bill of fare dishes with the most extraordinary names.

It was hard to understand a man so hard to please. Maybe it was from being a southerner. Lantier didn't like anything too rich and argued about every dish, sending back meat that was too salty or too peppery. He hated drafts. If a door was left open, he complained loudly. At the same time, he was very stingy, only giving the waiter a tip of two sous for a meal of seven or eight francs. He was treated with respect in spite of that.

The pair were well known along the exterior boulevards, from Batignolles to Belleville. They would go to the Grand Rue des Batignolles to eat tripe cooked in the Caen style. At the foot of Montmartre they obtained the best oysters in the neighborhood at the "Town of Bar-le-Duc." When they ventured to the top of the height as far as the "Galette Windmill" they had a stewed rabbit. The "Lilacs," in the Rue des Martyrs, had a reputation for their calf's head, while the restaurant of the "Golden Lion" and the "Two Chestnut Trees," in the Chaussee Clignancourt, served them stewed kidneys which made them lick their lips. Usually they went toward Belleville where they had tables reserved for them at some places of such excellent repute that you could order anything with your eyes closed. These eating sprees were always surreptitious and the next day they would refer to them indirectly while playing with the potatoes served by Gervaise. Once Lantier brought a woman with him to the "Galette Windmill" and Coupeau left immediately after dessert.

One naturally cannot both guzzle and work; so that ever since the hatter was made one of the family, the zinc-worker, who was already pretty lazy, had got to the point of never touching a tool. When tired of doing nothing, he sometimes let himself be prevailed upon to take a job. Then his comrade would look him up and chaff him unmercifully when he found him hanging to his knotty cord like a smoked ham, and he would call to him to come down and have a glass of wine. And that settled it. The zinc-worker would send the job to blazes and commence a booze which lasted days and weeks . . . it was a famous booze—a general review of all the dram shops of the neighborhood, the intoxication of the morning slept off by midday and renewed in the evening; the smells of "vitriol" succeeded one another, becoming lost in the depths of the night, like the Venetian lanterns of an illumination, until the last candle disappeared with the last glass. That rogue of a hatter never kept on to the end. He let the other get elevated, then gave him the slip and returned home smiling in his pleasant way. He could drink a great deal without people noticing it. When one got to know him well one could only tell it by his half-closed eyes and his overbold behavior to women. The zinc-worker, on the contrary, became quite disgusting, and could no longer drink without putting himself into a beastly state.

Thus, towards the beginning of November, Coupeau went in for a booze which ended in a most dirty manner, both for himself and the others. The day before he had been offered a job. This time Lantier was full of fine sentiments; he lauded work, because work ennobles a man. In the morning he even rose before it was light, for he gravely wished to accompany his friend to the workshop, honoring in him the workman really worthy of the name. But when they arrived before the "Little Civet," which was just opening, they entered to have a plum in brandy, only one, merely to drink together to the firm observance of a good resolution. On a bench opposite the counter, and with his back against the wall, Bibi-the-Smoker was sitting smoking with a sulky look on his face.

"Hallo. Here's Bibi having a snooze," said Coupeau. "Are you down in the dumps, old bloke?"

"No, no," replied the comrade, stretching his arm. "It's the employers who disgust me. I sent mine to the right about yesterday. They're all toads and scoundrels."

Bibi-the-Smoker accepted a plum. He was, no doubt, waiting there on that bench for someone to stand him a drink. Lantier, however, took the part of the employers; they often had some very hard times, as he who had been in business himself well knew. The workers were a bad lot, forever getting drunk. They didn't take their work seriously. Sometimes they quit in the middle of a job and only returned when they needed something in their pockets. Then Lantier would switch his attack to the employers. They were nasty exploiters, regular cannibals. But he could sleep with a clear conscience as he had always acted as a friend to his employees. He didn't want to get rich the way others did.

"Let's be off, my boy," he said, speaking to Coupeau. "We must be going or we shall be late."

Bibi-the-Smoker followed them, swinging his arms. Outside the sun was scarcely rising, the pale daylight seemed dirtied by the muddy reflection of the pavement; it had rained the night before and it was very mild. The gas lamps had just been turned out; the Rue des Poissonniers, in which shreds of night rent by the houses still floated, was gradually filling with the dull tramp of the workmen descending towards Paris. Coupeau, with his zinc-worker's bag slung over his shoulder, walked along in the imposing manner of a fellow who feels in good form for a change. He turned round and asked, "Bibi, do you want a job. The boss told me to bring a pal if I could."

"No thanks," answered Bibi-the-Smoker; "I'm purging myself. You should ask My-Boots. He was looking for something yesterday. Wait a minute. My-Boots is most likely in there."

And as they reached the bottom of the street they indeed caught sight of My-Boots inside Old Man Colombe's. In spite of the early hour The Saloon was flaring, the shutters down, the gas lighted. Lantier stood at the door, telling Coupeau to make haste, because they had only ten minutes left.

"What. You're going to work for that rascal Bourguignon?" yelled My-Boots, when the zinc-worker had spoken to him. "You'll never catch me in his hutch again. No, I'd rather go till next year with my tongue hanging out of my mouth. But, old fellow, you won't stay three days, and it's I who tell you so."

"Really now, is it such a dirty hole?" asked Coupeau anxiously.

". . . it's about the dirtiest. You can't move there. The ape's forever on your back. And such queer ways too—a missus who always says you're drunk, a shop where you mustn't spit. I sent them to the right about the first night, you know."

"Good; now I'm warned. I shan't stop there forever. I'll just go this morning to see what it's like; but if the boss bothers me, I'll catch him up and plant him upon his missus, you know, bang together like two fillets of sole."

Then Coupeau thanked his friend for the useful information and shook his hand. As he was about to leave, My-Boots cursed angrily. Was that lousy Bourguignon going to stop them from having a drink? Weren't they free anymore? He could well wait another five minutes. Lantier came in to share in the round and they stood together at the counter. My-Boots, with his smock black with dirt and his cap flattened on his head had recently been proclaimed king of pigs and drunks after he had eaten a salad of live beetles and chewed a piece of a dead cat.

"Say there, old Borgia," he called to Old Man Colombe, "give us some of your yellow stuff, first class mule's wine."

And when Old Man Colombe, pale and quiet in his blue-knitted waistcoat, had filled the four glasses, these gentlemen tossed them off, so as not to let the liquor get flat.

"That does some good when it goes down," murmured Bibi-the-Smoker.

The comic My-Boots had a story to tell. He was so drunk on the Friday that his comrades had stuck his pipe in his mouth with a handful of plaster. Anyone else would have died of it; he merely strutted about and puffed out his chest.

"Do you gentlemen require anything more?" asked Old Man Colombe in his oily voice.

"Yes, fill us up again," said Lantier. "It's my turn."

Now they were talking of women. Bibi-the-Smoker had taken his girl to an aunt's at Montrouge on the previous Sunday. Coupeau asked for the news of the "Indian Mail," a washerwoman of Chaillot who was known in the establishment. They were about to drink, when My-Boots loudly called to Goujet and Lorilleux who were passing by. They came just to the door, but would not enter. The blacksmith did not care to take anything. The chain-maker, pale and shivering, held in his pocket the gold chains he was going to deliver; and he coughed and asked them to excuse him, saying that the least drop of brandy would nearly make him split his sides.

"There are hypocrites for you." grunted My-Boots. "I bet they have their drinks on the sly."

And when he had poked his nose in his glass he attacked Old Man Colombe.

"Vile druggist, you've changed the bottle. You know it's no good your trying to palm your cheap stuff off on me."

The day had advanced; a doubtful sort of light lit up The Saloon, where the landlord was turning out the gas. Coupeau found excuses for his brother-in-law who could not stand drink, which after all was no crime. He even approved Goujet's behavior for it was a real blessing never to be thirsty. And as he talked of going off to his work Lantier, with his grand air of a gentleman, sharply gave him a lesson. One at least stood one's turn before sneaking off; one should not leave one's friends like a mean bastard, even when going to do one's duty.

"Is he going to badger us much longer about his work?" cried My-Boots.

"So this is your turn, sir?" asked Old Man Colombe of Coupeau.

The latter paid. But when it came to Bibi-the-Smoker's turn he whispered to the landlord who refused with a shake of the head. My-Boots understood, and again set to abusing the old Jew Colombe. What. A rascal like him dared to behave in that way to a comrade. Everywhere else one could get drink on tick. It was only in such low boozing-dens that one was insulted. The landlord remained calm, leaning his big fists on the edge of the counter. He politely said:

"Lend the gentleman some money—that will be far simpler."

"My God Yes, I'll lend him some," yelled My-Boots. "Here. Bibi, throw this money in his face, the limb of Satan."

Then, excited and annoyed at seeing Coupeau with his bag slung over his shoulder, he continued speaking to the zinc-worker, "You look like a wet-nurse. Drop your brat. It'll give you a hump-back."

Coupeau hesitated an instant; and then, quietly, as though he had only made up his mind after considerable reflection, he laid his bag on the ground saying, "It's too late now. I'll go to Bourguignon's after lunch. I'll tell him that the missus was ill. Listen, Old Man Colombe, I'll leave my tools under this seat and I'll call for them at twelve o'clock."

Lantier gave his blessing to this arrangement with an approving nod. Labor was necessary, yes, but when you're with good friends, courtesy comes first. Now the four had five hours of idleness before them. They were full of noisy merriment. Coupeau was especially relieved. They had another round and then went to a small bar that had a billiard table.

At first Lantier turned up his nose at this establishment because it was rather shabby. So much liquor had been spilled on the billiard table that the balls stuck to it. Once the game got started though, Lantier recovered his good humor and began to flaunt his extraordinary knack with a cue.

When lunch time came Coupeau had an idea. He stamped his feet and cried:

"We must go and fetch Salted-Mouth. I know where he's working. We'll take him to Mere Louis' to have some potatoes."

The idea was greeted with acclamation. Yes, Salted-Mouth, otherwise Drink-without-Thirst, was no doubt in want of some anchovies. They started off. Coupeau took them to the bolt factory in the Rue Marcadet. As they arrived a good half hour before the time the workmen came out, the zinc-worker gave a youngster two sous to go in and tell Salted-Mouth that his wife was ill and wanted him at once. The blacksmith made his appearance, waddling in his walk, looking very calm, and scenting a tuck-out.

"Ah, you jokers." said he, as soon as he caught sight of them hiding in a doorway. "I guessed it. Well, what are we going to eat?"

At mother Louis', while they sucked the little bones of the anchovies, they again fell to abusing the employers. Salted-Mouth, otherwise Drink-without-Thirst, related that they had a most pressing order to execute at the shop. . . . The ape was pleasant for the time being. One could be late, and he would say nothing; he no doubt considered himself lucky when one turned up at all. At any rate, no boss would dare to throw Salted-Mouth out the door, because you couldn't find lads of his capacity any more. After the anchovies they had an omelet. When each of them had emptied his bottle, Mere Louis brought out some Auvergne wine, thick enough to cut with a knife. The party was really warming up.

"What do you think is the ape's latest idea?" cried Salted-Mouth at dessert. "Why, he's been and put a bell up in his shed. A bell. That's good for slaves. Ah, well. It can ring today. They won't catch me again at the anvil. For five days past I've been sticking there; I may give myself a rest now. If he deducts anything, I'll send him to blazes."

"I," said Coupeau, with an air of importance, "I'm obliged to leave you;

I'm off to work. Yes, I promised my wife. Amuse yourselves; my spirit you know remains with my pals."

The others teased him. But he seemed so decided that they all accompanied him when he talked of going to fetch his tools from Old Man Colombe's. He took his bag from under the seat and laid it on the ground before him while they had a final drink. But at one o'clock the party was still standing drinks. Then Coupeau, with a bored gesture placed the tools back again under the seat. They were in his way; he could not get near the counter without stumbling against them. It was too absurd; he would go to Bourguignon's on the morrow. The other four, who were quarrelling about the question of salaries, were not at all surprised when the zinc-worker, without any explanation, proposed a little stroll on the Boulevard, just to stretch their legs. They didn't go very far. They seemed to have nothing to say to each other out in the fresh air. Without even consulting each other with so much as a nudge, they slowly and instinctively ascended the Rue des Poissonniers, where they went to Francois's and had a glass of wine out of the bottle. Lantier pushed his comrades inside the private room at the back; it was a narrow place with only one table in it, and was separated from the shop by a dull glazed partition. He liked to do his drinking in private rooms because it seemed more respectable. Didn't they like it here? It was as comfortable as being at home. You could even take a nap here without being embarrassed. He called for the newspaper, spread it out open before him, and looked through it, frowning the while. Coupeau and My-Boots had commenced a game of piquet. Two bottles of wine and five glasses were scattered about the table.

They emptied their glasses. Then Lantier read out loud, "A frightful crime has just spread consternation throughout the Commune of Gaillon, Department of Seine-et-Marne. A son has killed his father with blows from a spade in order to rob him of thirty sous."

They all uttered a cry of horror. There was a fellow whom they would have taken great pleasure in seeing guillotined. No, the guillotine was not enough; he deserved to be cut into little pieces. The story of an infanticide equally aroused their indignation; but the hatter, highly moral, found excuses for the woman, putting all the wrong on the back of her husband; for after all, if some beast of a man had not put the wretched woman into the way of bleak poverty, she could not have drowned it in a water closet.

They were most delighted though by the exploit of a Marquis who, coming out of a dance hall at two in the morning, had defended himself against an attack by three blackguards on the Boulevard des Invalides. Without taking off his gloves, he had disposed of the first two villains by ramming his head into their stomachs, and then had marched the third one off to the police. What a man. Too bad he was a noble.

"Listen to this now," continued Lantier. "Here's some society news: 'A marriage is arranged between the eldest daughter of the Countess de Bretigny and the young Baron de Valancay, aide-de-camp to His Majesty. The wedding trousseau will contain more than three hundred thousand francs' worth of lace.'"

"What's that to us?" interrupted Bibi-the-Smoker. "We don't want to know the color of her mantle. The girl can have no end of lace; nevertheless she'll see the folly of loving."

As Lantier seemed about to continue his reading, Salted-Mouth, otherwise Drink-without-Thirst, took the newspaper from him and sat upon it, saying, "Ah. No, that's enough. This is all the paper is good for."

Meanwhile, My-Boots, who had been looking at his hand, triumphantly banged his fist down on the table. He scored ninety-three.

"I've got the Revolution." he exulted.

"You're out of luck, comrade," the others told Coupeau.

They ordered two fresh bottles. The glasses were filled up again as fast as they were emptied, the booze increased. Towards five o'clock it began to get disgusting, so much so that Lantier kept very quiet, thinking of how to give the others the slip; brawling and throwing the wine about was no longer his style. Just then Coupeau stood up to make the drunkard's sign of the cross. Touching his head he pronounced Montpernasse, then Menilmonte as he brought his hand to his right shoulder, Bagnolet giving himself a blow in the chest, and wound up by saying stewed rabbit three times as he hit himself in the pit of the stomach. Then the hatter took advantage of the clamor which greeted the performance of this feat and quietly made for the door. His comrades did not even notice his departure. He had already had a pretty good dose. But once outside he shook himself and regained his self-possession; and he quietly made for the shop, where he told Gervaise that Coupeau was with some friends.

Two days passed by. The zinc-worker had not returned. He was reeling about the neighborhood, but no one knew exactly where. Several persons, however, stated that they had seen him at mother Baquet's, at the "Butterfly," and at the "Little Old Man with a Cough." Only some said that he was alone, while others affirmed that he was in the company of seven or eight drunkards like himself. Gervaise shrugged her shoulders in a resigned sort of way. My God. She just had to get used to it. She never ran about after her old man; she even went out of her way if she caught sight of him inside a wine shop, so as to not anger him; and she waited at home till he returned, listening at night-time to hear if he was snoring outside the door. He would sleep on a rubbish heap, or on a seat, or in a piece of waste land, or across a gutter. On the morrow, after having only badly slept off his booze of the day before, he would start off again, knocking at the doors of all the consolation dealers, plunging afresh into a furious wandering, in the midst of nips of spirits, glasses of wine, losing his friends and then finding them again, going regular voyages from which he returned in a state of stupor, seeing the streets dance, the night fall and the day break, without any other thought than to drink and sleep off the effects wherever he happened to be. When in the latter state, the world was ended so far as he was concerned. On the second day, however, Gervaise went to Old Man Colombe's The Saloon to find out something about him; he had been there another five times, they were unable to tell her anything more. All she could do was to take away his tools which he had left under a seat.

In the evening Lantier, seeing that the laundress seemed very worried, offered to take her to a music-hall, just by way of passing a pleasant hour or two. She refused at first, she was in no mood for laughing. Otherwise she would not have said, "No," for the hatter made the proposal in too straightforward a manner for her to feel any mistrust. He seemed to feel for her in quite a paternal way. Never before had Coupeau slept out two nights running. So that in spite of herself, she would go every ten minutes to the door, with her iron in her hand, and look up and down the street to see if her old man was coming.

It might be that Coupeau had broken a leg, or fallen under a wagon and been crushed and that might be good riddance to bad rubbish. She saw no reason for cherishing in her heart any affection for a filthy character like him, but it was irritating, all the same, to have to wonder every night whether he would come in or not. When it got dark, Lantier again suggested the music-hall, and this time she accepted. She decided it would be silly to deny herself a little pleasure when her husband had been out on the town for three days. If he wasn't coming in, then she might as well go out herself. Let the entire dump burn up if it felt like it. She might even put a torch to it herself. She was getting tired of the boring monotony of her present life.

They ate their dinner quickly. Then, when she went off at eight o'clock, arm-in-arm with the hatter, Gervaise told mother Coupeau and Nana to go to bed at once. The shop was shut and the shutters up. She left by the door opening into the courtyard and gave Madame Boche the key, asking her, if her pig of a husband came home, to have the kindness to put him to bed. The hatter was waiting for her under the big doorway, arrayed in his best and whistling a tune. She had on her silk dress. They walked slowly along the pavement, keeping close to each other, lighted up by the glare from the shop windows which showed them smiling and talking together in low voices.

The music-hall was in the Boulevard de Rochechouart. It had originally been a little cafe and had been enlarged by means of a kind of wooden shed erected in the courtyard. At the door a string of glass globes formed a luminous porch. Tall posters pasted on boards stood upon the ground, close to the gutter.

"Here we are," said Lantier. "To-night, first appearance of Mademoiselle Amanda, serio-comic."

Then he caught sight of Bibi-the-Smoker, who was also reading the poster. Bibi had a black eye; some punch he had run up against the day before.

"Well. Where's Coupeau?" inquired the hatter, looking about. "Have you, then, lost Coupeau?"

". . . long ago, since yesterday," replied the other. "There was a bit of a free-for-all on leaving mother Baquet's. I don't care for fisticuffs. We had a row, you know, with mother Baquet's pot-boy, because he wanted to make us pay for a quart twice over. Then I left. I went and had a bit of a snooze."

He was still yawning; he had slept eighteen hours at a stretch. He was, moreover, quite sobered, with a stupid look on his face, and his jacket smothered with fluff; for he had no doubt tumbled into bed with his clothes on.

"And you don't know where my husband is, sir?" asked the laundress.

"Well, no, not a bit. It was five o'clock when we left mother Baquet's. That's all I know about it. Perhaps he went down the street. Yes, I fancy now that I saw him go to the 'Butterfly' with a coachman. . . . How stupid it is. Really, we deserve to be shot."

Lantier and Gervaise spent a very pleasant evening at the music-hall. At eleven o'clock when the place closed, they strolled home without hurrying themselves. The cold was quite sharp. People seemed to be in groups. Some of the girls were giggling in the darkness as their men pressed close to them. Lantier was humming one of Mademoiselle Amanda's songs. Gervaise, with her head spinning from too much drink, hummed the refrain with him. It had been very warm at the music-hall and the two drinks she had had, along with all the smoke, had upset her stomach a bit. She had been quite impressed with Mademoiselle Amanda. She wouldn't dare to appear in public wearing so little, but she had to admit that the lady had lovely skin.

"Everyone's asleep," said Gervaise, after ringing three times without the Boches opening the door.

At length the door opened, but inside the porch it was very dark, and when she knocked at the window of the concierge's room to ask for her key, the concierge, who was half asleep, pulled out some rigmarole which she could make nothing of at first. She eventually understood that Poisson, the policeman, had brought Coupeau home in a frightful state, and that the key was no doubt in the lock.

"The deuce." murmured Lantier, when they had entered, "whatever has he been up to here? The stench is abominable."

There was indeed a most powerful stench. As Gervaise went to look for matches, she stepped into something messy. After she succeeded in lighting a candle, a pretty sight met their eyes. Coupeau appeared to have disgorged his very insides. The bed was splattered all over, so was the carpet, and even the bureau had splashes on its sides. Besides that, he had fallen from the bed where Poisson had probably thrown him, and was snoring on the floor in the midst of the filth like a pig wallowing in the mire, exhaling his foul breath through his open mouth. His gray hair was straggling into the puddle around his head.

". . . . The pig. The pig," repeated Gervaise, indignant and exasperated. "He's dirtied everything. No, a dog wouldn't have done that, even a dead dog is cleaner."

They both hesitated to move, not knowing where to place their feet. Coupeau had never before come home and put the bedroom into such a shocking state. This sight was a blow to whatever affection his wife still had for him. Previously she had been forgiving and not seriously offended, even when he had been blind drunk. But this made her sick; it was too much. She wouldn't have touched Coupeau for the world, and just the thought of this filthy bum touching her caused a repugnance such as she might have felt had she been required to sleep beside the corpse of someone who had died from a terrible disease.

". . . I must get into that bed," murmured she. "I can't go and sleep in the street . . . . I'll crawl into it foot first."

She tried to step over the drunkard, but had to catch hold of a corner of the chest of drawers to save herself from slipping in the mess. Coupeau completely blocked the way to the bed. Then, Lantier, who laughed to himself on seeing that she certainly could not sleep on her own pillow that night, took hold of her hand, saying, in a low and angry voice, "Gervaise; he is a pig."

She understood what he meant and pulled her hand free. She sighed to herself, and, in her bewilderment, addressed him familiarly, as in the old days.

"No, leave me alone, Auguste. Go to your own bed. I'll manage somehow to lie at the foot of the bed."

"Come, Gervaise, don't be foolish," resumed he. "It's too abominable; you can't remain here. Come with me. He won't hear us. What are you afraid of?"

"No," she replied firmly, shaking her head vigorously. Then, to show that she would remain where she was, she began to take off her clothes, throwing her silk dress over a chair. She was quickly in only her chemise and petticoat. Well, it was her own bed. She wanted to sleep in her own bed and made two more attempts to reach a clean corner of the bed.

Lantier, having no intention of giving up, whispered things to her.

What a predicament she was in, with a louse of a husband that prevented her from crawling under her own blankets and a low skunk behind her just waiting to take advantage of the situation to possess her again. She begged Lantier to be quiet. Turning toward the small room where Nana and mother Coupeau slept, she listened anxiously. She could hear only steady breathing.

"Leave me alone, Auguste," she repeated. "You'll wake them. Be sensible."

Lantier didn't answer, but just smiled at her. Then he began to kiss her on the ear just as in the old days.

Gervaise felt like sobbing. Her strength deserted her; she felt a great buzzing in her ears, a violent tremor passed through her. She advanced another step forward. And she was again obliged to draw back. It was not possible, the disgust was too great. She felt on the verge of vomiting herself. Coupeau, overpowered by intoxication, lying as comfortably as though on a bed of down, was sleeping off his booze, without life in his limbs, and with his mouth all on one side. The whole street might have entered and laughed at him, without a hair of his body moving.

"Well, I can't help it," she faltered. "It's his own fault. My God. He's forcing me out of my own bed. I've no bed any longer. No, I can't help it. It's his own fault."

She was trembling so she scarcely knew what she was doing. While Lantier was urging her into his room, Nana's face appeared at one of the glass panes in the door of the little room. The young girl, pale from sleep, had awakened and gotten out of bed quietly. She stared at her father lying in his vomit. Then, she stood watching until her mother disappeared into Lantier's room. She watched with the intensity and the wide-open eyes of a vicious child aflame with curiosity.

CHAPTER IX

That winter mother Coupeau nearly went off in one of her coughing fits. Each December she could count on her asthma keeping her on her back for two and three weeks at a time. She was no longer fifteen, she would be seventy-three on Saint-Anthony's day. With that she was very rickety, getting a rattling in her throat for nothing at all, though she was plump and stout. The doctor said she would go off coughing, just time enough to say: "Good-night, the candle's out."

When she was in her bed mother Coupeau became positively unbearable. It is true though that the little room in which she slept with Nana was not at all gay. There was barely room for two chairs between the beds. The wallpaper, a faded gray, hung loose in long strips. The small window near the ceiling let in only a dim light. It was like a cavern. At night, as she lay awake, she could listen to the breathing of the sleeping Nana as a sort of distraction; but in the day-time, as there was no one to keep her company from morning to night, she grumbled and cried and repeated to herself for hours together, as she rolled her head on the pillow:

"Good heavens. What a miserable creature I am. Good heavens. What a miserable creature I am. They'll leave me to die in prison, yes, in prison."

As soon as anyone called, Virginie or Madame Boche, to ask after her health, she would not reply directly, but immediately started on her list of complaints: ". . . I pay dearly for the food I eat here. I'd be much better off with strangers. I asked for a cup of tisane and they brought me an entire pot of hot water. It was a way of saying that I drank too much. I brought Nana up myself and she scurries away in her bare feet every morning and I never see her again all day. Then at night she sleeps so soundly that she never wakes up to ask me if I'm in pain. I'm just a nuisance to them. They're waiting for me to die. That will happen soon enough. I don't even have a son anymore; that laundress has taken him from me. She'd beat me to death if she wasn't afraid of the law."

Gervaise was indeed rather hasty at times. The place was going to the dogs, everyone's temper was getting spoilt and they sent each other to the right about for the least word. Coupeau, one morning that he had a hangover, exclaimed: "The old thing's always saying she's going to die, and yet she never does." The words struck mother Coupeau to the heart. They frequently complained of how much she cost them, observing that they would save a lot of money when she was gone.

When at her worst that winter, one afternoon, when Madame Lorilleux and Madame Lerat had met at her bedside, mother Coupeau winked her eye as a signal to them to lean over her. She could scarcely speak. She rather hissed than said in a low voice:

"It's becoming indecent. I heard them last night. Yes, Clump-clump and the hatter. And they were kicking up such a row together. Coupeau's too decent for her."

And she related in short sentences, coughing and choking between each, that her son had come home dead drunk the night before. Then, as she was not asleep, she was easily able to account for all the noises, of Clump-clump's bare feet tripping over the tiled floor, the hissing voice of the hatter calling her, the door between the two rooms gently closed, and the rest. It must have lasted till daylight. She could not tell the exact time, because, in spite of her efforts, she had ended by falling into a dose.

"What's most disgusting is that Nana might have heard everything," continued she. "She was indeed restless all the night, she who usually sleeps so sound. She tossed about and kept turning over as though there had been some lighted charcoal in her bed."

The other two women did not seem at all surprised.

"Of course." murmured Madame Lorilleux, "it probably began the very first night. But as it pleases Coupeau, we've no business to interfere. All the same, it's not very respectable."

"As for me," declared Madame Lerat through clenched teeth, "if I'd been there, I'd have thrown a fright into them. I'd have shouted something, anything. A doctor's maid told me once that the doctor had told her that a surprise like that, at a certain moment, could strike a woman dead. If she had died right there, that would have been well, wouldn't it? She would have been punished right where she had sinned."

It wasn't long until the entire neighborhood knew that Gervaise visited Lantier's room every night. Madame Lorilleux was loudly indignant, calling her brother a poor fool whose wife had shamed him. And her poor mother, forced to live in the midst of such horrors. As a result, the neighbors blamed Gervaise. Yes, she must have led Lantier astray; you could see it in her eyes. In spite of the nasty gossip, Lantier was still liked because he was always so polite. He always had candy or flowers to give the ladies. My God. Men shouldn't be expected to push away women who threw themselves at them. There was no excuse for Gervaise. She was a disgrace. The Lorilleuxs used to bring Nana up to their apartment in order to find out more details from her, their godchild. But Nana would put on her expression of innocent stupidity and lower her long silky eyelashes to hide the fire in her eyes as she replied.

In the midst of this general indignation, Gervaise lived quietly on, feeling tired out and half asleep. At first she considered herself very sinful and felt a disgust for herself. When she left Lantier's room she would wash her hands and scrub herself as if trying to get rid of an evil stain. If Coupeau then tried to joke with her, she would fly into a passion, and run and, while shivering, dress herself in the farthest corner of the shop; neither would she allow Lantier near her soon after her husband had kissed her. She would have liked to have changed her skin as she changed men. But she gradually became accustomed to it. Soon it was too much trouble to scrub herself each time. Her thirst for happiness led her to enjoy as much as she could the difficult situation. She had always been disposed to make allowances for herself, so why not for others? She only wanted to avoid causing trouble. As long as the household went along as usual, there was nothing to complain about.

Then, after all, she could not be doing anything to make Coupeau stop drinking; matters were arranged so easily to the general satisfaction. One is generally punished if one does what is not right. His dissoluteness had gradually become a habit. Now it was as regular an affair as eating and drinking. Each time Coupeau came home drunk, she would go to Lantier's room. This was usually on Mondays, Tuesdays and Wednesdays. Sometimes on other nights, if Coupeau was snoring too loudly, she would leave in the middle of the night. It was not that she cared more for Lantier, but just that she slept better in his room.

Mother Coupeau never dared speak openly of it. But after a quarrel, when the laundress had bullied her, the old woman was not sparing in her allusions. She would say that she knew men who were precious fools and women who were precious sluts, and she would mutter words far more biting, with the sharpness of language pertaining to an old waistcoat-maker. The first time this had occurred Gervaise looked at her straight in the face without answering. Then, also avoiding going into details, she began to defend herself with reasons given in a general sort of way. When a woman had a drunkard for a husband, a pig who lived in filth, that woman was to be excused if she sought for cleanliness elsewhere. Once she pointed out that Lantier was just as much her husband as Coupeau was. Hadn't she known him since she was fourteen and didn't she have children by him?

Anyway, she'd like to see anyone make trouble for her. She wasn't the only one around the Rue de la Goutte-d'Or. Madame Vigouroux, the coal-dealer had a merry dance from morning to night. Then there was the grocer's wife, Madame Lehongre with her brother-in-law. My God. What a slob of a fellow. He wasn't worth touching with a shovel. Even the neat little clockmaker was said to have carried on with his own daughter, a streetwalker. Ah, the entire neighborhood . . . she knew plenty of dirt.

One day when mother Coupeau was more pointed than usual in her observations, Gervaise had replied to her, clinching her teeth:

"You're confined to your bed and you take advantage of it. Listen. You're wrong. You see that I behave nicely to you, for I've never thrown your past life into your teeth . . . . I know all about it. No, don't cough. I've finished what I had to say. It's only to request you to mind your own business, that's all."

The old woman almost choked. On the morrow, Goujet having called about his mother's washing when Gervaise happened to be out, mother Coupeau called him to her and kept him some time seated beside her bed. She knew all about the blacksmith's friendship, and had noticed that for some time past he had looked dismal and wretched, from a suspicion of the melancholy things that were taking place. So, for the sake of gossiping, and out of revenge for the quarrel of the day before, she bluntly told him the truth, weeping and complaining as though Gervaise's wicked behavior did her some special injury. When Goujet quitted the little room, he leant against the wall, almost stifling with grief. Then, when the laundress returned home, mother Coupeau called to her that Madame Goujet required her to go round with her clothes, ironed or not; and she was so animated that Gervaise, seeing something was wrong, guessed what had taken place and had a presentiment of the unpleasantness which awaited her.

Very pale, her limbs already trembling, she placed the things in a basket and started off. For years past she had not returned the Goujets a sou of their money. The debt still amounted to four hundred and twenty-five francs. She always spoke of her embarrassments and received the money for the washing. It filled her with shame, because she seemed to be taking advantage of the blacksmith's friendship to make a fool of him. Coupeau, who had now become less scrupulous, would chuckle and say that Goujet no doubt had fooled around with her a bit, and had so paid himself. But she, in spite of the relations she had fallen into with Coupeau, would indignantly ask her husband if he already wished to eat of that sort of bread. She would not allow anyone to say a word against Goujet in her presence; her affection for the blacksmith remained like a last shred of her honor. Thus, every time she took the washing home to those worthy people, she felt a spasm of her heart the moment she put a foot on their stairs.

"Ah. It's you, at last." said Madame Goujet sharply, on opening the door to her. "When I'm in want of death, I'll send you to fetch him."

Gervaise entered, greatly embarrassed, not even daring to mutter an excuse. She was no longer punctual, never came at the time arranged, and would keep her customers waiting for days on end. Little by little she was giving way to a system of thorough disorder.

"For a week past I've been expecting you," continued the lace-mender. "And you tell falsehoods too; you send your apprentice to me with all sorts of stories; you are then busy with my things, you will deliver them the same evening, or else you've had an accident, the bundle's fallen into a pail of water. While all this is going on, I waste my time, nothing turns up, and it worries me exceedingly. No, you're most unreasonable. Come, what have you in your basket? Is everything there now? Have you brought me the pair of sheets you've been keeping back for a month past, and the chemise which was missing the last time you brought home the washing?"

"Yes, yes," murmured Gervaise, "I have the chemise. Here it is."

But Madame Goujet cried out. That chemise was not hers, she would have nothing to do with it. Her things were changed now; it was too bad. Only the week before, there were two handkerchiefs which hadn't her mark on them. It was not to her taste to have clothes coming from no one knew where. Besides that, she liked to have her own things.

"And the sheets?" she resumed. "They're lost, aren't they? Well. Woman, you must see about them, for I insist upon having them tomorrow morning, do you hear?"

There was a silence which particularly bothered Gervaise when she noticed that the door to Goujet's room was open. If he was in there, it was most annoying that he should hear these just criticisms. She made no reply, meekly bowing her head, and placing the laundry on the bed as quickly as possible.

Matters became worse when Madame Goujet began to look over the things, one by one. She took hold of them and threw them down again saying:

"Ah. You don't get them up nearly so well as you used to do. One can't compliment you every day now. Yes, you've taken to mucking your work—doing it in a most slovenly way. Just look at this shirt-front, it's scorched, there's the mark of the iron on the plaits; and the buttons have all been torn off. I don't know how you manage it, but there's never a button left on anything . . . . Now, here's a petticoat body which I shall certainly not pay you for. Look there. The dirt's still on it, you've simply smoothed it over. So now the things are not even clean."

She stopped while she counted the different articles. Then she exclaimed, "What. This is all you've brought? There are two pairs of stockings, six towels, a table-cloth, and several dish-cloths short. You're regularly trifling with me, it seems. I sent word that you were to bring me everything, ironed or not. If your apprentice isn't here on the hour with the rest of the things, we shall fall out, Madame Coupeau, I warn you."

At this moment Goujet coughed in his room. Gervaise slightly started. My God. How she was treated before him. And she remained standing in the middle of the rooms, embarrassed and confused and waiting for the dirty clothes; but after making up the account Madame Goujet had quietly returned to her seat near the window, and resumed the mending of a lace shawl.

"And the dirty things?" timidly inquired the laundress.

"No, thank you," replied the old woman, "there will be no laundry this week."

Gervaise turned pale. She was no longer to have the washing. Then she quite lost her head; she was obliged to sit down on a chair, for her legs were giving way under her. She did not attempt to vindicate herself. All that she would find to say was, "Is Monsieur Goujet ill?"

Yes, he was not well. He had been obliged to come home instead of returning to the forge, and he had gone to lie down on his bed to get a rest. Madame Goujet talked gravely, wearing her black dress as usual and her white face framed in her nun-like coif. The pay at the forge had been cut again. It was now only seven francs a day because the machines did so much of the work. This forced her to save money every way she could. She would do her own washing from now on. It would naturally have been very helpful if the Coupeaus had been able to return her the money lent them by her son; but she was not going to set the lawyers on them, as they were unable to pay. As she was talking about the debt, Gervaise lowered her eyes in embarrassment.

"All the same," continued the lace-maker, "by pinching yourselves a little you could manage to pay it off. For really now, you live very well; and spend a great deal, I'm sure. If you were only to pay off ten francs a month."

She was interrupted by the sound of Goujet's voice as he called, "Mamma. Mamma."

And when she returned to her seat, which was almost immediately, she changed the conversation. The blacksmith had doubtless begged her not to ask Gervaise for money; but in spite of herself she again spoke of the debt at the expiration of five minutes . . . . She had foreseen long ago what was now happening. Coupeau was drinking all that the laundry business brought in and dragging his wife down with him. Her son would never have loaned the money if he had only listened to her. By now he would have been married, instead of miserably sad with only unhappiness to look forward to for the rest of his life. She grew quite stern and angry, even accusing Gervaise of having schemed with Coupeau to take advantage of her foolish son. Yes, some women were able to play the hypocrite for years, but eventually the truth came out.

"Mamma. Mamma." again called Goujet, but louder this time.

She rose from her seat and when she returned she said, as she resumed her lace mending:

"Go in, he wishes to see you."

Gervaise, all in a tremble left the door open. This scene filled her with emotion because it was like an avowal of their affection before Madame Goujet. She again beheld the quiet little chamber, with its narrow iron bedstead, and walls covered over with pictures, the whole looking like the room of some girl of fifteen. Goujet's big body was stretched on the bed. Mother Coupeau's disclosures and the things his mother had been saying seemed to have knocked all the life out of his limbs. His eyes were red and swollen, his beautiful yellow beard was still wet. In the first moment of rage he must have punched away at his pillow with his terrible fists, for the ticking was split and the feathers were coming out.

"Listen, mamma's wrong," said he to the laundress in a voice that was scarcely audible. "You owe me nothing. I won't have it mentioned again."

He had raised himself up and was looking at her. Big tears at once filled his eyes.

"Do you suffer, Monsieur Goujet?" murmured she. "What is the matter with you? Tell me."

"Nothing, thanks. I tired myself with too much work yesterday. I will rest a bit."

Then, his heart breaking, he could not restrain himself and burst out, "My God Ah. My God. It was never to be—never. You swore it. And now it is—it is. Ah, it pains me too much, leave me."

And with his hand he gently and imploringly motioned to her to go. She did not draw nearer to the bed. She went off as he requested her to, feeling stupid, unable to say anything to soothe him. When in the other room she took up her basket; but she did not go home. She stood there trying to find something to say. Madame Goujet continued her mending without raising her head. It was she who at length said, "Well. Good-night; send me back my things and we will settle up afterwards."

"Yes, it will be best so—good-night," stammered Gervaise.

She took a last look around the neatly arranged room and thought as she shut the door that she seemed to be leaving some part of her better self behind. She plodded blindly back to the laundry, scarcely knowing where she was going.

When Gervaise arrived, she found mother Coupeau out of her bed, sitting on a chair by the stove. Gervaise was too tired to scold her. Her bones ached as though she had been beaten and she was thinking that her life was becoming too hard to bear. Surely a quick death was the only escape from the pain in her heart.

After this, Gervaise became indifferent to everything. With a vague gesture of her hand she would send everybody about their business. At each fresh worry she buried herself deeper in her only pleasure, which was to have her three meals a day. The shop might have collapsed. So long as she was not beneath it, she would have gone off willingly without a chemise to her back. And the little shop was collapsing, not suddenly, but little by little, morning and evening. One by one the customers got angry, and sent their washing elsewhere. Monsieur Madinier, Mademoiselle Remanjou, the Boches themselves had returned to Madame Fauconnier, where they could count on great punctuality. One ends by getting tired of asking for a pair of stockings for three weeks straight, and of putting on shirts with grease stains dating from the previous Sunday. Gervaise, without losing a bite, wished them a pleasant journey, and spoke her mind about them, saying that she was precious glad she would no longer have to poke her nose into their filth. The entire neighborhood could quit her; that would relieve her of the piles of stinking junk and give her less work to do.

Now her only customers were those who didn't pay regularly, the street-walkers, and women like Madame Gaudron, whose laundry smelled so bad that not one of the laundresses on the Rue Neuve would take it. She had to let Madame Putois go, leaving only her apprentice, squint-eyed Augustine, who seemed to grow more stupid as time passed. Frequently there was not even enough work for the two of them and they sat on stools all afternoon doing nothing.

While idleness and poverty entered, dirtiness naturally entered also. One would never have recognized that beautiful blue shop, the color of heaven, which had once been Gervaise's pride. Its window-frames and panes, which were never washed, were covered from top to bottom with the splashes of the passing vehicles. On the brass rods in the windows were displayed three gray rags left by customers who had died in the hospital. And inside it was more pitiable still; the dampness of the clothes hung up at the ceiling to dry had loosed all the wallpaper; the

Pompadour chintz hung in strips like cobwebs covered with dust; the big stove, broken and in holes from the rough use of the poker, looked in its corner like the stock in trade of a dealer in old iron; the work-table appeared as though it had been used by a regiment, covered as it was with wine and coffee stains, sticky with jam, greasy from spilled gravy.

Gervaise was so at ease among it all that she never even noticed the shop was getting filthy. She became used to it all, just as she got used to wearing torn skirts and no longer washing herself carefully. The disorder was like a warm nest.

Her own ease was her sole consideration; she did not care a pin for anything else. The debts, though still increasing, no longer troubled her. Her honesty gradually deserted her; whether she would be able to pay or not was altogether uncertain, and she preferred not to think about it. When her credit was stopped at one shop, she would open an account at some other shop close by. She was in debt all over the neighborhood; she owed money every few yards. To take merely the Rue de la Goutte-d'Or, she no longer dared pass in front of the grocer's, nor the charcoal-dealer's, nor the greengrocer's; and this obliged her, whenever she required to be at the wash-house, to go round by the Rue des Poissonniers, which was quite ten minutes out of her way. The tradespeople came and treated her as a swindler. One evening the dealer from whom she had purchased Lantier's furniture made a scene in the street. Scenes like this upset her at the time, but were soon forgotten and never spoiled her appetite. What a nerve to bother her like that when she had no money to pay. They were all robbers anyway and it served them right to have to wait. Well, she'd have to go bankrupt, but she didn't intend to fret about it now.

Meanwhile mother Coupeau had recovered. For another year the household jogged along. During the summer months there was naturally a little more work—the white petticoats and the cambric dresses of the street-walkers of the exterior Boulevard. The catastrophe was slowly approaching; the home sank deeper into the mire every week; there were ups and downs, however—days when one had to rub one's stomach before the empty cupboard, and others when one ate veal enough to make one burst. Mother Coupeau was forever being seen in the street, hiding bundles under her apron, and strolling in the direction of the pawn-place in the Rue Polonceau. She strutted along with the air of a devotee going to mass; for she did not dislike these errands; haggling about money amused her; this crying up of her wares like a second-hand dealer tickled the old woman's fancy for driving hard bargains. The clerks knew her well and called her "Mamma Four Francs," because she always demanded four francs when they offered three, on bundles no bigger than two sous' worth of butter.

At the start, Gervaise took advantage of good weeks to get things back from the pawn-shops, only to put them back again the next week. Later she let things go altogether, selling her pawn tickets for cash.

One thing alone gave Gervaise a pang—it was having to pawn her clock to pay an acceptance for twenty francs to a bailiff who came to seize her goods. Until then, she had sworn rather to die of hunger than to part with her clock. When mother Coupeau carried it away in a little bonnet-box, she sunk on to a chair, without a particle of strength left in her arms, her eyes full of tears, as though a fortune was being torn from her. But when mother Coupeau reappeared with twenty-five francs, the unexpected loan, the five francs profit consoled her; she at once sent the old woman out again for four sous' worth of brandy in a glass, just to toast the five-franc piece.

The two of them would often have a drop together, when they were on good terms with each other. Mother Coupeau was very successful at bringing back a full glass hidden in her apron pocket without spilling a drop. Well, the neighbors didn't need to know, did they. But the neighbors knew perfectly well. This turned the neighborhood even more against Gervaise. She was devouring everything; a few more mouthfuls and the place would be swept clean.

In the midst of this general demolishment, Coupeau continued to prosper. The confounded tippler was as well as well could be. The sour wine and the "vitriol" positively fattened him. He ate a great deal, and laughed at that stick Lorilleux, who accused drink of killing people, and answered him by slapping himself on the stomach, the skin of which was so stretched by the fat that it resembled the skin of a drum. He would play him a tune on it, the glutton's vespers, with rolls and beats loud enough to have made a quack's fortune. Lorilleux, annoyed at not having any fat himself, said that it was soft and unhealthy. Coupeau ignored him and went on drinking more and more, saying it was for his health's sake.

His hair was beginning to turn gray and his face to take on the drunkard's hue of purplish wine. He continued to act like a mischievous child. Well, it wasn't his concern if there was nothing about the place to eat. When he went for weeks without work he became even more difficult.

Still, he was always giving Lantier friendly slaps on the back. People swore he had no suspicion at all. Surely something terrible would happen if he ever found out. Madame Lerat shook her head at this. His sister said she had known of husbands who didn't mind at all.

Lantier wasn't wasting away either. He took great care of himself, measuring his stomach by the waist-board of his trousers, with the constant dread of having to loosen the buckle or draw it tighter; for he considered himself just right, and out of coquetry neither desired to grow fatter nor thinner. That made him hard to please in the matter of food, for he regarded every dish from the point of view of keeping his waist as it was. Even when there was not a sou in the house, he required eggs, cutlets, light and nourishing things. Since he was sharing the lady of the house, he considered himself to have a half interest in everything and would pocket any franc pieces he saw lying about. He kept Gervaise running here and there and seemed more at home than Coupeau. Nana was his favorite because he adored pretty little girls, but he paid less and less attention to Etienne, since boys, according to him, ought to know how to take care of themselves. If anyone came to see Coupeau while he was out, Lantier, in shirt sleeves and slippers, would come out of the back room with the bored expression of a husband who has been disturbed, saying he would answer for Coupeau as it was all the same.

Between these two gentlemen, Gervaise had nothing to laugh about. She had nothing to complain of as regards her health, thank goodness. She was growing too fat. But two men to coddle was often more than she could manage. Ah. My God. One husband is already too much for a woman. The worst was that they got on very well together, the rogues. They never quarreled; they would chuckle in each other's faces, as they sat of an evening after dinner, their elbows on the table; they would rub up against one another all the live-long day, like cats which seek and cultivate their pleasure. The days when they came home in a rage, it was on her that they vented it. Go at it. Hammer away at the animal. She had a good back; it made them all the better friends when they yelled together. And it never did for her to give them tit-for-tat. In the beginning, whenever one of them yelled at her, she would appeal to the other, but this seldom worked. Coupeau had a foul mouth and called her horrible things. Lantier chose his insults carefully, but they often hurt her even more.

But one can get used to anything. Soon their nasty remarks and all the wrongs done her by these two men slid off her smooth skin like water off a duck's back. It was even easier to have them angry, because when they were in good moods they bothered her too much, never giving her time to get a bonnet ironed.

Yes, Coupeau and Lantier were wearing her out. The zinc-worker, sure enough, lacked education; but the hatter had too much, or at least he had education in the same way that dirty people have a white shirt, with filth underneath it. One night, she dreamed that she was on the edge of a wall; Coupeau was knocking her into it with a blow of his fist, while Lantier was tickling her in the ribs to make her fall quicker. Well, that resembled her life. It was no surprise if she was becoming slipshod. The neighbors weren't fair in blaming her for the frightful habits she had fallen into. Sometimes a cold shiver ran through her, but things could have been worse, so she tried to make the best of it. Once she had seen a play in which the wife detested her husband and poisoned him for the sake of her lover. Wasn't it more sensible for the three of them to live together in peace? In spite of her debts and poverty she thought she was quite happy and could live in peace if only Coupeau and Lantier would stop yelling at her so much.

Towards the autumn, unfortunately, things became worse. Lantier pretended he was getting thinner, and pulled a longer face over the matter every day. He grumbled at everything, sniffed at the dishes of potatoes—a mess he could not eat, he would say, without having the colic. The least jangling now turned to quarrels, in which they accused one another of being the cause of all their troubles, and it was a devil of a job to restore harmony before they all retired for the night.

Lantier sensed a crisis coming and it exasperated him to realize that this place was already so thoroughly cleaned out that he could see the day coming when he'd have to take his hat and seek elsewhere for his bed and board. He had become accustomed to this little paradise where he was nicely treated by everybody. He should have blamed himself for eating himself out of house and home, but instead he blamed the Coupeaus for letting themselves be ruined in less than two years. He thought Gervaise was too extravagant. What was going to happen to them now?

One evening in December they had no dinner at all. There was not a radish left. Lantier, who was very glum, went out early, wandering about in search of some other den where the smell of the kitchen would bring a smile to one's face. He would now remain for hours beside the stove wrapt in thought. Then, suddenly, he began to evince a great friendship for the Poissons. He no longer teased the policeman and even went so far as to concede that the Emperor might not be such a bad fellow after all. He seemed to especially admire Virginie. No doubt he was hoping to board with them. Virginie having acquainted him with her desire to set up in some sort of business, he agreed with everything she said, and declared that her idea was a most brilliant one. She was just the person for trade—tall, engaging and active . . . . She would make as much as she liked. The capital had been available for some time, thanks to an inheritance from an aunt. Lantier told her of all the shopkeepers who were making fortunes. The time was right for it; you could sell anything these days. Virginie, however, hesitated; she was looking for a shop that was to be let, she did not wish to leave the neighborhood. Then Lantier would take her into corners and converse with her in an undertone for ten minutes at a time. He seemed to be urging her to do something in spite of herself; and she no longer said "no," but appeared to authorize him to act. It was as a secret between them, with winks and words rapidly exchanged, some mysterious understanding which betrayed itself even in their hand-shakings.

From this moment the hatter would covertly watch the Coupeaus while eating their dry bread, and becoming very talkative again, would deafen them with his continual jeremiads. All day long Gervaise moved in the midst of that poverty which he so obligingly spread out. My God. He wasn't thinking of himself; he would go on starving with his friends as long as they liked. But look at it with common sense. They owed at least five hundred francs in the neighborhood. Besides which, they were two quarters rent behind with the rent, which meant another two hundred and fifty francs; the landlord, Monsieur Marescot, even spoke of having them evicted if they did not pay him by the first of January. Finally the pawn-place had absorbed everything, one could not have got together three francs' worth of odds and ends, the clearance had been so complete; the nails remained in the walls and that was all and perhaps there were two pounds of them at three sous the pound. Gervaise, thoroughly entangled in it all, her nerves quite upset by this calculation, would fly into a passion and bang her fists down upon the table or else she would end by bursting into tears like a fool. One night she exclaimed:

"I'll be off to-morrow. I prefer to put the key under the door and to sleep on the pavement rather than continue to live in such frights."

"It would be wiser," said Lantier slyly, "to get rid of the lease if you could find someone to take it. When you are both decided to give up the shop."

She interrupted him more violently, "At once, at once. Ah. It'll be a good riddance."

Then the hatter became very practical. On giving up the lease one would no doubt get the new tenant to be responsible for the two overdue quarters. And he ventured to mention the Poissons, he reminded them that Virginie was looking for a shop; theirs would perhaps suit her. He remembered that he had heard her say she longed for one just like it. But when Virginie's name was mentioned the laundress suddenly regained her composure. We'll see how things go along. When you're angry you always talk of quitting, but it isn't so easy when you just stop to think about it.

During the following days it was in vain that Lantier harped upon the subject. Gervaise replied that she had seen herself worse off and had pulled through. How would she be better off when she no longer had her shop? That would not put bread into their mouths. She would, on the contrary, engage some fresh workwomen and work up a fresh connection.

Lantier made the mistake of mentioning Virginie again. This stirred Gervaise into furious obstinacy. No. Never. She had always had her suspicions of what was in Virginie's heart. Virginie only wanted to humiliate her. She would rather turn it over to the first woman to come in from the street than to that hypocrite who had been waiting for years to see her fail. Yes, Virginie still had in mind that fight in the wash-house. Well, she'd be wiser to forget about it, unless she wanted another one now.

In the face of this flow of angry retorts, Lantier began by attacking Gervaise. He called her stupid and stuck-up. He even went so far as to abuse Coupeau, accusing him of not knowing how to make his wife respect his friend. Then, realizing that passion would compromise everything, he swore that he would never again interest himself in the affairs of other people, for one always got more kicks than thanks; and indeed he appeared to have given up all idea of talking them into parting with the lease, but he was really watching for a favorable opportunity of broaching the subject again and of bringing the laundress round to his views.

January had now arrived; the weather was wretched, both damp and cold. Mother Coupeau, who had coughed and choked all through December, was obliged to take to her bed after Twelfth-night. It was her annuity, which she expected every winter. This winter though, those around her said she'd never come out of her bedroom except feet first. Indeed, her gaspings sounded like a death rattle. She was still fat, but one eye was blind and one side of her face was twisted. The doctor made one call and didn't return again. They kept giving her tisanes and going to check on her every hour. She could no longer speak because her breathing was so difficult.

One Monday evening, Coupeau came home totally drunk. Ever since his mother was in danger, he had lived in a continual state of deep emotion. When he was in bed, snoring soundly, Gervaise walked about the place for a while. She was in the habit of watching over mother Coupeau during a part of the night. Nana had showed herself very brave, always sleeping beside the old woman, and saying that if she heard her dying, she would wake everyone. Since the invalid seemed to be sleeping peacefully this night, Gervaise finally yielded to the appeals of Lantier to come into his room for a little rest. They only kept a candle alight, standing on the ground behind the wardrobe. But towards three o'clock Gervaise abruptly jumped out of bed, shivering and oppressed with anguish. She thought she had felt a cold breath pass over her body. The morsel of candle had burnt out; she tied on her petticoats in the dark, all bewildered, and with feverish hands. It was not till she got into the little room, after knocking up against the furniture, that

she was able to light a small lamp. In the midst of the oppressive silence
of night, the zinc-worker's snores alone sounded as two grave notes.
Nana, stretched on her back, was breathing gently between her pouting
lips. And Gervaise, holding down the lamp which caused big shadows
to dance about the room, cast the light on mother Coupeau's face, and
beheld it all white, the head lying on the shoulder, the eyes wide open.
Mother Coupeau was dead.

Gently, without uttering a cry, icy cold yet prudent, the laundress returned to Lantier's room. He had gone to sleep again. She bent over
him and murmured:

"Listen, it's all over, she's dead."

Heavy with sleep, only half awake, he grunted at first, "Leave me
alone, get into bed. We can't do her any good if she's dead."

Then he raised himself on his elbow and asked, "What's the time?"

"Three o'clock."

"Only three o'clock. Get into bed quick. You'll catch cold. When it's
daylight, we'll see what's to be done."

But she did not listen to him, she dressed herself completely.
Bundling himself in the blankets, Lantier muttered about how stub-
born women were. What was the hurry to announce a death in the
house? He was irritated at having his sleep spoiled by such gloomy matters.

Meanwhile, Gervaise had moved her things back into her own
room. Then she felt free to sit down and cry, no longer fearful of being
caught in Lantier's room. She had been fond of mother Coupeau and
felt a deep sorrow at her loss. She sat, crying by herself, her sobs loud
in the silence, but Coupeau never stirred. She had spoken to him and
even shaken him and finally decided to let him sleep. He would be more
of a nuisance if he woke up.

On returning to the body, she found Nana sitting up in bed rubbing
her eyes. The child understood, and with her vicious urchin's curiosity,
stretched out her neck to get a better view of her grandmother; she
said nothing but she trembled slightly, surprised and satisfied in the
presence of this death which she had been promising herself for two
days past, like some nasty thing hidden away and forbidden to children;
and her young cat-like eyes dilated before that white face all emaciated
at the last gasp by the passion of life, she felt that tingling in her back

which she felt behind the glass door when she crept there to spy on what was no concern of chits like her.

"Come, get up," said her mother in a low voice. "You can't remain here."

She regretfully slid out of bed, turning her head round and not taking her eyes off the corpse. Gervaise was much worried about her, not knowing where to put her till day-time. She was about to tell her to dress herself, when Lantier, in his trousers and slippers, rejoined her. He could not get to sleep again, and was rather ashamed of his behavior.

Then everything was arranged.

"She can sleep in my bed," murmured he. "She'll have plenty of room."

Nana looked at her mother and Lantier with her big, clear eyes and put on her stupid air, the same as on New Year's Day when anyone made her a present of a box of chocolate candy. And there was certainly no need for them to hurry her. She trotted off in her night-gown, her bare feet scarcely touching the tiled floor; she glided like a snake into the bed, which was still quite warm, and she lay stretched out and buried in it, her slim body scarcely raising the counterpane. Each time her mother entered the room she beheld her with her eyes sparkling in her motionless face—not sleeping, not moving, very red with excitement, and appearing to reflect on her own affairs.

Lantier assisted Gervaise in dressing mother Coupeau—and it was not an easy matter, for the body was heavy. One would never have thought that that old woman was so fat and so white. They put on her stockings, a white petticoat, a short linen jacket and a white cap—in short, the best of her linen. Coupeau continued snoring, a high note and a low one, the one sharp, the other flat. One could almost have imagined it to be church music accompanying the Good Friday ceremonies. When the corpse was dressed and properly laid out on the bed, Lantier poured himself out a glass of wine, for he felt quite upset. Gervaise searched the chest of drawers to find a little brass crucifix which she had brought from Plassans, but she recollected that mother Coupeau had, in all probability, sold it herself. They had lighted the stove, and they passed the rest of the night half asleep on chairs, finishing the bottle of wine that had been opened, worried and sulking, as though it was their own fault.

Towards seven o'clock, before daylight, Coupeau at length awoke. When he learnt his loss he at first stood still with dry eyes, stuttering and vaguely thinking that they were playing him some joke. Then he threw himself on the ground and went and knelt beside the corpse. His kissed it and wept like a child, with such a copious flow of tears that he quite wetted the sheet with wiping his cheeks. Gervaise had recommenced sobbing, deeply affected by her husband's grief, and the best of friends with him again. Yes, he was better at heart than she thought he was. Coupeau's despair mingled with a violent pain in his head. He passed his fingers through his hair. His mouth was dry, like after a binge, and he was still a little drunk in spite of his ten hours of sleep. And, clenching his fist, he complained aloud. My God, she was gone now, his poor mother, whom he loved so much. Ah. What a headache he had; it would settle him. It was like a wig of fire. And now they were tearing out his heart. No, it was not just of fate thus to set itself against one man.

"Come, cheer up, old fellow," said Lantier, raising him from the ground. "You must pull yourself together."

He poured him out a glass of wine, but Coupeau refused to drink.

"What's the matter with me? I've got copper in my throat. It's mamma. When I saw her I got a taste of copper in my mouth. Mamma. My God. Mamma, Mamma."

And he recommenced crying like a child. Then he drank the glass of wine, hoping to put out the flame searing his breast. Lantier soon left, using the excuse of informing the family and filing the necessary declaration at the town hall. Really though, he felt the need of fresh air, and so he took his time, smoking cigarettes and enjoying the morning air. When he left Madame Lerat's house, he went into a dairy place on Les Batignolles for a cup of hot coffee and remained there an hour, thinking things over.

Towards nine o'clock the family was all united in the shop, the shutters of which were kept up. Lorilleux did not cry. Moreover he had some pressing work to attend to, and he returned almost directly to his room, after having stalked about with a face put on for the occasion. Madame Lorilleux and Madame Lerat embraced the Coupeaus and wiped their eyes, from which a few tears were falling. But Madame Lorilleux, after giving a hasty glance round the death chamber, suddenly raised her voice to say that it was unheard of, that one never left a lighted lamp beside a corpse; there should be a candle, and Nana was sent to purchase a packet of tall ones. Ah, well. It made one long to die at Clump-clump's, she laid one out in such a fine fashion. What a fool, not even to know what to do with a corpse. Had she then never buried anyone in her life? Madame Lerat had to go to the neighbors and borrow a crucifix; she brought one back which was too big, a cross of black wood with a Christ in painted cardboard fastened to it, which covered the whole of mother Coupeau's chest, and seemed to crush her under its weight. Then they tried to obtain some holy water, but no one had any, and it was again Nana who was sent to the church to bring some back in a bottle. In practically no time the tiny room presented quite another appearance; on a little table a candle was burning beside a glass full of holy water into which a sprig of boxwood was dipped. Now, if anyone came, it would at least look decent. And they arranged the chairs in a circle in the shop for receiving people.

Lantier only returned at eleven o'clock. He had been to the undertaker's for information.

"The coffin is twelve francs," said he. "If you desire a mass, it will be ten francs more. Then there's the hearse, which is charged for according to the ornaments."

". . . . It's quite unnecessary to be fancy," murmured Madame Lorilleux, raising her head in a surprised and anxious manner. "We can't bring mamma to life again, can we? One must do according to one's means."

"Of course, that's just what I think," resumed the hatter. "I merely asked the prices to guide you. Tell me what you desire; and after lunch I will give the orders."

They were talking in lowered voices. Only a dim light came into the room through the cracks in the shutters. The door to the little room stood half open, and from it came the deep silence of death. Children's laughter echoed in the courtyard. Suddenly they heard the voice of Nana, who had escaped from the Boches to whom she had been sent. She was giving commands in her shrill voice and the children were singing a song about a donkey.

Gervaise waited until it was quiet to say, "We're not rich certainly; but all the same we wish to act decently. If mother Coupeau has left us nothing, it's no reason for pitching her into the ground like a dog. No;

we must have a mass, and a hearse with a few ornaments."

"And who will pay for them?" violently inquired Madame Lorilleux. "Not we, who lost some money last week; and you either, as you're stumped. Ah. You ought, however, to see where it has led you, this trying to impress people."

Coupeau, when consulted, mumbled something with a gesture of profound indifference, and then fell asleep again on his chair. Madame Lerat said that she would pay her share. She was of Gervaise's opinion, they should do things decently. Then the two of them fell to making calculations on a piece of paper: in all, it would amount to about ninety francs, because they decided, after a long discussion, to have a hearse ornamented with a narrow scallop.

"We're three," concluded the laundress. "We'll give thirty francs each. It won't ruin us."

But Madame Lorilleux broke out in a fury.

"Well. I refuse, yes, I refuse. It's not for the thirty francs. I'd give a hundred thousand, if I had them, and if it would bring mamma to life again. Only, I don't like vain people. You've got a shop, you only dream of showing off before the neighborhood. We don't fall in with it, we don't. We don't try to make ourselves out what we are not . . . . You can manage it to please yourself. Put plumes on the hearse if it amuses you."

"No one asks you for anything," Gervaise ended by answering. "Even though I should have to sell myself, I'll not have anything to reproach myself with. I've fed mother Coupeau without your help, and I can certainly bury her without your help also. I already once before gave you a bit of my mind; I pick up stray cats, I'm not likely to leave your mother in the mire."

Then Madame Lorilleux burst into tears and Lantier had to prevent her from leaving. The argument became so noisy that Madame Lerat felt she had to go quietly into the little room and glance tearfully at her dead mother, as though fearing to find her awake and listening. Just at this moment the girls playing in the courtyard, led by Nana, began singing again.

"My God how those children grate on one's nerves with their singing." said Gervaise, all upset and on the point of sobbing with impatience and sadness. Turning to the hatter, she said:

"Do please make them leave off, and send Nana back to the

concierge's with a kick."

Madame Lerat and Madame Lorilleux went away to eat lunch, promising to return. The Coupeaus sat down to eat a bite without much appetite, feeling hesitant about even raising a fork. After lunch Lantier went to the undertaker's again with the ninety francs. Thirty had come from Madame Lerat and Gervaise had run, with her hair all loose, to borrow sixty francs from Goujet.

Several of the neighbors called in the afternoon, mainly out of curiosity. They went into the little room to make the sign of the cross and sprinkle some holy water with the boxwood sprig. Then they sat in the shop and talked endlessly about the departed. Mademoiselle Remanjou had noticed that her right eye was still open. Madame Gaudron maintained that she had a fine complexion for her age. Madame Fauconnier kept repeating that she had seen her having coffee only three days earlier.

Towards evening the Coupeaus were beginning to have had enough of it. It was too great an affliction for a family to have to keep a corpse so long a time. The government ought to have made a new law on the subject. All through another evening, another night, and another morning—no. It would never come to an end. When one no longer weeps, grief turns to irritation; is it not so? One would end by misbehaving oneself. Mother Coupeau, dumb and stiff in the depths of the narrow chamber, was spreading more and more over the lodging and becoming heavy enough to crush the people in it. And the family, in spite of itself, gradually fell into the ordinary mode of life, and lost some portion of its respect.

"You must have a mouthful with us," said Gervaise to Madame Lerat and Madame Lorilleux, when they returned. "We're too sad; we must keep together."

They laid the cloth on the work-table. Each one, on seeing the plates, thought of the feastings they had had on it. Lantier had returned. Lorilleux came down. A pastry-cook had just brought a meat pie, for the laundress was too upset to attend to any cooking. As they were taking their seats, Boche came to say that Monsieur Marescot asked to be admitted, and the landlord appeared, looking very grave, and wearing a broad decoration on his frock-coat. He bowed in silence and went straight to the little room, where he knelt down. All the family, leaving the table, stood up, greatly impressed. Monsieur Marescot, having finished his devotions, passed into the shop and said to the Coupeaus:

"I have come for the two quarters' rent that's overdue. Are you prepared to pay?"

"No, sir, not quite," stammered Gervaise, greatly put out at hearing this mentioned before the Lorilleuxs. "You see, with the misfortune which has fallen upon us."

"No doubt, but everyone has their troubles," resumed the landlord, spreading out his immense fingers, which indicated the former workman. "I am very sorry, but I cannot wait any longer. If I am not paid by the morning after to-morrow, I shall be obliged to have you put out."

Gervaise, struck dumb, imploringly clasped her hands, her eyes full of tears. With an energetic shake of his big bony head, he gave her to understand that supplications were useless. Besides, the respect due to the dead forbade all discussion. He discreetly retired, walking backwards.

"A thousand pardons for having disturbed you," murmured he. "The morning after to-morrow; do not forget."

And as on withdrawing he again passed before the little room, he saluted the corpse a last time through the wide open door by devoutly bending his knee.

They began eating and gobbled the food down very quickly, so as not to seem to be enjoying it, only slowing down when they reached the dessert. Occasionally Gervaise or one of the sisters would get up, still holding her napkin, to look into the small room. They made plenty of strong coffee to keep them awake through the night. The Poissons arrived about eight and were invited for coffee.

Then Lantier, who had been watching Gervaise's face, seemed to seize an opportunity that he had been waiting for ever since the morning. In speaking of the indecency of landlords who entered houses of mourning to demand their money, he said:

"He's a Jesuit, the beast, with his air of officiating at a mass. But in your place, I'd just chuck up the shop altogether."

Gervaise, quite worn out and feeling weak and nervous, gave way and replied:

"Yes, I shall certainly not wait for the bailiffs. Ah. It's more than I can bear—more than I can bear."

The Lorilleuxs, delighted at the idea that Clump-clump would no longer have a shop, approved the plan immensely. One could hardly conceive the great cost a shop was. If she only earned three francs working for others she at least had no expenses; she did not risk losing large sums of money. They repeated this argument to Coupeau, urging him on; he drank a great deal and remained in a continuous fit of sensibility, weeping all day by himself in his plate. As the laundress seemed to be allowing herself to be convinced, Lantier looked at the Poissons and winked. And tall Virginie intervened, making herself most amiable.

"You know, we might arrange the matter between us. I would relieve you of the rest of the lease and settle your matter with the landlord. In short, you would not be worried nearly so much."

"No thanks," declared Gervaise, shaking herself as though she felt a shudder pass over her. "I'll work; I've got my two arms, thank heaven. To help me out of my difficulties."

"We can talk about it some other time," the hatter hastened to put in. "It's scarcely the thing to do so this evening. Some other time—in the morning for instance."

At this moment, Madame Lerat, who had gone into the little room, uttered a faint cry. She had had a fright because she had found the candle burnt out. They all busied themselves in lighting another; they shook their heads, saying that it was not a good sign when the light went out beside a corpse.

The wake commenced. Coupeau had gone to lie down, not to sleep, said he, but to think; and five minutes afterwards he was snoring. When they sent Nana off to sleep at the Boches' she cried; she had been looking forward ever since the morning to being nice and warm in her good friend Lantier's big bed. The Poissons stayed till midnight. Some hot wine had been made in a salad-bowl because the coffee affected the ladies' nerves too much. The conversation became tenderly effusive. Virginie talked of the country: she would like to be buried at the corner of a wood with wild flowers on her grave. Madame Lerat had already put by in her wardrobe the sheet for her shroud, and she kept it perfumed with a bunch of lavender; she wished always to have a nice smell under her nose when she would be eating the dandelions by the roots. Then, with no sort of transition, the policeman related that he had arrested a fine girl that morning who had been stealing from a pork-butcher's shop; on undressing her at the commissary of police's they had found ten sausages hanging round her body. And Madame Lorilleux having remarked, with a look of disgust, that she would not eat any of those sausages, the party burst into a gentle laugh. The wake became livelier, though not ceasing to preserve appearances.

But just as they were finishing the hot wine a peculiar noise, a dull trickling sound, issued from the little room. All raised their heads and looked at each other.

"It's nothing," said Lantier quietly, lowering his voice. "She's emptying."

The explanation caused the others to nod their heads in a reassured way, and they replaced their glasses on the table.

When the Poissons left for home, Lantier left also, saying he would sleep with a friend and leave his bed for the ladies in case they wanted to take turns napping. Lorilleux went upstairs to bed. Gervaise and the two sisters arranged themselves by the stove where they huddled together close to the warmth, talking quietly. Coupeau was still snoring.

Madame Lorilleux was complaining that she didn't have a black dress and asked Gervaise about the black skirt they had given mother Coupeau on her saint's day. Gervaise went to look for it. Madame Lorilleux then wanted some of the old linen and mentioned the bed, the wardrobe, and the two chairs as she looked around for other odds and ends. Madame Lerat had to serve as peace maker when a quarrel nearly broke out. She pointed out that as the Coupeaus had cared for their mother, they deserved to keep the few things she had left. Soon they were all dozing around the stove.

The night seemed terribly long to them. Now and again they shook themselves, drank some coffee and stretched their necks in the direction of the little room, where the candle, which was not to be snuffed, was burning with a dull red flame, flickering the more because of the black soot on the wick. Towards morning, they shivered, in spite of the great heat of the stove. Anguish and the fatigue of having talked too much was stifling them, while their mouths were parched, and their eyes ached. Madame Lerat threw herself on Lantier's bed, and snored as loud as a man; while the other two, their heads falling forward, and almost touching their knees, slept before the fire. At daybreak, a shudder awoke them. Mother Coupeau's candle had again gone out; and as,

in the obscurity, the dull trickling sound recommenced, Madame Lorilleux gave the explanation of it anew in a loud voice, so as to reassure
herself:

"She's emptying," repeated she, lighting another candle.

The funeral was to take place at half-past ten. A nice morning to
add to the night and the day before. Gervaise, though without a sou,
said she would have given a hundred francs to anybody who would have
come and taken mother Coupeau away three hours sooner. No, one
may love people, but they are too great a weight when they are dead; and
the more one has loved them, the sooner one would like to be rid of
their bodies.

The morning of a funeral is, fortunately, full of diversions. One
has all sorts of preparations to make. To begin with, they lunched. Then
it happened to be old Bazouge, the undertaker's helper, who lived on
the sixth floor, who brought the coffin and the sack of bran. He was
never sober, the worthy fellow. At eight o'clock that day, he was still
lively from the booze of the day before.

"This is for here, isn't it?" asked he.

And he laid down the coffin, which creaked like a new box. But as
he was throwing the sack of bran on one side, he stood with a look of
amazement in his eyes, his mouth opened wide, on beholding Gervaise
before him.

"Beg pardon, excuse me. I've made a mistake," stammered he. "I
was told it was for you."

He had already taken up the sack again, and the laundress was
obliged to call to him, "Leave it alone, it's for here."

"My God. Now I understand." resumed he, slapping his thigh. "It's
for the old lady."

Gervaise had turned quite pale. Old Bazouge had brought the coffin for her. By way of apology, he tried to be gallant, and continued,
"I'm not to blame, am I? It was said yesterday that someone on the
ground floor had passed away. Then I thought—you know, in our business, these things enter by one ear and go out by the other. All the same,
my compliments to you. As late as possible, eh? That's best, though life
isn't always amusing; ah. No, by no means."

As Gervaise listened to him, she draw back, afraid he would grab
her and take her away in the box. She remembered the time before,

when he had told her he knew of women who would thank him to come and get them. Well, she wasn't ready yet. My God. The thought sent chills down her spine. Her life may have been bitter, but she wasn't ready to give it up yet. No, she would starve for years first.

"He's abominably drunk," murmured she, with an air of disgust mingled with dread. "They at least oughtn't to send us tipplers. We pay dear enough."

Then he became insolent, and jeered, "See here, little woman, it's only put off until another time. I'm entirely at your service, remember. You've only to make me a sign. I'm the ladies' consoler. And don't spit on old Bazouge, because he's held in his arms finer ones than you, who let themselves be tucked in without a murmur, very pleased to continue their by-by in the dark."

"Hold your tongue, old Bazouge." said Lorilleux severely, having hastened to the spot on hearing the noise, "such jokes are highly improper. If we complained about you, you would get the sack. Come, be off, as you've no respect for principles."

Bazouge moved away, but one could hear him stuttering as he dragged along the pavement:

"Well. What? Principles? There's no such thing as principles, there's no such thing as principles—there's only common decency."

At length ten o'clock struck. The hearse was late. There were already several people in the shop, friends and neighbors—Monsieur Madinier, My-Boots, Madame Gaudron, Mademoiselle Remanjou; and every minute, a man's or a woman's head was thrust out of the gaping opening of the door between the closed shutters, to see if that creeping hearse was in sight. The family, all together in the back room, was shaking hands. Short pauses occurred interrupted by rapid whisperings, a tiresome and feverish waiting with sudden rushes of skirts—Madame Lorilleux who had forgotten her handkerchief, or else Madame Lerat who was trying to borrow a prayer-book. Everyone, on arriving, beheld the open coffin in the center of the little room before the bed; and in spite of oneself, each stood covertly studying it, calculating that plump mother Coupeau would never fit into it. They all looked at each other with this thought in their eyes, though without communicating it. But there was a slight pushing at the front door. Monsieur Madinier, extending his arms, came and said in a low grave voice, "Here they are."

It was not the hearse though. Four helpers entered hastily in single file, with their red faces, their hands all lumpy like persons in the habit of moving heavy things, and their rusty black clothes worn and frayed from constant rubbing against coffins. Old Bazouge walked first, very drunk and very proper. As soon as he was at work he found his equilibrium. They did not utter a word, but slightly bowed their heads, already weighing mother Coupeau with a glance. And they did not dawdle; the poor old woman was packed in, in the time one takes to sneeze. A young fellow with a squint, the smallest of the men, poured the bran into the coffin and spread it out. The tall and thin one spread the winding sheet over the bran. Then, two at the feet and two at the head, all four took hold of the body and lifted it. Mother Coupeau was in the box, but it was a tight fit. She touched on every side.

The undertaker's helpers were now standing up and waiting; the little one with the squint took the coffin lid, by way of inviting the family to bid their last farewell, while Bazouge had filled his mouth with nails and was holding the hammer in readiness. Then Coupeau, his two sisters and Gervaise threw themselves on their knees and kissed the mamma who was going away, weeping bitterly, the hot tears falling on and streaming down the stiff face now cold as ice. There was a prolonged sound of sobbing. The lid was placed on, and old Bazouge knocked the nails in with the style of a packer, two blows for each; and they none of them could hear any longer their own weeping in that din, which resembled the noise of furniture being repaired. It was over. The time for starting had arrived.

"What a fuss to make at such a time." said Madame Lorilleux to her husband as she caught sight of the hearse before the door.

The hearse was creating quite a revolution in the neighborhood. The tripe-seller called to the grocer's men, the little clockmaker came out on to the pavement, the neighbors leant out of their windows; and all these people talked about the scallop with its white cotton fringe. Ah. The Coupeaus would have done better to have paid their debts. But as the Lorilleuxs said, when one is proud it shows itself everywhere and in spite of everything.

"It's shameful," Gervaise was saying at the same moment, speaking of the chain-maker and his wife. "To think that those skinflints have not even brought a bunch of violets for their mother."

The Lorilleuxs, true enough, had come empty-handed. Madame Lerat had given a wreath of artificial flowers. And a wreath of immortelles and a bouquet bought by the Coupeaus were also placed on the coffin. The undertaker's helpers had to give a mighty heave to lift the coffin and carry it to the hearse. It was some time before the procession was formed. Coupeau and Lorilleux, in frock coats and with their hats in their hands, were chief mourners. The first, in his emotion which two glasses of white wine early in the morning had helped to sustain, clung to his brother-in-law's arm, with no strength in his legs, and a violent headache. Then followed the other men—Monsieur Madinier, very grave and all in black; My-Boots, wearing a great-coat over his blouse; Boche, whose yellow trousers produced the effect of a petard; Lantier, Gaudron, Bibi-the-Smoker, Poisson and others. The ladies came next—in the first row Madame Lorilleux, dragging the deceased's skirt, which she had altered; Madame Lerat, hiding under a shawl her hastily got-up mourning, a gown with lilac trimmings; and following them, Virginie, Madame Gaudron, Madame Fauconnier, Mademoiselle Remanjou and the rest. When the hearse started and slowly descended the Rue de la Goutte-d'Or, amidst signs of the cross and heads bared, the four helpers took the lead, two in front, the two others on the right and left. Gervaise had remained behind to close the shop. She left Nana with Madame Boche and ran to rejoin the procession, while the child, firmly held by the concierge under the porch, watched with a deeply interested gaze her grandmother disappear at the end of the street in that beautiful carriage.

At the moment when Gervaise caught up with the procession, Goujet arrived from another direction. He nodded to her so sympathetically that she was reminded of how unhappy she was, and began to cry again as Goujet took his place with the men.

The ceremony at the church was soon got through. The mass dragged a little, though, because the priest was very old. My-Boots and Bibi-the-Smoker preferred to remain outside on account of the collection. Monsieur Madinier studied the priests all the while, and communicated his observations to Lantier. Those jokers, though so glib with their Latin, did not even know a word of what they were saying. They buried a person just in the same way that they would have baptized or married him, without the least feeling in their heart.

Happily, the cemetery was not far off, the little cemetery of La Chapelle, a bit of a garden which opened on to the Rue Marcadet. The procession arrived disbanded, with stampings of feet and everybody talking of his own affairs. The hard earth resounded, and many would have liked to have moved about to keep themselves warm. The gaping hole beside which the coffin was laid was already frozen over, and looked white and stony, like a plaster quarry; and the followers, grouped round little heaps of gravel, did not find it pleasant standing in such piercing cold, while looking at the hole likewise bored them. At length a priest in a surplice came out of a little cottage. He shivered, and one could see his steaming breath at each *de profundis* that he uttered. At the final sign of the cross he bolted off, without the least desire to go through the service again. The sexton took his shovel, but on account of the frost, he was only able to detach large lumps of earth, which beat a fine tune down below, a regular bombardment of the coffin, an enfilade of artillery sufficient to make one think the wood was splitting. One may be a cynic; nevertheless that sort of music soon upsets one's stomach. The weeping recommenced. They moved off, they even got outside, but they still heard the detonations. My-Boots, blowing on his fingers, uttered an observation aloud.

"Mother of God; poor mother Coupeau won't feel very warm."

"Ladies and gentlemen," said the zinc-worker to the few friends who remained in the street with the family, "will you permit us to offer you some refreshments?"

He led the way to a wine shop in the Rue Marcadet, the "Arrival at the Cemetery." Gervaise, remaining outside, called Goujet, who was moving off, after again nodding to her. Why didn't he accept a glass of wine? He was in a hurry; he was going back to the workshop. Then they looked at each other a moment without speaking.

"I must ask your pardon for troubling you about the sixty francs," at length murmured the laundress. "I was half crazy, I thought of you."

". . . . Don't mention it; you're fully forgiven," interrupted the blacksmith. "And you know, I am quite at your service if any misfortune should overtake you. But don't say anything to mamma, because she has her ideas, and I don't wish to cause her annoyance."

She gazed at him. He seemed to her such a good man, and sad-looking, and so handsome. She was on the verge of accepting his former proposal, to go away with him and find happiness together somewhere else. Then an evil thought came to her. It was the idea of borrowing the six months' back rent from him.

She trembled and resumed in a caressing tone of voice, "We're still friends, aren't we?"

He shook his head as he answered, "Yes, we'll always be friends. It's just that, you know, all is over between us."

And he went off with long strides, leaving Gervaise bewildered, listening to his last words which rang in her ears with the clang of a big bell. On entering the wine shop, she seemed to hear a hollow voice within her which said, "All is over, well. All is over; there is nothing more for me to do if all is over." Sitting down, she swallowed a mouthful of bread and cheese, and emptied a glass full of wine which she found before her.

The wine shop was a single, long room with a low ceiling occupied by two large tables on which loaves of bread, large chunks of Brie cheese and bottles of wine were set out. They ate informally, without a tablecloth. Near the stove at the back the undertaker's helpers were finishing their lunch.

"My God" exclaimed Monsieur Madinier, "we each have our time. The old folks make room for the young ones. Your lodging will seem very empty to you now when you go home."

". . . . My brother is going to give notice," said Madame Lorilleux quickly. "That shop's ruined."

They had been working upon Coupeau. Everyone was urging him to give up the lease. Madame Lerat herself, who had been on very good terms with Lantier and Virginie for some time past, and who was tickled with the idea that they were a trifle smitten with each other, talked of bankruptcy and prison, putting on the most terrified airs. And suddenly, the zinc-worker, already overdosed with liquor, flew into a passion, his emotion turned to fury.

"Listen," cried he, poking his nose in his wife's face; "I intend that you shall listen to me. Your confounded head will always have its own way. But, this time, I intend to have mine, I warn you."

"Ah. Well," said Lantier, "no one can talk to her; it wants a mallet to drive it into her head."

For a time they both went on at her. Meanwhile, the Brie was quickly disappearing and the wine bottles were pouring like fountains. Gervaise began to weaken under this persistent pounding. She answered nothing, but hurried herself, her mouth ever full, as though she had been very hungry. When they got tired, she gently raised her head and said, "That's enough, isn't it? I don't give a damn for the shop. I want no more of it. Do you understand? It can go to hell."

Then they ordered some more bread and cheese and talked business. The Poissons took the rest of the lease and agreed to be answerable for the two quarters' rent overdue. Boche, moreover, pompously agreed to the arrangement in the landlord's name. He even then and there let a lodging to the Coupeaus—the vacant one on the sixth floor, in the same passage as the Lorilleuxs' apartment. As for Lantier, well, he would like to keep his room, if it did not inconvenience the Poissons. The policeman bowed; it did not inconvenience him at all; friends always get on together, in spite of any difference in their political ideas. And Lantier, without mixing himself up any more in the matter, like a man who has at length settled his little business, helped himself to an enormous slice of bread and cheese; he leant back in his chair and ate devoutly, his blood tingling beneath his skin, his whole body burning with a sly joy, and he blinked his eyes to peep first at Gervaise, and then at Virginie.

"Hi. Old Bazouge." called Coupeau, "come and have a drink. We're not proud; we're all workers."

The four undertaker's helpers, who had started to leave, came back to raise glasses with the group. They thought that the lady had weighed quite a bit and they had certainly earned a glass of wine. Old Bazouge gazed steadily at Gervaise without saying a word. It made her feel uneasy though and she got up and left the men who were beginning to show signs of being drunk. Coupeau began to sob again, saying he was feeling very sad.

That evening when Gervaise found herself at home again, she remained in a stupefied state on a chair. It seemed to her that the rooms were immense and deserted. Really, it would be a good riddance. But it was certainly not only mother Coupeau that she had left at the bottom of the hole in the little garden of the Rue Marcadet. She missed too many things, most likely a part of her life, and her shop, and her pride of being an employer, and other feelings besides, which she had buried on that day. Yes, the walls were bare, and her heart also; it was a complete clear out, a tumble into the pit. And she felt too tired; she would pick herself up again later on if she could.

At ten o'clock, when undressing, Nana cried and stamped. She wanted to sleep in mother Coupeau's bed. Her mother tried to frighten her; but the child was too precocious. Corpses only filled her with a great curiosity; so that, for the sake of peace, she was allowed to lie down in mother Coupeau's place. She liked big beds, the chit; she spread herself out and rolled about. She slept uncommonly well that night in the warm and pleasant feather bed.

CHAPTER X

The Coupeaus' new lodging was on the sixth floor, staircase B. After passing Mademoiselle Remanjou's door, you took the corridor to the left, and then turned again further along. The first door was for the apartment of the Bijards. Almost opposite, in an airless corner under a small staircase leading to the roof, was where Old Man Bru slept. Two doors further was Bazouge's room and the Coupeaus were opposite him, overlooking the court, with one room and a closet. There were only two more doors along the corridor before reaching that of the Lorilleuxs at the far end.

A room and a closet, no more. The Coupeaus perched there now. And the room was scarcely larger than one's hand. And they had to do everything in there—eat, sleep, and all the rest. Nana's bed just squeezed into the closet; she had to dress in her father and mother's room, and her door was kept open at night-time so that she should not be suffocated. There was so little space that Gervaise had left many things in the shop for the Poissons. A bed, a table, and four chairs completely filled their new apartment but she didn't have the courage to part with her old bureau and so it blocked off half the window. This made the room dark and gloomy, especially since one shutter was stuck shut. Gervaise was now so fat that there wasn't room for her in the limited window space and she had to lean sideways and crane her neck if she wanted to see the courtyard.

During the first few days, the laundress would continually sit down and cry. It seemed to her too hard, not being able to move about in her home, after having been used to so much room. She felt stifled; she remained at the window for hours, squeezed between the wall and the drawers and getting a stiff neck. It was only there that she could breathe freely. However, the courtyard inspired rather melancholy thoughts. Opposite her, on the sunny side, she would see that same window she had dreamed about long ago where the spring brought scarlet vines. Her own room was on the shady side where pots of mignonette died within a week . . . this wasn't at all the sort of life she had dreamed of.

She had to wallow in filth instead of having flowers all about her.

On leaning out one day, Gervaise experienced a peculiar sensation: she fancied she beheld herself down below, near the concierge's room under the porch, her nose in the air, and examining the house for the first time; and this leap thirteen years backwards caused her heart to throb. The courtyard was a little dingier and the walls more stained, otherwise it hadn't changed much. But she herself felt terribly changed and worn. To begin with, she was no longer below, her face raised to heaven, feeling content and courageous and aspiring to a handsome lodging. She was right up under the roof, among the most wretched, in the dirtiest hole, the part that never received a ray of sunshine. And that explained her tears; she could scarcely feel enchanted with her fate.

However, when Gervaise had grown somewhat used to it, the early days of the little family in their new home did not pass off so badly. The winter was almost over, and the trifle of money received for the furniture sold to Virginie helped to make things comfortable. Then with the fine weather came a piece of luck, Coupeau was engaged to work in the country at Etampes; and he was there for nearly three months without once getting drunk, cured for a time by the fresh air. One has no idea what a quench it is to the tippler's thirst to leave Paris where the very streets are full of the fumes of wine and brandy. On his return he was as fresh as a rose, and he brought back in his pocket four hundred francs with which they paid the two overdue quarters' rent at the shop that the Poissons had become answerable for, and also the most pressing of their little debts in the neighborhood. Gervaise thus opened two or three streets through which she had not passed for a long time.

She had naturally become an ironer again. Madame Fauconnier was quite good-hearted if you flattered her a bit, and she was happy to take Gervaise back, even paying her the same three francs a day as her best worker. This was out of respect for her former status as an employer. The household seemed to be getting on well and Gervaise looked forward to the day when all the debts would be paid. Hard work and economy would solve all their money troubles. Unfortunately, she dreamed of this in the warm satisfaction of the large sum earned by her husband. Soon, she said that the good things never lasted and took things as they came.

What the Coupeaus most suffered from at that time was seeing the

Poissons installing themselves at their former shop. They were not naturally of a particularly jealous disposition, but people aggravated them by purposely expressing amazement in their presence at the embellishments of their successors. The Boches and the Lorilleuxs especially, never tired. According to them, no one had ever seen so beautiful a shop. They were also continually mentioning the filthy state in which the Poissons had found the premises, saying that it had cost thirty francs for the cleaning alone.

After much deliberation, Virginie had decided to open a shop specializing in candies, chocolate, coffee and tea. Lantier had advised this, saying there was much money to be made from such delicacies. The shop was stylishly painted black with yellow stripes. Three carpenters worked for eight days on the interior, putting up shelves, display cases and counters. Poisson's small inheritance must have been almost completely used, but Virginie was ecstatic. The Lorilleuxs and the Boches made sure that Gervaise did not miss a single improvement and chuckled to themselves while watching her expression.

There was also a question of a man beneath all this. It was reported that Lantier had broken off with Gervaise. The neighborhood declared that it was quite right. In short, it gave a moral tone to the street. And all the honor of the separation was accorded to the crafty hatter on whom all the ladies continued to dote. Some said that she was still crazy about him and he had to slap her to make her leave him alone. Of course, no one told the actual truth. It was too simple and not interesting enough.

Actually Lantier climbed to the sixth floor to see her whenever he felt the impulse. Mademoiselle Remanjou had often seen him coming out of the Coupeaus' at odd hours.

The situation was even more complicated by neighborhood gossip linking Lantier and Virginie. The neighbors were a bit too hasty in this also; he had not even reached the stage of buttock-pinching with her. Still, the Lorilleuxs delighted in talking sympathetically to Gervaise about the affair between Lantier and Virginie. The Boches maintained they had never seen a more handsome couple. The odd thing in all this was that the Rue de la Goutte-d'Or seemed to have no objection to this new arrangement which everyone thought was progressing nicely. Those who had been so harsh to Gervaise were now quite lenient toward Virginie.

Gervaise had previously heard numerous reports about Lantier's affairs with all sorts of girls on the street and they had bothered her so little that she hadn't even felt enough resentment to break off the affair. However, this new intrigue with Virginie wasn't quite so easy to accept because she was sure that the two of them were just out to spite her. She hid her resentment though to avoid giving any satisfaction to her enemies. Mademoiselle Remanjou thought that Gervaise had words with Lantier over this because one afternoon she heard the sound of a slap. There was certainly a quarrel because Lantier stopped speaking to Gervaise for a couple of weeks, but then he was the first one to make up and things seemed to go along the same as before.

Coupeau found all this most amusing. The complacent husband who had been blind to his own situation laughed heartily at Poisson's predicament. Then Coupeau even teased Gervaise. Her lovers always dropped her. First the blacksmith and now the hat-maker. The trouble was that she got involved with undependable trades. She should take up with a mason, a good solid man. He said such things as if he were joking, but they upset Gervaise because his small gray eyes seemed to be boring right into her.

On evenings when Coupeau became bored being alone with his wife up in their tiny hole under the roof, he would go down for Lantier and invite him up. He thought their dump was too dreary without Lantier's company so he patched things up between Gervaise and Lantier whenever they had a falling out.

In the midst of all this Lantier put on the most consequential airs. He showed himself both paternal and dignified. On three successive occasions he had prevented a quarrel between the Coupeaus and the Poissons. The good understanding between the two families formed a part of his contentment. Thanks to the tender though firm glances with which he watched over Gervaise and Virginie, they always pretended to entertain a great friendship for each other. He reigned over both blonde and brunette with the tranquility of a pasha and fattened on his cunning. The rogue was still digesting the Coupeaus when he already began to devour the Poissons . . . it did not inconvenience him much. As soon as one shop was swallowed, he started on a second. It was only men of his sort who ever have any luck.

It was in June of that year that Nana was confirmed. She was then nearly thirteen years old, as tall as an asparagus shoot run to seed, and had a bold, impudent air about her. The year before she had been sent away from the catechism class on account of her bad behavior; and the priest had only allowed her to join it this time through fear of losing her altogether, and of casting one more heathen onto the street. Nana danced for joy as she thought of the white dress. The Lorilleuxs, being godfather and godmother, had promised to provide it, and took care to let everyone in the house know of their present. Madame Lerat was to give the veil and the cap, Virginie the purse, and Lantier the prayerbook; so that the Coupeaus looked forward to the ceremony without any great anxiety. Even the Poissons, wishing to give a house-warming, chose this occasion, no doubt on the hatter's advice. They invited the Coupeaus and the Boches, whose little girl was also going to be confirmed. They provided a leg of mutton and trimmings for the evening in question.

It so happened that on the evening before, Coupeau returned home in a most abominable condition, just as Nana was lost in admiration before the presents spread out on the top of the chest of drawers. The Paris atmosphere was getting the better of him again; and he fell afoul of his wife and child with drunken arguments and disgusting language which no one should have uttered at such a time. Nana herself was beginning to get hold of some very bad expressions in the midst of the filthy conversations she was continually hearing. On the days when there was a row, she would often call her mother an old camel and a cow.

"Where's my food?" yelled the zinc-worker. "I want my soup, you whores. There's bitches for you, always thinking of finery. I'll shit right here, you know, if I don't get my soup."

"He's unbearable when he's drunk," murmured Gervaise, out of patience; and turning towards him, she exclaimed, "It's warming up, don't bother us."

Nana was being modest, because she thought it nice on such a day. She continued to look at the presents on the chest of drawers, affectedly lowering her eyelids and pretending not to understand her father's naughty words. But the zinc-worker was an awful plague on the nights when he had had too much. Poking his face right against her neck, he said, "I'll give you white dresses. So the finery tickles your fancy. They excite your imagination. Just you cut away from there, you ugly little brat. Move your hands about, bundle them all into a drawer."

Nana, with bowed head, did not answer a word. She had taken up the little tulle cap and was asking her mother how much it cost. And as Coupeau thrust out his hand to seize hold of the cap, it was Gervaise who pushed him aside exclaiming, "Do leave the child alone. She's very good, she's doing no harm."

Then the zinc-worker let out in real earnest, "Ah. The bastards. The mother and daughter, they make the pair. It's a nice thing to go to church just to leer at the men. Dare to say it isn't true, little slattern. I'll dress you in a sack, just to disgust you, you and your priests. I don't want you to be taught anything worse than you know already. My God. Just listen to me, both of you."

At this Nana turned round in a fury, while Gervaise had to spread out her arms to protect the things which Coupeau talked of tearing. The child looked her father straight in the face; then, forgetting the modest bearing inculcated by her confessor, she said, clinching her teeth: "Pig."

As soon as the zinc-worker had had his soup he went off to sleep. On the morrow he awoke in a very good humor. He still felt a little of the booze of the day before but only just sufficient to make him amiable. He assisted at the dressing of the child, deeply affected by the white dress and finding that a mere nothing gave the little vermin quite the look of a young lady.

The two families started off together for the church. Nana and Pauline walked first, their prayer-books in their hands and holding down their veils on account of the wind; they did not speak but were bursting with delight at seeing people come to their shop-doors, and they smiled primly and devoutly every time they heard anyone say as they passed that they looked very nice. Madame Boche and Madame Lorilleux lagged behind, because they were interchanging their ideas about Clump-clump, a gobble-all, whose daughter would never have been confirmed if the relations had not found everything for her; yes, everything, even a new chemise, out of respect for the holy altar. Madame Lorilleux was rather concerned about the dress, calling Nana a dirty thing every time the child got dust on her skirt by brushing against the store fronts.

At church Coupeau wept all the time. It was stupid but he could not help it. It affected him to see the priest holding out his arms and all the little girls, looking like angels, pass before him, clasping their hands; and the music of the organ stirred up his stomach and the pleasant smell of the incense forced him to sniff, the same as though someone had thrust a bouquet of flowers into his face. In short he saw everything cerulean, his heart was touched. Anyway, other sensitive souls around him were wetting their handkerchiefs. This was a beautiful day, the most beautiful of his life. After leaving the church, Coupeau went for a drink with Lorilleux, who had remained dry-eyed.

That evening the Poissons' house-warming was very lively. Friendship reigned without a hitch from one end of the feast to the other. When bad times arrive one thus comes in for some pleasant evenings, hours during which sworn enemies love each other. Lantier, with Gervaise on his left and Virginie on his right, was most amiable to both of them, lavishing little tender caresses like a cock who desires peace in his poultry-yard. But the queens of the feast were the two little ones, Nana and Pauline, who had been allowed to keep on their things; they sat bolt upright through fear of spilling anything on their white dresses and at every mouthful they were told to hold up their chins so as to swallow cleanly. Nana, greatly bored by all this fuss, ended by slobbering her wine over the body of her dress, so it was taken off and the stains were at once washed out in a glass of water.

Then at dessert the children's future careers were gravely discussed.

Madame Boche had decided that Pauline would enter a shop to learn how to punch designs on gold and silver. That paid five or six francs a day. Gervaise didn't know yet because Nana had never indicated any preference.

"In your place," said Madame Lerat, "I would bring Nana up as an artificial flower-maker. It is a pleasant and clean employment."

"Flower-makers?" muttered Lorilleux. "Every one of them might as well walk the streets."

"Well, what about me?" objected Madame Lerat, pursing her lips. "You're certainly not very polite. I assure you that I don't lie down for anyone who whistles."

Then all the rest joined together in hushing her. "Madame Lerat. .

. . Madame Lerat." By side glances they reminded her of the two girls, fresh from communion, who were burying their noses in their glasses to keep from laughing out loud. The men had been very careful, for propriety's sake, to use only suitable language, but Madame Lerat refused to follow their example. She flattered herself on her command of language, as she had often been complimented on the way she could say anything before children, without any offence to decency.

"Just you listen, there are some very fine women among the flower-makers." she insisted. "They're just like other women and they show good taste when they choose to commit a sin."

"My God" interrupted Gervaise, "I've no dislike for artificial flower-making. Only it must please Nana, that's all I care about; one should never thwart children on the question of a vocation. Come Nana, don't be stupid; tell me now, would you like to make flowers?"

The child was leaning over her plate gathering up the cake crumbs with her wet finger, which she afterwards sucked. She did not hurry herself. She grinned in her vicious way.

"Why yes, mamma, I should like to," she said.

Then the matter was at once settled. Coupeau was quite willing that Madame Lerat should take the child with her on the morrow to the place where she worked in the Rue du Caire. And they all talked very gravely of the duties of life. Boche said that Nana and Pauline were women now that they had partaken of communion. Poisson added that for the future they ought to know how to cook, mend socks and look after a house. Something was even said of their marrying, and of the children they would someday have. The youngsters listened, laughing to themselves, elated by the thought of being women. What pleased them the most was when Lantier teased them, asking if they didn't already have little husbands. Nana eventually admitted that she cared a great deal for Victor Fauconnier, son of her mother's employer.

"Ah well," said Madame Lorilleux to the Boches, as they were all leaving, "she's our goddaughter, but as they're going to put her into artificial flower-making, we don't wish to have anything more to do with her. Just another whore. She'll be leading them a merry chase before six months are over."

On going up to bed, the Coupeaus agreed that everything had passed off well and that the Poissons were not at all bad people. Gervaise even considered the shop was nicely got up. She was surprised to discover that it hadn't pained her at all to spend an evening there. While Nana was getting ready for bed she contemplated her white dress and asked her mother if the young lady on the third floor had had one like it when she was married last month.

This was their last happy day. Two years passed by, during which they sank deeper and deeper. The winters were especially hard for them. If they had bread to eat during the fine weather, the rain and cold came accompanied by famine, by drubbings before the empty cupboard, and by dinner-hours with nothing to eat in the little Siberia of their larder. Villainous December brought numbing freezing spells and the black misery of cold and dampness.

The first winter they occasionally had a fire, choosing to keep warm rather than to eat. But the second winter, the stove stood mute with its rust, adding a chill to the room, standing there like a cast-iron gravestone. And what took the life out of their limbs, what above all utterly crushed them was the rent . . . . The January quarter, when there was not a radish in the house and old Boche came up with the bill. It was like a bitter storm, a regular tempest from the north. Monsieur Marescot then arrived the following Saturday, wrapped up in a good warm overcoat, his big hands hidden in woolen gloves; and he was forever talking of turning them out, while the snow continued to fall outside, as though it were preparing a bed for them on the pavement with white sheets. To have paid the quarter's rent they would have sold their very flesh. It was the rent which emptied the larder and the stove.

No doubt the Coupeaus had only themselves to blame. Life may be a hard fight, but one always pulls through when one is orderly and economical—witness the Lorilleuxs, who paid their rent to the day, the money folded up in bits of dirty paper. But they, it is true, led a life of starved spiders, which would disgust one with hard work. Nana as yet earned nothing at flower-making; she even cost a good deal for her keep. At Madame Fauconnier's Gervaise was beginning to be looked down upon. She was no longer so expert. She bungled her work to such an extent that the mistress had reduced her wages to two francs a day, the price paid to the clumsiest bungler. But she was still proud, reminding everyone of her former status as boss of her own shop. When Madame Fauconnier hired Madame Putois, Gervaise was so annoyed at having to work beside her former employee that she stayed away for two weeks.

As for Coupeau, he did perhaps work, but in that case he certainly made a present of his labor to the Government, for since the time he returned from Etampes Gervaise had never seen the color of his money. She no longer looked in his hands when he came home on pay-days. He arrived swinging his arms, his pockets empty, and often without his handkerchief; well, yes, he had lost his rag, or else some rascally comrade had sneaked it. At first he always fibbed; there was a donation to charity, or some money slipped through the hole in his pocket, or he paid off some imaginary debts. Later, he didn't even bother to make up anything. He had nothing left because it had all gone into his stomach.

Madame Boche suggested to Gervaise that she go to wait for him at the shop exit. This rarely worked though, because Coupeau's comrades would warn him and the money would disappear into his shoe or someone else's pocket.

Yes, it was their own fault if every season found them lower and lower. But that's the sort of thing one never tells oneself, especially when one is down in the mire. They accused their bad luck; they pretended that fate was against them. Their home had become a regular shambles where they wrangled the whole day long. However, they had not yet come to blows, with the exception of a few impulsive smacks, which somehow flew about at the height of their quarrels. The saddest part of the business was that they had opened the cage of affection; all their better feelings had taken flight, like so many canaries. The genial warmth of father, mother and child, when united together and wrapped up in each other, deserted them, and left them shivering, each in his or her own corner. All three—Coupeau, Gervaise and Nana—were always in the most abominable tempers, biting each other's noses off for nothing at all, their eyes full of hatred; and it seemed as though something had broken the mainspring of the family, the mechanism which, with happy people, causes hearts to beat in unison. Ah. It was certain Gervaise was no longer moved as she used to be when she saw Coupeau at the edge of a roof forty or fifty feet above the pavement. She would not have pushed him off herself, but if he had fallen accidentally, in truth it would have freed the earth of one who was of but little account. The days when they were more especially at enmity she would ask him why he didn't come back on a stretcher. She was awaiting it. It would be her good luck they were bringing back to her. What use was he—that drunkard? To make her weep, to devour all she possessed, to drive her to sin. Well. Men so useless as he should be thrown as quickly as possible into the hole and the polka of deliverance be danced over them. And when the mother said "Kill him," the daughter responded, "Knock him on the head." Nana read all of the reports of accidents in the newspapers, and made reflections that were unnatural for a girl. Her father had such good luck an omnibus had knocked him down without even sobering him. Would the beggar never croak?

In the midst of her own poverty Gervaise suffered even more because other families around her were also starving to death. Their corner of the tenement housed the most wretched. There was not a family that ate every day.

Gervaise felt the most pity for Old Man Bru in his cubbyhole under the staircase where he hibernated. Sometimes he stayed on his bed of straw without moving for days. Even hunger no longer drove him out since there was no use taking a walk when no one would invite him to dinner. Whenever he didn't show his face for several days, the neighbors would push open his door to see if his troubles were over. No, he was still alive, just barely. Even Death seemed to have neglected him. Whenever Gervaise had any bread she gave him the crusts. Even when she hated all men because of her husband, she still felt sincerely sorry for Old Man Bru, the poor old man. They were letting him starve to death because he could no longer hold tools in his hand.

The laundress also suffered a great deal from the close neighborhood of Bazouge, the undertaker's helper. A simple partition, and a very thin one, separated the two rooms. He could not put his fingers down his throat without her hearing it. As soon as he came home of an evening she listened, in spite of herself, to everything he did. His black leather hat landed with a dull thud on the chest of drawers, like a shovelful of earth; the black cloak hung up and rustling against the walls like the wings of some night bird; all the black clothing flung into the middle of the room and filling it with the trappings of mourning. She heard him stamping about, felt anxious at the least movement, and was quite startled if he knocked against the furniture or rattled any of his crockery. This confounded drunkard was her preoccupation, filling her with a secret fear mingled with a desire to know. He, jolly, his belly full every day, his head all upside down, coughed, spat, sang "Mother Godichon," made use of many dirty expressions and fought with the four walls before finding his bedstead. And she remained quite pale, wondering what he could be doing in there. She imagined the most atrocious things. She got into her head that he must have brought a corpse home, and was stowing it away under his bedstead. Well, the newspapers had related something of the kind—an undertaker's helper who collected the coffins of little children at his home, so as to save himself trouble and to make only one journey to the cemetery.

For certain, directly Bazouge arrived, a smell of death seemed to permeate the partition. One might have thought oneself lodging against the Old Man Lachaise cemetery, in the midst of the kingdom of moles. He was frightful, the animal, continually laughing all by himself, as though his profession enlivened him. Even when he had finished his rumpus and had laid himself on his back, he snored in a manner so extraordinary that it caused the laundress to hold her breath. For hours she listened attentively, with an idea that funerals were passing through her neighbor's room.

The worst was that, in spite of her terrors, something incited Gervaise to put her ear to the wall, the better to find out what was taking place. Bazouge had the same effect on her as handsome men have on good women: they would like to touch them. Well. If fear had not kept her back, Gervaise would have liked to have handled death, to see what it was like. She became so peculiar at times, holding her breath, listening attentively, expecting to unravel the secret through one of Bazouge's movements, that Coupeau would ask her with a chuckle if she had a fancy for that gravedigger next door. She got angry and talked of moving, the close proximity of this neighbor was so distasteful to her; and yet, in spite of herself, as soon as the old chap arrived, smelling like a cemetery, she became wrapped again in her reflections, with the excited and timorous air of a wife thinking of passing a knife through the marriage contract. Had he not twice offered to pack her up and carry her off with him to some place where the enjoyment of sleep is so great, that in a moment one forgets all one's wretchedness? Perhaps it was really very pleasant. Little by little the temptation to taste it became stronger. She would have liked to have tried it for a fortnight or a month

. . . to sleep a month, especially in winter, the month when the rent became due, when the troubles of life were killing her. But it was not possible—one must sleep forever, if one commences to sleep for an hour; and the thought of this froze her, her desire for death departed before the eternal and stern friendship which the earth demanded.

However, one evening in January she knocked with both her fists against the partition. She had passed a frightful week, hustled by everyone, without a sou, and utterly discouraged. That evening she was not at all well, she shivered with fever, and seemed to see flames dancing about her. Then, instead of throwing herself out of the window, as she had at one moment thought of doing, she set to knocking and calling, "Old Bazouge. Old Bazouge."

The undertaker's helper was taking off his shoes and singing, "There were three lovely girls." He had probably had a good day, for he seemed even more maudlin than usual.

"Old Bazouge. Old Bazouge." repeated Gervaise, raising her voice.

Did he not hear her then? She was ready to give herself at once; he might come and take her on his neck, and carry her off to the place where he carried his other women, the poor and the rich, whom he consoled. It pained her to hear his song, "There were three lovely girls," because she discerned in it the disdain of a man with too many sweethearts.

"What is it? What is it?" stuttered Bazouge; "who's unwell? We're coming, little woman."

But the sound of this husky voice awoke Gervaise as though from a nightmare. And a feeling of horror ascended from her knees to her shoulders at the thought of seeing herself lugged along in the old fellow's arms, all stiff and her face as white as a china plate.

"Well, is there no one there now?" resumed Bazouge in silence. "Wait a bit; we're always ready to oblige the ladies."

"It's nothing, nothing," said the laundress at length in a choking voice. "I don't require anything, thanks."

She remained anxious, listening to old Bazouge grumbling himself to sleep, afraid to stir for fear he would think he heard her knocking again.

In her corner of misery, in the midst of her cares and the cares of others, Gervaise had, however, a beautiful example of courage in the home of her neighbors, the Bijards. Little Lalie, only eight years old and no larger than a sparrow, took care of the household as competently as a grown person. The job was not an easy one because she had two little tots, her brother Jules and her sister Henriette, aged three and five, to watch all day long while sweeping and cleaning.

Ever since Bijard had killed his wife with a kick in the stomach, Lalie had become the little mother of them all. Without saying a word, and of her own accord, she filled the place of one who had gone, to the extent that her brute of a father, no doubt to complete the resemblance, now belabored the daughter as he had formerly belabored the mother. Whenever he came home drunk, he required a woman to massacre. He did not even notice that Lalie was quite little; he would not have beaten some old trollop harder. Little Lalie, so thin it made you cry, took it all without a word of complaint in her beautiful, patient eyes. Never would she revolt. She bent her neck to protect her face and stifled her sobs so as not to alarm the neighbors. When her father got tired of kicking her, she would rest a bit until she got her strength back and then resume her work. It was part of her job, being beaten daily.

Gervaise entertained a great friendship for her little neighbor. She treated her as an equal, as a grown-up woman of experience. It must be said that Lalie had a pale and serious look, with the expression of an old girl. One might have thought her thirty on hearing her speak. She knew very well how to buy things, mend the clothes, attend to the home, and she spoke of the children as though she had already gone through two or three nurseries in her time. It made people smile to hear her talk thus at eight years old; and then a lump would rise in their throats, and they would hurry away so as not to burst out crying. Gervaise drew the child towards her as much as she could, gave her all she could spare of food and old clothing. One day as she tried one of Nana's old dresses on her, she almost choked with anger on seeing her back covered with bruises, the skin off her elbow, which was still bleeding, and all her innocent flesh martyred and sticking to her bones. Well. Old Bazouge could get a box ready; she would not last long at that rate. But the child had begged the laundress not to say a word. She would not have her father bothered on her account. She took his part, affirming that he would not have been so wicked if it had not been for the drink. He was mad; he did not know what he did . . . . She forgave him, because one ought to forgive madmen everything.

From that time Gervaise watched and prepared to interfere directly she heard Bijard coming up the stairs. But on most of the occasions she only caught some whack for her trouble. When she entered their room in the day-time, she often found Lalie tied to the foot of the iron bedstead; it was an idea of the locksmith's, before going out, to tie her legs and her body with some stout rope, without anyone being able to find out why—a mere whim of a brain diseased by drink, just for the sake, no doubt, of maintaining his tyranny over the child when he was no longer there. Lalie, as stiff as a stake with pins and needles in her legs, remained whole days at the post. She once even passed a night there, Bijard having forgotten to come home. Whenever Gervaise, carried away by her indignation, talked of unfastening her, she implored her not to disturb the rope, because her father became furious if he did not find the knots tied the same way he had left them. Really, it wasn't so bad, it gave her a rest. She smiled as she said this though her legs were swollen and bruised. What upset her the most was that she couldn't do her work while tied to the bed. She could watch the children though, and even did some knitting, so as not to entirely waste the time.

The locksmith had thought of another little game too. He heated sous in the frying pan, then placed them on a corner of the mantlepiece; and he called Lalie, and told her to fetch a couple of pounds of bread. The child took up the sous unsuspectingly, uttered a cry and threw them on the ground, shaking her burnt hand. Then he flew into a fury. Who had saddled him with such a piece of carrion? She lost the money now. And he threatened to beat her to a jelly if she did not pick the sous up at once. When the child hesitated she received the first warning, a clout of such force that it made her see thirty-six candles. Speechless and with two big tears in the corners of her eyes, she would pick up the sous and go off, tossing them in the palm of her hand to cool them.

No, one could never imagine the ferocious ideas which may sprout from the depths of a drunkard's brain. One afternoon, for instance, Lalie having made everything tidy was playing with the children. The window was open, there was a draught, and the wind blowing along the passage gently shook the door.

"It's Monsieur Hardy," the child was saying. "Come in, Monsieur

Hardy. Pray have the kindness to walk in."

And she curtsied before the door, she bowed to the wind. Henriette and Jules, behind her, also bowed, delighted with the game and splitting their sides with laughing, as though being tickled. She was quite rosy at seeing them so heartily amused and even found some pleasure in it on her own account, which generally only happened to her on the thirty-sixth day of each month.

"Good day, Monsieur Hardy. How do you do, Monsieur Hardy?"

But a rough hand pushed open the door, and Bijard entered. Then the scene changed. Henriette and Jules fell down flat against the wall; while Lalie, terrified, remained standing in the very middle of the curtsey. The locksmith held in his hand a big wagoner's whip, quite new, with a long white wooden handle, and a leather thong, terminating with a bit of whip-cord. He placed the whip in the corner against the bed and did not give the usual kick to the child who was already preparing herself by presenting her back. A chuckle exposed his blackened teeth and he was very lively, very drunk, his red face lighted up by some idea that amused him immensely.

"What's that?" said he. "You're playing the deuce, eh, you confounded young bitch. I could hear you dancing about from downstairs. Now then, come here. Nearer and full face. I don't want to sniff you from behind. Am I touching you that you tremble like a mass of giblets? Take my shoes off."

Lalie turned quite pale again and, amazed at not receiving her usual drubbing, took his shoes off. He had seated himself on the edge of the bed. He lay down with his clothes on and remained with his eyes open, watching the child move about the room. She busied herself with one thing and another, gradually becoming bewildered beneath his glance, her limbs overcome by such a fright that she ended by breaking a cup. Then, without getting off the bed, he took hold of the whip and showed it to her.

"See, little chickadee, look at this. It's a present for you. Yes, it's another fifty sous you've cost me. With this plaything I shall no longer be obliged to run after you, and it'll be no use you getting into the corners. Will you have a try? Ah. You broke a cup. Now then, get up. Dance away; make your curtsies to Monsieur Hardy."

He did not even raise himself but lay sprawling on his back, his head buried in his pillow, making the big whip crack about the room with the noise of a pistol shot starting his horses. Then, lowering his arm he lashed Lalie in the middle of the body, encircling her with the whip and unwinding it again as though she were a top. She fell and tried to escape on her hands and knees; but lashing her again he jerked her to her feet.

"Giddy up, giddy up." yelled he. "It's the donkey race. Eh, it'll be fine of a cold morning in winter. I can lie snug without getting cold or hurting my chilblains and catch the calves from a distance. In that corner there, a hit, you bitch. And in that other corner, a hit again. And in that one, another hit. Ah. If you crawl under the bed I'll whack you with the handle. Gee up, you jade. Gee up. Gee up."

A slight foam came to his lips, his yellow eyes were starting from their black orbits. Lalie, maddened, howling, jumped to the four corners of the room, curled herself up on the floor and clung to the walls; but the lash at the end of the big whip caught her everywhere, cracking against her ears with the noise of fireworks, streaking her flesh with burning welts. A regular dance of the animal being taught its tricks. This poor kitten waltzed. It was a sight. Her heels in the air like little girls playing at skipping, and crying "Father." She was all out of breath, rebounding like an India-rubber ball, letting herself be beaten, unable to see or any longer to seek a refuge. And her wolf of a father triumphed, calling her a virago, asking her if she had had enough and whether she understood sufficiently that she was in future to give up all hope of escaping from him.

But Gervaise suddenly entered the room, attracted by the child's howls.

On beholding such a scene she was seized with a furious indignation.

"Ah, you brute of a man." cried she. "Leave her alone, you brigand. I'll put the police on to you."

Bijard growled like an animal being disturbed, and stuttered, "Mind your own business a bit, Limper. Perhaps you'd like me to put gloves on when I stir her up. It's merely to warm her, as you can plainly see— simply to show her that I've a long arm."

And he gave a final lash with the whip which caught Lalie across the face. The upper lip was cut, the blood flowed. Gervaise had seized a chair, and was about to fall on to the locksmith; but the child held her hands towards her imploringly, saying that it was nothing and that it was all over. She wiped away the blood with the corner of her apron and quieted the babies, who were sobbing bitterly, as though they had received all the blows.

Whenever Gervaise thought of Lalie, she felt she had no right to complain for herself. She wished she had as much patient courage as the little girl who was only eight years old and had to endure more than the rest of the women on their staircase put together. She had seen Lalie living on stale bread for months and growing thinner and weaker. Whenever she smuggled some remnants of meat to Lalie, it almost broke her heart to see the child weeping silently and nibbling it down only by little bits because her throat was so shrunken. Gervaise looked on Lalie as a model of suffering and forgiveness and tried to learn from her how to suffer in silence.

In the Coupeau household the vitriol of The Saloon was also commencing its ravages. Gervaise could see the day coming when her husband would get a whip like Bijard's to make her dance.

Yes, Coupeau was spinning an evil thread. The time was past when a drink would make him feel good. His unhealthy soft fat of earlier years had melted away and he was beginning to wither and turn a leaden gray. He seemed to have a greenish tint like a corpse putrefying in a pond. He no longer had a taste for food, not even the most beautifully prepared stew. His stomach would turn and his decayed teeth refuse to touch it. A pint a day was his daily ration, the only nourishment he could digest. When he awoke in the mornings he sat coughing and spitting up bile for at least a quarter of an hour. It never failed; you might as well have the basin ready. He was never steady on his pins till after his first glass of consolation, a real remedy, the fire of which cauterized his bowels; but during the day his strength returned. At first he would feel a tickling sensation, a sort of pins-and-needles in his hands and feet; and he would joke, relating that someone was having a lark with him, that he was sure his wife put horse-hair between the sheets. Then his legs would become heavy, the tickling sensation would end by turning into the most abominable cramps, which gripped his flesh as though in a vise. That though did not amuse him so much. He no longer laughed; he stopped suddenly on the pavement in a bewildered way with a ringing in his ears and his eyes blinded with sparks. Everything appeared to him to be yellow; the houses danced and he reeled about for three seconds with the fear of suddenly finding himself sprawling on the ground. At other times, while the sun was shining full on his back, he would shiver as though iced water had been poured down his shoulders. What bothered him the most was a slight trembling of both his hands; the right hand especially must have been guilty of some crime, it suffered from so many nightmares. My God, was he then no longer a man? He was becoming an old woman. He furiously strained his muscles; he seized hold of his glass and bet that he would hold it perfectly steady as with a hand of marble; but in spite of his efforts the glass danced about, jumped to the right, jumped to the left with a hurried and regular trembling movement. Then in a fury he emptied it into his gullet, yelling that he would require dozens like it, and afterwards he undertook to carry a cask without so much as moving a finger. Gervaise, on the other hand, told him to give up drink if he wished to cease trembling, and he laughed at her, emptying quarts until he experienced the sensation again, flying into a rage and accusing the passing omnibuses of shaking up his liquor.

In the month of March Coupeau returned home one evening soaked through. He had come with My-Boots from Montrouge, where they had stuffed themselves full of eel soup, and he had received the full force of the shower all the way from the Barriere des Fourneaux to the Barriere Poissonniere, a good distance. During the night he was seized with a confounded fit of coughing. He was very flushed, suffering from a violent fever and panting like a broken bellows. When the Boches' doctor saw him in the morning and listened against his back he shook his head, and drew Gervaise aside to advise her to have her husband taken to the hospital. Coupeau was suffering from pneumonia.

Gervaise did not worry herself, you may be sure. At one time she would have been chopped into pieces before trusting her old man to the saw-bones. After the accident in the Rue de la Nation she had spent their savings in nursing him. But those beautiful sentiments don't last when men take to wallowing in the mire. No, no; she did not intend to make a fuss like that again. They might take him and never bring him back; she would thank them heartily. Yet, when the litter arrived and Coupeau was put into it like an article of furniture, she became all pale and bit her lips; and if she grumbled and still said it was a good job, her heart was no longer in her words. Had she but ten francs in her drawer she would not have let him go.

She accompanied him to the Lariboisiere Hospital, saw the nurses put him to bed at the end of a long hall, where the patients in a row, looking like corpses, raised themselves up and followed with their eyes the comrade who had just been brought in. It was a veritable death chamber. There was a suffocating, feverish odor and a chorus of coughing. The long hall gave the impression of a small cemetery with its double row of white beds looking like an aisle of marble tombs. When Coupeau remained motionless on his pillow, Gervaise left, having nothing to say nor anything in her pocket that could comfort him.

Outside, she turned to look up at the monumental structure of the hospital and recalled the days when Coupeau was working there, putting on the zinc roof, perched up high and singing in the sun. He wasn't drinking in those days. She used to watch for him from her window in the Hotel Boncoeur and they would both wave their handkerchiefs in greeting. Now, instead of being on the roof like a cheerful sparrow, he was down below. He had built his own place in the hospital where he had come to die. My God. It all seemed so far way now, that time of young love.

On the day after the morrow, when Gervaise called to obtain news of him, she found the bed empty. A Sister of Charity told her that they had been obliged to remove her husband to the Asylum of Sainte-Anne, because the day before he had suddenly gone wild . . . . A total leave-taking of his senses; attempts to crack his skull against the wall; howls which prevented the other patients from sleeping. It all came from drink, it seemed. Gervaise went home very upset. Well, her husband had gone crazy. What would it be like if he came home? Nana insisted that they should leave him in the hospital because he might end by killing both of them.

Gervaise was not able to go to Sainte-Anne until Sunday. It was a tremendous journey. Fortunately, the omnibus from the Boulevard Rochechouart to La Glaciere passed close to the asylum. She went down the Rue de la Sante, buying two oranges on her way, so as not to arrive empty-handed. It was another monumental building, with gray courtyards, interminable corridors and a smell of rank medicaments, which did not exactly inspire liveliness. But when they had admitted her into a cell she was quite surprised to see Coupeau almost jolly. He was just then seated on the throne, a spotlessly clean wooden case, and they both laughed at her finding him in this position. Well, one knows what an invalid is. He squatted there like a pope with his cheek of earlier days . . . . He was better, as he could do this.

"And the pneumonia?" inquired the laundress.

"Done for," replied he. "They cured it in no time. I still cough a little, but that's all that is left of it."

Then at the moment of leaving the throne to get back into his bed, he joked once more. "It's lucky you have a strong nose and are not bothered."

They laughed louder than ever. At heart they felt joyful. It was by way of showing their contentment without a host of phrases that they thus joked together. One must have had to do with patients to know the pleasure one feels at seeing all their functions at work again.

When he was back in bed she gave him the two oranges and this filled him with emotion. He was becoming quite nice again ever since he had had nothing but tisane to drink. She ended by venturing to speak to him about his violent attack, surprised at hearing him reason like in the good old times.

"Ah, yes," said he, joking at his own expense; "I talked a precious lot of nonsense. Just fancy, I saw rats and ran about on all fours to put a grain of salt under their tails. And you, you called to me, men were trying to kill you. In short, all sorts of stupid things, ghosts in broad daylight . . . . I remember it well, my noodle's still solid. Now it's over, I dream a bit when I'm asleep. I have nightmares, but everyone has nightmares."

Gervaise remained with him until the evening. When the house surgeon came, at the six o'clock inspection, he made him spread his hands; they hardly trembled at all, scarcely a quiver at the tips of the fingers. However, as night approached, Coupeau was little by little seized with uneasiness. He twice sat up in bed looking on the ground and in the dark corners of the room. Suddenly he thrust out an arm and appeared to crush some vermin against the wall.

"What is it?" asked Gervaise, frightened.

"The rats. The rats," murmured he.

Then, after a pause, gliding into sleep, he tossed about, uttering disconnected phrases.

"My God they're tearing my skin….. . the filthy beasts…keep steady. Hold your skirts right round you. Beware of the dirty bastard behind you. My God she's down and the scoundrels laugh. Scoundrels. Cocksuckers. Scumbags."

He dealt blows into space, caught hold of his blanket and rolled it into a bundle against his chest, as though to protect the latter from the violence of the bearded men whom he beheld. Then, an attendant having hastened to the spot, Gervaise withdrew, quite frozen by the scene.

But when she returned a few days later, she found Coupeau completely cured. Even the nightmares had left him; he could sleep his ten hours right off as peacefully as a child and without stirring a limb. So his wife was allowed to take him away. The house surgeon gave him the usual good advice on leaving and advised him to follow it. If he recommenced drinking, he would again collapse and would end by dying. Yes, it solely depended upon himself. He had seen how jolly and healthy one could become when one did not get drunk. Well, he must continue at home the sensible life he had led at Sainte-Anne, fancy himself under lock and key and that dram-shops no longer existed.

"The gentleman's right," said Gervaise in the omnibus which was taking them back to the Rue de la Goutte-d'Or.

"Of course he's right," replied Coupeau.

Then, after thinking a minute, he resumed, ". . . you know, a little glass now and again can't kill a man; it helps the digestion."

And that very evening he swallowed a glass of bad spirit, just to keep his stomach in order. For eight days he was pretty reasonable. He was a great coward at heart; he had no desire to end his days in the Bicetre mad-house. But his passion got the better of him; the first little glass led him, in spite of himself, to a second, to a third and to a fourth, and at the end of a fortnight, he had got back to his old ration, a pint of vitriol a day. Gervaise, exasperated, could have beaten him. To think that she had been stupid enough to dream once more of leading a worthy life, just because she had seen him at the asylum in full possession of his good sense. Another joyful hour had flown, the last one no doubt. Now, as nothing could reclaim him, not even the fear of his near death, she swore she would no longer put herself out; the home might be all at sixes and sevens, she did not care any longer; and she talked also of leaving him.

Then hell upon earth recommenced, a life sinking deeper into the mire, without a glimmer of hope for something better to follow. Nana, whenever her father clouted her, furiously asked why the brute was not at the hospital. She was waiting the time when she would be earning money, she would say, to treat him to brandy and make him croak quicker. Gervaise, on her side, flew into a passion one day that Coupeau was regretting their marriage. Ah. She had brought him her saucy children; she had got herself picked up from the pavement, wheedling him with rosy dreams. My God. He had a rare cheek. So many words, so many lies. She hadn't wished to have anything to do with him; that was the truth. He had dragged himself at her feet to make her give way, while she was advising him to think well what he was about. And if it was all to come over again, he would hear how she would just say "no." She would sooner have an arm cut off. Yes, she'd had a lover before him; but a woman who has had a lover, and who is a worker, is worth more than a sluggard of a man who sullies his honor and that of his family in all the dram-shops. That day, for the first time, the Coupeaus went in for a general brawl, and they whacked each other so hard that an old umbrella and the broom were broken.

Gervaise kept her word. She sank lower and lower; she missed going to her work oftener, spent whole days in gossiping, and became as soft as a rag whenever she had a task to perform. If a thing fell from her hands, it might remain on the floor; it was certainly not she who would have stooped to pick it up. She took her ease about everything, and never handled a broom except when the accumulation of filth almost brought her to the ground. The Lorilleuxs now made a point of holding something to their noses whenever they passed her room; the stench was poisonous, said they. Those hypocrites slyly lived at the end of the passage, out of the way of all these miseries which filled the corner of the house with whimpering, locking themselves in so as not to have to lend twenty sou pieces . . . . Kind-hearted folks, neighbors awfully obliging. Yes, you may be sure. One had only to knock and ask for a light or a pinch of salt or a jug of water, one was certain of getting the door banged in one's face. With all that they had vipers' tongues. They protested everywhere that they never occupied themselves with other people. This was true whenever it was a question of assisting a neighbor; but they did so from morning to night, directly they had a chance of pulling any one to pieces. With the door bolted and a rug hung up to cover the chinks and the key-hole, they would treat themselves to a spiteful gossip without leaving their gold wire for a moment.

The fall of Clump-clump in particular kept them purring like pet cats. Completely ruined. Not a sou remaining. They smiled gleefully at the small piece of bread she would bring back when she went shopping and kept count of the days when she had nothing at all to eat. And the clothes she wore now. Disgusting rags. That's what happened when one tried to live high.

Gervaise, who had an idea of the way in which they spoke of her, would take her shoes off, and place her ear against their door; but the rug over the door prevented her from hearing much. She was heartily sick of them; she continued to speak to them, to avoid remarks, though expecting nothing but unpleasantness from such nasty persons, but no longer having strength even to give them as much as they gave her, passed the insults off as a lot of nonsense. And besides she only wanted her own pleasure, to sit in a heap twirling her thumbs, and only moving when it was a question of amusing herself, nothing more.

One Saturday Coupeau had promised to take her to the circus. It was well worth while disturbing oneself to see ladies galloping along on horses and jumping through paper hoops. Coupeau had just finished a fortnight's work, he could well spare a couple of francs; and they had also arranged to dine out, just the two of them, Nana having to work very late that evening at her employer's because of some pressing order. But at seven o'clock there was no Coupeau; at eight o'clock it was still the same. Gervaise was furious. Her drunkard was certainly squandering his earnings with his comrades at the dram-shops of the neighborhood. She had washed a cap and had been slaving since the morning over the holes of an old dress, wishing to look decent. At last, towards nine o'clock, her stomach empty, her face purple with rage, she decided to go down and look for Coupeau.

"Is it your husband you want?" called Madame Boche, on catching sight of Gervaise looking very glum. "He's at Old Man Colombe's. Boche has just been having some cherry brandy with him."

Gervaise uttered her thanks and stalked stiffly along the pavement with the determination of flying at Coupeau's eyes. A fine rain was falling which made the walk more unpleasant still. But when she reached The Saloon, the fear of receiving the drubbing herself if she badgered her old man suddenly calmed her and made her prudent. The shop was ablaze with the lighted gas, the flames of which were as brilliant as suns, and the bottles and jars illuminated the walls with their colored glass. She stood there an instant stretching her neck, her eyes close to the window, looking between two bottle placed there for show, watching Coupeau who was right at the back; he was sitting with some comrades at a little zinc table, all looking vague and blue in the tobacco smoke; and, as one could not hear them yelling, it created a funny effect to see them gesticulating with their chins thrust forward and their eyes popping out of their heads. Good heavens. Was it really possible that men could leave their wives and their homes to shut themselves up thus in a hole where they were choking?

The rain trickled down her neck; she drew herself up and went off to the exterior Boulevard, wrapped in thought and not daring to enter. Ah. Well Coupeau would have welcomed her in a pleasant way, he who objected to be spied upon. Besides, it really scarcely seemed to her the proper place for a respectable woman. Twice she went back and stood before the shop window, her eyes again riveted to the glass, annoyed at still beholding those confounded drunkards out of the rain and yelling and drinking. The light of The Saloon was reflected in the puddles on the pavement, which simmered with little bubbles caused by the downpour. At length she thought she was too foolish, and pushing open the door, she walked straight up to the table where Coupeau was sitting. After all it was her husband she came for, was it not? And she was authorized in doing so, because he had promised to take her to the circus that evening. So much the worse. She had no desire to melt like a cake of soap out on the pavement.

"Hullo. It's you, old woman." exclaimed the zinc-worker, half choking with a chuckle. "Ah. That's a good joke. Isn't it a good joke now?"

All the company laughed. Gervaise remained standing, feeling rather bewildered. Coupeau appeared to her to be in a pleasant humor, so she ventured to say:

"You remember, we've somewhere to go. We must hurry. We shall still be in time to see something."

"I can't get up, I'm glued, . . . without joking," resumed Coupeau, who continued laughing. "Try, just to satisfy yourself; pull my arm with all your strength; try it. Harder than that, tug away, up with it. You see it's that louse Old Man Colombe who's screwed me to his seat."

Gervaise had humored him at this game, and when she let go of his arm, the comrades thought the joke so good that they tumbled up against one another, braying and rubbing their shoulders like donkeys being groomed. The zinc-worker's mouth was so wide with laughter that you could see right down his throat.

"You great noodle." said he at length, "you can surely sit down a minute. You're better here than splashing about outside. Well, yes; I did-n't come home as I promised, I had business to attend to. Though you may pull a long face, it won't alter matters. Make room, you others."

"If madame would accept my knees she would find them softer than the seat," gallantly said My-Boots.

Gervaise, not wishing to attract attention, took a chair and sat down at a short distance from the table. She looked at what the men were drinking, some rotgut brandy which shone like gold in the glasses; a lit-tle of it had dropped upon the table and Salted-Mouth, otherwise Drink-without-Thirst, dipped his finger in it while conversing and wrote a woman's name—"Eulalie"—in big letters. She noticed that Bibi-the-Smoker looked shockingly jaded and thinner than a hundred-weight of nails. My-Boot's nose was in full bloom, a regular purple Burgundy dahlia. They were all quite dirty, their beards stiff, their smocks ragged and stained, their hands grimy with dirt. Yet they were still quite polite.

Gervaise noticed a couple of men at the bar. They were so drunk that they were spilling the drink down their chins when they thought they were wetting their whistles. Fat Old Man Colombe was calmly serv-ing round after round.

The atmosphere was very warm, the smoke from the pipes as-cended in the blinding glare of the gas, amidst which it rolled about like dust, drowning the customers in a gradually thickening mist; and from this cloud there issued a deafening and confused uproar, cracked voices, clinking of glasses, oaths and blows sounding like detonations. So Gervaise pulled a very wry face, for such a sight is not funny for a woman, especially when she is not used to it; she was stifling, with a smarting sensation in her eyes, and her head already feeling heavy from the alcoholic fumes exhaled by the whole place. Then she suddenly experienced the sensation of something more unpleasant still behind her back. She turned round and beheld the still, the machine which manufactured drunkards, working away beneath the glass roof of the narrow courtyard with the profound trepidation of its hellish cookery. Of an evening, the copper parts looked more mournful than ever, lit up only on their rounded surface with one big red glint; and the shadow of the apparatus on the wall at the back formed most abominable figures, bodies with tails, monsters opening their jaws as though to swallow everyone up.

"Listen, mother Talk-too-much, don't make any of your grimaces," cried Coupeau. "To blazes, you know, with all wet blankets. What'll you drink?"

"Nothing, of course," replied the laundress. "I haven't dined yet."

"Well. That's all the more reason for having a glass; a drop of something sustains one."

But, as she still retained her glum expression, My-Boots again did the gallant.

"Madame probably likes sweet things," murmured he.

"I like men who don't get drunk," retorted she, getting angry. "Yes, I like a fellow who brings home his earnings, and who keeps his word when he makes a promise."

"Ah. So that's what upsets you?" said the zinc-worker, without ceasing to chuckle. "Yes, you want your share. Then, big goose, why do you refuse a drink? Take it; it's so much to the good."

She looked at him fixedly, in a grave manner, a wrinkle marking her forehead with a black line. And she slowly replied, "Why, you're right, it's a good idea. That way, we can drink up the coin together."

Bibi-the-Smoker rose from his seat to fetch her a glass of anisette. She drew her chair up to the table. While she was sipping her anisette, a recollection suddenly flashed across her mind, she remembered the plum she had taken with Coupeau, near the door, in the old days, when he was courting her. At that time, she used to leave the juice of fruits preserved in brandy. And now, here was she going back to liqueurs . . . . She knew herself well, she had not two thimblefuls of will. One would only have had to have given her a walloping across the back to have made her regularly wallow in drink. The anisette even seemed to be very good, perhaps rather too sweet and slightly sickening. She went on sipping as she listened to Salted-Mouth, otherwise Drink-without-Thirst, tell of his affair with fat Eulalie, a fish peddler and very shrewd at locating him. Even if his comrades tried to hide him, she could usually sniff him out when he was late. Just the night before she had slapped his face with a flounder to teach him not to neglect going to work. Bibi-the-Smoker and My-Boots nearly split their sides laughing. They slapped Gervaise on the shoulder and she began to laugh also, finding it amusing in spite of herself. They then advised her to follow Eulalie's example and bring an iron with her so as to press Coupeau's ears on the counters of the wine shops.

"Ah, well, no thanks," cried Coupeau as he turned upside down the glass his wife had emptied. "You pump it out pretty well. Just look, you fellows, she doesn't take long over it."

"Will madame take another?" asked Salted-Mouth, otherwise Drink-without-Thirst.

No, she had had enough. Yet she hesitated. The anisette had slightly bothered her stomach. She should have taken straight brandy to settle her digestion.

She cast side glances at the drunkard manufacturing machine behind her. That confounded pot, as round as the stomach of a tinker's fat wife, with its nose that was so long and twisted, sent a shiver down her back, a fear mingled with a desire. Yes, one might have thought it the metal pluck of some big wicked woman, of some witch who was discharging drop by drop the fire of her entrails. A fine source of poison, an operation which should have been hidden away in a cellar, it was so brazen and abominable. But all the same she would have liked to have poked her nose inside it, to have sniffed the odor, have tasted the filth, though the skin might have peeled off her burnt tongue like the rind off an orange.

"What's that you're drinking?" asked she slyly of the men, her eyes lighted up by the beautiful golden color of their glasses.

"That, old woman," answered Coupeau, "is Old Man Colombe's camphor. Don't be silly now and we'll give you a taste."

And when they had brought her a glass of the vitriol, the rotgut, and her jaws had contracted at the first mouthful, the zinc-worker resumed, slapping his thighs:

"Ha. It tickles your gullet. Drink it off at one go. Each glassful cheats the doctor of six francs."

At the second glass Gervaise no longer felt the hunger which had been tormenting her. Now she had made it up with Coupeau, she no longer felt angry with him for not having kept his word. They would go to the circus some other day; it was not so funny to see jugglers galloping about on houses. There was no rain inside Old Man Colombe's and if the money went in brandy, one at least had it in one's body; one drank it bright and shining like beautiful liquid gold. Ah. She was ready to send the whole world to blazes. Life was not so pleasant after all, besides it seemed some consolation to her to have her share in squandering the cash. As she was comfortable, why should she not remain? One might have a discharge of artillery; she did not care to budge once she had settled in a heap. She nursed herself in a pleasant warmth, her bodice sticking to her back, overcome by a feeling of comfort which benumbed her limbs. She laughed all to herself, her elbows on the table, a vacant look in her eyes, highly amused by two customers, a fat heavy fellow and a tiny shrimp, seated at a neighboring table, and kissing each other lovingly. Yes, she laughed at the things to see in The Saloon, at Old Man Colombe's full moon face, a regular bladder of lard, at the customers smoking their short clay pipes, yelling and spitting, and at the big flames of gas which lighted up the looking-glasses and the bottles of liqueurs. The smell no longer bothered her, on the contrary it tickled her nose, and she thought it very pleasant. Her eyes slightly closed, while she breathed very slowly, without the least feeling of suffocation, tasting the enjoyment of the gentle slumber which was overcoming her. Then, after her third glass, she let her chin fall on her hands; she now only saw Coupeau and his comrades, and she remained nose to nose with them, quite close, her cheeks warmed by their breath, looking at their dirty beards as though she had been counting the hairs. My-Boots drooled, his pipe between his teeth, with the dumb and grave air of a dozing ox. Bibi-the-Smoker was telling a story—the manner in which he emptied a bottle at a swallow, giving it such a kiss that one instantly saw its bottom. Meanwhile Salted-Mouth, otherwise Drink-without-Thirst, had gone and fetched the wheel of fortune from the counter, and was playing with Coupeau for drinks.

"Two hundred. You're lucky; you get high numbers every time."

The needle of the wheel grated, and the figure of Fortune, a big red woman placed under glass, turned round and round until it looked like a mere spot in the center, similar to a wine stain.

"Three hundred and fifty. You must have been inside it, you confounded lascar. Ah. I shan't play anymore."

Gervaise amused herself with the wheel of fortune. She was feeling awfully thirsty, and calling My-Boots "my child." Behind her the machine for manufacturing drunkards continued working, with its murmur of an underground stream; and she despaired of ever stopping it, of exhausting it, filled with a sullen anger against it, feeling a longing to spring upon the big still as upon some animal, to kick it with her heels and stave in its belly. Then everything began to seem all mixed up. The machine seemed to be moving itself and she thought she was being grabbed by its copper claws, and that the underground stream was now flowing over her body.

Then the room danced round, the gas-jets seemed to shoot like stars. Gervaise was drunk. She heard a furious wrangle between Salted-Mouth, otherwise Drink-without-Thirst, and that rascal Old Man Colombe. There was a thief of a landlord who wanted one to pay for what one had not had. Yet one was not at a gangster's hang-out. Suddenly there was a scuffling, yells were heard and tables were upset. It was Old Man Colombe who was turning the party out without the least hesitation, and in the twinkling of an eye. On the other side of the door they insulted him and called him a cocksucker. It still rained and blew icy cold. Gervaise lost Coupeau, found him and then lost him again. She wished to go home; she felt the shops to find her way. This sudden darkness surprised her immensely. At the corner of the Rue des Poissonniers, she sat down in the gutter thinking she was at the wash-house. The water which flowed along caused her head to swim, and made her very ill. At length she arrived, she passed stiffly before the concierge's room where she perfectly recognized the Lorilleuxs and the Poissons seated at the table having dinner, and who made grimaces of disgust on beholding her in that sorry state.

She never remembered how she had got up all those flights of stairs. Just as she was turning into the passage at the top, little Lalie, who heard her footsteps, hastened to meet her, opening her arms caressingly, and saying, with a smile:

"Madame Gervaise, papa has not returned. Just come and see my little children sleeping . . . . They look so pretty."

But on beholding the laundress' besotted face, she tremblingly drew back. She was acquainted with that brandy-laden breath, those pale eyes, that convulsed mouth. Then Gervaise stumbled past without uttering a word, while the child, standing on the threshold of her room, followed her with her dark eyes, grave and speechless.

CHAPTER XI

Nana was growing up and becoming wayward. At fifteen years old she had expanded like a calf, white-skinned and very fat; so plump, indeed, you might have called her a pincushion. Yes, such she was—fifteen years old, full of figure and no stays. A saucy magpie face, dipped in milk, a skin as soft as a peach skin, a funny nose, pink lips and eyes sparkling like tapers, which men would have liked to light their pipes at. Her pile of fair hair, the color of fresh oats, seemed to have scattered gold dust over her temples, freckle-like as it were, giving her brow a sunny crown. Ah. A pretty doll, as the Lorilleuxs say, a dirty nose that needed wiping, with fat shoulders, which were as fully rounded and as powerful as those of a full-grown woman. Nana no longer needed to stuff wads of paper into her bodice, her breasts were grown. She wished they were larger though and dreamed of having breasts like a wet-nurse.

What made her particularly tempting was a nasty habit she had of protruding the tip of her tongue between her white teeth. No doubt on seeing herself in the looking-glasses she had thought she was pretty like this; and so, all day long, she poked her tongue out of her mouth, in view of improving her appearance.

"Hide your lying tongue." cried her mother.

Coupeau would often get involved, pounding his fist, swearing and shouting:

"Make haste and draw that red rag inside again."

Nana showed herself very coquettish. She did not always wash her feet, but she bought such tight boots that she suffered martyrdom in St. Crispin's prison; and if folks questioned her when she turned purple with pain, she answered that she had the stomach ache, so as to avoid confessing her coquetry. When bread was lacking at home it was difficult for her to trick herself out. But she accomplished miracles, brought ribbons back from the workshop and concocted toilettes—dirty dresses set off with bows and puffs. The summer was the season of her greatest triumphs. With a cambric dress which had cost her six francs she filled the whole neighborhood of the Goutte-d'Or with her fair beauty. Yes, she was known from the outer Boulevards to the Fortifications, and from the Chaussee de Clignancourt to the Grand Rue of La Chapelle. Folks called her "chickadee," for she was really as tender and as fresh-looking as a chicken.

There was one dress which suited her perfectly, a white one with pink dots. It was very simple and without a frill. The skirt was rather short and revealed her ankles. The sleeves were deeply slashed and loose, showing her arms to the elbow. She pinned the neck back into a wide V as soon as she reached a dark corner of the staircase to avoid getting her ears boxed by her father for exposing the snowy whiteness of her throat and the golden shadow between her breasts. She also tied a pink ribbon round her blond hair.

Sundays she spent the entire day out with the crowds and loved it when the men eyed her hungrily as they passed. She waited all week long for these glances. She would get up early to dress herself and spend hours before the fragment of mirror that was hung over the bureau. Her mother would scold her because the entire building could see her through the window in her chemise as she mended her dress.

Ah. She looked cute like that, said father Coupeau, sneering and jeering at her, a real Magdalene in despair. She might have turned into a whore at the drop of a hat and have shown her tits for a sou. Hide your meat, he used to say, and let me eat my bread. In fact, she was adorable, white and dainty under her overhanging golden fleece, blushing to the point that her skin turned pink, not daring to answer her father, but cutting her thread with her teeth with a hasty, furious jerk, which shook her plump, youthful breasts.

Then immediately after breakfast she tripped down the stairs into the courtyard. The entire tenement seemed to be resting sleepily in the peacefulness of a Sunday afternoon. The workshops on the ground floor were closed. Gaping windows revealed tables in some apartments that were already set for dinner, awaiting families out working up an appetite by strolling along the fortifications.

Then, in the midst of the empty, echoing courtyard, Nana, Pauline and other big girls engaged in games of tag and shuttlecock. They had grown up together and were now becoming queens of their building.

Whenever a man crossed the court, flutelike laugher would arise, and then starched skirts would rustle like the passing of a gust of wind.

The games were only an excuse for them to make their escape. Suddenly stillness fell upon the tenement. The girls had glided out into the street and made for the outer Boulevards. Then, linked arm-in-arm across the full breadth of the pavement, they went off, the whole six of them, clad in light colors, with ribbons tied around their bare heads. With bright eyes darting stealthy glances through their partially closed eyelids, they took note of everything, and constantly threw back their necks to laugh, displaying the fleshy part of their chins. They would swing their hips, or group together tightly, or flaunt along with awkward grace, all for the purpose of calling attention to the fact that their breasts and rumps were filling out.

Nana was in the center with her pink dress all aglow in the sunlight. She gave her arm to Pauline, whose costume, yellow flowers on a white ground, glared in similar fashion, dotted as it were with little flames. As they were the tallest of the band, the most woman-like and most unblushing, they led the troop and drew themselves up with breasts well forward whenever they detected glances or heard complimentary remarks. The others extended right and left, puffing themselves out in order to attract attention. Nana and Pauline resorted to the complicated devices of experienced coquettes. If they ran till they were out of breath, it was in view of showing their white stockings and making the ribbons of their chignons wave in the breeze. When they stopped, pretending complete breathlessness, you would certainly spot someone they knew quite near, one of the young fellows of the neighborhood. This would make them dawdle along languidly, whispering and laughing among themselves, but keeping a sharp watch through their downcast eyelids.

They went on these strolls of a Sunday mainly for the sake of these chance meetings. Tall lads, wearing their Sunday best, would stop them, joking and trying to catch them round their waists. Pauline was forever running into one of Madame Gaudron's sons, a seventeen-year-old carpenter, who would treat her to fried potatoes. Nana could spot Victor Fauconnier, the laundress's son and they would exchange kisses in dark corners. It never went farther than that, but they told each other some tall tales.

Then when the sun set, the great delight of these young sluts was to stop and look at the mountebanks. Conjurors and strong men turned up and spread threadbare carpets on the soil of the avenue. Loungers collected and a circle formed while the mountebank in the center tried his muscles under his faded tights. Nana and Pauline would stand for hours in the thickest part of the crowd. Their pretty, fresh frocks would get crushed between great-coats and dirty work smocks. In this atmosphere of wine and sweat they would laugh gaily, finding amusement in everything, blooming naturally like roses growing out of a dunghill. The only thing that vexed them was to meet their fathers, especially when the hatter had been drinking. So they watched and warned one another.

"Look, Nana," Pauline would suddenly cry out, "here comes father Coupeau."

"Well, he's drunk too . . . dear," said Nana, greatly bothered. "I'm going to beat it, you know. I don't want him to give me a wallop. Hullo. How he stumbles. Good Lord, if he could only break his neck."

At other times, when Coupeau came straight up to her without giving her time to run off, she crouched down, made herself small and muttered, "Just you hide me, you others. He's looking for me, and he promised he'd knock my head off if he caught me hanging about."

Then when the drunkard had passed them she drew herself up again, and all the others followed her with bursts of laughter. He'll find her—he will—he won't. It was a true game of hide and seek. One day, however, Boche had come after Pauline and caught her by both ears, and Coupeau had driven Nana home with kicks.

Nana was now a flower-maker and earned forty sous a day at Titreville's place in the Rue du Caire, where she had served as apprentice. The Coupeaus had kept her there so that she might remain under the eye of Madame Lerat, who had been forewoman in the workroom for ten years. Of a morning, when her mother looked at the cuckoo clock, off she went by herself, looking very pretty with her shoulders tightly confined in her old black dress, which was both too narrow and too short; and Madame Lerat had to note the hour of her arrival and tell it to Gervaise. She was allowed twenty minutes to go from the Rue de la Goutte-d'Or to the Rue du Caire, and it was enough, for these young sluts have the legs of racehorses. Sometimes she arrived exactly on time but so breathless and flushed that she must have covered most of the distance at a run after dawdling along the way. More often she was a few minutes late. Then she would fawn on her aunt all day, hoping to soften her and keep her from telling. Madame Lerat understood what it was to be young and would lie to the Coupeaus, but she also lectured Nana, stressing the dangers a young girl runs on the streets of Paris. My God. She herself was followed often enough.

". . . . I watch, you needn't fear," said the widow to the Coupeaus. "I will answer to you for her as I would for myself. And rather than let a fucker squeeze her, why I'd step between them."

The workroom at Titreville's was a large apartment on the first floor, with a broad work-table standing on trestles in the center. Round the four walls, the plaster of which was visible in parts where the dirty yellowish-gray paper was torn away, there were several stands covered with old cardboard boxes, parcels and discarded patterns under a thick coating of dust. The gas had left what appeared to be like a daub of soot on the ceiling. The two windows opened so wide that without leaving the work-table the girls could see the people walking past on the pavement over the way.

Madame Lerat arrived first, in view of setting an example. Then for a quarter of an hour the door swayed to and fro, and all the work girls scrambled in, perspiring with tumbled hair. One July morning Nana arrived the last, as very often happened. "Ah, me." she said, "It won't be a pity when I have a carriage of my own." And without even taking off her hat, one which she was weary of patching up, she approached the window and leant out, looking to the right and the left to see what was going on in the street.

"What are you looking at?" asked Madame Lerat, suspiciously. "Did your father come with you?"

"No, you may be sure of that," answered Nana coolly. "I'm looking at nothing—I'm seeing how hot it is. It's enough to make anyone sweat having to run like that."

It was a stifling hot morning. The work-girls had drawn down the Venetian blinds, between which they could spy out into the street; and they had at last begun working on either side of the table, at the upper end of which sat Madame Lerat. They were eight in number, each with her pot of glue, pincers, tools and curling stand in front of her. On the work-table lay a mass of wire, reels, cotton wool, green and brown paper, leaves and petals cut out of silk, satin or velvet. In the center, in the neck of a large decanter, one flower-girl had thrust a little penny nosegay which had been fading on her breast since the day before.

"... I have some news," said a pretty brunette named Leonie as she leaned over her cushion to crimp some rose petals. "Poor Caroline is very unhappy about that fellow who used to wait for her every evening."

"Ah." said Nana, who was cutting thin strips of green paper. "A man who cheats on her every day."

Madame Lerat had to display severity over the muffled laughter. Then Leonie whispered suddenly, "Quiet. The boss."

It was indeed Madame Titreville who entered. The tall thin woman usually stayed down in the shop. The girls were quite in awe of her because she never joked with them. All the heads were now bent over the work in diligent silence. Madame Titreville slowly circled the work-table. She told one girl her work was sloppy and made her do the flower over. Then she stalked out as stiffly as she had come in.

The complaining and low laughter began again.

"Really, young ladies." said Madame Lerat, trying to look more severe than ever. "You will force me to take measures."

The work-girls paid no attention to her. They were not afraid of her. She was too easy-going because she enjoyed being surrounded by these young girls whose zest for life sparkled in their eyes. She enjoyed taking them aside to hear their confidences about their lovers. She even told their fortunes with cards whenever a corner of the work-table was free. She was only offended by coarse expressions. As long as you avoided those you could say what you pleased.

To tell the truth, Nana perfected her education in nice style in the workroom. No doubt she was already inclined to go wrong. But this was the finishing stroke—associating with a lot of girls who were already worn out with misery and vice. They all hobnobbed and rotted together, just the story of the baskets of apples when there are rotten ones among them. They maintained a certain propriety in public, but the smut flowed freely when they got to whispering together in a corner.

For inexperienced girls like Nana, there was an undesirable atmosphere around the workshop, an air of cheap dance halls and unorthodox evenings brought in by some of the girls. The laziness of mornings after a gay night, the shadows under the eyes, the lounging, the hoarse voices, all spread an odor of dark perversion over the work-table which contrasted sharply with the brilliant fragility of the artificial flowers. Nana eagerly drank it all in and was dizzy with joy when she found herself beside a girl who had been around. She always wanted to sit next to big Lisa, who was said to be pregnant, and she kept glancing curiously at her neighbor as though expecting her to swell up suddenly.

"It's hot enough to make one stifle," Nana said, approaching a window as if to draw the blind farther down; but she leant forward and again looked out both to the right and left.

At the same moment Leonie, who was watching a man stationed at the foot of the pavement over the way, exclaimed, "What's that old fellow about? He's been spying here for the last quarter of an hour."

"Some tom cat," said Madame Lerat. "Nana, just come and sit down. I told you not to stand at the window."

Nana took up the stems of some violets she was rolling, and the whole workroom turned its attention to the man in question. He was a well-dressed individual wearing a frock coat and he looked about fifty years old. He had a pale face, very serious and dignified in expression, framed round with a well-trimmed gray beard. He remained for an hour in front of a herbalist's shop with his eyes fixed on the Venetian blinds of the workroom. The flower-girls indulged in little bursts of laughter which died away amid the noise of the street, and while leaning forward, to all appearance busy with their work, they glanced askance so as not to lose sight of the gentleman.

"Ah." remarked Leonie, "he wears glasses. He's a swell. He's waiting for Augustine, no doubt."

But Augustine, a tall, ugly, fair-haired girl, sourly answered that she did not like old men; whereupon Madame Lerat, jerking her head, answered with a smile full of underhand meaning:

"That is a great mistake on your part, my dear; the old ones are more affectionate."

At this moment Leonie's neighbor, a plump little body, whispered something in her ear and Leonie suddenly threw herself back on her chair, seized with a fit of noisy laughter, wriggling, looking at the gentleman and then laughing all the louder. "That's it . . . . That's it," she stammered. "How dirty that Sophie is."

"What did she say? What did she say?" asked the whole workroom, aglow with curiosity.

Leonie wiped the tears from her eyes without answering. When she became somewhat calmer, she began curling her flowers again and declared, "It can't be repeated."

The others insisted, but she shook her head, seized again with a gust of gaiety. Then Augustine, her left-hand neighbor, besought her to whisper it to her; and finally Leonie consented to do so with her lips close to Augustine's ear. Augustine threw herself back and wriggled with convulsive laughter in her turn. Then she repeated the phrase to a girl next to her, and from ear to ear it traveled round the room amid exclamations and stifled laughter. When they were all of them acquainted with Sophie's disgusting remark they looked at one another and burst out laughing together although a little flushed and confused. Madame Lerat alone was not in the secret and she felt extremely vexed.

"That's very impolite behavior on your part, young ladies," said she. "It is not right to whisper when other people are present. Something indecent no doubt. Ah. That's becoming."

She did not dare go so far as to ask them to pass Sophie's remark on to her although she burned to hear it. So she kept her eyes on her work, amusing herself by listening to the conversation. Now no one could make even an innocent remark without the others twisting it around and connecting it with the gentleman on the sidewalk. Madame Lerat herself once sent them into convulsions of laughter when she said, "Mademoiselle Lisa, my fire's gone out. Pass me yours."

". . . . Madame Lerat's fire's out." laughed the whole shop.

They refused to listen to any explanation, but maintained they were going to call in the gentleman outside to rekindle Madame Lerat's fire.

However, the gentleman over the way had gone off. The room grew calmer and the work was carried on in the sultry heat. When twelve o'clock struck—meal-time—they all shook themselves. Nana, who had hastened to the window again, volunteered to do the errands if they liked. And Leonie ordered two sous worth of shrimps, Augustine a screw of fried potatoes, Lisa a bunch of radishes, Sophie a sausage. Then as Nana was doing down the stairs, Madame Lerat, who found her partiality for the window that morning rather curious, overtook her with her long legs.

"Wait a bit," said she. "I'll go with you. I want to buy something too."

But in the passage below she perceived the gentleman, stuck there like a candle and exchanging glances with Nana. The girl flushed very red, whereupon her aunt at once caught her by the arm and made her trot over the pavement, while the individual followed behind. Ah. So the tom cat had come for Nana. Well, that was nice. At fifteen years and a half to have men trailing after her. Then Madame Lerat hastily began to question her. My God. Nana didn't know; he had only been following her for five days, but she could not poke her nose out of doors without stumbling on men. She believed he was in business; yes, a manufacturer of bone buttons. Madame Lerat was greatly impressed. She turned round and glanced at the gentleman out of the corner of her eye.

"One can see he's got a deep purse," she muttered. "Listen to me, kitten; you must tell me everything. You have nothing more to fear now."

While speaking they hastened from shop to shop—to the pork butcher's, the fruiterer's, the cook-shop; and the errands in greasy paper were piled up in their hands. Still they remained amiable, flouncing along and casting bright glances behind them with gusts of gay laughter. Madame Lerat herself was acting the young girl, on account of the button manufacturer who was still following them.

"He is very distinguished looking," she declared as they returned into the passage. "If he only has honorable views...."

Then, as they were going up the stairs she suddenly seemed to remember something. "By the way, tell me what the girls were whispering to each other—you know, what Sophie said?"

Nana did not make any ceremony. Only she caught Madame Lerat by the hand, and caused her to descend a couple of steps, for, really, it wouldn't do to say it aloud, not even on the stairs. When she whispered it to her, it was so obscene that Madame Lerat could only shake her head, opening her eyes wide, and pursing her lips. Well, at least her curiosity wasn't troubling her any longer.

From that day forth Madame Lerat regaled herself with her niece's first love adventure. She no longer left her, but accompanied her morning and evening, bringing her responsibility well to the fore. This somewhat annoyed Nana, but all the same she expanded with pride at see-ing herself guarded like a treasure; and the talk she and her aunt in-dulged in in the street with the button manufacturer behind them flattered her, and rather quickened her desire for new flirtations . . . . Her aunt understood the feelings of the heart; she even compassion-ated the button manufacturer, this elderly gentleman, who looked so respectable, for, after all, sentimental feelings are more deeply rooted among people of a certain age. Still she watched. And, yes, he would have to pass over her body before stealing her niece.

One evening she approached the gentleman, and told him, as straight as a bullet, that his conduct was most improper. He bowed to her politely without answering, like an old satyr who was accustomed to hear parents tell him to go about his business. She really could not be cross with him, he was too well mannered.

Then came lectures on love, allusions to dirty bastards and all sorts of stories about sluts who had repented of flirtations, which left Nana in a state of pouting, with eyes gleaming brightly in her pale face.

One day, however, in the Rue du Faubourg-Poissonniere the button manufacturer ventured to poke his nose between the aunt and the niece to whisper some things which ought not to have been said. Then Madame Lerat was so frightened that she declared she no longer felt able to handle the matter and she told the whole business to her brother. Then came another fight. There were some pretty rumpuses in the Coupeaus' room. To begin with, the zinc-worker gave Nana a hid-ing. What was that he learnt? The bitch was flirting with old men. All right. Only let her be caught philandering out of doors again, she'd be done for; he, her father, would cut off her head in a jiffy. Had the like ever been seen before. A slut who thought of beggaring her family. Then he shook her, declaring in God's name that she'd have to walk straight, for he'd watch her himself in future. He now looked her over every night when she came in, even going so far as to sniff at her and make her turn round before him.

One evening she got another hiding because he discovered a mark on her neck that he maintained was the mark of a kiss. Nana insisted it was a bruise that Leonie had given her when they were having a bit of a rough-house. Yet at other times her father would tease her, saying she was certainly a choice morsel for men. Nana began to display the sullen submissiveness of a trapped animal. She was raging inside.

"Why don't you leave her alone?" repeated Gervaise, who was more reasonable. "You will end by making her wish to do it by talking to her about it so much."

Ah. Yes, indeed, she did wish to do it. She itched all over, longing to break loose and gad all the time, as father Coupeau said. He insisted so much on the subject that even an honest girl would have fired up. Even when he was abusing her, he taught her a few things she did not know as yet, which, to say the least was astonishing. Then, little by little she acquired some singular habits. One morning he noticed her rummaging in a paper bag and rubbing something on her face. It was rice powder, which she plastered on her delicate satin-like skin with perverse taste. He caught up the paper bag and rubbed it over her face violently enough to graze her skin and called her a miller's daughter. On another occasion she brought some ribbon home, to do up her old black hat which she was so ashamed of. He asked her in a furious voice where she had got those ribbons from. Had she earned them by lying on her back or had she bagged them somewhere? A whore or a thief, and perhaps both by now?

More than once he found her with some pretty little doodad. She had found a little interlaced heart in the street on Rue d'Aboukir. Her father crushed the heart under his foot, driving her to the verge of throwing herself at him to ruin something of his. For two years she had been longing for one of those hearts, and now he had smashed it. This was too much, she was reaching the end of the line with him.

Coupeau was often in the wrong in the manner in which he tried to rule Nana. His injustice exasperated her. She at last left off attending the workshop and when the zinc-worker gave her a hiding, she declared she would not return to Titreville's again, for she was always placed next to Augustine, who must have swallowed her feet to have such a foul breath. Then Coupeau took her himself to the Rue du Caire and requested the mistress of the establishment to place her always next to Augustine, by way of punishment. Every morning for a fortnight he took the trouble to come down from the Barriere Poissonniere to escort Nana to the door of the flower shop. And he remained for five minutes on the footway, to make sure that she had gone in. But one morning while he was drinking a glass with a friend in a wine shop in the Rue Saint-Denis, he perceived the bitch darting down the street. For a fortnight she had been deceiving him; instead of going into the workroom, she climbed a story higher, and sat down on the stairs, waiting till he had gone off. When Coupeau began casting the blame on Madame Lerat, the latter flatly replied that she would not accept it. She had told her niece all she ought to tell her, to keep her on her guard against men, and it was not her fault if the girl still had a liking for the nasty beasts. Now, she washed her hands of the whole business; she swore she would not mix up in it, for she knew what she knew about scandalmongers in her own family, yes, certain persons who had the nerve to accuse her of going astray with Nana and finding an indecent pleasure in watching her take her first misstep. Then Coupeau found out from the proprietress that Nana was being corrupted by that little floozie Leonie, who had given up flower-making to go on the street. Nana was being tempted by the jingle of cash and the lure of adventure on the streets.

In the tenement in the Rue de la Goutte-d'Or, Nana's old fellow was talked about as a gentleman everyone was acquainted with. He remained very polite, even a little timid, but awfully obstinate and patient, following her ten paces behind like an obedient poodle. Sometimes, indeed, he ventured into the courtyard. One evening, Madame Gaudron met him on the second floor landing, and he glided down alongside the balusters with his nose lowered and looking as if on fire, but frightened. The Lorilleuxs threatened to move out if that wayward niece of theirs brought men trailing in after her. It was disgusting. The staircase was full of them. The Boches said that they felt sympathy for the old gentleman because he had fallen for a tramp. He was really a respectable businessman; they had seen his button factory on the Boulevard de la Villette. He would be an excellent catch for a decent girl.

For the first month Nana was greatly amused with her old flirt. You should have seen him always dogging her—a perfect great nuisance, who followed far behind, in the crowd, without seeming to do so. And his legs were matchsticks. No more moss on his head, only four straight hairs falling on his neck, so that she was always tempted to ask him where his hairdresser lived. Ah. What an old geezer, he was comical and no mistake, nothing to get excited over.

Then, on finding him always behind her, she no longer thought him so funny. She became afraid of him and would have called out if he had approached her. Often, when she stopped in front of a jeweler's shop, she heard him stammering something behind her. And what he said was true; she would have liked to have had a cross with a velvet neck-band, or a pair of coral earrings, so small you would have thought they were drops of blood.

More and more, as she plodded through the mire of the streets, getting splashed by passing vehicles and being dazzled by the magnificence of the window displays, she felt longings that tortured her like hunger pangs, yearnings for better clothes, for eating in restaurants, for going to the theatre, for a room of her own with nice furniture. Right at those moments, it never failed that her old gentleman would come up to whisper something in her ear . . . if only she wasn't afraid of him, how readily she would have taken up with him.

When the winter arrived, life became impossible at home. Nana had her hiding every night. When her father was tired of beating her, her mother smacked her to teach her how to behave. And there were free-for-alls; as soon as one of them began to beat her, the other took her part, so that all three of them ended by rolling on the floor in the midst of the broken crockery. And with all this, there were short rations and they shivered with cold. Whenever the girl bought anything pretty, a bow or a pair of buttons, her parents confiscated the purchase and drank what they could get for it. She had nothing of her own, excepting her allowance of blows, before coiling herself up between the rags of a sheet, where she shivered under her little black skirt, which she stretched out by way of a blanket. No, that cursed life could not continue; she was not going to leave her skin in it. Her father had long since ceased to count for her; when a father gets drunk like hers did, he isn't a father, but a dirty beast one longs to be rid of. And now, too, her mother was doing down the hill in her esteem. She drank as well. She liked to go and fetch her husband at Old Man Colombe's, so as to be treated; and she willingly sat down, with none of the air of disgust that she had assumed on the first occasion, draining glasses indeed at one gulp, dragging her elbows over the table for hours and leaving the place with her eyes staring out of her head.

When Nana passed in front of The Saloon and saw her mother inside with her nose in her glass, fuddled in the midst of the disputing men, she was seized with anger; for youth which has other dainty thoughts uppermost does not understand drink. On these evenings it was a pretty sight. Father drunk, mother drunk, a hell of a home that stunk with liquor and where there was no bread. To tell the truth, a saint would not have stayed in the place. So much the worse if she flew the coop one of these days; her parents would have to say their mea culpa, and own that they had driven her out themselves.

One Saturday when Nana came home she found her father and her mother in a lamentable condition. Coupeau, who had fallen across the bed was snoring. Gervaise, crouching on a chair was swaying her head, with her eyes vaguely and threateningly staring into vacancy. She had forgotten to warm the dinner, the remains of a stew. A tallow dip which she neglected to snuff revealed the shameful misery of their hovel.

"It's you, shrimp?" stammered Gervaise. "Ah, well, your father will take care of you."

Nana did not answer, but remained pale, looking at the cold stove, the table on which no plates were laid, the lugubrious hovel which this pair of drunkards invested with the pale horror of their callousness. She did not take off her hat but walked round the room; then with her teeth tightly set, she opened the door and went out.

"You are doing down again?" asked her mother, who was unable even to turn her head.

"Yes; I've forgotten something. I shall come up again. Good evening."

And she did not return. On the morrow when the Coupeaus were sobered they fought together, reproaching each other with being the cause of Nana's flight. Ah. She was far away if she were running still. As children are told of sparrows, her parents might set a pinch of salt on her tail, and then perhaps they would catch her. It was a great blow, and crushed Gervaise, for despite the impairment of her faculties, she realized perfectly well that her daughter's misconduct lowered her still more; she was alone now, with no child to think about, able to let herself sink as low as she could fall. She drank steadily for three days. Coupeau prowled along the exterior Boulevards without seeing Nana and then came home to smoke his pipe peacefully. He was always back in time for his soup.

In this tenement, where girls flew off every month like canaries whose cages are left open, no one was astonished to hear of the Coupeaus' mishap. But the Lorilleuxs were triumphant. Ah, they had predicted that the girl would reward her parents in this fashion. It was deserved; all artificial flower-girls went that way. The Boches and the Poissons also sneered with an extraordinary display and outlay of grief. Lantier alone covertly defended Nana. My God, said he, with his puritanical air, no doubt a girl who so left her home did offend her parents; but, with a gleam in the corner of his eyes, he added that damn it, the girl was, after all, too pretty to lead such a life of misery at her age.

"Do you know?" cried Madame Lorilleux, one day in the Boches' room, where the party were taking coffee; "well, as sure as daylight, Clump-clump sold her daughter. Yes, she sold her, and I have proof of it. That old fellow, who was always on the stairs morning and night, went up to pay something on account. It stares one in the face. They were seen together at the Ambigu Theatre—the young wench and her old tom cat. Upon my word of honor, they're living together; it's quite plain."

They discussed the scandal thoroughly while finishing their coffee. Yes, it was quite possible. Soon most of the neighborhood accepted the conclusion that Gervaise had actually sold her daughter.

Gervaise now shuffled along in her slippers, without caring a rap for anyone. You might have called her a thief in the street, she wouldn't have turned round. For a month past she hadn't looked at Madame Fauconnier's; the latter had had to turn her out of the place to avoid disputes. In a few weeks' time she had successively entered the service of eight washerwomen; she only lasted two or three days in each place before she got the sack, so badly did she iron the things entrusted to her, careless and dirty, her mind failing to such a point that she quite forgot her own craft. At last realizing her own incapacity she abandoned ironing; and went out washing by the day at the wash-house in the Rue Neuve, where she still jogged on, floundering about in the water, fighting with filth, reduced to the roughest but simplest work, a bit lower on the down-hill slopes. The wash-house scarcely beautified her. A real mud-splashed dog when she came out of it, soaked and showing her blue skin. At the same time she grew stouter and stouter, despite her frequent dances before the empty sideboard, and her leg became so crooked that she could no longer walk beside anyone without the risk of knocking him over, so great indeed was her limp.

Naturally enough when a woman falls to this point all her pride leaves her. Gervaise had divested herself of all her old self-respect, coquetry and need of sentiment, propriety and politeness. You might have kicked her, no matter where, she did not feel kicks for she had become too fat and flabby. Lantier had altogether neglected her; he no longer escorted her or even bothered to give her a pinch now and again. She did not seem to notice this finish of a long liaison slowly spun out, and ending in mutual insolence. It was a chore the less for her. Even Lantier's intimacy with Virginie left her quite calm, so great was her indifference now for all that she had been so upset about in the past. She would even have held a candle for them now.

Everyone was aware that Virginie and Lantier were carrying on. It was much too convenient, especially with Poisson on duty every other night. Lantier had thought of himself when he advised Virginie to deal in dainties. He was too much of a Provincial not to adore sugared things; and in fact he would have lived off sugar candy, lozenges, pastilles, sugar plums and chocolate. Sugared almonds especially left a little froth on his lips so keenly did they tickle his palate. For a year he had been living only on sweetmeats. He opened the drawers and stuffed himself whenever Virginie asked him to mind the shop. Often, when he was talking in the presence of five or six other people, he would take the lid off a jar on the counter, dip his hand into it and begin to nibble at something sweet; the glass jar remained open and its contents diminished. People ceased paying attention to it, it was a mania of his so he had declared. Besides, he had devised a perpetual cold, an irritation of the throat, which he always talked of calming.

He still did not work, for he had more and more important schemes than ever in view. He was contriving a superb invention—the umbrella hat, a hat which transformed itself into an umbrella on your head as soon as a shower commenced to fall; and he promised Poisson half shares in the profit of it, and even borrowed twenty franc pieces from him to defray the cost of experiments. Meanwhile, the shop melted away on his tongue. All the stock-in-trade followed suit down to the chocolate cigars and pipes in pink caramel. Whenever he was stuffed with sweetmeats and seized with a fit of tenderness, he paid himself with a last lick on the grocery girl in a corner, who found him all sugar with lips which tasted like burnt almonds. Such a delightful man to kiss. He was positively becoming all honey. The Boches said he merely had to dip a finger into his coffee to sweeten it.

Softened by this perpetual dessert, Lantier showed himself paternal towards Gervaise. He gave her advice and scolded her because she no longer liked to work. Indeed. A woman of her age ought to know how to turn herself round. And he accused her of having always been a glutton. Nevertheless, as one ought to hold out a helping hand, even to folks who don't deserve it, he tried to find her a little work. Thus he had prevailed upon Virginie to let Gervaise come once a week to scrub the shop and the rooms. That was the sort of thing she understood and on each occasion she earned her thirty sous. Gervaise arrived on the Saturday morning with a pail and a scrubbing brush, without seeming to suffer in the least at having to perform a dirty, humble duty, a charwoman's work in the dwelling-place where she had reigned as the beautiful fair-haired mistress. It was a last humiliation, the end of her pride.

One Saturday she had a hard job of it. It had rained for three days and the customers seemed to have brought all the mud of the neighborhood into the shop on the soles of their boots. Virginie was at the counter doing the grand, with her hair well combed, and wearing a little white collar and a pair of lace cuffs. Beside her, on the narrow seat covered with red oil-cloth, Lantier did the dandy, looking for the world as if he were at home, as if he were the real master of the place, and from time to time he carelessly dipped his hand into a jar of peppermint drops, just to nibble something sweet according to his habit.

"Look here, Madame Coupeau." cried Virginie, who was watching the scrubbing with compressed lips, "you have left some dirt over there in the corner. Scrub that rather better please."

Gervaise obeyed. She returned to the corner and began to scrub again. She bent double on her knees in the midst of the dirty water, with her shoulders protruding, her arms stiff and purple with cold. Her old skirt, fairly soaked, stuck to her figure. And there on the floor she looked a dirty, ill-combed drab, the rents in her jacket showing her puffy form, her fat, flabby flesh which heaved, swayed and floundered about as she went about her work; and all the while she perspired to such a point that from her moist face big drops of sweat fell on to the floor.

"The more elbow grease one uses, the more it shines," said Lantier, sententiously, with his mouth full of peppermint drops.

Virginie, who sat back with the demeanor of a princess, her eyes partly open, was still watching the scrubbing, and indulging in remarks. "A little more on the right there. Take care of the wainscot. You know I was not very well pleased last Saturday. There were some stains left."

And both together, the hatter and the grocery girl assumed a more important air, as if they had been on a throne while Gervaise dragged herself through the black mud at their feet. Virginie must have enjoyed herself, for a yellowish flame darted from her cat's eyes, and she looked at Lantier with an insidious smile. At last she was revenged for that hiding she had received at the wash-house, and which she had never forgotten.

Whenever Gervaise ceased scrubbing, a sound of sawing could be heard from the back room. Through the open doorway, Poisson's profile stood out against the pale light of the courtyard. He was off duty that day and was profiting by his leisure time to indulge in his mania for making little boxes. He was seated at a table and was cutting out arabesques in a cigar box with extraordinary care.

"Say, Badingue." cried Lantier, who had given him this surname again, out of friendship. "I shall want that box of yours as a present for a young lady."

Virginie gave him a pinch and he reached under the counter to run his fingers like a creeping mouse up her leg.

"Quite so," said the policeman. "I was working for you, Auguste, in view of presenting you with a token of friendship."

"Ah, if that's the case, I'll keep your little memento." rejoined Lantier with a laugh. "I'll hang it round my neck with a ribbon."

Then suddenly, as if this thought brought another one to his memory, "By the way," he cried, "I met Nana last night."

This news caused Gervaise such emotion that she sunk down in the dirty water which covered the floor of the shop.

"Ah." she muttered speechlessly.

"Yes; as I was going down the Rue des Martyrs, I caught sight of a girl who was on the arm of an old fellow in front of me, and I said to myself: I know that shape. I stepped faster and sure enough found myself face to face with Nana. There's no need to pity her, she looked very happy, with her pretty woolen dress on her back, a gold cross and an awfully pert expression."

"Ah," repeated Gervaise in a husky voice.

Lantier, who had finished the pastilles, took some barley-sugar out of another jar.

"She's sneaky," he resumed. "She made a sign to me to follow her, with wonderful composure. Then she left her old fellow somewhere in a cafe—. . . a wonderful chap, the old bloke, quite used up. And she came and joined me under the doorway. A pretty little serpent, pretty, and acting fancy and fawning on you like a little dog. Yes, she kissed me, and wanted to have news of everyone—I was very pleased to meet her."

"Ah." said Gervaise for the third time. She drew herself together and still waited. Hadn't her daughter had a word for her then? In the silence Poisson's saw could be heard again. Lantier, who felt gay, was sucking his barley-sugar, and smacking his lips.

"Well, if I saw her, I should go over to the other side of the street," interposed Virginie, who had just pinched the hatter again most ferociously. "It isn't because you are there, Madame Coupeau, but your daughter is rotten to the core. Why, every day Poisson arrests girls who are better than she is."

Gervaise said nothing, nor did she move; her eyes staring into space. She ended by jerking her head to and fro, as if in answer to her thoughts, while the hatter, with a gluttonous mien, muttered, "Ah, a man wouldn't mind getting a bit of indigestion from that sort of rottenness. It's as tender as chicken."

But the grocer gave him such a terrible look that he had to pause and quiet her with some delicate attention. He watched the policeman, and perceiving that he had his nose lowered over his little box again, he profited of the opportunity to shove some barley-sugar into Virginie's mouth. Then she laughed at him good-naturedly and turned all her anger against Gervaise.

"Just make haste, eh? The work doesn't do itself while you remain stuck there like a street post. Come, look alive, I don't want to flounder about in the water till night time."

And she added hatefully in a lower tone, "It isn't my fault if her daughter's gone and left her."

No doubt Gervaise did not hear. She had begun to scrub the floor again, with her back bent and dragging herself along with a frog-like motion. She still had to sweep the dirty water out into the gutter, and then do the final rinsing.

After a pause, Lantier, who felt bored, raised his voice again, "Do you know, Badingue," he cried, "I met your boss yesterday in the Rue de Rivoli. He looked awfully down in the mouth. He hasn't six months' life left in his body. Ah. After all, with the life he leads."

He was talking about the Emperor. The policeman did not raise his eyes, but curtly answered: "If you were the Government you wouldn't be so fat."

". . . my dear fellow, if I were the Government," rejoined the hatter, suddenly affecting an air of gravity, "things would go on rather better, I give you my word for it. Thus, their foreign policy—why, for some time past it has been enough to make a fellow sweat. If I—I who speak to you—only knew a journalist to inspire him with my ideas."

He was growing animated, and as he had finished crunching his barley-sugar, he opened a drawer from which he took a number of jujubes, which he swallowed while gesticulating.

"It's quite simple. Before anything else, I should give Poland her independence again, and I should establish a great Scandinavian state to keep the Giant of the North at bay. Then I should make a republic out of all the little German states. As for England, she's scarcely to be feared; if she budged ever so little I should send a hundred thousand men to India. Add to that I should send the Sultan back to Mecca and the Pope to Jerusalem, belaboring their backs with the butt end of a rifle. Eh? Europe would soon be clean. Come, Badingue, just look here."

He paused to take five or six jujubes in his hand. "Why, it wouldn't take longer than to swallow these." And he threw one jujube after another into his open mouth.

"The Emperor has another plan," said the policeman, after reflecting for a couple of minutes.

". . . forget it," rejoined the hatter. "We know what his plan is. All Europe is laughing at us. Every day the Tuilleries footmen find your boss under the table between a couple of high society floozies."

Poisson rose to his feet. He came forward and placed his hand on his heart, saying: "You hurt me, Auguste. Discuss, but don't involve personalities."

Then Virginie intervened, bidding them stop their fight. She didn't care a fig for Europe. How could two men, who shared everything else, always be disputing about politics? For a minute they mumbled some indistinct words. Then the policeman, in view of showing that he harbored no spite, produced the cover of his little box, which he had just finished; it bore the inscription in marquetry: "To Auguste, a token of friendship." Lantier, feeling exceedingly flattered, lounged back and spread himself out so that he almost sat upon Virginie. And the husband viewed the scene with his face the color of an old wall and his bleared eyes fairly expressionless; but all the same, at moments the red hairs of his moustaches stood up on end of their own accord in a very singular fashion, which would have alarmed any man who was less sure of his business than the hatter.

This beast of a Lantier had the quiet cheek which pleases ladies. As Poisson turned his back he was seized with the idea of printing a kiss on Madame Poisson's left eye. As a rule he was stealthily prudent, but when he had been disputing about politics he risked everything, so as to show the wife his superiority. These gloating caresses, cheekily stolen behind the policeman's back, revenged him on the Empire which had turned France into a house of quarrels. Only on this occasion he had forgotten Gervaise's presence. She had just finished rinsing and wiping the shop and she stood near the counter waiting for her thirty sous. However, the kiss on Virginie's eye left her perfectly calm, as being quite natural, and as part of a business she had no right to mix herself up in. Virginie seemed rather vexed. She threw the thirty sous on to the counter in front of Gervaise. The latter did not budge but stood there waiting, still palpitating with the effort she had made in scrubbing, and looking as soaked and as ugly as a dog fished out of the sewer.

"Then she didn't tell you anything?" she asked the hatter at last.

"Who?" he cried. "Ah, yes; you mean Nana. No, nothing else. What a tempting mouth she has, the little bitch. Real strawberry jam."

Gervaise went off with her thirty sous in her hand. The holes in her shoes spat water forth like pumps; they were real musical shoes, and played a tune as they left moist traces of their broad soles along the pavement.

In the neighborhood the feminine tipplers of her own class now related that she drank to console herself for her daughter's misconduct. She herself, when she gulped down her dram of spirits on the counter, assumed a dramatic air, and tossed the liquor into her mouth, wishing it would "do" for her. And on the days when she came home boozed she stammered that it was all through grief. But honest folks shrugged their shoulders. They knew what that meant: ascribing the effects of the peppery fire of The Saloon to grief, indeed. At all events, she ought to have called it bottled grief. No doubt at the beginning she couldn't digest Nana's flight. All the honest feelings remaining in her revolted at the thought, and besides, as a rule a mother doesn't like to have to think that her daughter, at that very moment, perhaps, is being familiarly addressed by the first chance comer. But Gervaise was already too stultified with a sick head and a crushed heart, to think of the shame for long. With her it came and went. She remained sometimes for a week together without thinking of her daughter, and then suddenly a tender or an angry feeling seized hold of her, sometimes when she had her stomach empty, at others when it was full, a furious longing to catch Nana in some corner, where she would perhaps have kissed her or perhaps have beaten her, according to the fancy of the moment.

Whenever these thoughts came over her, Gervaise looked on all sides in the streets with the eyes of a detective. Ah. If she had only seen her little sinner, how quickly she would have brought her home again. The neighborhood was being turned topsy-turvy that year. The Boulevard Magenta and the Boulevard Ornano were being pierced; they were doing away with the old Barriere Poissonniere and cutting right through the outer Boulevard. The district could not be recognized. The whole of one side of the Rue des Poissonniers had been pulled down. From the Rue de la Goutte-d'Or a large clearing could now be seen, a dash of sunlight and open air; and in place of the gloomy buildings which had hidden the view in this direction there rose up on the Boulevard Ornano a perfect monument, a six-storied house, carved all over like a church, with clear windows, which, with their embroidered curtains, seemed symbolical of wealth. This white house, standing just in front of the street, illuminated it with a jet of light, as it were, and every day it caused discussions between Lantier and Poisson.

Gervaise had several times had tidings of Nana. There are always ready tongues anxious to pay you a sorry compliment. Yes, she had been told that the bitch had left her old gentleman, just like the inexperienced girl she was. She had gotten along famously with him, petted, adored, and free, too, if she had only known how to manage the situation. But youth is foolish, and she had no doubt gone off with some young rake, no one knew exactly where. What seemed certain was that one afternoon she had left her old fellow on the Place de la Bastille, just for half a minute and he was still waiting for her to return. Other persons swore they had seen her since, dancing on her heels at the "Grand Hall of Folly," in the Rue de la Chapelle. Then it was that Gervaise took it into her head to frequent all the dancing places of the neighborhood. She did not pass in front of a public ball-room without going in. Coupeau accompanied her. At first they merely made the round of the room, looking at the drabs who were jumping about. But one evening, as they had some coin, they sat down and ordered a large bowl of hot wine in view of regaling themselves and waiting to see if Nana would turn up. At the end of a month or so they had practically forgotten her, but they frequented the halls for their own pleasure, liking to look at the dancers. They would remain for hours without exchanging a word, resting their elbows on the table, stultified amidst the quaking of the floor, and yet no doubt amusing themselves as they stared with pale eyes at the Barriere women in the stifling atmosphere and ruddy glow of the hall.

It happened one November evening that they went into the "Grand Hall of Folly" to warm themselves. Out of doors a sharp wind cut you across the face. But the hall was crammed. There was a thundering big swarm inside; people at all the tables, people in the middle, people up above, quite an amount of flesh. Yes, those who cared for tripes could enjoy themselves. When they had made the round twice without finding a vacant table, they decided to remain standing and wait till somebody went off. Coupeau was teetering on his legs, in a dirty blouse, with an old cloth cap which had lost its peak flattened down on his head. And as he blocked the way, he saw a scraggy young fellow who was wiping his coat-sleeve after elbowing him.

"Say." cried Coupeau in a fury, as he took his pipe out of his black mouth. "Can't you apologize? And you play the disgusted one? Just because a fellow wears a blouse."

The young man turned round and looked at the zinc-worker from head to foot.

"I'll just teach you, you scraggy young scamp," continued Coupeau, "that the blouse is the finest garment out; yes, the garment of work. I'll wipe you if you like with my fists. Did one ever hear of such a thing— a ne'er-do-well insulting a workman."

Gervaise tried to calm him, but in vain. He drew himself up in his rags, in full view, and struck his blouse, roaring: "There's a man's chest under that."

Then the young man dived into the midst of the crowd, muttering, "What a dirty bastard."

Coupeau wanted to follow and catch him. He wasn't going to let himself be insulted by a fellow with a coat on. Probably it wasn't even paid for. Some second-hand rag to impress a girl with, without having to fork out a centime. If he caught the chap again, he'd bring him down on his knees and make him bow to the blouse. But the crush was too great; there was no means of walking. He and Gervaise turned slowly round the dancers; there were three rows of sightseers packed close together, whose faces lighted up whenever any of the dancers showed off. As Coupeau and Gervaise were both short, they raised themselves up on tiptoe, trying to see something besides the chignons and hats that were bobbing about. The cracked brass instruments of the orchestra were furiously thundering a quadrille, a perfect tempest which made the hall shake; while the dancers, striking the floor with their feet, raised a cloud of dust which dimmed the brightness of the gas. The heat was unbearable.

"Look there," said Gervaise suddenly.

"Look at what?"

"Why, at that velvet hat over there."

They raised themselves up on tiptoe. On the left hand there was an old black velvet hat trimmed with ragged feathers bobbing about—regular hearse's plumes. It was dancing a devil of a dance, this hat—bouncing and whirling round, diving down and then springing up again. Coupeau and Gervaise lost sight of it as the people round about moved their heads, but then suddenly they saw it again, swaying farther off with such droll effrontery that folks laughed merely at the sight of this dancing hat, without knowing what was underneath it.

"Well?" asked Coupeau.

"Don't you recognize that head of hair?" muttered Gervaise in a stifled voice. "May my head be cut off if it isn't her."

With one shove the zinc-worker made his way through the crowd. My God yes, it was Nana. And in a nice pickle too. She had nothing on her back but an old silk dress, all stained and sticky from having wiped the tables of boozing dens, and with its flounces so torn that they fell in tatters round about. Not even a bit of a shawl over her shoulders. And to think that the bitch had had such an attentive, loving gentleman, and had yet fallen to this condition, merely for the sake of following some rascal who had beaten her, no doubt. Nevertheless she had remained fresh and insolent, with her hair as frizzy as a poodle's, and her mouth bright pink under that rascally hat of hers.

"Just wait a bit, I'll make her dance." resumed Coupeau.

Naturally enough, Nana was not on her guard. You should have seen how she wriggled about. She twisted to the right and to the left, bending double as if she were going to break herself in two, and kicking her feet as high as her partner's face. A circle had formed about her and this excited her even more. She raised her skirts to her knees and really let herself go in a wild dance, whirling and turning, dropping to the floor in splits, and then jigging and bouncing.

Coupeau was trying to force his way through the dancers and was disrupting the quadrille.

"I tell you, it's my daughter." he cried; "let me pass."

Nana was now dancing backwards, sweeping the floor with her flounces, rounding her figure and wriggling it, so as to look all the more tempting. She suddenly received a masterly blow just on the right cheek. She raised herself up and turned quite pale on recognizing her father and mother. Bad luck and no mistake.

"Turn him out." howled the dancers.

But Coupeau, who had just recognized his daughter's cavalier as the scraggy young man in the coat, did not care a fig for what the people said.

"Yes, it's us," he roared. "Eh? You didn't expect it. So we catch you here, and with a whipper-snapper, too, who insulted me a little while ago."

Gervaise, whose teeth were tight set, pushed him aside, exclaiming, "Shut up. There's no need of so much explanation."

And, stepping forward, she dealt Nana a couple of hearty cuffs. The first knocked the feathered hat on one side, and the second left a red mark on the girl's white cheek. Nana was too stupefied either to cry or resist. The orchestra continued playing, the crowd grew angry and repeated savagely, "Turn them out. Turn them out."

"Come, make haste." resumed Gervaise. "Just walk in front, and don't try to run off. You shall sleep in prison if you do."

The scraggy young man had prudently disappeared. Nana walked ahead, very stiff and still stupefied by her bad luck. Whenever she showed the least unwillingness, a cuff from behind brought her back to the direction of the door. And thus they went out, all three of them, amid the jeers and banter of the spectators, while the orchestra finished playing the finale with such thunder that the trombones seemed to be spitting bullets.

The old life began again. After sleeping for twelve hours in her closet, Nana behaved very well for a week or so. She had patched herself a modest little dress, and wore a cap with the strings tied under her chignon. Seized indeed with remarkable fervor, she declared she would work at home, where one could earn what one liked without hearing any nasty work-room talk; and she procured some work and installed herself at a table, getting up at five o'clock in the morning on the first few days to roll her sprigs of violets. But when she had delivered a few gross, she stretched her arms and yawned over her work, with her hands cramped, for she had lost her knack of stem-rolling, and suffocated, shut up like this at home after allowing herself so much open air freedom during the last six months. Then the glue dried, the petals and the green paper got stained with grease, and the flower-dealer came three times in person to make a row and claim his spoiled materials.

Nana idled along, constantly getting a hiding from her father, and wrangling with her mother morning and night—quarrels in which the two women flung horrible words at each other's head. It couldn't last; the twelfth day she took herself off, with no more luggage than her modest dress on her back and her cap perched over one ear. The Lorilleuxs, who had pursed their lips on hearing of her return and repentance, nearly died of laughter now. Second performance, Act number two, all aboard for the train for Saint-Lazare, the prison-hospital for streetwalkers. No, it was really too comical. Nana took herself off in such an amusing style. Well, if the Coupeaus wanted to keep her in the future, they must shut her up in a cage.

In the presence of other people the Coupeaus pretended they were very glad to be rid of the girl, though in reality they were enraged. However, rage can't last forever, and soon they heard without even blinking that Nana was seen in the neighborhood. Gervaise, who accused her of doing it to enrage them, set herself above the scandal; she might meet her daughter on the street, she said; she wouldn't even dirty her hand to cuff her; yes, it was all over; she might have seen her lying in the gutter, dying on the pavement, and she would have passed by without even admitting that such a bitch was her own child.

Nana meanwhile was enlivening the dancing halls of the neighborhood. She was known from the "Ball of Queen Blanche" to the "Great Hall of Folly." When she entered the "Elysee-Montmartre," folks climbed onto the tables to see her do the "sniffling crawfish" during the pastourelle. As she had twice been turned out of the "Chateau Rouge" hall, she walked outside the door waiting for someone she knew to escort her inside. The "Black Ball" on the outer Boulevard and the "Grand Turk" in the Rue des Poissonniers, were respectable places where she only went when she had some fine dress on. Of all the jumping places of the neighborhood, however, those she most preferred were the "Hermitage Ball" in a damp courtyard and "Robert's Ball" in the Impasse du Cadran, two dirty little halls, lighted up with a half dozen oil lamps, and kept very informally, everyone pleased and everyone free, so much so that the men and their girls kissed each other at their ease, in the dances, without being disturbed. Nana had ups and downs, perfect transformations, now tricked out like a stylish woman and now all dirt. Ah. She had a fine life.

On several occasions the Coupeaus fancied they saw her in some shady dive. They turned their backs and decamped in another direction so as not to be obliged to recognize her. They didn't care to be laughed at by a whole dancing hall again for the sake of bringing such a dolt home. One night as they were going to bed, however, someone knocked at the door. It was Nana who matter-of-factly came to ask for a bed; and in what a state. My God, her head was bare, her dress in tatters, and her boots full of holes—such a toilet as might have led the police to run her in, and take her off to the Depot. Naturally enough she received a hiding, and then she gluttonously fell on a crust of stale bread and went to sleep, worn out, with the last mouthful between her teeth.

Then this sort of life continued. As soon as she was somewhat recovered she would go off and not a sight or sound of her. Weeks or months would pass and she would suddenly appear with no explanation. The Coupeaus got used to these comings and goings. Well, as long as she didn't leave the door open. What could you expect?

There was only one thing that really bothered Gervaise. This was to see her daughter come home in a dress with a train and a hat covered with feathers. No, she couldn't stomach this display. Nana might indulge in riotous living if she chose, but when she came home to her mother's she ought to dress like a work-girl. The dresses with trains caused quite a sensation in the house; the Lorilleuxs sneered; Lantier, whose mouth sneered, turned the girl round to sniff at her delicious aroma; the Boches had forbidden Pauline to associate with this baggage in her frippery. And Gervaise was also angered by Nana's exhausted slumber, when after one of her adventures, she slept till noon, with her blouse undone, her breasts exposed and her head still full of hair pins, looking so white and breathing so feebly that she seemed to be dead. Her mother shook her five or six times in the course of the morning, threatening to throw a jug full of water over her. The sight of this handsome lazy girl, half-naked and soaked with wine, exasperated her, as she saw her lying there. Sometimes Nana opened an eye, closed it again, and then stretched herself out all the more.

One day after reproaching her with the life she led and asking her if she had taken on an entire battalion of soldiers, Gervaise put her threat into execution to the extent of shaking her dripping hand over Nana's body. Quite infuriated, the girl pulled herself up in the sheet, and cried out, "That's enough, mamma. It would be better not to talk of men. You did as you liked, and now I do the same."

"What? What?" stammered the mother.

"Yes, I never spoke to you about it, for it didn't concern me; but you didn't used to be very fussy. I often saw you when we lived at the shop sneaking off as soon as papa started snoring. So just shut up; you shouldn't have set me the example."

Gervaise remained pale, with trembling hands, turning round without knowing what she was about, while Nana, flattened on her breast, embraced her pillow with both arms and subsided into the torpor of her leaden slumber.

Coupeau growled, no longer sane enough to think of launching out a whack. He was altogether losing his mind. And really there was no need to call him an unprincipled father, for liquor had deprived him of all consciousness of good and evil.

Now it was a settled thing. He wasn't sober once in six months; then he was laid up and had to go into the Sainte-Anne hospital; a pleasure trip for him. The Lorilleuxs said that the Duke of Bowel-Twister had gone to visit his estates. At the end of a few weeks he left the asylum, repaired and set together again, and then he began to pull himself to bits once more, till he was down on his back and needed another mending. In three years he went seven times to Sainte-Anne in this fashion. The neighborhood said that his cell was kept ready for him. But the worst of the matter was that this obstinate tippler demolished himself more and more each time so that from relapse to relapse one could foresee the final tumble, the last cracking of this shaky cask, all the hoops of which were breaking away, one after the other.

At the same time, he forgot to improve in appearance; a perfect ghost to look at. The poison was having terrible effects. By dint of imbibing alcohol, his body shrunk up like the embryos displayed in glass jars in chemical laboratories. When he approached a window you could see through his ribs, so skinny had he become. Those who knew his age, only forty years just gone, shuddered when he passed by, bent and unsteady, looking as old as the streets themselves. And the trembling of his hands increased, the right one danced to such an extent, that sometimes he had to take his glass between both fists to carry it to his lips . . . . That cursed trembling. It was the only thing that worried his addled brains. You could hear him growling ferocious insults against those hands of his.

This last summer, during which Nana usually came home to spend her nights, after she had finished knocking about, was especially bad for Coupeau. His voice changed entirely as if liquor had set a new music in his throat. He became deaf in one ear. Then in a few days his sight grew dim, and he had to clutch hold of the stair railings to prevent himself from falling. As for his health, he had abominable headaches and dizziness. All on a sudden he was seized with acute pains in his arms and legs; he turned pale; was obliged to sit down, and remained on a chair witless for hours; indeed, after one such attack, his arm remained paralyzed for the whole day. He took to his bed several times; he rolled himself up and hid himself under the sheet, breathing hard and continuously like a suffering animal. Then the strange scenes of Sainte-Anne began again. Suspicious and nervous, worried with a burning fever, he rolled about in a mad rage, tearing his blouse and biting the furniture with his convulsed jaws; or else he sank into a great state of emotion, complaining like a child, sobbing and lamenting because nobody loved him. One night when Gervaise and Nana returned home together they were surprised not to find him in his bed. He had laid the bolster in his place. And when they discovered him, hiding between the bed and the wall, his teeth were chattering, and he related that some men had come to murder him. The two women were obliged to put him to bed again and quiet him like a child.

Coupeau knew only one remedy, to toss down a pint of spirits; a whack in his stomach, which set him on his feet again. This was how he doctored his gripes of a morning. His memory had left him long ago, his brain was empty; and he no sooner found himself on his feet than he poked fun at illness. He had never been ill. Yes, he had got to the point when a fellow kicks the bucket declaring that he's quite well. And his wits were going a-wool-gathering in other respects too. When Nana came home after gadding about for six weeks or so he seemed to fancy she had returned from doing some errand in the neighborhood. Often when she was hanging on an acquaintance's arm she met him and laughed at him without his recognizing her. In short, he no longer counted for anything; she might have sat down on him if she had been at a loss for a chair.

When the first frosts came Nana took herself off once more under the pretense of going to the fruiterer's to see if there were any baked pears. She scented winter and didn't care to let her teeth chatter in front of the fireless stove. The Coupeaus had called her no good because they had waited for the pears. No doubt she would come back again. The other winter she had stayed away three weeks to fetch her father two sous' worth of tobacco. But the months went by and the girl did not show herself. This time she must have indulged in a hard gallop. When June arrived she did not even turn up with the sunshine. Evidently it was all over, she had found a new meal ticket somewhere or other. One day when the Coupeaus were totally broke they sold Nana's iron bedstead for six francs, which they drank together at Saint-Ouen. The bedstead had been in their way.

One morning in July Virginie called to Gervaise, who was passing by, and asked her to lend a hand in washing up, for Lantier had entertained a couple of friends on the day before. And while Gervaise was cleaning up the plates and dishes, greasy with the traces of the spread, the hatter, who was still digesting in the shop, suddenly called out, "Say, I saw Nana the other day."

Virginie, who was seated at the counter looking very careworn in front of the jars and drawers which were already three parts emptied, jerked her head furiously. She restrained herself so as not to say too much, but really it was angering her. Lantier was seeing Nana often . . . . She was by no means sure of him; he was a man to do much worse than that, when a fancy for a woman came into his head. Madame Lerat, very intimate just then with Virginie, who confided in her, had that moment entered the shop, and hearing Lantier's remark, she pouted ridiculously, and asked, "What do you mean, you saw her?"

". . . in the street here," answered the hatter, who felt highly flattered, and began to laugh and twirl his moustaches. "She was in a carriage and I was floundering on the pavement. Really it was so, I swear it. There's no use denying it, the young fellows of position who are on friendly terms with her are terribly lucky."

His eyes had brightened and he turned towards Gervaise who was standing in the rear of the shop wiping a dish.

"Yes, she was in a carriage, and wore such a stylish dress. I didn't recognize her, she looked so much like a lady of the upper set, with her white teeth and her face as fresh as a flower. It was she who waved her glove to me. She has caught a count, I believe . . . . She's launched for good. She can afford to do without any of us; she's head over heels in happiness, the little beggar. What a love of a little kitten. No, you've no idea what a little kitten she is."

Gervaise was still wiping the same plate, although it had long since been clean and shiny. Virginie was reflecting, anxious about a couple of bills which fell due on the morrow and which she didn't know how to pay; while Lantier, stout and fat, perspiring the sugar he fed off, ventured his enthusiasm for well-dressed little sluts. The shop, which was already three parts eaten up, smelt of ruin. Yes, there were only a few more burnt almonds to nibble, a little more barley-sugar to suck, to clean the Poissons' business out. Suddenly, on the pavement over the way, he perceived the policeman, who was on duty, pass by all buttoned up with his sword dangling by his side. And this made him all the gayer. He compelled Virginie to look at her husband.

"Dear me," he muttered, "Badingue looks fine this morning. Just look, see how stiff he walks. He must have stuck a glass eye in his back to surprise people."

When Gervaise went back upstairs, she found Coupeau seated on the bed, in the torpid state induced by one of his attacks. He was looking at the window-panes with his dim expressionless eyes. She sat herself down on a chair, tired out, her hands hanging beside her dirty skirt; and for a quarter of an hour she remained in front of him without saying a word.

"I've had some news," she muttered at last. "Your daughter's been seen. Yes, your daughter's precious stylish and hasn't any more need of you. She's awfully happy, she is. Ah. My God. I'd give a great deal to be in her place."

Coupeau was still staring at the window-pane. But suddenly he raised his ravaged face, and stammered with an idiotic laugh, "Well, my little lamb, I'm not stopping you. You're not yet so bad looking when you wash yourself. As folks say, however old a pot may be, it ends by finding its lid. And, after all, I wouldn't care if it only buttered our bread."

CHAPTER XII

It must have been the Saturday after quarter day, something like the 12th or 13th of January—Gervaise didn't quite know. She was losing her wits, for it was centuries since she had had anything warm in her stomach. Ah, what an infernal week. A complete clear out. Two loaves of four pounds each on Tuesday, which had lasted till Thursday; then a dry crust found the night before, and finally not a crumb for thirty-six hours, a real dance before the cupboard. What did she know, by the way, what she felt on her back, was the frightful cold, a black cold, the sky as grimy as a frying-pan, thick with snow which obstinately refused to fall. When winter and hunger are both together in your guts, you may tighten your belt as much as you like, it hardly feeds you.

Perhaps Coupeau would bring back some money in the evening. He said that he was working. Anything is possible, isn't it? And Gervaise, although she had been caught many and many a time, had ended by relying on this coin. After all sorts of incidents, she herself couldn't find as much as a duster to wash in the whole neighborhood; and even an old lady, whose rooms she did, had just given her the sack, charging her with swilling her liqueurs. No one would engage her, she was washed up everywhere; and this secretly suited her, for she had fallen to that state of indifference when one prefers to croak rather than move one's fingers. At all events, if Coupeau brought his pay home they would have something warm to eat. And meanwhile, as it wasn't yet noon, she remained stretched on the mattress, for one doesn't feel so cold or so hungry when one is lying down.

The bed was nothing but a pile of straw in a corner. Bed and bedding had gone, piece by piece, to the second-hand dealers of the neighborhood. First she had ripped open the mattress to sell handfuls of wool at ten sous a pound. When the mattress was empty she got thirty sous for the sack so as to be able to have coffee. Everything else had followed. Well, wasn't the straw good enough for them?

Gervaise bent herself like a gun-trigger on the heap of straw, with her clothes on and her feet drawn up under her rag of a skirt, so as to keep them warm. And huddled up, with her eyes wide open, she turned some scarcely amusing ideas over in her mind that morning. Ah. No, they couldn't continue living without food. She no longer felt her hunger, only she had a leaden weight on her chest and her brain seemed empty. Certainly there was nothing gay to look at in the four corners of the hovel. A real shithole now, where greyhounds who wear jackets in the streets, would not even have pissed. Her pale eyes stared at the bare walls. Everything had long since gone to "uncle's." All that remained were the chest of drawers, the table and a chair. Even the marble top of the chest of drawers and the drawers themselves, had evaporated in the same direction as the bedstead. A fire could not have cleaned them out more completely; the little knick-knacks had melted, beginning with the ticker, a twelve franc watch, down to the family photos, the frames of which had been bought by a woman keeping a second-hand store; a very obliging woman, by the way, to whom Gervaise carried a saucepan, an iron, a comb and who gave her five, three or two sous in exchange, according to the article; enough, at all events to go upstairs again with a bit of bread. But now there only remained a broken pair of candle snuffers, which the woman refused to give her even a sou for.

. . . if she could only have sold the rubbish and refuse, the dust and the dirt, how speedily she would have opened shop, for the room was filthy. She only saw cobwebs in the corners and although cobwebs are good for cuts, there are, so far, no merchants who buy them. Then turning her head, abandoning the idea of doing a bit of trade, Gervaise gathered herself together more closely on her straw, preferring to stare through the window at the snow-laden sky, at the dreary daylight, which froze the marrow in her bones.

What a lot of worry. Though, after all, what was the use of putting herself in such a state and puzzling her brains? If she had only been able to have a snooze. But her hole of a home wouldn't go out of her mind. Monsieur Marescot, the landlord had come in person the day before to tell them that he would turn them out into the street if the two quarters' rent now overdue were not paid during the ensuing week. Well, so he might, they certainly couldn't be worse off on the pavement. Fancy this ape, in his overcoat and his woolen gloves, coming upstairs to talk to them about rent, as if they had had a treasure hidden somewhere.

Just the same with that brute of a Coupeau, who couldn't come home now without beating her; she wished him in the same place as the landlord. She sent them all there, wishing to rid herself of everyone, and of life too. She was becoming a real storehouse for blows. Coupeau had a cudgel, which he called his ass's fan, and he fanned his old woman. You should just have seen him giving her abominable thrashings, which made her perspire all over. She was no better herself, for she bit and scratched him. Then they stamped about in the empty room and gave each other such drubbings as were likely to ease them of all taste for bread for good. But Gervaise ended by not caring a fig for these thwacks, not more than she did for anything else. Coupeau might celebrate Saint Monday for weeks altogether, go off on the spree for months at a time, come home mad with liquor, and seek to sharpen her as he said, she had grown accustomed to it, she thought him tiresome, but nothing more. It was on these occasions that she wished him somewhere else. Yes, somewhere, her beast of a man and the Lorilleuxs, the Boches, and the Poissons too; in fact, the whole neighborhood, which she had such contempt for. She sent all Paris there with a gesture of supreme carelessness, and was pleased to be able to revenge herself in this style.

One could get used to almost anything, but still, it is hard to break the habit of eating. That was the one thing that really annoyed Gervaise, the hunger that kept gnawing at her insides . . . those pleasant little snacks she used to have. Now she had fallen low enough to gobble anything she could find.

On special occasions, she would get waste scraps of meat from the butcher for four sous a pound. Blacked and dried out meat that couldn't find a purchaser. She would mix this with potatoes for a stew. On other occasions, when she had some wine, she treated herself to a sop, a true parrot's pottage. Two sous' worth of Italian cheese, bushels of white potatoes, quarts of dry beans, cooked in their own juice, these also were dainties she was not often able to indulge in now. She came down to leavings from low eating dens, where for a sou she had a pile of fish-bones, mixed with the parings of moldy roast meat. She fell even lower—she begged a charitable eating-house keeper to give her his customers' dry crusts, and she made herself a bread soup, letting the

crusts simmer as long as possible on a neighbor's fire. On the days when she was really hungry, she searched about with the dogs, to see what might be lying outside the tradespeople's doors before the dustmen went by; and thus at times she came across rich men's food, rotten melons, stinking mackerel and chops, which she carefully inspected for fear of maggots.

Yes, she had come to this. The idea may be a repugnant one to delicate-minded folks, but if they hadn't chewed anything for three days running, we should hardly see them quarreling with their stomachs; they would go down on all fours and eat filth like other people. Ah. The death of the poor, the empty entrails, howling hunger, the animal appetite that leads one with chattering teeth to fill one's stomach with beastly refuse in this great Paris, so bright and golden. And to think that Gervaise used to fill her belly with luscious goose. Now the thought of it brought tears to her eyes. One day, when Coupeau bagged two bread tickets from her to go and sell them and get some liquor, she nearly killed him with the blow of a shovel, so hungered and so enraged was she by this theft of a bit of bread.

However, after a long contemplation of the pale sky, she had fallen into a painful doze. She dreamed that the snow-laden sky was falling on her, so cruelly did the cold pinch. Suddenly she sprang to her feet, awakened with a start by a shudder of anguish. My God. Was she going to die? Shivering and haggard she perceived that it was still daylight. Wouldn't the night ever come? How long the time seems when the stomach is empty. Hers was waking up in its turn and beginning to torture her. Sinking down on the chair, with her head bent and her hands between her legs to warm them, she began to think what they would have for dinner as soon as Coupeau brought the money home: a loaf, a quart of wine and two platefuls of tripe in the Lyonnaise fashion. Three o'clock struck by father Bazouge's clock. Yes, it was only three o'clock. Then she began to cry. She would never have strength enough to wait until seven. Her body swayed backwards and forwards, she oscillated like a child nursing some sharp pain, bending herself double and crushing her stomach so as not to feel it. A beating is less painful than hunger. And unable to ease herself, seized with rage, she rose and stamped about, hoping to send her hunger to sleep by walking it to and fro like an infant. For half an hour or so, she knocked against the four corners of the empty room. Then, suddenly, she paused with a fixed stare. So much the worse. They might say what they liked; she would lick their feet if needs be, but she would go and ask the Lorilleuxs to lend her ten sous.

At winter time, up these stairs of the house, the paupers' stairs, there was a constant borrowing of ten sous and twenty sous, petty services which these hungry beggars rendered each other. Only they would rather have died than have applied to the Lorilleuxs, for they knew they were too tight-fisted. Thus Gervaise displayed remarkable courage in going to knock at their door. She felt so frightened in the passage that she experienced the sudden relief of people who ring a dentist's bell.

"Come in." cried the chain-maker in a sour voice.

How warm and nice it was inside. The forge was blazing, its white flame lighting up the narrow workroom, while Madame Lorilleux set a coil of gold wire to heat. Lorilleux, in front of his worktable, was perspiring with the warmth as he soldered the links of a chain together. And it smelt nice. Some cabbage soup was simmering on the stove, exhaling a steam which turned Gervaise's heart topsy-turvy and almost made her faint.

"Ah. It's you," growled Madame Lorilleux, without even asking her to sit down. "What do you want?"

Gervaise did not answer for a moment. She had recently been on fairly good terms with the Lorilleuxs, but she saw Boche sitting by the stove. He seemed very much at home, telling funny stories.

"What do you want?" repeated Lorilleux.

"You haven't seen Coupeau?" Gervaise finally stammered at last. "I thought he was here."

The chain-makers and the concierge sneered. No, for certain, they hadn't seen Coupeau. They didn't stand treat often enough to interest Coupeau.

Gervaise made an effort and resumed, stuttering, "It's because he promised to come home. Yes, he's to bring me some money. And as I have absolute need of something...."

Silence followed. Madame Lorilleux was roughly fanning the fire of the stove; Lorilleux had lowered his nose over the bit of chain between his fingers, while Boche continued laughing, puffing out his face till it looked like the full moon.

"If I only had ten sous," muttered Gervaise, in a low voice.
The silence persisted.

"Couldn't you lend me ten sous? . . . . I would return them to you this evening."

Madame Lorilleux turned round and stared at her. Here was a weasel trying to get round them. Today she asked them for ten sous, tomorrow it would be for twenty, and there would be no reason to stop. No, indeed; it would be a cold day in hell if they lent her anything.

"But, my dear," cried Madame Lorilleux. "You know very well that we haven't any money. Look. There's the lining of my pocket. You can search us. If we could, it would be with a willing heart, of course."

"The heart's always there," growled Lorilleux. "Only when one can't, one can't."

Gervaise looked very humble and nodded her head approvingly. However, she did not take herself off. She squinted at the gold, at the gold tied together hanging on the walls, at the gold wire the wife was drawing out with all the strength of her little arms, at the gold links lying in a heap under the husband's knotty fingers. And she thought that the least bit of this ugly black metal would suffice to buy her a good dinner. The workroom was as dirty as ever, full of old iron, coal dust and sticky oil stains, half wiped away; but now, as Gervaise saw it, it seemed resplendent with treasure, like a money changer's shop. And so she ventured to repeat softly: "I would return them to you, return them without fail. Ten sous wouldn't inconvenience you."

Her heart was swelling with the effort she made not to own that she had had nothing to eat since the day before. Then she felt her legs give way. She was frightened that she might burst into tears, and she still stammered:

"It would be kind of you. You don't know. Yes, I'm reduced to that, good Lord—reduced to that."

Then the Lorilleuxs pursed their lips and exchanged covert glances. So Clump-clump was begging now. Well, the fall was complete. But they did not care for that kind of thing by any means. If they had known, they would have barricaded the door, for people should always be on their guard against beggars—folks who make their way into apartments under a pretext and carry precious objects away with them; and especially so in this place, as there was something worthwhile stealing. One might lay one's fingers no matter where, and carry off thirty or forty francs by merely closing the hands. They had felt suspicious several times already on noticing how strange Gervaise looked when she stuck herself in front of the gold. This time, however, they meant to watch her. And as she approached nearer, with her feet on the board, the chain-maker roughly called out, without giving any further answer to her question: "Look out, bitch—take care; you'll be carrying some scraps of gold away on the soles of your shoes. One would think you had greased them on purpose to make the gold stick to them."

Gervaise slowly drew back. For a moment she leant against a rack, and seeing that Madame Lorilleux was looking at her hands, she opened them and showed them, saying softly, without the least anger, like a fallen women who accepts anything, "I have taken nothing; you can look."

And then she went off, because the strong smell of the cabbage soup and the warmth of the workroom made her feel too ill.

The Lorilleuxs did not detain her. Good riddance; just see if they opened the door to her again. They had seen enough of her face. They didn't want other people's misery in their rooms, especially when that misery was so well deserved. They reveled in their selfish delight at being seated so cozily in a warm room, with a dainty soup cooking. Boche also stretched himself, puffing with his cheeks still more and more, so much, indeed, that his laugh really became indecent. They were all nicely revenged on Clump-clump, for her former manners, her blue shop, her spreads, and all the rest. It had all worked out just as it should, proving where a love of showing-off would get you.

"So that is the style now? Begging for ten sous," cried Madame Lorilleux as soon as Gervaise had gone. "Wait a bit; I'll lend her ten sous, and no mistake, to go and get drunk with."

Gervaise shuffled along the passage in her slippers, bending her back and feeling heavy. On reaching her door she did not open it—her room frightened her. It would be better to walk about, she would learn patience. As she passed by she stretched out her neck, peering into Old Man Bru's kennel under the stairs. There, for instance, was another one who must have a fine appetite, for he had breakfasted and dined by heart during the last three days. However, he wasn't at home, there was only his hole, and Gervaise felt somewhat jealous, thinking that perhaps he had been invited somewhere. Then, as she reached the Bijards' she heard Lalie moaning, and, as the key was in the lock as usual, she opened the door and went in.

"What is the matter?" she asked.

The room was very clean. One could see that Lalie had carefully swept it, and arranged everything during the morning. Misery might blow into the room as much as it liked, carry off the chattels and spread all the dirt and refuse about. Lalie, however, came behind and tidied everything, imparting, at least, some appearance of comfort within. She might not be rich, but you realized that there was a housewife in the place. That afternoon her two little ones, Henriette and Jules, had found some old pictures which they were cutting out in a corner. But Gervaise was greatly surprised to see Lalie herself in bed, looking very pale, with the sheet drawn up to her chin. In bed, indeed, then she must be seriously ill.

"What is the matter with you?" inquired Gervaise, feeling anxious.

Lalie no longer groaned. She slowly raised her white eyelids, and tried to compel her lips to smile, although they were convulsed by a shudder.

"There's nothing the matter with me," she whispered very softly. "Really nothing at all."

Then, closing her eyes again, she added with an effort, "I made myself too tired during the last few days, and so I'm doing the idle; I'm nursing myself, as you see."

But her childish face, streaked with livid stains, assumed such an expression of anguish that Gervaise, forgetting her own agony, joined her hands and fell on her knees near the bed. For the last month she had seen the girl clinging to the walls for support when she went about, bent double indeed, by a cough which seemed to presage a coffin. Now the poor child could not even cough. She had a hiccough and drops of blood oozed from the corners of her mouth.

"It's not my fault if I hardly feel strong," she murmured, as if relieved. "I've tired myself today, trying to put things to rights. It's pretty tidy, isn't it? And I wanted to clean the windows as well, but my legs failed me. How stupid. However, when one has finished one can go to bed."

She paused, then said, "Pray, see if my little ones are not cutting themselves with the scissors."

And then she relapsed into silence, trembling and listening to a heavy footfall which was approaching up the stairs. Suddenly father Bijard brutally opened the door. As usual he was far gone, and his eyes shone with the furious madness imparted by the vitriol he had swallowed. When he perceived Lalie in bed, he tapped on his thighs with a sneer, and took the whip from where it hung.

"Ah. By blazes, that's too much," he growled, "we'll soon have a laugh. So the cows lie down on their straw at noon now. Are you poking fun at me, you lazy beggar? Come, quick now, up you get."

And he cracked the whip over the bed. But the child replied, "Please, papa, don't—don't strike me. I swear to you, you'll regret it. Don't strike."

"Will you jump up?" he roared still louder, "or else I'll tickle your ribs. Jump up, you little bitch."

Then she softly said, "I can't—do you understand? I'm going to die."

Gervaise had sprung upon Bijard and torn the whip away from him. He stood bewildered in front of the bed. What was the filthy brat talking about? Do girls die so young without even having been ill? Some excuse to get sugar out of him no doubt. Ah. He'd make inquiries, and if she lied, let her look out.

"You'll see, it's the truth," she continued. "As long as I could I avoided worrying you; but be kind now, and bid me good-bye, papa."

Bijard wriggled his nose as if he fancied she was deceiving him. And yet it was true she had a sick look, the serious look of a grown up person. The breath of death which passed through the room in some measure sobered him. He gazed around like a man awakened from a long sleep, saw the room so tidy, the two children clean, playing and laughing. And then he sank on to a chair stammering, "Our little mother; our little mother."

Those were the only words he could find to say, and yet they were very tender ones to Lalie who had never been much spoiled. She consoled her father. What especially worried her was to go off like this without having completely brought up the little ones. He would take care of them, wouldn't he? With her dying breath she told him how they ought to be cared for and kept clean. But drunk with the fumes of drink seizing hold of him again, he wagged his head, watching her with an uncertain stare as she was dying. All kind of things were touched in him, but he could find no more to say and he was too utterly burnt with liquor to shed a tear.

"Listen," resumed Lalie, after a pause. "We owe four francs and seven sous to the baker; you must pay that. Madame Gaudron borrowed an iron of ours, which you must get from her. I wasn't able to make any soup this evening, but there's some bread left and you can warm up the potatoes."

Till her last rattle, the poor kitten still remained the little mother. Surely she could never be replaced. She was dying because she had had, at her age, a true mother's reason, because her breast was too small and weak for so much maternity. And if her ferocious beast of a father lost his treasure, it was his own fault. After kicking the mother to death, hadn't he murdered the daughter as well? The two good angels would lie in the pauper's grave and all that could be in store for him was to kick the bucket like a dog in the gutter.

Gervaise restrained herself not to burst out sobbing. She extended her hands, desirous of easing the child and as the shred of a sheet was falling, she wished to tack it up and arrange the bed. Then the dying girl's poor little body was exposed. My God, what misery. What woe. Stones would have wept. Lalie was naked with only the remnants of a camisole on her shoulders; yes, naked with the grievous, bleeding nudity of a martyr. She had no flesh left; her bones seemed to protrude through the skin. From her ribs to her thighs were a number of violet stripes—the marks of the whip forcibly imprinted on her. A livid bruise, moreover, encircled her left arm, as if the tender limb, scarcely larger than a matchstick, had been crushed in a vise. There was also an imperfectly closed wound on her right leg, left there by some ugly blow and which opened again and again every morning when she went about doing her errands. From head to foot, indeed, she was but one bruise. This murdering of childhood; those heavy hands crushing this lovely girl; how abominable that such weakness should have such a weighty cross to bear. Again did Gervaise crouch down, no longer thinking of tucking in the sheet, but overwhelmed by the pitiful sight of this martyrdom and her trembling lips seemed to be seeking for words of prayer.

"Madame Coupeau," murmured the child, "I beg you."

With her little arms she tried to draw up the sheet again, ashamed for her father. Bijard, as boozed as ever, with his eyes on the corpse which was his own work, still wagged his head, but more slowly, like a worried animal might do.

When she had covered Lalie up again, Gervaise felt she could not remain there any longer. The dying girl was growing weaker and ceased speaking; all that was left to her was her gaze—the dark look she had had as a resigned and thoughtful child and which she now fixed on her two little ones who were still cutting out their pictures. The room was growing gloomy and Bijard was working off his liquor while the poor girl was in her death agonies. No, no, life was too hideous. How dreadful it was. How frightful. And Gervaise left and went down the stairs, not knowing what she was doing, her head wandering and so full of disgust that she would willingly have thrown herself under the wheels of an omnibus to have finished with her own existence.

As she hastened on, growling against cursed fate, she suddenly found herself in front of the place where Coupeau pretended that he worked. Her legs had taken her there and now her stomach began singing its song again, the complaint of hunger in ninety verses—a complaint she knew by heart. However, if she caught Coupeau as he left, she would be able to pounce upon the coin at once and buy some grub. A short hour's waiting at the utmost; she could surely stay that out, though she had sucked her thumbs since the day before.

She was at the corner of Rue de la Charbonniere and Rue de Chartres. A chill wind was blowing and the sky was an ugly leaden gray. The impending snow hung over the city but not a flake had fallen as yet. She tried stamping her feet to keep warm, but soon stopped as there was no use working up an appetite.

There was nothing amusing about. The few passers-by strode rapidly along, wrapped up in comforters; naturally enough one does not care to tarry when the cold is nipping at your heels. However, Gervaise perceived four or five women who were mounting guard like herself outside the door of the zinc-works; unfortunate creatures of course—wives watching for the pay to prevent it going to the dram-shop. There was a tall creature as bulky as a gendarme leaning against the wall, ready to spring on her husband as soon as he showed himself. A dark little

woman with a delicate humble air was walking about on the other side
of the way. Another one, a fat creature, had brought her two brats with
her and was dragging them along, one on either hand, and both of
them shivering and sobbing. And all these women, Gervaise like the
others, passed and re-passed, exchanging glances, but without speaking to one another. A pleasant meeting and no mistake. They didn't
need to make friends to learn what number they lived at. They could all
hang out the same sideboard, "Misery & Co." It seemed to make one
feel even colder to see them walk about in silence, passing each other
in this terrible January weather.

However, nobody as yet left the zinc-works. But presently one
workman appeared, then two, and then three, but these were no doubt
decent fellows who took their pay home regularly, for they jerked their
heads significantly as they saw the shadows wandering up and down.
The tall creature stuck closer than ever to the side of the door, and suddenly fell upon a pale little man who was prudently poking his head out
. . . . It was soon settled. She searched him and collared his coin. Caught,
no more money, not even enough to pay for a dram. Then the little
man, looking very vexed and cast down, followed his gendarme, weeping like a child. The workmen were still coming out; and as the fat
mother with the two brats approached the door, a tall fellow, with a
cunning look, who noticed her, went hastily inside again to warn her
husband; and when the latter arrived he had stuffed a couple of cart
wheels away, two beautiful new five franc pieces, one in each of his
shoes. He took one of the brats on his arm, and went off telling a variety of lies to his old woman who was complaining. There were other
workmen also, mournful-looking fellows, who carried in their clinched
fists the pay for the three or five days' work they had done during a
fortnight, who reproached themselves with their own laziness, and took
drunkards' oaths. But the saddest thing of all was the grief of the dark
little woman, with the humble, delicate look; her husband, a handsome
fellow, took himself off under her very nose, and so brutally indeed
that he almost knocked her down, and she went home alone, stumbling
past the shops and weeping all the tears in her body.

At last the defile finished. Gervaise, who stood erect in the middle
of the street, was still watching the door. The look-out seemed a bad
one. A couple of workmen who were late appeared on the threshold,

but there were still no signs of Coupeau. And when she asked the work-men if Coupeau wasn't coming, they answered her, being up to snuff, that he had gone off by the back-door with Lantimeche. Gervaise understood what this meant. Another of Coupeau's lies; she could whistle for him if she liked. Then shuffling along in her worn-out shoes, she went slowly down the Rue de la Charbonniere. Her dinner was going off in front of her, and she shuddered as she saw it running away in the yellow twilight. This time it was all over. Not a copper, not a hope, nothing but night and hunger. Ah. A fine night to kick the bucket, this dirty night which was falling over her shoulders.

She was walking heavily up the Rue des Poissonniers when she suddenly heard Coupeau's voice. Yes, he was there in the Little Civet, letting My-Boots treat him. That comical chap, My-Boots, had been cunning enough at the end of last summer to espouse in authentic fashion a lady who, although rather advanced in years, had still preserved considerable traces of beauty. She was a lady-of-the-evening of the Rue des Martyrs, none of your common street sluts. And you should have seen this fortunate mortal, living like a man of means, with his hands in his pockets, well clad and well fed. He could hardly be recognized, so fat had he grown. His comrades said that his wife had as much work as she liked among the gentlemen of her acquaintance. A wife like that and a country-house is all one can wish for to embellish one's life. And so Coupeau squinted admiringly at My-Boots. Why, the lucky dog even had a gold ring on his little finger.

Gervaise touched Coupeau on the shoulder just as he was coming out of the little Civet.

"Say, I'm waiting; I'm hungry. I've got an empty stomach which is all I ever get from you."

But he silenced her in a capital style, "You're hungry, eh? Well, eat your fist, and keep the other for to-morrow."

He considered it highly improper to do the dramatic in other people's presence. What, he hadn't worked, and yet the bakers kneaded bread all the same. Did she take him for a fool, to come and try to frighten him with her stories?

"Do you want me to turn thief?" she muttered, in a dull voice.

My-Boots stroked his chin in conciliatory fashion. "No, that's forbidden," said he. "But when a woman knows how to handle herself."

And Coupeau interrupted him to call out "Bravo." Yes, a woman always ought to know how to handle herself, but his wife had always been a helpless thing. It would be her fault if they died on the straw. Then he relapsed into his admiration for My-Boots. How awfully fine he looked. A regular landlord; with clean linen and swell shoes. They were no common stuff. His wife, at all events, knew how to keep the pot boiling.

The two men walked towards the outer Boulevard, and Gervaise followed them. After a pause, she resumed, talking behind Coupeau's back, "I'm hungry; you know, I relied on you. You must find me something to nibble."

He did not answer, and she repeated, in a tone of despairing agony: "Is that all I get from you?"

"My God, I'm broke," he roared, turning round in a fury. "Just leave me alone, eh? Or else I'll hit you."

He was already raising his fist. She drew back, and seemed to make up her mind. "All right, I'll leave you. I guess I can find a man."

The zinc-worker laughed at this. He pretended to make a joke of the matter, and strengthened her purpose without seeming to do so. That was a fine idea of hers, and no mistake. In the evening, by gaslight, she might still hook a man. He recommended her to try the Capuchin restaurant where one could dine very pleasantly in a small private room. And, as she went off along the Boulevard, looking pale and furious he called out to her: "Listen, bring me back some dessert. I like cakes. And if your gentleman is well dressed, ask him for an old overcoat. I could use one."

With these words ringing in her ears, Gervaise walked softly away. But when she found herself alone in the midst of the crowd, she slackened her pace. She was quite resolute. Between thieving and the other, well she preferred the other; for at all events she wouldn't harm anyone. No doubt it wasn't proper. But what was proper and what was improper was sorely muddled together in her brain. When you are dying of hunger, you don't philosophize; you eat whatever bread turns up. She had gone along as far as the Chaussee-Clignancourt. It seemed as if the night would never come. However, she followed the Boulevards like a lady who is taking a stroll before dinner. The neighborhood in which she felt so ashamed was now full of fresh air.

Lost in the crowd on the broad footway, walking past the little plane trees, Gervaise felt alone and abandoned. The vistas of the avenues seemed to empty her stomach all the more. And to think that among this flood of people there were many in easy circumstances, and yet not a Christian who could guess her position, and slip a ten sous piece into her hand. Yes, it was too great and too beautiful; her head swam and her legs tottered under this broad expanse of gray sky stretched over so vast a space. The twilight had the dirty-yellowish tinge of Parisian evenings, a tint that gives you a longing to die at once, so ugly does street life seem. The horizon was growing indistinct, assuming a mud-colored tinge. Gervaise, who was already weary, met all the workers returning home. At this hour of the day the ladies in bonnets and the well-dressed gentlemen living in the new houses mingled with the people, with the files of men and women still pale from inhaling the tainted atmosphere of workshops and workrooms. From the Boulevard Magenta and the Rue du Faubourg-Poissonniere, came bands of people, rendered breathless by their uphill walk. As the coaches and the cabs rolled by less noiselessly among the vans and trucks returning home empty at a gallop, an ever-increasing swarm of blouses and blue vests covered the pavement. Commissionaires returned with their crotchets on their backs. Two workmen took long strides side by side, talking to each other in loud voices, with any amount of gesticulation, but without looking at one another; others who were alone in overcoats and caps walked along the curbstones with lowered noses; others again came in parties of five or six, following each other, with pale eyes and their hands in their pockets and not exchanging a word. Some still had their pipes, which had gone out between their teeth. Four masons poked their white faces out of the windows of a cab which they had hired between them, and on the roof of which their mortar-troughs rocked to and fro. House-painters were swinging their pots; a zinc-worker was returning laden with a long ladder, with which he almost poked people's eyes out; while a belated plumber, with his box on his back, played the tune of "The Good King Dagobert" on his little trumpet. Ah, the sad music, a fitting accompaniment to the tread of the flock, the tread of the weary beasts of burden.

Suddenly on raising her eyes she noticed the old Hotel Boncoeur in front of her. After being an all-night cafe, which the police had closed

down, the little house was now abandoned; the shutters were covered
with posters, the lantern was broken, and the whole building was rotting and crumbling away from top to bottom, with its smudgy claret-
colored paint, quite moldy. The stationer's and the tobacconist's were
still there. In the rear, over some low buildings, you could see the lep-
rous facades of several five-storied houses rearing their tumble-down
outlines against the sky. The "Grand Balcony" dancing hall no longer
existed; some sugar-cutting works, which hissed continually, had been
installed in the hall with the ten flaming windows. And yet it was here,
in this dirty den—the Hotel Boncoeur—that the whole cursed life had
commenced. Gervaise remained looking at the window of the first
floor, from which hung a broken shutter, and recalled to mind her youth
with Lantier, their first rows and the ignoble way in which he had abandoned her. Never mind, she was young then, and it all seemed gay to
her, seen from a distance. Only twenty years. And yet she had fallen to
street-walking. Then the sight of the lodging house oppressed her and
she walked up the Boulevard in the direction of Montmartre.

The night was gathering, but children were still playing on the heaps
of sand between the benches. The march past continued, the work girls
went by, trotting along and hurrying to make up for the time they had
lost in looking in at the shop windows; one tall girl, who had stopped,
left her hand in that of a big fellow, who accompanied her to within
three doors of her home; others as they parted from each other, made
appointments for the night at the "Great Hall of Folly" or the "Black
Ball." In the midst of the groups, piece-workmen went by, carrying
their clothes folded under their arms. A chimney sweep, harnessed with
leather braces, was drawing a cart along, and nearly got himself crushed
by an omnibus. Among the crowd which was now growing scantier,
there were several women running with bare heads; after lighting the
fire, they had come downstairs again and were hastily making their purchases for dinner; they jostled the people they met, darted into the bakers' and the pork butchers', and went off again with all dispatch, their
provisions in their hands. There were little girls of eight years old, who
had been sent out on errands, and who went along past the shops,
pressing long loaves of four pounds' weight, as tall as they were themselves, against their chests, as if these loaves had been beautiful yellow
dolls; at times these little ones forgot themselves for five minutes or so,

in front of some pictures in a shop window, and rested their cheeks against the bread. Then the flow subsided, the groups became fewer and farther between, the working classes had gone home; and as the gas blazed now that the day's toil was over, idleness and amusement seemed to wake up.

Ah. Yes; Gervaise had finished her day. She was wearier even than all this mob of toilers who had jostled her as they went by. She might lie down there and croak, for work would have nothing more to do with her, and she had toiled enough during her life to say: "Whose turn now? I've had enough." At present everyone was eating. It was really the end, the sun had blown out its candle, the night would be a long one. My God. To stretch one's self at one's ease and never get up again; to think one had put one's tools by for good and that one could ruminate like a cow forever. That's what is good, after tiring one's self out for twenty years. And Gervaise, as hunger twisted her stomach, thought in spite of herself of the party days, the spreads and the revelry of her life. On one occasion especially, an awfully cold day, a mid-Lent Thursday, she had enjoyed herself wonderfully well. She was very pretty, fair-haired and fresh looking at that time. Her wash-house in the Rue Neuve had chosen her as queen in spite of her leg. And then they had had an outing on the boulevards in carts decked with greenery, in the midst of stylish people who ogled her. Real gentlemen put up their glasses as if she had been a true queen. In the evening there was a wonderful spread, and then they had danced till daylight. Queen; yes Queen. With a crown and a sash for twenty-four hours—twice round the clock. And now oppressed by hunger, she looked on the ground, as if she were seeking for the gutter in which she had let her fallen majesty tumble.

She raised her eyes again. She was in front of the slaughter-houses which were being pulled down; through the gaps in the walls one could see the dark, stinking courtyards, still damp with blood. And when she had gone down the Boulevard again, she also saw the Lariboisiere Hospital, with its long gray wall, above which she could distinguish the mournful, fan-like wings, pierced with windows at even spaces. A door in the wall filled the neighborhood with dread; it was the door of the dead in solid oak, and without a crack, as stern and as silent as a tombstone. Then to escape her thoughts, she hurried further down till she reached the railway bridge. The high parapets of riveted sheet-iron hid the line from view; she could only distinguish a corner of the station standing out against the luminous horizon of Paris, with a vast roof black with coal-dust. Through the clear space she could hear the engines whistling and the cars being shunted, in token of colossal hidden activity. Then a train passed by, leaving Paris, with puffing breath and a growing rumble. And all she perceived of this train was a white plume, a sudden gust of steam which rose above the parapet and then evaporated. But the bridge had shaken and she herself seemed impressed by this departure at full speed. She turned around as if to follow the invisible engine, the noise of which was dying away.

She caught a glimpse of open country through a gap between tall buildings . . . if only she could have taken a train and gone away, far away from this poverty and suffering. She might have started an entirely new life. Then she turned to look at the posters on the bridge sidings. One was on pretty blue paper and offered a fifty-franc reward for a lost dog. Someone must have really loved that dog.

Gervaise slowly resumed her walk. In the smoky fog which was falling, the gas lamps were being lighted up; and the long avenues, which had grown bleak and indistinct, suddenly showed themselves plainly again, sparkling to their full length and piercing through the night, even to the vague darkness of the horizon. A great gust swept by; the widened spaces were lighted up with streaks of little flames shining under the far-stretching moonless sky. It was the hour when, from one end of the Boulevard to the other, the bars and the dancing-halls flamed gayly as the first glasses were merrily drunk and the first dance began. It was the great fortnightly pay-day and the pavement was crowded with jostling revelers on the spree. There was a breath of merrymaking in the air—damned fine revelry, but not objectionable so far. Fellows were filling themselves in the pubs; through the lighted windows you could see people feeding, with their mouths full and laughing without taking the trouble to swallow first. Drunkards were already installed in the wine shops, squabbling and gesticulating. And there was a cursed noise on all sides, voices shouting amid the constant clatter of feet on the pavement.

"Say, are you coming to sip?" "Make haste, old man; I'll pay for a glass of bottled wine." "Here's Pauline. Shan't we just laugh." The doors swung to and fro, letting a smell of wine and a sound of coronet playing escape into the open air. There was a gathering in front of Old Man Colombe's The Saloon, which was lighted up like a cathedral for high mass. My God, you would have said a real celebration was going on, for several capital fellows, with rounded paunches and swollen cheeks, looking for all the world like professional choristers, were singing inside. They were celebrating Saint-Pay, of course—a very amiable saint, who no doubt keeps the cash box in Paradise. Only, on seeing how gaily the evening began, the retired petty tradesmen who had taken their wives out for a stroll wagged their heads and repeated that there would be any number of drunken men in Paris that night. And the night stretched very dark, dead-like and icy, above this revelry, perforated only with lines of gas lamps extending to the four corners of heaven.

Gervaise stood in front of The Saloon, thinking that if she had had a couple of sous she could have gone inside and drunk a dram. No doubt a shot would have quieted her hunger. Ah, what a number of drams she had drunk in her time. Liquor seemed good stuff to her after all. And from outside she watched the drunk-making machine, realizing that her misfortune was due to it, and yet dreaming of finishing herself off with brandy on the day she had some coin. But a shudder passed through her hair as she saw it was now almost dark. Well, the night time was approaching. She must have some courage and sell herself coaxingly if she didn't wish to kick the bucket in the midst of the general revelry. Looking at other people gorging themselves didn't precisely fill her own stomach. She slackened her pace again and looked around her. There was a darker space under the trees. Few people passed along, only folks in a hurry, who swiftly crossed the Boulevards. And on the broad, dark, deserted footway, where the sound of the revelry died away, women were standing and waiting. They remained for long intervals motionless, patient and as stiff-looking as the scrubby little plane trees; then they slowly began to move, dragging their slippers over the frozen soil, taking ten steps or so and then waiting again, rooted as it were to the ground. There was one of them with a fat body and insect-like arms and legs, wearing a black silk rag, with a yellow scarf over her head; there was another one, tall and bony, who was bareheaded and wore a servant's apron; and others, too—old ones plastered up and young ones so dirty that a rag picker would not have picked them up. However, Gervaise tried to learn what to do by imitating them;

girlish-like emotion tightened her throat; she was hardly aware whether she felt ashamed or not; she seemed to be living in a horrible dream. For a quarter of an hour she remained standing erect. Men hurried by without even turning their heads. Then she moved about in her turn, and venturing to accost a man who was whistling with his hands in his pockets, she murmured, in a strangled voice, "Sir, listen a moment..."

The man gave her a side glance and then went off, whistling all the louder.

Gervaise grew bolder and, with her stomach empty, she became absorbed in this chase, fiercely rushing after her dinner, which was still running away. She walked about for a long while, without thinking of the flight of time or of the direction she took. Around her the dark, mute women went to and fro under the trees like wild beasts in a cage. They stepped out of the shade like apparitions, and passed under the light of a gas lamp with their pale masks fully apparent; then they grew vague again as they went off into the darkness, with a white strip of petticoat swinging to and fro. Men let themselves be stopped at times, talked jokingly, and then started off again laughing. Others would quietly follow a woman to her room, discreetly, ten paces behind. There was a deal of muttering, quarreling in an undertone and furious bargaining, which suddenly subsided into profound silence. And as far as Gervaise went she saw these women standing like sentinels in the night. They seemed to be placed along the whole length of the Boulevard. As soon as she met one she saw another twenty paces further on, and the file stretched out unceasingly. Entire Paris was guarded. She grew enraged on finding herself disdained, and changing her place, she now walked between the Chaussee de Clignancourt and the Grand Rue of La Chapelle. All were beggars.

"Sir, just listen."

But the men passed by. She started from the slaughter-houses which stank of blood. She glanced on her way at the old Hotel Boncoeur, now closed. She passed in front of the Lariboisiere Hospital, and mechanically counted the number of windows that were illuminated with a pale quiet glimmer, like that of night-lights at the bedside of some agonizing sufferers. She crossed the railway bridge as the trains rushed by with a noisy rumble, rending the air in twain with their shrill whistling. Ah, how sad everything seemed at night-time. Then she turned on her heels again and filled her eyes with the sight of the same houses, doing this ten and twenty times without pausing, without resting for a minute on a bench. No; no one wanted her. Her shame seemed to be increased by this contempt. She went down towards the hospital again, and then returned towards the slaughter-houses. It was her last promenade—from the blood-stained courtyards, where animals were slaughtered, down to the pale hospital wards, where death stiffened the patients stretched between the sheets. It was between these two establishments that she had passed her life.

"Sir, excuse me."

But suddenly she perceived her shadow on the ground. When she approached a gas-lamp it gradually became less vague, till it stood out at last in full force—an enormous shadow it was, positively grotesque, so portly had she become. Her stomach, breast and hips, all equally flabby jostled together. She walked with such a limp that the shadow bobbed almost topsy-turvy at every step she took; she looked like a giant puppet. Then as she left the street lamp behind her, the puppet grew taller, becoming in fact gigantic, filling the whole Boulevard, bobbing to and fro in such style that it seemed fated to smash its nose against the trees or the houses. My God, how frightful she was. She had never realized her disfigurement so thoroughly. And she could not help looking at her shadow; indeed, she waited for the gas-lamps, still watching the puppet as it bobbed about. Ah, she had a pretty companion beside her. What a figure. It ought to attract the men at once. And at the thought of her unsightliness, she lowered her voice, and only just dared to stammer behind the passers-by, "Sir, excuse me...."

It was now getting quite late. Matters were growing bad in the neighborhood. The eating-houses had closed and voices, gruff with drink, could be heard disputing in the wine shops. Revelry was turning to quarreling and brawls. A big ragged chap roared out, "I'll knock yer to bits; just count yer bones." A large woman had quarreled with a fellow outside a dancing place, and was calling him a "dirty fucker" and "asshole," while he on his side just muttered under his breath. Drink seemed to have imparted a fierce desire to fight and the passers-by, who were now less numerous, had pale contracted faces. There was a brawl at last; one drunken fellow came down on his back with all four limbs raised in the air, while his comrade, thinking he had killed him, ran off with his heavy shoes clattering over the pavement. Groups of men sang bawdy songs and then there would be long silences broken only by belches or the thud of a drunk falling down.

Gervaise still hobbled about, going up and down, with the idea of walking forever. At times, she felt drowsy and almost went to sleep, rocked by her lame leg; then she looked round her with a start, and noticed she had walked a hundred yards unconsciously. Her feet were swelling in her ragged shoes. The last clear thought that occupied her mind was that her bitch of a daughter was perhaps eating oysters at that very moment. Then everything became cloudy; she remained with open eyes. It required too great an effort for her to think. The only sensation that remained to her, in her utter annihilation, was that it was frightfully cold, so sharply, mortally cold, she had never known the like before. Why, even dead people could not feel so cold in their graves. With an effort she raised her head, and something seemed to lash her face. It was the snow, which had at last decided to fall from the smoky sky—fine thick snow, which the breeze swept round and round. For three days it had been expected and what a splendid moment it chose to appear.

Woken up by the first gusts, Gervaise began to walk faster. Eager to get home, men were running along, with their shoulders already white. And as she suddenly saw one who, on the contrary, was coming slowly towards her under the trees, she approached him and again said: "Sir, excuse me…."

The man stopped. But he did not seem to have heard her. He held out his hand, and muttered in a low voice, "Charity, if you please."

They looked at one another. My God. They were reduced to this— Old Man Bru begging, Madame Coupeau walking the streets. They remained stupefied in front of each other. They could join hands as equals now. The old workman had prowled about the whole evening, not daring to stop anyone, and the first person he accosted was as hungry as himself. Lord, was it not pitiful. To have toiled for fifty years and be obliged to beg. To have been one of the most prosperous laundresses in the Rue de la Goutte-d'Or and to end in the gutter. They still looked at one another. Then, without saying a word, they went off in different directions under the lashing snow.

It was a terrible storm. On these heights, in the midst of this open space, the fine snow revolved round and round as if the wind came from the four corners of heaven. You could not see ten paces off; everything was confused in the midst of this flying ice. The world had disappeared; the Boulevard seemed to be dead, as if the storm had stretched the silence of its white sheet over the vomit of the last drunkards. Gervaise still went on, blinded, lost. She felt her way by touching the trees. As she advanced, the gas-lamps shone out amidst the whiteness like torches. Then, suddenly, whenever she crossed an open space, these lights failed her; she was enveloped in the whirling snow, unable to distinguish anything to guide her. Below stretched the ground, vaguely white; gray walls surrounded her, and when she paused, hesitating and turning her head, she divined that behind this icy veil extended the immense avenue with interminable vistas of gas-lamps—the black and deserted Infinity of Paris asleep.

She was standing where the outer Boulevard meets the Boulevards Magenta and Ornano, thinking of lying down on the ground, when suddenly she heard a footfall. She began to run, but the snow blinded her, and the footsteps went off without her being able to tell whether it was to the right or to the left. At last, however, she perceived a man's broad shoulders, a dark form which was disappearing amid the snow. . . . she wouldn't let this man get away. And she ran on all the faster, reached him, and caught him by the blouse: "Sir, sir, excuse me."

The man turned round. It was Goujet.

So now she had accosted Golden-Beard. But what had she done on earth to be tortured like this by Providence? It was the crowning blow—to stumble against Goujet, and be seen by her blacksmith friend, pale and begging, like a common street walker. And it happened just under a gas-lamp; she could see her deformed shadow swaying on the snow like a monster. You would have said she was drunk. My God, not to have a crust of bread, or a drop of wine in her body, and to be taken for a drunken woman. It was her own fault, why did she booze? Goujet no doubt thought she had been drinking, and that she was up to some nasty pranks.

He looked at her while the snow scattered daisies over his beautiful yellow beard. Then as she lowered her head and stepped back he detained her.

"Come," said he.

And he walked on first. She followed him. They both crossed the silent district, gliding noiselessly along the walls. Poor Madame Goujet had died of rheumatism in the month of October. Goujet still resided in the little house in the Rue Neuve, living gloomily alone. On this occasion he was late because he had sat up nursing a wounded comrade. When he had opened the door and lighted a lamp, he turned towards Gervaise, who had remained humbly on the threshold. Then, in a low voice, as if he were afraid his mother could still hear him, he exclaimed, "Come in."

The first room, Madame Goujet's, was piously preserved in the state she had left it. On a chair near the window lay the table by the side of the large arm-chair, which seemed to be waiting for the old lace-worker. The bed was made, and she could have stretched herself beneath the sheets if she had left the cemetery to come and spend the evening with her child. There was something solemn, a perfume of honesty and goodness about the room.

"Come in," repeated the blacksmith in a louder tone. She went in, half frightened, like a disreputable woman gliding into a respectable place. He was quite pale, and trembled at the thought of ushering a woman like this into his dead mother's home. They crossed the room on tip-toe, as if they were ashamed to be heard. Then when he had pushed Gervaise into his own room he closed the door. Here he was at home. It was the narrow closet she was acquainted with; a schoolgirl's room, with the little iron bedstead hung with white curtains. On the walls the engravings cut out of illustrated newspapers had gathered and spread, and they now reached to the ceiling. The room looked so pure that Gervaise did not dare to advance, but retreated as far as she could from the lamp. Then without a word, in a transport as it were, he tried to seize hold of her and press her in his arms. But she felt faint and murmured, ". . . . My God . . . my God."

The fire in the stove, having been covered with coke-dust, was still alight, and the remains of a stew which Goujet had put to warm, thinking he should return to dinner, was smoking in front of the cinders. Gervaise, who felt her numbness leave her in the warmth of this room, would have gone down on all fours to eat out of the saucepan. Her hunger was stronger than her will; her stomach seemed rent in two; and she stooped down with a sigh. Goujet had realized the truth. He placed the stew on the table, cut some bread, and poured her out a glass of wine.

"Thank you. Thank you." said she. ". . . how kind you are. Thank you."

She stammered; she could hardly articulate. When she caught hold of her fork she began to tremble so acutely that she let it fall again. The hunger that possessed her made her wag her head as if senile. She carried the food to her mouth with her fingers. As she stuffed the first potato into her mouth, she burst out sobbing. Big tears coursed down her cheeks and fell onto her bread. She still ate, gluttonously devouring this bread thus moistened by her tears, and breathing very hard all the while. Goujet compelled her to drink to prevent her from stifling, and her glass chinked, as it were, against her teeth.

"Will you have some more bread?" he asked in an undertone.

She cried, she said "no," she said "yes," she didn't know. Ah, how nice and yet how painful it is to eat when one is starving.

And standing in front of her, Goujet looked at her all the while; under the bright light cast by the lamp-shade he could see her well. How aged and altered she seemed. The heat was melting the snow on her hair and clothes, and she was dripping. Her poor wagging head was quite gray; there were any number of gray locks which the wind had disarranged. Her neck sank into her shoulders and she had become so fat and ugly you might have cried on noticing the change. He recollected their love, when she was quite rosy, working with her irons, and showing the child-like crease which set such a charming necklace round her throat. In those times he had watched her for hours, glad just to look at her. Later on she had come to the forge, and there they had enjoyed themselves while he beat the iron, and she stood by watching his hammer dance. How often at night, with his head buried in his pillow, had he dreamed of holding her in his arms.

Gervaise rose; she had finished. She remained for a moment with her head lowered, and ill at ease. Then, thinking she detected a gleam in his eyes, she raised her hand to her jacket and began to unfasten the first button. But Goujet had fallen on his knees, and taking hold of her hands, he exclaimed softly:

"I love you, Madame Gervaise; . . . . I love you still, and in spite of everything, I swear it to you."

"Don't say that, Monsieur Goujet." she cried, maddened to see him like this at her feet. "No, don't say that; you grieve me too much."

And as he repeated that he could never love twice in his life, she became yet more despairing.

"No, no, I am too ashamed. For the love of God, get up. It is my place to be on the ground."

He rose, he trembled all over and stammered: "Will you allow me to kiss you?"

Overcome with surprise and emotion she could not speak, but she assented with a nod of the head. After all she was his; he could do what he chose with her. But he merely kissed her.

"That suffices between us, Madame Gervaise," he muttered. "It sums up all our friendship, doesn't it?"

He had kissed her on the forehead, on a lock of her gray hair. He had not kissed anyone since his mother's death. His sweetheart Gervaise alone remained to him in life. And then, when he had kissed her with so much respect, he fell back across his bed with sobs rising in his throat. And Gervaise could not remain there any longer. It was too sad and too terrible to meet again under such circumstances when one loved. "I love you, Monsieur Goujet," she exclaimed. "I love you dearly, also . . . . It isn't possible you still love me. Good-bye, good-bye; it would kill us both; it would be more than we could stand."

And she darted through Madame Goujet's room and found herself outside on the pavement again. When she recovered her senses she had rung at the door in the Rue de la Goutte-d'Or and Boche was pulling the string. The house was quite dark and in the black night the yawning, dilapidated porch looked like an open mouth. To think that she had always wanted to live in this terrible place. Had her ears been stopped up then, she might have missed the cursed music of despair which sounded behind the walls. Since she had set foot in the place she had begun to go downhill. Yes, it must bring bad luck to shut oneself up in these big workmen's houses; the cholera of misery was contagious there. That night everyone seemed to have died. She only heard the Boches snoring on the right-hand side, while Lantier and Virginie on the left were purring like a couple of cats who were not asleep but have their eyes closed and feel warm. In the courtyard, she fancied she was in a perfect cemetery; the snow paved the ground with white; the high walls, livid gray in tint, rose up unlighted like ruined walls, and not a sigh could be heard. It seemed as if a whole village, stiffened with cold and hunger, were buried here. She had to step over a black gutter—water from the dye-works—which smoked and streaked the whiteness of the snow with its muddy course. It was the color of her thoughts. The beautiful light blue and light pink waters had long since flowed away.

Then, while ascending the six flights of stairs in the dark, she could not prevent herself from laughing, an ugly laugh which hurt her. She recalled her ideal of former days: to work quietly, always have bread to eat and a tidy house to sleep in, to bring up her children, not to be beaten and to die in her bed. No, really, it was comical how all that had vanished. She no longer worked, she no longer ate, she slept on filth, her husband frequented all sorts of bars, and her husband drubbed her at all hours of the day; all that was left for her to do was to die on the pavement and it would not take long if on getting into her room, she could only pluck up courage to fling herself out of the window. Was it not enough to make one think that she had hoped to earn thirty thousand francs a year, and no end of respect? Ah, really, in this life it is no use being humble; one only gets sat upon. Nothing from nothing.

What increased her ugly laugh was the recollection of her grand hope of retiring into the country after twenty years passed in ironing. Well, she was on her way to the country. She was going to have her green corner in the Pere-Lachaise cemetery.

When she entered the passage she was like a lunatic. Her poor head was whirling around. At heart her real grief was having bid the blacksmith an eternal farewell. All was ended between them; they would never see each other again. Then, besides that, all her other thoughts of misfortune pressed upon her and almost caused her head to split. As she passed she poked her nose in at the Bijards' and beheld Lalie dead, with a look of contentment on her face at having at last been laid out, slumbering forever. Ah, well, children were luckier than grown-up people. As a glimmer of light passed under old Bazouge's door, she walked boldly in, seized with a yearning to go on the same journey as the little one.

That old joker, Bazouge, had come home that night in an extraordinary state of gaiety. He had had such a boozing that he was snoring on the ground in spite of the cold. No doubt that did not prevent him from dreaming something pleasant, for he seemed to be laughing from within as he slept. The candle, which he had not put out, lighted up his old garments, his black cloak, which he had drawn over his knees as though it had been a blanket.

On beholding him Gervaise uttered such a deep wailing that he awoke.

"My God shut the door. It's so cold. Ah, it's you. What's the matter? What do you want?"

Then, Gervaise, stretching out her arms, no longer knowing what she stuttered, began passionately to implore him, ". . . take me away. I've had enough; I want to go. You mustn't bear me any grudge. I didn't know. One never knows until one's ready . . . yes; one's glad to go one day. Take me away. Take me away and I shall thank you."

She fell on her knees, all shaken with a desire which caused her to turn ghastly pale. Never before had she thus dragged herself at a man's feet. Old Bazouge's ugly mug, with his mouth all on one side and his hide grimy with the dust of funerals, seemed to her as beautiful and resplendent as a sun. The old fellow, who was scarcely awake thought, however, that it was some sort of bad joke.

"Look here," murmured he, *"no jokes."*

"Take me away," repeated Gervaise more ardently still. "You remember, I knocked one evening against the partition; then I said that it wasn't true, because I was still a fool. But see. Give me your hands. I'm no longer frightened. Take me away to death. You'll see how still I'll be . . . sleep, that's all I care for . . . . I'll love you so much."

Bazouge, ever gallant, thought that he ought not to be hasty with a lady who appeared to have taken such a fancy to him. She was falling to pieces, but all the same, what remained was very fine, especially when she was excited.

"What you say is very true," he said with conviction. "I packed up three more today who would only have been too glad to have given me something for myself, could they but have got their hands to their pockets. But, little woman, it's not so easily settled as all that."

"Take me away, take me away," continued Gervaise, "I want to die."

"Ah, but there's a little operation to be gone through beforehand— you know…"And he made a noise in his throat, as though swallowing his tongue.

Then, thinking it a good joke, he chuckled.

Gervaise slowly rose to her feet. So he too could do nothing for her. She went to her room and threw herself on her straw, feeling stupid, and regretting she had eaten. Ah. No indeed, misery did not kill quickly enough.

CHAPTER XIII

That night Coupeau went on a binge. Next day, Gervaise received ten francs from her son Etienne, who was a mechanic on some railway. The youngster sent her a few francs from time to time, knowing that they were not very well off at home. She made some soup, and ate it all alone, for that scoundrel Coupeau did not return. On Monday he was still absent, and on Tuesday also. The whole week went by. Ah, it would be good luck if some woman took him in.

On Sunday Gervaise received a printed document. It was to inform her that her husband was dying at the Sainte-Anne asylum.

Gervaise did not disturb herself. He knew the way; he could very well get home from the asylum by himself. They had cured him there so often that they could once more do him the sorry service of putting him straight and sober. Had she not heard that very morning that for the week before Coupeau had been seen as round as a ball, rolling about Belleville from one saloon to another in the company of My-Boots. Exactly so; and it was My-Boots, too, who stood treat. He must have hooked his missus's stocking with all the savings gained at very hard work. It wasn't clean money they had used, but money that could infect them with any manner of vile diseases. Well, anyway, they hadn't thought to invite her for a drink. If you wanted to drink by yourself, you could croak by yourself.

However, on Monday, as Gervaise had a nice little meal planned for the evening, the remains of some beans and a pint of wine, she pretended to herself that a walk would give her an appetite. The letter from the asylum which she had left lying on the bureau bothered her. The snow had melted, the day was mild and gray and on the whole fine, with just a slight keenness in the air which was invigorating. She started at noon for her walk was a long one. She had to cross Paris and her bad leg always slowed her. The streets were crowded but the people amused her; she reached her destination very pleasantly. When she had given her name, she was told a most astounding story to the effect that Coupeau had been fished out of the Seine close to the Pont-Neuf. He had jumped over the parapet under the impression that a bearded man was barring his way. A fine jump, wasn't it? And as for finding out how Coupeau got to be on the Pont-Neuf, that was a matter he could not even explain himself.

One of the keepers escorted Gervaise. She was ascending a staircase, when she heard howlings which made her shiver to her very bones.

"He's playing nice music, isn't he?" observed the keeper.

"Who is?" asked she.

"Why, your old man. He's been yelling like that ever since the day before yesterday; and he dances, you'll just see."

My God, what a sight. She stood as one transfixed. The cell was padded from the floor to the ceiling. On the floor there were two straw mats, one piled on top of the other; and in a corner were spread a mattress and a bolster, nothing more. Inside, Coupeau was dancing and yelling, his blouse in tatters and his limbs beating the air. He wore the mask of one about to die. What a breakdown. He bumped up against the window then fell backwards, beating time with his arms and shaking his hands as though he were trying to wrench them off and fling them in somebody's face. Buffoons in low dancing places imitate the delirium tremens, only they do it badly. This drunkard's dance was the real thing. The song also has its merits, a continuous yell worthy of carnival-time, a mouth wide open uttering the same hoarse trombone notes for hours together. Coupeau had the howl of a beast with a crushed paw. Strike up, music. Gentlemen, choose your partners.

"My God what is the matter with him? What is the matter with him?" repeated Gervaise, seized with fear.

A house surgeon, a big fair fellow with a rosy countenance, and wearing a white apron, was quietly sitting taking notes. The case was a curious one; the doctor did not leave the patient.

"Stay a while if you like," said he to the laundress; "but keep quiet. Try and speak to him, he will not recognize you."

Coupeau indeed did not even appear to see his wife. She had only a bad view of him on entering, he was wriggling about so much. When she looked him full in the face, she stood aghast. My God, was it possible he had a countenance like that, his eyes full of blood and his lips covered with scabs? She would certainly never have known him. To begin with, he was making too many grimaces, without saying why, his mouth suddenly out of all shape, his nose curled up, his cheeks drawn in: a perfect animal's muzzle. His skin was so hot the air steamed around him; and his hide was as though varnished, covered with a heavy sweat which trickled off him. In his mad dance, one could see all the same that he was not at his ease, his head was heavy and his limbs ached.

Gervaise drew near to the house surgeon, who was strumming a tune with the tips of his fingers on the back of his chair.

"Tell me, sir, it's serious this time?"

The house surgeon nodded his head without answering.

"Isn't he jabbering to himself? Eh. Don't you hear? What's it about?"

"About things he sees," murmured the young man. "Keep quiet, let me listen."

Coupeau was speaking in a spastic voice. A glimmer of amusement lit up his eyes. He looked on the floor, to the right, to the left, and turned about as though he had been strolling in the Bois de Vincennes, conversing with himself.

"Ah, that's nice, that's grand. There're cottages, a regular fair. And some jolly fine music. What a Balthazar's feast. They're smashing the crockery in there. Awfully swell. Now it's being lit up; red balls in the air, and it jumps, and it flies . . . . What a lot of lanterns in the trees. It's confoundedly pleasant. There's water flowing everywhere, fountains, cascades, water which sings . . . . With the voice of a chorister. The cascades are grand."

And he drew himself up, as though the better to hear the delicious song of the water; he sucked in forcibly, fancying he was drinking the fresh spray blown from the fountains. But, little by little, his face resumed an agonized expression. Then he crouched down and flew quicker than ever around the walls of the cell, uttering vague threats.

"More traps, all that. I thought as much. Silence, you set of swindlers. Yes, you're making a fool of me. It's for that that you're drinking and bawling inside there with your whores. I'll demolish you, you and your cottage. Damnation. Will you leave me in peace?"

He clinched his fists; then he uttered a hoarse cry, stooping as he ran.

And he stuttered, his teeth chattering with fright. "It's so that I may kill myself. No, I won't throw myself in. All that water means that I've no heart. No, I won't throw myself in."

The cascades, which fled at his approach, advanced when he retired. And all of a sudden, he looked stupidly around him, mumbling, in a voice which was scarcely audible, "It isn't possible, they set conjurers against me."

"I'm off, sir. I've got to go. Good-night." said Gervaise to the house surgeon. "It upsets me too much; I'll come again."

She was quite white. Coupeau was continuing his breakdown from the window to the mattress and from the mattress to the window, perspiring, toiling, always beating the same rhythm. Then she hurried away. But though she scrambled down the stairs, she still heard her husband's confounded jig until she reached the bottom. Ah. My God, how pleasant it was out of doors, one could breathe there.

That evening everyone in the tenement was discussing Coupeau's strange malady. The Boches invited Gervaise to have a drink with them, even though they now considered Clump-clump beneath them, in order to hear all the details. Madame Lorilleux and Madame Poisson were there also. Boche told of a carpenter he had known who had been a drinker of absinthe. The man shed his clothes, went out in the street and danced the polka until he died. That rather struck the ladies as comic, even though it was very sad.

Gervaise got up in the middle of the room and did an imitation of Coupeau. Yes, that's just how it was. Can anyone feature a man doing that for hours on end? If they didn't believe they could go see for themselves.

On getting up the next morning, Gervaise promised herself she would not return to the Sainte-Anne again. What use would it be? She did not want to go crazy too. However, every ten minutes, she fell to musing and became absent-minded. It would be curious though, if he were still throwing his legs about. When twelve o'clock struck, she could no longer resist; she started off and did not notice how long the walk was, her brain was so full of her desire to go and the dread of what awaited her.

There was no need for her to ask for news. She heard Coupeau's song the moment she reached the foot of the staircase. Just the same tune, just the same dance. She might have thought herself going up again after having only been down for a minute. The attendant of the day before, who was carrying some jugs of disinfectant along the corridor, winked his eye as he met her, by way of being amiable.

"Still the same, then?" said she.

"Yes, still the same." he replied without stopping.

She entered the room, but she remained near the door, because there were some people with Coupeau. The fair, ruddy house surgeon was standing up, having given his chair to a bald old gentleman who was decorated and had a pointed face like a weasel. He was no doubt the head doctor, for his glance was as sharp and piercing as a fox. All the dealers in sudden death have a glance like that.

No, really, it was not a pretty sight and Gervaise, all in a tremble, asked herself why she had returned. To think that the evening before they accused her at the Boches' of exaggerating the picture. Now she saw better how Coupeau set about it, his eyes wide open looking into space, and she would never forget it. She overheard a few words between the house surgeon and the head doctor. The former was giving some details of the night: her husband had talked and thrown himself about, that was what it amounted to. Then the bald-headed old gentleman, who was not very polite by the way, at length appeared to become aware of her presence; and when the house surgeon had informed him that she was the patient's wife, he began to question her in the harsh manner of a commissary of the police.

"Did this man's father drink?"

"Yes, sir; just a little like everyone. He killed himself by falling from a roof one day when he was tipsy."

"Did his mother drink?"

"Well, sir, like everyone else, you know; a drop here, a drop there. The family is very respectable. There was a brother who died very young in convulsions."

The doctor looked at her with his piercing eye. He resumed in his rough voice:

"And you, you drink too, don't you?"

Gervaise stammered, protested, and placed her hand upon her heart, as though to take her solemn oath.

"You drink. Take care; see where drink leads to. One day or other you will die thus."

Then she remained close to the wall. The doctor had turned his back to her. He squatted down, without troubling himself as to whether his overcoat trailed in the dust of the matting; for a long while he studied Coupeau's trembling, waiting for its reappearance, following it with his glance. That day the legs were going in their turn, the trembling had descended from the hands to the feet; a regular puppet with his strings being pulled, throwing his limbs about, while the trunk of his body remained as stiff as a piece of wood. The disease progressed little by little. It was like a musical box beneath the skin; it started off every three or four seconds and rolled along for an instant; then it stopped and then it started off again, just the same as the little shiver which shakes stray dogs in winter, when cold and standing in some doorway for protection. Already the middle of the body and the shoulders quivered like water on the point of boiling. It was a funny demolition all the same, going off wriggling like a girl being tickled.

Coupeau, meanwhile, was complaining in a hollow voice. He seemed to suffer a great deal more than the day before. His broken murmurs disclosed all sorts of ailments. Thousands of pins were pricking him. He felt something heavy all about his body; some cold, wet animal was crawling over his thighs and digging its fangs into his flesh. Then there were other animals sticking to his shoulders, tearing his back with their claws.

"I'm thirsty, ... I'm thirsty." groaned he continually.

The house surgeon handed him a little lemonade from a small shelf;

Coupeau seized the mug in both hands and greedily took a mouthful, spilling half the liquid over himself; but he spat it out at once with furious disgust, exclaiming:

"Damnation. It's brandy."

Then, on a sign from the doctor, the house surgeon tried to make him drink some water without leaving go of the bottle. This time he swallowed the mouthful, yelling as though he had swallowed fire.

"It's brandy; damnation. It's brandy."

Since the night before, everything he had had to drink was brandy. It redoubled his thirst and he could no longer drink, because everything burnt him. They had brought him some broth, but they were evidently trying to poison him, for the broth smelt of vitriol. The bread was sour and moldy. There was nothing but poison around him. The cell stank of sulphur. He even accused persons of rubbing matches under his nose to infect him.

All on a sudden he exclaimed:

"The rats, there're the rats now."

There were black balls that were changing into rats. These filthy animals got fatter and fatter, then they jumped onto the mattress and disappeared. There was also a monkey which came out of the wall, and went back into the wall, and which approached so near him each time, that he drew back through fear of having his nose bitten off. Suddenly there was another change, the walls were probably cutting capers, for he yelled out, choking with terror and rage:

"That's it, giddy up. Shake me, I don't care. Giddy up. Tumble down. Yes, ring the bells, you black crows. Play the organ to prevent my calling the police. They've put a bomb behind the wall, the lousy bastards. I can hear it, it snorts, they're going to blow us up. Fire. Damnation, fire. There's a cry of fire. There it blazes. It's getting lighter, lighter. All the sky's burning, red fires, green fires, yellow fires. Hi. Help. Fire."

His cries became lost in a rattle. He now only mumbled disconnected words, foaming at the mouth, his chin wet with saliva. The doctor rubbed his nose with his finger, a movement no doubt habitual with him in the presence of serious cases. He turned to the house surgeon, and asked him in a low voice:

"And the temperature, still the hundred degrees, is it not?"

"Yes, sir."

The doctor pursed his lips. He continued there another two minutes, his eyes fixed on Coupeau. Then he shrugged his shoulders, adding:

"The same treatment, broth, milk, lemonade, and the potion of extract of quinine. Do not leave him, and call me if necessary."

He went out and Gervaise followed him, to ask him if there was any hope. But he walked so stiffly along the corridor, that she did not dare approach him. She stood rooted there a minute, hesitating whether to return and look at her husband. The time she had already passed had been far from pleasant. As she again heard him calling out that the lemonade smelt of brandy, she hurried away, having had enough of the performance. In the streets, the galloping of the horses and the noise of the vehicles made her fancy that all the inmates of Saint-Anne were at her heels. And that the doctor had threatened her. Really, she already thought she had the complaint.

In the Rue de la Goutte-d'Or the Boches and the others were naturally awaiting her. The moment she appeared they called her into the concierge's room. Well. Was old Coupeau still in the land of the living? My God, yes, he still lived. Boche seemed amazed and confounded; he had bet a bottle that old Coupeau would not last till the evening. What. He still lived. And they all exhibited their astonishment, and slapped their thighs. There was a fellow who lasted. Madame Lorilleux reckoned up the hours; thirty-six hours and twenty-four hours, sixty hours. Sacre Dieu. Already sixty hours that he had been doing the jig and screaming. Such a feat of strength had never been seen before. But Boche, who was upset that he had lost the bet, questioned Gervaise with an air of doubt, asking her if she was quite sure he had not filed off behind her back . . . . No, he had no desire to, he jumped about too much. Then Boche, still doubting, begged her to show them again a little how he was acting, just so they could see. Yes, yes, a little more. The request was general. The company told her she would be very kind if she would oblige, for just then two neighbors happened to be there who had not been present the day before, and who had come down purposely to see the performance. The concierge called to everybody to make room, they cleared the center of the apartment, pushing one another with their elbows, and quivering with curiosity. Gervaise, however, hung down her head. Really, she was afraid it might upset her. Desirous though of showing that she did not refuse for the sake of being pressed, she tried two or three little leaps; but she became quite queer, and stopped; on her word of honor, she was not equal to it. There was a murmur of disappointment; it was a pity, she imitated it perfectly. However, she could not do it, it was no use insisting. And when Virginie left to return to her shop, they forgot all about old Coupeau and began to gossip about the Poissons and their home, a real mess now. The day before, the bailiffs had been; the policeman was about to lose his place; as for Lantier, he was now making up to the daughter of the restaurant keeper next door, a fine woman, who talked of setting up as a tripe-seller. Ah. It was amusing, everyone already beheld a tripe-seller occupying the shop; after the sweets should come something substantial. And that blind Poisson. How could a man whose profession required him to be so smart fail to see what was going on in his own home?

They stopped talking suddenly when they noticed that Gervaise was off in a corner by herself imitating Coupeau. Her hands and feet were jerking. Yes, they couldn't ask for a better performance. Then Gervaise started as if waking from a dream and hurried away calling out good-night to everyone.

On the morrow, the Boches saw her start off at twelve, the same as on the two previous days. They wished her a pleasant afternoon. That day the corridor at Sainte-Anne positively shook with Coupeau's yells and kicks. She had not left the stairs when she heard him yelling:

"What a lot of bugs. Come this way again that I may squash you. They want to kill me. The bugs. I'm a bigger swell than the lot of you. Clear out, damnation. Clear out."

For a moment she stood panting before the door. Was he then fighting against an army? When she entered, the performance had increased and was embellished even more than on previous occasions. Coupeau was a raving madman, the same as one sees at the Charenton mad-house. He was throwing himself about in the center of the cell, slamming his fists everywhere, on himself, on the walls, on the floor, and stumbling about punching empty space. He wanted to open the window, and he hid himself, defended himself, called, answered, produced all this uproar without the least assistance, in the exasperated way of a man beset by a mob of people. Then Gervaise understood that he fancied he was on a roof, laying down sheets of zinc. He imitated the bellows with his mouth, he moved the iron about in the fire and knelt down so as to pass his thumb along the edges of the mat, thinking that he was soldering it. Yes, his handicraft returned to him at the moment of croaking; and if he yelled so loud, if he fought on his roof, it was because ugly scoundrels were preventing him doing his work properly. On all the neighboring roofs were villains mocking and tormenting him. Besides that, the jokers were letting troops of rats loose about his legs. Ah. The filthy beasts, he saw them always. Though he kept crushing them, bringing his foot down with all his strength, fresh hordes of them continued passing, until they quite covered the roof. And there were spiders there too. He roughly pressed his trousers against his thigh to squash some big spiders which had crept up his leg. He would never finish his day's work, they wanted to destroy him, his employer would send him to prison. Then, while making haste, he suddenly imagined he had a steam-engine in his stomach; with his mouth wide open, he puffed out the smoke, a dense smoke which filled the cell and found an outlet by the window; and, bending forward, still puffing, he looked outside of the cloud of smoke as it unrolled and ascended to the sky, where it hid the sun.

"Look." cried he, "there's the band of the Chaussee Clignancourt, disguised as bears with drums, putting on a show."

He remained crouching before the window, as though he had been watching a procession in a street, from some rooftop.

"There's the cavalcade, lions and panthers making grimaces—there's brats dressed up as dogs and cats—there's tall Clemence, with her wig full of feathers. Ah. My God. She's turning head over heels; she's showed everything—you'd better run, Duckie. Hey, the cops, leave her alone…just you leave her alone—don't shoot. Don't shoot."

His voice rose, hoarse and terrified and he stooped down quickly, saying that the police and the military were below, men who were aiming at him with rifles. In the wall he saw the barrel of a pistol emerging, pointed at his breast. They had dragged the girl away.

"Don't shoot. My God. Don't shoot."

Then, the buildings were tumbling down, he imitated the cracking of a whole neighborhood collapsing; and all disappeared, all flew off. But he had no time to take breath, other pictures passed with extraordinary rapidity. A furious desire to speak filled his mouth full of words which he uttered without any connection, and with a gurgling sound in his throat. He continued to raise his voice, louder and louder.

"Hallow, it's you? Good-day. No jokes. Don't make me nuzzle your hair."

And he passed his hand before his face, he blew to send the hairs away.

The house surgeon questioned him.

"Who is it you see?"

"My wife, of course."

He was looking at the wall with his back to Gervaise. The latter had a rare fright, and she examined the wall, to see if she also could catch sight of herself there. He continued talking.

"Now, you know, none of your wheedling—I won't be tied down. You are pretty, you have got a fine dress. Where did you get the money for it, you cow? You've been at a party, camel. Wait a bit and I'll do for you. Ah. You're hiding your boyfriend behind your skirts. Who is it? Stoop down that I may see. Damnation, it's him again."

With a terrible leap, he went head first against the wall; but the padding softened the blow. One only heard his body rebounding onto the matting, where the shock had sent him.

"Who is it you see?" repeated the house surgeon.

"The hatter. The hatter." yelled Coupeau.

And the house surgeon questioning Gervaise, the latter stuttered without being able to answer, for this scene stirred up within her all the worries of her life. The zinc-worker thrust out his fists.

"We'll settle this between us, my lad. It's full time I did for you. Ah, you coolly come, with that scoundrel on your arm, to make a fool of me before everyone. Well. I'm going to throttle you—yes, yes, I. And without putting any gloves on either. I'll stop your swaggering. Take that. And that. And that."

He hit about in the air viciously. Then a wild rage took possession of him. Having bumped against the wall in walking backwards, he thought he was being attacked from behind. He turned round, and fiercely hammered away at the padding. He sprang about, jumped from one corner to another, knocked his stomach, his back, his shoulder, rolled over, and picked himself up again. His bones seemed softened, his flesh had a sound like damp oakum. He accompanied this pretty game with atrocious threats, and wild and guttural cries. However the battle must have been going badly for him, for his breathing became quicker, his eyes were starting out of his head, and he seemed little by little to be seized with the cowardice of a child.

"Murder. Murder. Be off with you both . . . . You brutes, they're laughing. There she is on her back, the virago. She must give in, it's settled. Ah. The brigand, he's murdering her. He's cutting off her leg with his knife. The other leg's on the ground, the stomach's in two, it's full of blood. My God. My God."

And, covered with perspiration, his hair standing on end, looking a frightful object, he retired backwards, violently waving his arms, as though to send the abominable sight from him. He uttered two heart-rending wails, and fell flat on his back on the mattress, against which his heels had caught.

"He's dead, sir, he's dead." said Gervaise, clasping her hands.

The house surgeon had drawn near, and was pulling Coupeau into the middle of the mattress. No, he was not dead. They had taken his shoes off. His bare feet hung off the end of the mattress and they were dancing all by themselves, one beside the other, in time, a little hurried and regular dance.

Just then the head doctor entered. He had brought two of his colleagues—one thin, the other fat, and both decorated like himself. All three stooped down without saying a word, and examined the man all over; then they rapidly conversed together in a low voice. They had uncovered Coupeau from his thighs to his shoulders, and by standing on tiptoe Gervaise could see the naked trunk spread out. Well. It was complete. The trembling had descended from the arms and ascended from the legs, and now the trunk itself was getting lively.

"He's sleeping," murmured the head doctor.

And he called the two others' attention to the man's countenance. Coupeau, his eyes closed, had little nervous twinges which drew up all his face. He was more hideous still, thus flattened out, with his jaw projecting, and his visage deformed like a corpse's that had suffered from nightmare; but the doctors, having caught sight of his feet, went and poked their noses over them, with an air of profound interest. The feet were still dancing. Though Coupeau slept the feet danced. Their owner might snore, that did not concern them, they continued their little occupation without either hurrying or slackening. Regular mechanical feet, feet which took their pleasure wherever they found it.

Gervaise having seen the doctors place their hands on her old man, wished to feel him also. She approached gently and laid a hand on his shoulder and she kept it there a minute. Whatever was taking place inside? It danced down into the very depths of the flesh, the bones themselves must have been jumping. Quiverings, undulations, coming from afar, flowed like a river beneath the skin. When she pressed a little she felt she distinguished the suffering cries of the marrow. What a fearful thing, something was boring away like a mole. It must be the rotgut from The Saloon that was hacking away inside him. His entire body had been soaked in it.

The doctors had gone away. At the end of an hour Gervaise, who had remained with the house surgeon, repeated in a low voice:

"He's dead, sir; he's dead."

But the house surgeon, who was watching the feet, shook his head. The bare feet, projecting beyond the mattress, still danced on. They were not particularly clean and the nails were long. Several more hours passed. All on a sudden they stiffened and became motionless. Then the house surgeon turned towards Gervaise, saying:

"It's over now."

Death alone had been able to stop those feet.

When Gervaise got back to the Rue de la Goutte-d'Or she found at the Boches' a number of women who were cackling in excited tones. She thought they were awaiting her to have the latest news, the same as the other days.

"He's gone," said she, quietly, as she pushed open the door, looking tired out and dull.

But no one listened to her. The whole building was topsy-turvy. A most extraordinary story. Poisson had caught his wife with Lantier. Exact details were not known, because everyone had a different version. However, he had appeared just when they were not expecting him. Some further information was given, which the ladies repeated to one another as they pursed their lips. A sight like that had naturally brought Poisson out of his shell. He was a regular tiger. This man, who talked but little and who always seemed to walk with a stick up his ass, had begun to roar and jump about. Then nothing more had been heard. Lantier had evidently explained things to the husband. Anyhow, it could not last much longer, and Boche announced that the girl of the restaurant was for certain going to take the shop for selling tripe. That rogue of a hatter adored tripe.

On seeing Madame Lorilleux and Madame Lerat arrive, Gervaise repeated, faintly:

"He's gone. My God. Four days' dancing and yelling."

Then the two sisters could not do otherwise than pull out their handkerchiefs. Their brother had had many faults, but after all he was their brother. Boche shrugged his shoulders and said, loud enough to be heard by everyone:

"Bah. It's a drunkard the less."

From that day, as Gervaise often got a bit befuddled, one of the amusements of the house was to see her imitate Coupeau. It was no longer necessary to press her; she gave the performance gratis, her hands and feet trembling as she uttered little involuntary shrieks. She must have caught this habit at Sainte-Anne from watching her husband too long.

Gervaise lasted in this state several months. She fell lower and lower still, submitting to the grossest outrages and dying of starvation a little every day. As soon as she had four sous she drank and pounded on the walls. She was employed on all the dirty errands of the neighborhood. Once they even bet her she wouldn't eat someone else's vomit, but she did it in order to earn ten sous. Monsieur Marescot had decided to turn her out of her room on the sixth floor. But, as Old Man Bru had just been found dead in his cubbyhole under the staircase, the landlord had allowed her to turn into it. Now she roosted there in the place of Old Man Bru. It was inside there, on some straw, that her teeth chattered, while her stomach was empty and her bones were frozen. Even the earth refused her. She was becoming idiotic. She did not even think of making an end of herself by jumping out of the sixth floor window onto the pavement of the courtyard below. Death had to take her little by little, bit by bit, dragging her thus to the end through the accursed existence she had made for herself. It was never exactly known what she did die of. There was some talk of a cold, but the truth was she died of privation and of the filth and hardship of her ruined life. Overeating and dissoluteness killed her, according to the Lorilleuxs. One morning, as there was a bad smell in the passage, it was remembered that she had not been seen for two days, and she was discovered already green in her hole.

It happened to be old Bazouge who came with the pauper's coffin under his arm to pack her up. He was again drunk that day, but a jolly fellow all the same, and as lively as a cricket. When he recognized the customer he had to deal with he uttered several philosophical reflections, while performing his little business.

"Everyone has to go. There's no occasion for jostling, there's room for everyone. And it's stupid being in a hurry that just slows you up. All I want to do is to please everybody. Some will, others won't. What's the result? Here's one who wouldn't, then she would. So she was made to wait. Anyhow, it's all right now, and faith. She's earned it. Merrily, just take it easy."

And when he took hold of Gervaise in his big, dirty hands, he was seized with emotion, and he gently raised this woman who had had so great a longing for his attentions. Then, as he laid her out with paternal care at the bottom of the coffin, he stuttered between two belches:

"You know—now listen—it's me, Bibi-the-Gay, called the ladies' consoler. There, you're happy now. Go by-by, my beauty."

CPSIA information can be obtained at www.ICGtesting.com
Printed in the USA
BVOW072106050612

291879BV00003B/3/P